LOVE ON THE LINE

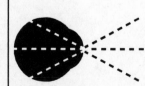

LOVE ON THE LINE

DEEANNE GIST

THORNDIKE PRESS
A part of Gale, Cengage Learning

Detroit • New York • San Francisco • New Haven, Conn • Waterville, Maine • London

GALE
CENGAGE Learning®

ALL RIGHTS RESERVED
Thorndike Press® Large Print Christian Romance.
The text of this Large Print edition is unabridged.
Other aspects of the book may vary from the original edition.
Set in 16 pt. Plantin.

LIBRARY OF CONGRESS CATALOGING-IN-PUBLICATION DATA

Gist, Deeanne.
   Love on the line / by Deeanne Gist.
     p. cm. — (Thorndike Press large print Christian romance)
   ISBN-13: 978-1-4104-4256-7 (hardcover)
   ISBN-10: 1-4104-4256-X (hardcover)
   1. Texas Rangers—Fiction. 2. Bird watchers—Fiction. 3. Texas—Fiction.
   4. Large type books. I. Title.
   PS3607.I55L68 2012
   813'.6—dc23   2011037969

Published in 2012 by arrangement with Bethany House Publishers, a division of Baker Publishing Group.

Printed in the United States of America
1 2 3 4 5 6 7 16 15 14 13 12

To my PIT Crew
(Personal Intercessory Team)

Carolyn Hall
Harold and Sharon Hearn
Brian and Elaine Mustain

who agreed to pray for me daily
during the writing of this novel.

This was such a big commitment
and I want you to know
your prayers were felt in a palpable way.
Your encouraging
words meant so much and lifted me
when I most needed
it. Thank you for walking this
road with me. You are
so very, very precious to me and a
delight to Him.

I love you,
Dee

ACKNOWLEDGMENTS

No matter how much research I do, there are some things I simply have to ask an expert about. One of the most delightful specialists I spoke with this time was Kenny Ray Estes, Museum Director of the Trapshooting Hall of Fame in Vandalia, Ohio. Oh, my goodness. Somebody put him on the payroll. He was *amazing* and so incredibly giving of his time. We spent days, no lie, on the phone and swapping emails. If he didn't know the answer to my question, he researched it until he did. My hat is off to you, Kenny Ray. Thank you, thank you, thank you.

Since the hero of this book is a Texas Ranger, I needed lots of help in the gun department. I connected with local vintage gun collector, Randal Hankla. He showed me a genuine turn-of-the-century rifle. He taught me how to load it, aim it, and fire it. He answered lots of questions, lots of emails, and he even took time out of a reenactment to show me what was what. Thank you, Randal!

In order to spread the love a little, I also called on longtime friend and world-renowned shooting instructor and title-holder, Gil Ash. (I know, Gil, you're not supposed to look down the barrel, but it's so much simpler in prose to say, "He looked down the barrel." But you and I will know, he's really looking where the target currently is, and shooting where it's going to be!)

The heroine in our story contributed her own challenges as a telephone operator. I searched and searched but could never find a "How to Use a Switchboard" instructional video. But Oleta Porter of the Doc Porter Museum of Telephone History gave me books, articles, pamphlets, and a personal tour of the museum. She gave me a hands-on demonstration of how to work a turn-of-the-century rural switchboard. I took a picture of it, and it is the one our heroine uses in the story. If you're ever in Houston, go to the museum and ask Oleta to point it out to you. She'll know just the one you're talking about.

Jack Dowling, of Houston, gave me lessons on how to climb a telephone pole back in the day. Imagine my shock when he informed me they didn't use safety straps. Instead, they simply wrapped one leg around the pole to keep themselves in place. Crazy!

Diane Probst out of Rockport, Texas, gave me special attention during their annual Hummingbird Celebration, where *thousands* of hummingbirds stop in Rockport each September to fill up on sugar water before their six-hundred-mile overnight migration to South America. What a treat it was to see all those exquisite birds up close and personal.

With our antagonists being train robbers, I needed someone to tell me what a steam engine sounds and smells like when it idles. Lori Pennington and John Garbutt with the Texas State Railroad not only answered my questions, they sent me photos and an actual audio clip!

Amazing what a team effort a book is, isn't it? And without these fine folks, *Love on the Line* wouldn't have the historical depth and accuracy I so love to include. That said, any mistakes within these pages are indisputably mine.

CHAPTER ONE

"Everybody off the train."

Jostled by other passengers, Georgie Gail raised her arms and shuffled past the man brandishing a gun. She strained her neck trying to obtain a closer look, but the aisle was too crowded.

No one said a word, even children sensing a need for silence. The press of bodies generated a touch of moisture beneath her brown wool traveling gown. A whiff of cinnamon from her homemade cologne water merged with the sweet perfumes and hair pomade of neighboring passengers.

At the door, two members of the Comer Gang stood on the ground flanking her exit. The February sun dipped behind the trees, blurring the sky with pinks and purples.

"Watch yer step, miss." Like the desperado inside, a Stetson shaded his eyes while a neckerchief covered his face. Holding a gun in one hand, he lifted his other in assistance.

Swallowing, she slipped her gloved hand into his. He squeezed, helping her make the leap from car to ground.

"Thank you." The automatic response was out before she could recall it.

"Ma'am. Hands up, now."

She glanced at him and lifted her hands, but he'd already turned to help the next lady.

Is he Frank Comer? she wondered. He was certainly polite enough to be, but she'd expected someone taller. Broader. Larger than life.

The outside air cooled her skin, though the warmth of an impending Texas spring tempered its bite. A jangle of bridles pulled her attention to a group of horses a few yards away. A palomino the color of a newly minted gold coin snorted and swished its white tail.

She took a quick peek toward the front of the train but found no evidence of the conductor or engineer. A thread of smoke and steam wafted from the smokestack.

A member of the gang stepped forward and did a double take before directing her to a line where three outlaws held several dozen passengers at gunpoint. A young girl with brown braids bumped her from behind.

"Careful there," Georgie whispered, reaching down to steady her. "Where's your mother?"

"I lost her." The girl's lip trembled. "I lost my hat, too, and when Mama finds out she'll give me a whupping."

Squatting down, Georgie brushed a loose strand of hair from the girl's face. "No, she won't. I'm sure she'll understand."

Tears welled in her eyes. "She said if I lose another, I'm gonna be in big trouble. And that means a whupping."

"What's your name?"

"Rosella Platt."

"Well, Rosella. I'm Miss Gail and I'm a telephone operator."

The girl's eyes widened. "You are?"

"I am. And when this is all over, I'll help you find your mother. I'll even —"

"Is there a problem, miss?"

Georgie lifted her gaze, then slowly rose, her hands following suit. A dirty vest hung open on the masked, powerfully built man. His thick gun belt cinched tight-fitting trousers at his waist.

"Rosella lost her hat," she said.

"Well, now." He looked at the girl. "I do believe there was a hat left behind on the train. Did it have a fetching brown ribbon wrapped around a straw crown?"

"Yes, sir," Rosella breathed. "It did."

"That'd probably be it, then. So don't you worry none."

A full head taller than Georgie, he turned his attention to her. "Might I have a look-see inside your reticule, miss?"

Blue. His eyes were definitely blue with thick brows above them.

Lowering her arms, she slid her handbag to her wrist.

"She's a telephone operator," Rosella offered, her voice filled with awe.

The man paused and looked again at Georgie. "That a fact? You run a switchboard?"

"I do."

"Where abouts?"

"Washington County."

Leaning back, he angled his head for a better view beneath her hat. "Don't reckon I've ever met a real switchboard operator."

"Then I'd say we're even, sir." She slid her fingers into the mouth of her bag, loosening its strings. "I've never met a real train robber."

His eyes crinkled; then he peeked inside the reticule and gently pushed it back toward her. "Thank you, miss."

"But . . . don't you want the money?"

"You on your own?"

"I am."

"You earn that money telephone operatin'?"

"I did."

"Well, you go on and keep it, then."

Her shoulders relaxed. "Thank you."

"My pleasure." He continued down the line, but instead of grabbing purses or yanking watches from their chains, he reassured an elderly woman, refusing her handbag and telling her to put her arms down. "I reckon they're awfully tired by now."

A few steps later, he gave a thin, pallid youth a few coins he'd taken from the express car.

"Is that Frank Comer?" Rosella whispered. "The *real* Frank Comer?"

"I believe it is," Georgie answered, excitement bubbling.

"He likes you."

Shushing the girl with her hand, Georgie willed away the heat springing to her cheeks and sliced another glance at the famous outlaw.

Comer clapped a man's shoulder, said something to make them both laugh, then tensed and swung his gaze to the left. "That's it, boys! Run for it!"

The gang members broke for their horses, their bags of loot banging against them as they ran. Some leapt onto their animals;

15

others tried to grab hold of their frightened mounts.

From the opposite end of the train, a man on horseback burst from the forest. "Get down!"

The command sailed above their heads and broached no argument. Like dominos, the passengers tumbled to the ground. Rosella kicked, trying to wriggle as close to Georgie as possible.

"Shhh." Georgie squeezed her shoulder. "Hold still."

The men exchanged gunfire, and with each loud crack, Georgie jerked. The temptation to cover her ears was great, but she didn't dare.

A woman close by screamed, setting off a chain reaction. Georgie felt as if she stood in a bell tower while every bell tolled. Still, she wondered if some of the screams were coming from wounded members of the gang.

She hoped not. *Please, Lord, let Frank Comer and his men make it to safety.*

Like the rest of the state's population, she closely followed the stories of Comer's escapades and his continual benevolence toward the old, the infirm, and the poor.

The man beside her shifted. Dirt puffed into her nose and mouth, grit sticking to her teeth. Sputtering, she lifted her head just a mite and swiped a glove across her lips. A zing tore through the air, perilously close above her.

Flattening herself back down, she ignored the awkward angle of her hat and its holding pin, which pressed against her scalp. Instead, she absorbed the sound of hooves reverberating beneath her, amazed at how the earth trembled in response to the scrambling men and beasts.

Rosella began to whimper. Curling up, Georgie pulled the child closer, murmuring words of comfort.

As quickly as it started, the clash between the outlaws and the charging lawman ended. The tremors, the gunshots, the shouts . . . all replaced with stillness. Georgie remained frozen on the ground. Rhythmic hisses of steam escaped the train's cylinders. The smell of coal and oil mixed with gunpowder.

Before long her head began to throb where the hatpin pressed. A rock beneath her skirts gouged her hip. The top of her left foot itched within her boot. And dirt continued to tickle her nose.

"Can we get up?" Rosella whispered.

But the men were already rising and assisting women and children to their feet.

"Rosella!" a woman cried.

"Mama!" Rosella scrambled upright. "I didn't lose my hat; it's still on the train."

The mother's response was lost to Georgie as the woman hugged her daughter and moved away, talking excitedly.

"It's okay, miss. You can get up now." A fellow passenger extended a large, beefy hand into Georgie's line of vision.

She tried to use it for leverage, but her skirts had been hopelessly tangled by Rosella and she couldn't rise.

"Beg your pardon, miss." Grasping her waist, he swung her up, plunking her to her feet.

She swallowed a cry of surprise. "Thank you, sir."

Even with his hat, he was an inch or two shorter than she and quite stout. "There now, no need to be frightened. Looks like one o' them Texas Rangers got wind of Comer's plans and hightailed it this way."

Shaking her skirts, she glanced toward the engine car at the front of the train. The engineer stood toe to toe with a man whose features she couldn't make out, particularly with the sun now having set and twilight fully upon them. But she could see his silhouette.

Tall. Broad. Muscular. And cocky.

"Where is everybody?" The engineer's

voice shook with anger. "They stole everything out of the safe, then emptied the passenger cars, and now Comer's long gone. You fellas were supposed to be patrolling this whole area."

"We were. We are. We're spread out all along this route and have been for weeks."

"Spread out?" the engineer screeched, arms waving. "You mean one by one? You aren't gathered in large groups?"

" 'Course not."

"Are you crazy? That was the Comer Gang. You could have gotten us all killed."

Georgie frowned. Comer wasn't a killer. He was a . . . a kindhearted thief who, according to the papers, helped more people than he harmed.

The Ranger's chest bowed out. "Listen, old-timer. One Ranger's all you need. You only had one train being robbed, didn't you?"

Georgie lifted a brow. It might take only one Ranger to make the Comer Gang scatter, but it'd take a great deal more to bring in its members.

With a sense of self-satisfaction, she glanced toward the woods, then froze. A half dozen bandits lay hog-tied together on the ground.

Her breath stuck in her throat. One

19

Ranger did all that? She scanned the ker-
chiefed men but could barely make them
out in the fading light. Still, from what the
engineer said, Comer wasn't among them.

"Maybe one Ranger would be enough."
The engineer leaned forward. "So long as
that Ranger wasn't you. Seems Comer gives
you the slip ever' time. The way I see it, you
have about as much chance catching Comer
as a jackrabbit at a coyote convention."

Bunching his fists, the Ranger tensed, then
turned and strode toward the passengers.

"Must be Lucious Landrum," the stout
man in front of her whispered to his wife.
"He's been after Comer for almost a year
now. And look at the way he's dressed, all
spiffy-like."

Georgie eyed the Ranger, unable to determine what he was wearing in this light,
much less the clothing's quality. All she
could see was a cowboy hat, a vest, and a
gun belt with two holsters.

"LOO-she-us," his wife replied, drawing
out the syllables. "Such a strange name. And
look at his beard. I thought he wore a big,
bushy mustache."

"Normally he does. But you heard him;
he's been on the trail for weeks."

The Ranger stopped several yards away
and questioned two men at the front of the

line. A woman in a black mourning gown began to quietly sob.

"We'll know soon enough." The portly man lowered his voice even more. "If his guns have bone handles carved with a boy on the right pistol and a girl on the left — closest to his heart — then it's Landrum."

The conductor emerged from the train with a lantern and walked it over to the Ranger, who moved within a few feet of Georgie. The light revealed a fine white Stetson. A big bushy beard. An olive shirt. A black string tie. And a gun belt strapped about his hips. A massive emblem buckle made of gold and silver held it together. She squinted, but couldn't make out the handles of his pistols.

"And you didn't see anything?" Landrum asked the short man and his wife. "Hear anything? Nothing at all?"

"Well, they kept saying, 'Hands up,' " the wife offered.

Landrum rubbed his eyes. Between the shadow from his hat and the full beard, his face was every bit as hard to discern as the outlaws'. "Any distinguishing features, ma'am? A disfigured eye, a scar? Anything at all would be helpful."

The couple looked at each other, as if it would help them remember something profound. But Georgie knew the Ranger was wasting his time. Frank Comer was nothing short of a legend in Texas. He rode fast horses, robbed trains, outwitted the law, and spread his newfound wealth wherever he went. Georgie had no doubt the man could knock on any door in the state and be welcomed, fed, and harbored.

No. The passengers on this train would become celebrities in their own right and would carry tales of Comer for many months to come.

The weeping woman refused to be consoled, her hysterics gaining momentum, her sobs sounding like a saw rasping through wood.

Landrum looked her direction. "Is she hurt or just scared?"

The gruffness of his voice whipped Georgie up to her full height. She opened her mouth to defend the woman, but the widow herself answered him.

"Neither, sir. I'm overcome with gratitude. When Mr. Comer found out I was on my way to my childhood home after burying Henry and losing everything, he gave me this." She opened a gloved hand to reveal a handful of gold coins.

"He took my gun," a man farther down shouted, "but then he emptied it and gave it right back."

"He signed my dime novel." A boy with a bow tie and short pants held up his pulp fiction pamphlet. Georgie had seen him reading it earlier on the train. Its cover held a colorful illustration of a masked man with kindly eyes. Thick block letters across the top read, The Legend of FRANK COMER.

Ranger Landrum moved his attention back to the widow. "That money belongs to the Texas & Pacific, ma'am. I'm going to have to ask you to turn it over."

The widow pulled back, then narrowed her eyes, loosened her collar, and dropped the coins right down her bodice.

Landrum took a step forward. "You oughtn't have done that, ma'am."

Readjusting her collar, she held the Ranger's gaze. "I'm rather fatigued, sir. If you'll excuse me, I believe I'll return to my seat on the train."

The woman sailed past him, daring him to stop her, her skirts swishing with each step.

Georgie bit her cheeks. Any cooperation Landrum might have received had vanished the moment he challenged the widow. And she had a feeling he knew it.

His fierce gaze moved to the boy with the dime novel.

"No!" the little fellow screamed, throwing himself into his mother's arms.

Swooping him up and hugging him tight, she followed the same path as the widow. The rest of the passengers did the same, all giving a wide berth to Texas Ranger Lucious Landrum.

CHAPTER TWO

"A telephone salesman?" Lucious stared at his captain, aghast. "You want me to go undercover as a *telephone salesman?*"

"And repairman." Captain Heywood didn't even look up from his desk, his pen skating across the paper in front of him.

"You must be joking."

"Do I look like I'm joking?"

The wooden blinds in the dusty office of Ranger headquarters were tightly closed against the noon sun, but the captain still wore his silver-gray Stetson. Lucious didn't need to see beneath its brim, though, to know the man wasn't joking. He'd heard that tone of voice many times before.

"Sir, I think going undercover is a mistake. My reputation as a Ranger will help flush Comer out."

"Like it did last time, and the time before that, and the time before that?" The scratching of the captain's pen competed with the clicking of the overhead fan.

"Yes, with all due respect. Just like that."

The pen stopped. The brim of the Stetson slowly lifted. "If you'll recall, Landrum, all those campaigns were unsuccessful."

"Not at flushing him out, sir. Only at apprehending him."

Skin weathered from years on the trail was as much a badge of the job as the five-pointed star on the captain's lapel. "And apprehending him is the result we're after."

"Which I plan to do. I will do. But he could rob a dozen more trains in the time it would take me to discover his whereabouts were I to go undercover. If you'd let me have a company of men, we could go into Washington County, flush him out, and then I'd have him."

Heywood returned his pen to its holder and leaned back in a wooden chair almost as old as he was. Its springs creaked in protest. "That's what you said last time."

"I brought in six of his men."

"None of whom are talking."

"We found out Comer's laying low. We found out he and his men own land in Washington County. That they're holing up in their farmsteads and splitting their time between farming and thieving."

"We already suspected that."

"And now it's confirmed."

"You got nothing from the train passengers."

Lucious tightened his jaw. "They protect him, sir. They believe the newspapers and he plays on it. They have no idea of his real nature."

Heywood placed his elbows on the arms of the chair, lacing his fingers together. "You don't have to go undercover, Landrum."

Lucious allowed himself the first easy breath he'd had since entering the office. "Thank you, sir."

"I'll send Harvey in. He won't mind going undercover."

"No."

Heywood lifted a brow. "No?"

"I don't need Harvey or anyone else doing my job for me."

"Good." Heywood sprang forward and shuffled through a stack of papers, sending dust wafting through the air. "You'll check in with . . ." He extracted a page from the middle of the pile, dropped it in front of Lucious, then tapped it with his fingernail. "A Miss Georgie Gail. She's switchboard operator for the Southwestern Telegraph and Telephone Company. She's been told a troubleman is on his way."

Lucious skimmed the assignment.

NAME: *Lucious Landrum*
COMPANY: *"A"*
ALIAS: *Luke Palmer*
POSITION: *Telephone salesman/ repairman. Incl. bill collection, books, accounting*
LOCATION: *Brenham, Texas*
OFFICES OF: *Georgie Gail, Operator Southwestern Telegraph and Telephone Company*

Lucious looked up. "Luke Palmer, sir?"

Heywood had already returned to the document he'd been working on previously. "Thought it would be easy to answer to, Luke being a shortened version of Lucious and Palmer being your mother's maiden name."

Lucious dragged a hand across his mouth. "Would it be all right if I just did repairs and the bookkeeping?"

"You got something against selling telephones?"

"As a matter of fact, I do. It's dishonest, sir."

Heywood whipped up his head, brows lifted. "Dishonest?"

"Those contraptions aren't reliable. They barely work under the best of circumstances, but you can always count on them to go down in emergencies. They'll lull people into a false sense of security. I'd just as soon not be party to it."

Had he voiced his concerns to anyone else, they wouldn't have understood. But Captain Heywood did. He knew better than any the distrust Lucious had for modern communications.

"You're the best tracker we have, Lucious," the captain said, gentling his voice. "And I need you. But I didn't sign off on this without some reservations. The sheriff of Washington County is incompetent. The townsfolk think Comer's a hero. And you tend to grow a mite impatient with that kind of thing. It's occurred to me, more than once, you might not be the right man for the job."

Had Heywood walloped him in the gut, it couldn't have caught him more off guard. He'd looked up to this man his entire life. Working for him had been a privilege. An honor. To discover his captain had doubts did not bear thinking.

"Is there a manual of some kind?" Lucious asked. "I don't know the first thing about telephones."

Heywood had the grace not to smile, but Lucious could see he was pleased. Opening a drawer, he removed a pale blue booklet.

"Take this. It's a repair and sales manual. You need to read it start to finish and become proficient as quickly as possible. It took some mighty convincing to get SWT&T to let us use one of our men."

"SWT&T?"

"Southwestern Telegraph and Telephone Company. They want to expand their business. I assured them I was sending my best man and that he'd sell a lot of phones for them."

Lucious held his face in check. "I'll see to it, sir."

"Good."

Picking up the manual, he headed to the door.

"Landrum?"

Lucious turned.

The captain's expression grew steely. "I want him. Alive if you can. Dead if you have to. But I want him. If he slips through your grasp again, I'm putting Harvey on it."

"I'll bring him in, sir." As he pulled the door open, it took every bit of control he had not to slam it behind him.

Luke caught his first glimpse of Brenham, a predominantly German town, astride a paint horse and on a tenderfoot saddle no respectable lawman would own. During his five-day ride in from Alice, he'd memorized the twenty-three Rules for Troublemen as presented in his SWT&T manual.

Rule #1: *Put up a good front. It is not necessary to advertise any tailor shop; neither is it necessary to go about your work looking like a coal heaver. Overalls can look as respectable as anything else, but they must at least show they are on speaking terms with the laundryman; and shoes must have a bowing acquaintance with the bootblack.*

He hated this. No Stetson. No Lucchese boots. No gun belt. No Padgitt saddle. No mustache. No trousers, for crying out loud. He'd hidden his pistols — Odysseus and Penelope — along with his badge, inside a specially designed compartment of his suitcase.

His mahogany-and-white tobiano shook her mane, no doubt in protest to the indignity of having to ride through town with this godforsaken saddle strapped to her back. He'd picked up the mare last week, and though he'd compromised his standards on everything else, he drew the line at horseflesh. If the unexpected happened, he wanted an animal he could rely on.

Patting the mare's neck, he murmured words of sympathy and urged her onto a wooden bridge crossing the Hog Branch

River. Her clopping hooves captured the attention of a couple of boys with rolled-up pant legs and minnow nets. They quit their wading along the bank to stretch out and wave.

Luke tugged his hat. The moment his fingertips touched the rim, he was again reminded he'd had to pack his Stetson away. In place of the fine nutria fur was a brown duck farm hat, which — if Sears, Roebuck could be believed — would hold up in any kind of weather. He'd spent all week dirtying it and beating it, along with his new overalls and plow boots. Hopefully they looked well-worn, yet still decent enough to suit SWT&T.

A breeze whisked across the river, the leaves of a live oak flapping like coattails of men on the run. With the wind came the aroma of spring. In the distance, a quail whistled in appreciation.

He scanned the terrain, zeroing in on the bird's call, narrowing its hiding place to either the yaupon or the mesquite. He was almost on top of it before it burst from the mesquite and startled his horse.

Controlling Honey Dew with one hand, he "drew" with his other, pointed his finger and clicked his thumb down. "Pow," he murmured. "Gotchya."

Hunting quail ranked right up there with hunting outlaws. He loved how the bob-whites hunkered down until the last second, then erupted from their refuge, giving him but a split second to take the shot. Not with a pistol, of course, but with his Remington. Still, he'd had to leave his shotgun behind. For manhunts he needed his rifle. He adjusted the 1895 Winchester encased in a long scabbard on the left side of his horse, then looked for more birds.

He'd flushed out Comer just as he had the quail. Three times. And each time, Comer had either known he was coming, or he was receiving divine intervention. Whatever the case, Luke was in this untenable position because of it.

He allowed himself a long sigh. It wouldn't have been so bad if the men were holed up in one place like a typical gang. Then he'd just track them, find them, and capture them.

But nothing about Comer was typical. He took his time. He thought ahead. And he garnered citizen support.

Now he was spreading out his men. Turning them into farmers while things cooled down.

Luke repositioned himself in the saddle. For all he knew, they'd been farmers all along. Maybe they'd been living in Washington County for generations and came back to warm, cozy homes after every single job.

The boys he'd gathered up at this last robbery hadn't told them much, but it would sure explain why he'd had such a confounded time finding a hideout. The only time he came close to catching them was right after a holdup.

He'd be right on them, then — *poof.* They were gone.

He lifted his hat, then settled it back on his head. Their living as farmers was going to complicate the tracking. Especially if they really did farm — which he figured they must or it would arouse suspicion.

Either way, he was going to have to cozy up to every farmer around. He'd have to sit there drinking coffee and spitting chew until he could encourage them to talk freely about themselves and their neighbors. It was bound to take the rest of spring and maybe even the summer.

He rubbed his eyes. A telephone salesman. He hated telephones — any communication that relied on man-made devices. He clearly remembered his hometown of Indianola after it had been hit by one of the biggest hurricanes the U.S. had ever seen. Trees were uprooted. Entire buildings were gone.

Telegraph wires were down. Horses couldn't get through. And two and a half miles of railroad tracks had been destroyed.

None of it had stopped Captain Heywood, then a young Ranger just starting out. Luke was ten when Heywood rode in sitting tall and ramrod straight in the saddle while wading through the debris which had, the week before, been a thriving coastal town. He'd helped clean up. Helped the injured. And helped bury Luke's father, who'd lost his life in the tragedy.

Now, not only was Luke going to have to hoodwink folks into investing in those newfangled claptraps, he was going to have to waste time with niceties and social chatter. As different from Lucious Landrum as he could be.

Rule #11: *Be courteous and polite, and don't be afraid to hand out a little jolly occasionally. It doesn't hurt anybody's feelings to be jollied a little.*

Slowing down his mare, he picked his way across a series of railroad tracks and reined in at the depot.

Inside the small clapboard building, every surface was covered with polished oak — the walls, the floor, the rafters, the bench. Two arched ticket windows directly opposite the entrance held a series of vertical

35

wooden bars. No one stood behind them.

To his right, a group of boys between the ages of five and twelve faced the wall. They'd pressed themselves together so tightly, their bums looked like a cluster of oversized grapes.

Above them and mounted to the wall was a three-box telephone. The hand of the tallest boy covered its mouthpiece. The receiver was somewhere in the midst of them.

Sniggers, snorts, and giggles erupted spontaneously, followed by a series of shushes. Amusement tugged at Luke. Whoever was on the party line would have their business known all over town within the hour.

An explosion of guffaws rocked the boys backward, loosening the taller one's grip on the mouthpiece. Several grabbed their stomachs and bent over. Another fell to the ground in an effort to outdo the rest. Their boisterous laughter bowed the walls of the depot.

Chuckling, Luke took a step toward the ticket window to ask for directions. Before he could reach it, the door flew open. A girl of about nine stomped in.

"Fellers! That is *quite* enough." She stood in rolled-up, baggy overalls with feet spread, fists on her hips. If it hadn't been for the dirty braids resting on her shoulders, he wasn't sure he'd have even known it was a girl.

She marched into the pack of them, shoving them aside as if they were swinging doors to a saloon. The boys, still caught up in hilarity, allowed her to manhandle them . . . until she tried to take the receiver from the oldest boy. He immediately lifted his arm, putting it well out of reach.

"Give me the phone, Kyle."

"Come and get it, Bettina Hyena."

The nickname didn't even faze her. Clearly, it was one she'd heard many a time before. "Miss Georgie sent me down here, so hand it over."

Luke glanced at the ticket counter. An old-timer with round glasses and bushy white brows watched from behind the grill, but made no effort to assist the girl. If anything, he appeared amused by the boy's challenge.

Bettina flipped a braid behind her. "I'll go up there and git that thing, Kyle. You know I will."

"I'd like to see you try."

All laughter and fidgeting stopped. Luke tensed.

Slim as a bed slat, the boy had gotten a jump on his height. A tiny collection of facial hair tickled his chin and along the spot where sideburns would eventually grow. This was not just a boy, but a boy on the cusp of manhood. The only way that gal could reach the receiver was if she were to climb him like a flagpole. And Kyle knew it.

Luke stepped up to the group. "I believe this little lady's asked you for the phone, son."

Kyle started, as did the other boys. Clearly, they'd not even noticed him.

"Who're you?"

"Mr. Palmer. The new telephone man." Forcing himself to relax his shoulders and temper his tone, he gave a friendly smile. "I'll be working with Miss Gail. And if she says to hang up the phone, then I'm thinking you need to hang up the phone."

"I don't need yer help, mister," Bettina said. "I can do my own job by my own self."

He didn't take his eyes off Kyle. The boy wavered, unsure of which way to make the scales tip.

Don't do it, Luke thought. *I'm supposed to be nice. I need to be nice.*

The boy lifted his chin. "Hyena's right, sir. This don't concern you."

Quicker than the first rattle out of the box, Luke snatched the receiver and handed it to the girl. "Thank you, Kyle. And I believe her name is Bettina. I suggest you use it."

A murmur of awe rippled through the group of boys. Luke gave himself a mental shake. He hadn't meant to be so fast. He'd been disarming men for so long, he didn't even think. Just acted.

Thank goodness only kids and an old-timer saw. If they recounted the exchange, folks would assume they were exaggerating.

He ran his gaze across the group. "Party's over, boys. You run on, now. I'm sure I'll be seeing you around."

The boys looked to their leader.

Kyle hitched up the waistband of his trousers. "Come on, fellas. The smell's getting so thick in here the candles'll be ashamed to burn afore long."

Be nice. You need to be nice.

Luke let him walk out the door in one piece, then turned to Bettina.

"I coulda gotten it," she said, scowling.

"I'm sure you could have, but a gentleman doesn't stand by while a young lady's being abused."

She snorted. "I ain't no lady. Ever'body knows that. I'm the town drunk's whelp."

He stifled his reaction, reminding himself she was only repeating what she'd no doubt been told countless times. "You're a lady to me, miss." He could also see she was too short to hang up the receiver. "Would you like me to hang that up for you?"

"I can do it."

He sighed. "I'm sure you can, but I'd be honored if you'd let me assist you."

She scrunched up her face. "You ain't one of those grown-ups who's a little shy on brains, is ya?"

He reached out to grasp her waist and lift her up, but stopped short when she jerked back and covered her head with her arms.

Not only a town drunk, but a mean town drunk.

He knit his fingers together instead, making a stirrup. "How about a boost?"

She slowly lowered her arms, then plopped a filthy boot, which had to be two sizes too big, into his hands.

He lifted and she dropped the receiver into the cradle. The minute he lowered her back down, she was off and out the door.

He glanced at the ticket clerk. The man rolled a wad of chew from one side of his mouth to the other, then turned his head and spit.

Ping.

Stepping up to the window, Luke took a deep breath and asked for directions to Cottonwood Lane.

40

CHAPTER THREE

"Hello, Central." Georgie scooted her chair closer to a switchboard which resembled a very skinny upright piano, but where the sheet music would go was a black-bordered grid of jacks and round metal plates. In place of piano keys was a forest of plugs and toggle switches.

Speaking into a mouthpiece hanging from a pulley, she adjusted its height and grabbed a pencil. Number twelve was the doctor's residence.

"Von Hardenberg here, Georgie. I'm going to check on Mrs. Blesinger, then'll swing by the Shultes and Zientiks. Should be back around three."

She scribbled down his schedule. "I've got it. Would you tell Mr. Shulte the post office called and he has a package?"

Ding.

"Sure will. Talk to you later."

She removed the cable from line twelve

and plugged it into line twenty-two. "Hello, Central."

Ding. She glanced at her board. Number fifteen had also dropped.

"Don't ring me, Georgie. The baby's finally gone down for a nap."

"Oh, good. Maybe you should rest, too, Mrs. Bargus. Either way, I'll hold your calls. Don't forget to let me know when Martie Jr. wakes up."

She unplugged Mrs. Bargus and plugged into line fifteen. "Hello, Central."

"Can you get Agnes on the line for me, Georgie? I want to find out what she puts in her tomato aspic. It's divine —"

Ding. Number eight.

"— and mine never comes out right. She brought it to the Ladies' Reading Circle Tuesday morning. We read *Last of the Mohicans,* you know, and were just beginning to discuss the part where the girls were captured by Indians when I placed a bite of Agnes's aspic in my mouth. Oh, heaven on earth. I didn't hear another —"

Ding. Georgie placed one hand on a toggle key and the other on a plug, then eyed the rows of jacks on her board. Each had a tiny hinged plate above it, no bigger than a nickel. And each plate had a number engraved on it. Whenever anyone called, the plate, or drop-line, would fall open, alerting Georgie as to who was calling. Right now, it was number eight.

"— word. I'm telling you, you haven't lived until —"

"Mrs. Oodson, I'm sorry to interrupt, but —"

"— you've had Agnes's aspic. Of course, her hushpuppies don't hold a candle to mine. Mine are crisp on the outside, soft on the inside. The secret, I don't mind telling you, is —"

Ding.

Georgie took a firm breath. "One moment, Mrs. Oodson."

She flipped the toggle key to neutral, then lifted a plug, unrolling its cable, and inserting it into number eight.

"Please hold. I'll be right with you."

She positioned number eight's key to the middle, then grasped a cable on the same circuit as Mrs. Oodson. She plugged it into line twenty-five, pulled its rear key backward, and turned the crank for one long and two short rings.

"Hello?"

Georgie pushed the key forward, allowing her and the two women she'd connected to all hear one another. Mrs. Oodson had never quit talking.

"— was wearing the most awful shade of red. I don't know why women with orange hair insist on wearing red. Do they not have a mirror, for heaven's sake? It simply —"

"Hello?" Agnes repeated.

"Go ahead, please." Georgie flicked the key to neutral, retaining the connection between the women but disconnecting herself.

Returning to number eight, she pressed that circuit's key forward. "I'm so sorry for the wait. This is Central."

"Vat time to do you have, Georgie?" Burch Leatherman barked. "My timepiece stop again."

She looked at her watch pin. "I have eleven fifty-three, sir."

"Gut. Danke."

She removed the cable, deactivated the key, leaned back in her chair, and rubbed her ear beneath the earpiece. It had been busy for a Thursday. The ladies usually didn't start visiting until ten, but they'd gotten a jump on things today and had never slowed down. Lunch would be on their tables soon, though, so she should have a lull over the next hour.

She swiped a dust cloth around the ten sets of plugs on her switchboard. Each pair made up a line — one cable connected the first person, the other cable connected the second. Of her ten lines, six were currently being used. The crisscrossed cables looked like giant red earthworms stretching from the table portion of her burnished oak switchboard to the jacks on its hutch.

If the rest of them rang, she'd have to break into Fred and Birdie's conversation. The young sparking couple had been on the phone all morning and had provided no small amount of entertainment for the boys down at the depot.

She wondered if Bettina had been successful in chasing them off. She pulled line one's key back, activating her earpiece but not her mouthpiece.

"— should have seen Chili slip the dog-catcher's noose," Birdie said. "He threw it right over her, but instead of running, she backed up, so he couldn't tighten it."

"That Chili's a smart one, all right," Fred answered.

The line was much clearer and louder than before, which meant fewer people were listening in. Returning the key to neutral, Georgie smiled. That was one way to ensure some privacy — talk so long everyone grew tired of listening and just hung up.

Placing her hands on her back, she arched and glanced out the giant bay window overlooking her backyard. The pink columbine had just begun to bloom, beckoning birds, bees, and butterflies. Even now, a ruby-throated hummingbird hovered over one of its bell-like flowers, sipping sweet nectar from deep within.

Georgie reached blindly for her opera glasses, then focused on the tiniest of the bird species. As if sensing its audience, the showy male flew sideways, backward, and hovered in midair before zipping out of view.

A sense of awe and delight filled her. Winter's quilt had been thrown off, leaving the way for spring. She hoped it would bring even more birds to her doorstep than last year.

She examined her yard as if from a bird's point of view. It offered plenty of open sky for flying and chasing. Yet surrounding its perimeter were trees, brush, vines, and ground cover specifically designed to entice.

Evergreens for the grackles, holly for the songbirds, Mexican plum for the fruit birds. Honeysuckle and Virginia creeper for a whole array of feathered friends. Wild rye for nesting material. And at the top of a five-foot pole, a wooden starch box with a rounded-out entrance and perches at either end. In just a few short months, some lucky family would have a private, cozy cabin for nesting. She wondered who it would be this time.

Under her back porch eaves hung alternating containers of sugar water and birdseed. Scattered throughout the garden were three different kinds of birdbaths, for more young birds died from lack of water than from any other cause. She had even planted items for coaxing insects to her yard, knowing they were an essential food source for her birds.

She returned her opera glasses to the corner of the switchboard table. One by one, she pulled each toggle key backward to see if anyone was still on the line. All had disconnected — even Fred and Birdie had finally hung up. She unplugged a cable, activating its spring-loaded reel, which coiled it up beneath the desktop, leaving only the metal plug visible. When all cables were in ready position, she checked her watch. Lunchtime.

Luke eyed the giant telephone pole in front of a quaint cottage on Cottonwood Lane. Thick wires radiated out in all directions. Yet every single one originated from the roof of the cottage. He assumed they terminated at the switchboard inside.

Tying Honey Dew to the hitching rail, he let himself through the front gate. A covered veranda stretched across the tiny yellow clapboard house, offering a haven for a green bench to the right of the door and two rattan rockers and a porch swing to the left. A squirrel on a lawn settee beneath a giant burr oak sat on its hind legs and twitched its nose.

Luke wondered if the telephone company provided the outdoor furniture. While preparing to go undercover, he'd been surprised to learn SWT&T gave their rural switchboard operators a fully furnished home. He could see doing that for a married woman, but a single gal?

That kind of independence was unheard of, even for one as old as Miss Gail. According to his report, she was twenty and unwed. Not for the first time, he wondered why.

Adjusting his hat, he climbed the steps. The front door was open, leaving only a screen between him and her.

He knocked. No movement, no noise. He could see the door led to a large living area.

He knocked again. "Hello? Anybody home?"

Nothing. He stepped back. The double window above the green bench looked into the same big room. He circled around the rockers on the left and peeked inside an

48

open smaller window.

Lacy curtains billowed out, giving him a glimpse of a bed, a washstand, and a wardrobe. He immediately straightened, though there was no need. No one had been inside the bedroom.

Sighing, he looked up and down the street. Hers was definitely the smallest house on the block. Cattycorner and three lots down was the Campbellite church. But there was no activity there, nor anywhere else.

Honey Dew swished her tail and gave a slow blink.

Returning to the door, he knocked again, then cupped his eyes with his hands and rested them against the screen. A bank of windows lined the entire southern wall of the living area. Spaced across it was a large, cluttered office desk, the switchboard, and a boxed-in contraption. The frame for all the cables, perhaps?

Centered along the west wall was a stone fireplace, bookcases on either side. He lifted his brows. Surely SWT&T didn't supply her with books, too. But where else would all those have come from?

An overstuffed divan, an easy chair, and a rocker crowded the center of the room, facing the dormant fireplace.

No rug. No wall hangings. No ornaments on the mantel. No zillions of tiny knick-knacks, which stifled every parlor he'd ever seen.

He frowned. The phone company said she'd come from their Dallas exchange and had been here for over a year. Seems like she'd have given it a woman's touch by now.

Straightening, he swiped at a gnat buzzing about his ear. Maybe he should check the back. He was halfway down the side of the house when it occurred to him she might be at the outhouse.

He slowed his pace. He'd just look around the corner. If she was making a trip to or from, he'd dart back to the street and start all over.

"Dad-blast it, Ivan." A woman's strident voice. "I've told you never to come around here. How many times do I have to tell you?"

Luke froze. An unwelcome suitor? A woman living alone would be mighty vulnerable. He crouched down, inching his way forward.

"I'm sick and tired of you coming over here licking your lips while drool drips from your mouth. I've had enough, I tell you. Enough."

Luke stopped midstride. What kind of

woman would say something like that? Only one kind he knew of. And it wasn't the kind who had a respectable address in a respectable neighborhood.

"Stop it." Her voice jumped an octave. "No! Get!" *Whack.* "I mean it. Get away from here." *Whack. Whack.*

Luke took several running hops, removed his hat, and peeked around the corner.

A little wisp of a woman held up the hem of her brown skirt with one hand and swung a broom with the other.

"Botheration," she mumbled, jumping over a clump of pink flowers. "Missed again."

He slowly eased away from the house. Whatever creature she was whacking, it wasn't of the two-legged variety.

"Out!" She swung.

"Rrrrraaaaaaarrh!" A reddish-brown cat leapt to the edge of the property, the woman keeping pace.

"You find your dinner somewhere else, Ivan. You cannot dine here." She swung and missed. "Ever. Do you hear me?"

Ivan jumped onto the trunk of an elderberry, then onto a fence and over the other side.

"And stay there," she shouted, shaking her fist. "Because the next time you come back,

I'll . . . I'll . . . I'll shoot you with a slingshot. Just see if I don't!"

Luke rubbed a hand across his mouth. What the deuce was wrong with cats?

She stood with her back to him, a swath of blond hair tumbling over one heaving shoulder while she gripped the broom's handle so tight her knuckles turned white.

Looking up into the tree, she shaded her eyes with her hand. "It's all right, little ones. You can come out now."

Ah. There were some kids up there who were afraid of cats.

But no one answered her call. No leaves in the tree shook. He took a couple steps forward and for the first time noticed the magnificence of her backyard.

At first glance, it looked almost random. But upon closer inspection, he realized there was nothing arbitrary about it. It was more like a precisely arranged orchestra, with wildflowers in the front where the strings go. Tall grasses in place of the woodwinds. Shrubs in lieu of brass. Vine-covered fences for percussion. And midsized trees interspersed throughout. At the edge of the property, three giant shade trees provided a backdrop.

She stepped toward the elderberry, rested the broom against its trunk, then stuck two little fingers in her mouth.

Cheeeeeeeo . . . wheet wheet wheet wheet wheet wheet wheet. Cheeeeeo, cheeeeeo, cheeeeeo . . . wheet wheet wheet wheet wheet wheet.

His mouth slackened. Her whistle was strong, loud, and sounded exactly like some bird he'd heard a million times. He had no idea which bird it was. Wouldn't know it if he saw it. But he'd sure heard it sing like that. Plenty of times.

She did it again, and lo and behold, if something didn't answer her back. His gaze flew to the branches of the tree but saw nothing.

Laughing, she propped her hands against her waist, arched her back, and lifted her chin. A breeze wafted the hair that had come loose.

"Don't you worry, handsome," she said. "I've chased that mean ol' cat away. You're safe now."

"Well," Luke drawled. "I'm mighty relieved to know that. Thank you."

Squeaking, she spun around. A bird darted from the elderberry, but he didn't look. No longer cared which bird made that noise.

"I wasn't talking to you," she breathed.

He settled his hat on his head. "Weren't you?"

"No." She stood in a patch of autumn sage, its rich red blooms forming a three-foot hedge around her.

He sauntered closer. "You must be Miss Gail."

"That's right. Who're you?"

"Luke Palmer. The new troubleman."

"Oh!" She jumped forward, skirting the sage bush, brushing her skirt, tucking in her blouse. "I wasn't . . . I didn't . . . I . . ." Sighing, she stopped. "Hello."

He tugged his hat. "Hello."

"Welcome to Brenham."

"Thank you."

Her eyes were green. He'd seen hazel before — a bit of blue with a bit of green. But these were all-out green like a Scandinavian goddess's, except she was no bigger than a mite. She had all the requisite curves, though.

"When did you get to town?" she asked.

"Just rode in."

She clasped her hands. "Oh my. Just in. Are you hungry? Have you had your dinner?"

"Yes, ma'am. Had it on the trail."

"Well. I see. Good." Swallowing, she made no move to invite him in. Just stood there wringing her hands.

He glanced at the yard. "Nice garden."

She turned toward it, showing him her profile. Smooth forehead. Small nose. Full lips. Defined chin. Long neck.

"Do you think so?"

It took him a second. The garden. "Yes, I do."

Everything about her softened. "I hope the birds think so, too."

In a flash, his subconscious brought forth items he'd seen, but not noticed. Birdbaths. Bird feeders. And a birdhouse made from an old starch box. "I'm sure they will."

She turned back to him and smiled. He blinked. She was pretty before, but when she smiled her whole face lit, especially her eyes. Multiple laugh lines framed her mouth. Straight white teeth peeked out. And a teeny brown mole to the left of her lower lip quivered.

"Well, we'd best get inside, Mr. Palmer, so I can show you where everything is. After the lunchtime lull, folks will be ready for some neighborly visiting, and every line on the board will drop." She swept past him, her hips offering a suggestion of sway.

It must be mental, whatever kept her from being married. Because there sure wasn't a thing wrong with the way that gal was put together.

Removing his hat, he followed her through the back door.

CHAPTER FOUR

"Your first priority is stringing lines onto the new telephone poles." Georgie stood between the troubleman and her desk.

She'd known he was coming, she just didn't know it was going to be today. Now. This minute. And he wasn't at all what she'd expected.

There'd been lots of troublemen in Dallas and none of them had been so . . . virile. It wasn't an attribute she often assigned to men of her acquaintance. None, actually, now that she thought on it.

Tilting her head, she considered exactly what it was that made him so. When studying her birds, she made note of every feature. Her gaze moved to the top of Mr. Palmer's head.

Crown: curly brown hair, which no comb had tamed. Eye ring: blue, the exact shade of an indigo bunting. Forehead: perfectly normal. Nothing of note there. Bill: intoxicating smile he flashed at the most unexpected moments. Chin: square jaw, which would need a shave by the end of the day. Throat: prominent Adam's apple. Chest: a physique any pugilist would envy. Plumage: Denim work overalls and white chambray shirt.

She sighed. No, it wasn't any one thing. Rather, the entire body, from head to tail, back to belly.

"I'm sorry," she said. "Calling upon nonsubscribers will have to wait until all urgent matters have been completed."

"My orders come from SWT&T, not you." He took a step forward, crowding her. "So, I'd appreciate it if you gave me the list of who has service and who doesn't."

She offered him a patient smile. "You don't seem to understand, Mr. Palmer. We have to take care of the customers we have first; then we can start introducing more."

He held out his hand. Wing: calloused, large, and strong.

"The list, please," he said.

"Don't you think you'll have a much better chance of drawing in new customers once we have real telephone wire fastened to real telephone poles, instead of common wire tacked onto trees, fences, and anything else which happens to be available? For heaven's sake, some folks are receiving service over barbed wire."

He kept his hand where it was. "I will string the wire, Miss Gail. But first, I'd like that list."

"I'm afraid I must insist. First, you string the wire."

Ding.

She glanced at the switchboard. Number nine had dropped. Suppressing her frustration, she skirted around him, slipped on her earpiece, plugged in a cable, and pushed the key forward. "Hello, Central."

"It's L.J. I hear tell the new troubleman's done made it to town. Is he comin' to get his cart and all this stuff them linemen left fer him? I really need the space back."

She glanced at Mr. Palmer. He brushed his fingers across some papers on her desk, fanning them out.

"I'll send him right over, Mr. Lockett. I know he's anxious to get started."

Palmer shot her a sideways glance, then returned to his nosing around.

She pulled out the cable. "That was the livery. Your installer's cart is there, along with miles of galvanized wire, insulators, brackets, climbers, and everything else you need to get started."

He ignored her. A brown curl fell across

his forehead.

"Mr. Palmer, would you kindly step away from my desk?"

Scooping the papers together, he set them on end and tapped their edges straight. "I believe, Miss Gail, this is my desk."

She stiffened. "I beg your pardon? That desk belongs to —"

"The Southwestern Telegraph and Telephone Company. And they have asked me to take over the billing, collecting, and trouble tickets. Since this is where the offices of SWT&T are located, well, it makes sense this is where the billing, collecting, and trouble tickets are generated. So this, Miss Gail, is now *my* desk."

She'd been told he was to take over those duties, but she had no intention of giving up either them or her desk. And when she'd asked Mr. Marshall in the Dallas office about it, he'd chuckled. "Well, of course he'll do those things," he'd said. "With a man there, we've no need to depend on a woman any longer."

Just thinking about it made her want to snatch him baldheaded.

She took a deep breath. "You're not going to have time for that just yet, Mr. Palmer. As I mentioned before, your first priority is to string wire."

60

He set her papers on the corner of the desk. "And as I mentioned before, I will begin the paperwork immediately. I will assume control of this desk. And I will have that list of subscribers."

Ding.

She snatched up a cable and stuffed it into number twenty-eight. "Hello, Central."

"Georgie, it's Mattieleene. How old is he? What does he look like? You have met him, haven't you?"

She didn't pretend to misunderstand. "Yes."

He tried to open one of the drawers, but it was locked. With a great deal of satisfaction, she smoothed her skirt beneath her and adjusted herself in her chair.

"Well?" Mattieleene asked.

"He's big and he's grouchy."

He pierced her with his gaze.

She shifted, facing forward. She could still see him, but only in her peripheral vision.

"Never say so!" Mattieleene moaned. "Is he old?"

"Very old."

He jiggled the second and third drawers. Locked.

"Is he ugly?"

"Long in tooth and raised on sour milk."

Balling his fists, he placed them on the

desktop and leaned against it. The fabric of his sleeves tightened around his upper arms.

"Oh, crumbs." Mattieleene sounded near tears. "Why couldn't they have sent a man with a little fur on his brisket?"

"Party lines, Mattieleene. Anyone can hear." And from the crackling on the line, it was a sure bet half the town was listening in. "I'm going to have to let you go now. We'll talk later." She unplugged the cable.

"Where is the key to these drawers, Miss Gail?" His tone was soft with a steely undercurrent.

She immediately thought of the woman on the train after the arrogant Ranger had demanded her coins. Georgie ran a finger along her neckline. "It's in a safe place."

His gaze touched her bodice. He narrowed his eyes. "Don't play games with me, ma'am."

"Or what?"

He slowly straightened. A mockingbird began running through an entire repertoire of songs, some his own, others imitations. A whiff of lemon pie cooling on someone's windowsill touched Georgie's nose, making her stomach growl.

Still, she held his gaze. She was the one who'd been doing all the work. She was the one with the seniority. She was the one who knew the customers. She'd be deviled if she was going to roll over and play dead simply because he was a man and she wasn't.

"If I have to involve Mr. Marshall," he said, "I will. But I'd rather not."

She lifted her chin. "If you feel the need to tattle, by all means, go ahead. But to do so will require a long-distance call. Do you know how to place one?"

A tick began in his jaw.

That's what she thought.

Ding.

She plugged in number nine. "Hello, Central."

"Is he comin' or not?"

"He hasn't left yet, Mr. Lockett. I'll remind him again." She unplugged. "The livery is waiting."

Reaching up, he slid his fingers across the lip of the kitchen doorframe. Had he not believed the key was tucked inside her bodice? It wasn't, but he didn't know that.

So long as he didn't look into her bedroom — which of course he wouldn't — then all was safe. But the moment he left, she'd retrieve it off her washstand, where it sat in plain sight.

He tipped up the desk chair, looking beneath its seat.

Ding.

"Hello, Central."

"Do you know where the doc is? Little Shirley has taken ill."

Georgie checked the doctor's schedule. "He's at the Shultes', the Zientiks', or somewhere in between. He's expected to be back by three."

"Would you have him call me when he returns?"

"Of course. Tell Shirley I hope she feels better."

Mr. Palmer had moved to her bookshelves, making no pretense of doing anything other than snooping. The key would certainly not be hidden inside any of the volumes, yet he thumbed through one book after the other.

"Mr. Palmer, the livery —"

Ding.

Sighing, she plugged into line seventeen. "Hello, Central." At Mrs. Dobbing's request, Georgie rang and connected her to Mrs. Folschinski. "Go ahead, please."

Mr. Palmer held up her Nellie Bly board game. "What the deuce is this?"

"It is personal property, Mr. Palmer. Property you do not have permission to rifle through. This may be the headquarters of SWT&T here in Brenham, but it is also my home, and I would ask you to respect my privacy."

"Give me the key."

"No."

He opened the box and took pieces out of her game, examining them.

Whipping off her earpiece, she jumped to her feet. "That is quite enough, sir."

"What are you, some kind of Nellie Bly follower?"

She snatched up the box and began to replace the pieces. "Nellie Bly is one of the greatest women of our time."

"She's a troublesome female who puts ideas into the heads of our women."

Tightening her lips, Georgie returned the game to the shelf. "Exactly what ideas are you referring to? The ones which say women are good for more than just cleaning, sewing, and keeping house? The ones which say a woman should be permitted to have a career if she so chooses? A career like — I don't know, a telephone operator? Would that be the kind of idea you object to?"

"It certainly would be. If you were a man, you'd have allowed me to prioritize my job the way I wanted to. You'd have shown me the list of subscribers. You'd have given me the key the moment I asked." With each statement he puffed up like a grackle. "Now, stop all this nonsense and either do as I've requested or go back to your sewing, clean-

65

ing, and keeping house."

Walking to the screen door, she opened it. "Get out of my home, Mr. Palmer."

"Give me the key, Miss Gail."

"When pigs fly, sir." Her entire body trembled. She clearly remembered her mother being told the farm they'd spent their whole life working would be taken from them without Papa. Didn't matter he'd died. Didn't matter he wanted Mama to have it. All that mattered was Mama had been a woman and therefore unworthy of being a landowner.

But Nellie Bly was different. She'd secured a job as a newspaper journalist. She'd pretended to be insane so she could expose the atrocities occurring in asylums. She'd broken a world record by traveling around the world in seventy-two days. *By herself.* At age twenty-five she'd become the most famous woman in the world.

And Georgie owned every product Miss Bly had ever endorsed except for her hat. But one day, when she'd saved enough, Georgie would buy herself a Nellie Bly hat.

In the meanwhile, she had no use for men who were so narrow-minded they could look through a keyhole with both eyes at the same time.

Mr. Palmer grabbed his hat from the

stand. "I'm going to pick up my supplies. When I get back, you better have that key sitting on top of my desk or I'll rip out every drawer in it. Don't think I won't."

"I wouldn't advise it. You'd be damaging company property."

"When I tell Marshall why, I have a feeling no one will be blaming me." He jammed on his hat. "You have thirty minutes, missy." He stormed out the door.

She slammed the screen behind him. It bounced open and closed before settling. But she knew he was right. If Palmer destroyed the desk, Mr. Marshall would hold her responsible and it would be her pay which was docked.

She watched Palmer swing up into his saddle, then take off at a full gallop.

Opening the screen door, she slammed it one more time, but it didn't change anything. He was still a male and she wasn't. Which meant her desk — and its key — would now be his.

CHAPTER FIVE

Luke gently shook the reins, prodding Honey Dew and the green installer's cart he rode. The smell of fresh bread billowed out of a bakery, making him glance up at the sun to judge how long before supper.

He sighed. Several hours yet. Carriages of every sort parked along the street, stepping blocks at their sides. Ladies flitted in and out of shops. A woman sporting a top-heavy hat slipped beneath a faded red awning leading to Scobey's Curiosity Shop.

He squinted, trying to see through the glass. He loved curiosity shops. As a boy he'd once seen a two-headed calf preserved in spirits. The aged cowboy running the place had said two heads made him half as difficult to rope. Luke smiled at the memory.

The syncopated rhythm of horses' hooves clashed with the sound of whistling coming from an open window. A man with a measuring tape about his neck stood inside the millinery's display window, setting a new monstrosity toward the front. A driver waiting for his mistress caught Luke's eye and gave a nod.

Responding in kind, he couldn't help but feel the difference between riding down the street in his overalls and riding down the street with his badge and gun belt. Ordinarily, men, women, and children of every age and walk of life quit whatever they were doing just to watch him and his sorrel pass through. Yet today, he wasn't worthy of even a glance — other than a brief acknowledgment from another of his ilk.

He shouldn't have minded. Shouldn't have even noticed. Yet he did.

The whitewashed Exchange Hotel took up almost an entire block. A gentleman and his lady stepped outside onto its roomy veranda. She opened a bright blue parasol the same color as her dress, then took her man's arm.

Luke followed them with his gaze, appreciating the sway of her skirts. *That* was how a lady should comport herself. She wasn't supposed to chase down cats with her broom, flounce around with her hair coming loose, nor square up to a man.

He became riled just thinking about it.

The mystery of why Miss Gail wasn't married had certainly been solved in a hurry. She just better have that key for him when he returned or he'd . . . he'd what?

What could he do? That desk was solid oak. He'd have to take an ax to it before he could break it open. And despite what he'd said to Miss Gail, SWT&T was none too happy to have him here. He didn't want to give them any excuse for removing him from his position and sending in a real troubleman.

Honey Dew snorted, drawing his attention. The installer's cart wasn't very big, but the giant reel of wire in the back weighed close to nine hundred pounds. It'd be slow going until he could lighten his load.

Rule #12: *Treat everybody as you like to be treated, not forgetting your horse; if you want to know the horse's side of it, just take off your coat and hat some zero day, hitch yourself to the same post with your belt, and stand there for a few hours. Hereafter don't forget his blanket.*

He spoke to Honey Dew in soothing tones, but the only way to lighten their load was to string the blasted stuff. Pushing up the brim of his hat, he glanced at the web of telephone wires above him, the bright sky making him squint. The wires ran every direction imaginable.

He tried to follow one from pole to point of entry into a building, but couldn't. The tangle was too complex. What a colossal mess. If one of those lines went down, how would he ever figure out which was which?

Guiding Honey Dew to the right, he turned onto Sycamore. What he needed was to string the wire he was hauling. It would give him practice with the lines and would get him out of town, where he could take a look at the surrounding farms. But he sure didn't want Miss Gail thinking he was doing it because she said so.

Making a left, he passed the church, then pulled up into the side yard of 114 Cottonwood Lane. The little yellow house looked so welcoming. So warm. You'd never suspect a shrew lived inside.

Jumping to the ground, he unhitched the cart. The list of telephone subscribers was critical to starting his investigation. It would familiarize him with who lived where, how long they'd been there, and if they had phone service.

To do that, though, he needed access to her desk. What would he do if the key wasn't where he'd told her to put it? He couldn't bust out the drawers. And he wasn't about to telegraph the captain. But neither could he do nothing.

He saddled his mare, then secured her to the hitching rail. He would have to think of something, because one way or the other, he was getting inside that desk.

Squaring his hat, he let himself through the gate. The closer he came to the porch, the quieter he moved, one ear cocked. No sound came from within. So either no one was on the phone or she was out back whacking cats.

Easing up the steps, he crossed the veranda and peeked inside. She sat at the switchboard, her back to the door, her earpiece tethering her to the machine. The brown of her skirt was lost against the oak switchboard, but her crisp white shirtwaist clearly outlined petite shoulders and tiny waist.

She slowly fanned herself with a large straw fan, her attention fixed on something outside. She'd repaired her hair. He wondered when she realized it was all askew from cat whacking. She'd certainly been unaware of it while he'd been there.

Unusual for a female. All the women he knew had a sixth sense if something about their person was amiss. Not Miss Gail. She'd had no idea.

Even now he could see she'd missed a few

wispys. They lifted and fell with each wave of her fan. He took another moment to enjoy the view, because that's all it was. Once he made his presence known, Jekyll would vanish and Hyde would appear.

He moved his attention to the desk, but the mesh screen kept him from seeing whether a key lay on top of it. Miss Gail pulled a lever on the board, then unplugged two cables. She pulled another lever but left those cables in.

He tapped the doorframe. Glancing over her shoulder, she tensed, then turned back around. No invitation inside, but no command to go away, either.

Opening the screen, he hooked his hat on the stand and crossed to the desk. A key lay smack in the middle of it. He let out a silent breath.

She picked up a pair of binoculars and pointed them in the opposite direction from where he stood. He followed her line of vision out the window. There was nothing to see. Yet she kept them against her eyes, pretending fascination with . . . a leaf?

He rubbed his mouth. Should he thank her? Probably not. Apologize? Absolutely not. So he pulled out a chair, sat down, and unlocked the top drawer.

Ding.

She set down the binoculars. "Hello, Central."

He tuned her out and went through every file, every document, every ledger. She kept excellent records. Her penmanship was first-rate. Her math flawless.

He began memorizing the names and locations of those receiving service outside of town. When his eyes began to cross, he stretched, linking his hands behind his head and twisting to the left. He twisted to the right and froze. She was staring at him, only she wasn't taking in the view the way he'd done earlier. No, she was looking at him as if he was a polecat at a picnic.

He lowered his arms.

"How does everything look?" she asked.

It was the best record keeping he'd ever seen. And he'd seen plenty. "It'll do."

Her lips thinned. The little mole beneath them shifted. "Do you have any questions?"

"Not as yet."

"How long are you going to sit there?"

He leaned back in his chair. "Am I bothering you?"

"Yes."

He didn't try to hide his amusement.

"Gloating?" she asked.

"No, ma'am."

She crossed her arms. "How long are you

going to sit there?"

"Miss Georgie, Miss Georgie!"

The two of them turned. The little gal from the depot scurried across the veranda, hunching over something in her hands. He stood, but before he could open the screen, she one-handed it. Her overalls had taken a turn for the worse, dirt marring their knees and seat.

"Sorry that last message took me so long to deliver," the girl said. "But lookit what I found. You'll never believe it." She stopped short, gaping at him. "What're you doin' here?"

"I work here," he said.

"No foolin'?"

"No fooling."

She accepted his claim with the unquestioning faith of youth, continued to Miss Gail's side, then held out her prize.

Miss Gail lurched back in her chair. Was it something poisonous? He was there in two strides, but it was only a bird's nest with three tiny eggs inside.

"Oh, Bettina." Miss Gail pressed her knuckles against her mouth. "Where did you find this?"

"In the big ol' pecan tree over there in Germania Park. Some fellers were throwing rocks at it, but I chased 'em off. Then I got to thinking, they'd fer sure come back later, you know, on account o' Ottfried's offer? So I done climbed up that tree and rescued it. Wanna help me put it in yer birdhouse?" She headed toward the kitchen.

"Bettina." A sadness edged Miss Gail's tone.

The girl stopped.

"We can't put that nest in the birdhouse, I'm afraid."

Bettina's eyes widened. "You done got somebody in there already?"

"No. Not yet."

"Then how come I can't put it in there?"

Miss Gail clasped her hands in her lap. "The mother and father bird won't be able to find it."

"Why, sure they will. All them birds round here come to yer place. It's the best spot in town."

"All the same, this nest has to stay right where the parents put it."

The girl looked at the nest, clearly unconvinced. "I can't put it back. Them boys'll get it. How 'bout I put it in yer mulberry tree? Why, that tree's as busy as Charlie's place on a Saturdee night."

Luke lifted his brows.

Bright spots of pink colored Miss Gail's cheeks. "You mustn't say things like that," she whispered.

"I ain't lying." Bettina whipped herself up.

"Of course not. I meant . . ." She sighed. "Never mind. We'll talk about it later. For now, tell me what you mean about Mr. Ottfried's offer."

"You know, the cash money offer."

"For his millinery? I haven't heard anything about it."

Bettina clucked her tongue. "You're the town operator, Miss Georgie. You're supposed to know about this kinda stuff."

The pink in Miss Gail's cheeks flushed bright red and filled her entire face. He slid his hands in his pockets and leaned against the desk.

"Perhaps you'd best tell me," she said.

Ding. She handled the call, then turned back to Bettina.

"Mr. Ottfried's givin' out money fer any kind o' bird stuff you bring in."

Miss Gail frowned. "What kind of bird stuff?"

"You know, feathers, nests, eggs, even whole birds — dead or alive."

With each item listed, Miss Gail's posture straightened a bit more, as if a pulley stretched her one crank at a time. "You cannot be serious."

"I ain't lying." Bettina's face crumpled. "That's twice now you haven't believed me."

Miss Gail held out a hand, but the girl didn't take it, so she let it drop.

"I believe you, Bettina. It's Mr. Ottfried I can't believe."

"Well, he ain't lying, neither. There's a big ol' sign in his window."

She removed her earpiece, careful not to muss her hair, and rose to her feet. "Can you do me a favor, Mr. Palmer?"

He crossed his ankles. "Depends on what it is."

"Will you watch the switchboard for me? I need to run to town for a few minutes."

The switchboard? She wanted him to work the switchboard? But that was a woman's job.

He couldn't say that, of course. Not after the big stink he'd made about women working. Still, he didn't fancy himself sitting there answering the phone. However . . .

He looked at the toes of his boots, then back up at her. "I do my job my way, on my time frame. No questions asked."

"Deal."

"I'm not finished."

She gripped the back of her chair. "Well, hurry up. What else?"

"The desk is mine. The key is mine."

Her lips fell open. "That's not fair."

"It's mine anyway and we both know it."

She drummed her fingernail on the seat-back. "Can we share it?"

He pursed his lips. "We might could work something out."

"Good." She yanked her chair back. "Sit down and let me show you how to use this thing."

CHAPTER SIX

Georgie hurried down Market Street. She'd never missed a moment of work since arriving in Brenham. Too many people depended on her. She wasn't at all comfortable leaving them in Mr. Palmer's hands, but he'd caught on fast, this was an emergency, and he was, after all, an employee of SWT&T.

Bettina did her best to keep up, but her oversized boots slowed her down and she was still trying to preserve the nest of eggs. "I'm tellin' ya, if I put 'em back, them boys will get 'em."

The little eggs were doomed no matter what. Georgie had seen birds take on snakes to protect their young. If boys had thrown rocks and Bettina had stolen the nest — all without repercussions — then the parents had long since abandoned their babies.

Still, if there was any chance . . . "I want you to put it back just the same. Perhaps the mama and daddy birds will return."

"What if they don't?" The girl looked at her treasure. "No tellin' what Mr. Ottfried would pay for a nest and three whole eggs."

Georgie pulled up short. "You may *not* sell those to Mr. Ottfried."

"But what if he pays me a nickel? I'd be rich as Will Cummings if I had me a whole nickel."

Georgie's heart squeezed. Lifting one of the girl's brown braids, she fanned a finger across its tail. It was time for a hair wash. "Is the money you're earning as my errand girl running out too fast?"

Bettina pulled back, breaking the connection between her braid and Georgie. "Me and Pa are getting by. But that don't mean I wouldn't like a sarsaparilla stick or one of them rock-and-rye drops. And sometimes, I get me a powerful thirst fer a Dr. Pepper. I could get all that fer a nickel and still have money left over."

Normally Bettina kept her vulnerabilities well hidden. That she would reveal such a wish list spoke volumes.

"What if the mama and daddy birds are there right now?" Georgie asked. "Looking for their babies?"

"What if they aren't?"

She took a deep breath. "If you sell those to Mr. Ottfried, they'll end up on some

81

lady's hat. How would you feel if you ran into somebody wearing those poor baby eggs?"

"I'd wanna know how much she paid fer her hat."

Georgie looked up the street toward the milliner's. "More than a nickel, I can promise you that."

"How much more?"

She lifted her shoulders. "Bird hats are the most expensive ones. They run anywhere from five dollars on up."

"Five dollars!" Bettina's eyes bugged. "He ought not offer a nickel for these, then. It ain't right a'tall."

"No, using birds for fashion is criminal, I think."

"I think buying these fer a nickel, then selling the hat fer five dollars is crim'nal." Her brows scrunched together in a fierce frown. "I can tell ya this, if he offers me anything less than fifty cents, I ain't givin' none of it to him. Not so much as a twig from the nest."

Georgie placed two fingers against her forehead. "You're missing the point. You shouldn't sell them to him at all. Don't you see? He's killing innocent creatures just so he can turn them into ornaments."

Bettina inched backward. "I know you

82

love yer birds and all, Miss Georgie, but lots o' folks kill 'em. Even you eat eggs."

She followed the girl step for step. "I'm not talking about hunting them for food or gathering eggs from a henhouse. I'm talking about killing birds for no other reason than to put them on a hat. If we keep it up, we'll have no birds left."

Bettina gave her a skeptical look. "We ain't likely to run outta birds."

"That's what they said about passenger pigeons. We had millions of them, billions even. Their flocks were so dense they'd block the noonday sun clean out, and where are they now? Gone, or very nearly so. And for what purpose? To satisfy a bunch of trap-shooting men and to trim the clothing of a bunch of fashion-conscious women."

Bettina scratched her hip. "I'm right sorry, Miss Georgie. I don't wanna make ya mad. I mighta put it back if it meant a nickel, but fifty cents? Well, me and Pa could live a long time on fifty cents." She whirled around and jogged down the boardwalk, boots clomping.

Georgie watched her go, her throat swelling. Those eggs would never hatch whether Bettina sold them or not. But that wasn't the point. The fifty cents she'd earn was as tainted as the thirty pieces of silver Judas earned. The difference was, Bettina didn't understand what she was doing. But Judas and Mr. Ottfried did.

Setting her jaw, she looked neither left nor right, but straight ahead. Marching down Market Street, she determined she would put a stop to his grotesque offer if it was the last thing she did.

In her resolve to reach the millinery, she didn't immediately hear her name being called. When it finally penetrated, she looked around, a bit dazed.

Mrs. Ottfried, the milliner's wife, stood in front of the curiosity shop, waving her over. "Georgie, dear. Whatever are you doing? Who's working the switchboard? Has some calamity befallen? You look utterly pallid. I hope no one has . . ."

The rest was lost on Georgie as her vision cleared and she had her first real glimpse at Mrs. Ottfried's outfit. An owl's head with blank staring eyes perched upon her hat. Swallows' wings edged her cape. And heads of yellow finches hemmed her skirt.

Georgie slammed her eyes shut, but the image remained stamped on her mind.

Mrs. Ottfried slipped her arm around Georgie's waist. "My dear, you look ready to faint. Quick, come inside Ernst's shop and catch your breath."

A swallow's wing brushed against Georgie's arm. Yelping, she jumped out of reach, bile quickly rising. Pressing a handkerchief to her mouth, she looked for an alley or someplace she could go, but there was nothing.

Instead, she ran. Back down Market Street, right on Sycamore, and left on Cottonwood, no longer able to hold her tears or distress at bay.

Adjusting the earpiece, Luke stretched his legs in front of him and crossed his feet. "Well, thank you for asking, Miss Honnkernamp. I reckon my favorite is pork belly. I don't suppose there's any place in town you might recommend, is there?"

"Oh my. It takes a person who knows what she's doing to rub, brine, and braise a belly, Mr. Palmer."

He allowed himself a smile. "That so?"

"Yes, indeed. And I can't think of anyone in town who does it up right."

"That's some mighty sorry news you're giving me, ma'am." Picking up the pencil he'd been keeping notes with, he scribbled *fast or naïve?* beside Mattieleene Honnkernamp's name. "Just how do the fellas round here survive without pork belly?"

She made him wait a few seconds before

answering. "I guess they get themselves invited to dinner by someone who has experience."

He stilled. Her voice was low and full of suggestion. He crossed out *naïve*. "I reckon you're right about that." Sitting up, he tucked his legs beneath the chair. "Well, I better —"

The gate out front slammed, rapid footfalls in its wake.

Frowning, he looked over his shoulder. "I better let you go, Miss Honnkernamp, and free up some of these other lines. It was a pleasure —"

Miss Gail yanked open the screen door and charged straight into her room, immediately to the left of the front entrance. He jumped to his feet, the cord of the earpiece pulling him up short like a dog on a leash.

She slapped the door shut behind her. In the brief seconds he had, he catalogued mussed hair, pale face, red nose, and fresh tears.

"Would you like to join my family for supper, Mr. Palmer?" Miss Honnkernamp asked. "Now that we know what your favorite is, I'm sure —"

Throwing off the earpiece, he yanked the cable from the jack and rushed to her bedroom door. "Miss Gail? Are you all right? Are you hurt? What's happened?"

No answer. He cocked his ear and held himself still. The sound of suppressed sobs came from the direction of the veranda. Pushing open the screen, he stuck his head out.

The crying was louder. He looked toward the swing, then remembered. Her window. It was open. Easing onto the porch, he stood and listened.

Whatever happened had been catastrophic. She took deep, broken breaths, followed by a long series of quiet, staccato sobs. He rubbed his mouth. What in tarnation?

Ding.

He pictured her prone on the bed, face cradled in the crook of her arm. Closing his eyes, he called to mind as much of her room as he could. The bed had been shoved against the window. Its quilt reminded him of a little girl's, all pinks, yellows, and blues with large squares patched together. A washstand had been on the opposite wall, a wardrobe against the right, a fireplace in the mix. That was all he could remember.

Ding.

His mother had spent a good portion of her life crying, but she never troubled to hide it. It had been so much a part of his childhood, he was buying his first shaving mug before he realized all women weren't like that.

Still, it had been a long time. And it was the last thing he'd expected from Miss Gail.

Ding.

She started to wind down, taking deep breaths, then releasing them in exhausted exhales. After a moment, all was still and quiet.

Ding.

He scowled, wishing he knew how to disconnect the stupid bell, but that hadn't been covered in his manual. As hushed as it was, he knew she was waiting for him to answer it. If he went in there now, she'd hear the screen door and realize he was eavesdropping. He rubbed his eyes. What was he doing out here?

Ding.

Her bed creaked; then she blew her nose. He quickly slipped inside. Several drop lines had fallen. Settling into the chair, he started answering.

"Central."

"Who's this? Where's Georgie?"

"This is Luke Palmer. I'm the new troubleman. Miss Gail ran to town. She'll be back any minute. Who can I get for you?"

"I need to talk to Roscoe over at the bank."

"Just a minute." He flipped the key to center position, looked at the list Miss Gail left him, plugged the corresponding cable into number five, pulled the rear key backward, checked his notes again, and cranked a handle to the right of his knee with three quick turns.

"Hello?"

Luke flipped the key forward. "Go ahead."

Returning the key to center, he continued answering the waiting calls. Everything went pretty well unless someone wanted to know what the price of turkeys was, who could deliver wood, or who'd come in on today's train.

The time spent on the board gave him an appreciation for what Miss Gail did all day — and the pulse she had on the comings and goings of every person in the county. During today's stint, he'd visited with several subscribers in town and a few out on farms. He'd do well to be a bit more friendly toward SWT&T's operator. She no doubt had information that would speed up his investigation.

Ding.

"Central."

"What happened, Mr. Palmer? One

minute you were there and the next you weren't."

"Please accept my apologies, Miss Honnkernamp. My hand slipped and I jarred loose the cable."

Miss Gail's bedroom door opened.

Luke quickly folded his notes with one hand and tapped them into his shirt pocket.

"I called back and there was no answer," Miss Honnkernamp replied.

He glanced over his shoulder. The setting sun sliced through the front window and screen, turning Miss Gail's hair the color of cornsilk. She'd repaired it and her face was pink from a recent scrubbing, but there was no hiding the red nose and puffy eyes.

"I was attending to other calls," he said into the phone.

"Were you?" Miss Honnkernamp's voice took on a pout. "I didn't hear anything on the line."

Miss Gail crossed to the bookshelves and took out a stack of publications. He'd not had a chance to look through all of them, but he knew the ones on top were from the Audubon Society.

"Hello? Mr. Palmer?"

"Yes, ma'am. Who can I connect you with?" He stayed turned around in the chair, watching Miss Gail sift through the pile. She was clearly looking for something in particular.

"Actually, I was calling to, well . . ."

Ding.

Miss Gail looked up, her eyes going from the board to him. But he couldn't read her expression, backlit as she was by the fading sun. Could she even see what she was perusing?

"Shouldn't you light a lantern?" he asked.

"Shouldn't you answer the phone?" she replied.

"I'm sorry?" Miss Honnkernamp said. "Light a lantern? I'm not sure I heard you right. You sound far away. Are you speaking into the mouthpiece?"

Shifting back around, he adjusted the speaking disc. "There are calls coming in, ma'am. Was there someone you wanted to talk to?"

"Well, I . . . of course," she snapped. "I'd like to speak with Mr. Schmid at the mercantile, please."

"One moment." He checked his list, connected her to number four, then answered the waiting call. When he had everyone settled, he took off the earpiece and twisted around, hooking his arm over the back of the chair.

He wanted to come right out and ask her

what was wrong, but truth was, it was none of his business. "When does the switchboard shut down?"

"Tired?" She didn't look up, just kept searching through her stack.

"It's been a long day."

"Switchboard closes at five o'clock unless it's an emergency."

"How do you know if it's an emergency?"

"The phone will ring."

He popped open his timepiece. Four fifty-five.

"You need to check lines two and six," she said. "They've been plugged in for a while."

Holding the earpiece to his ear, he pulled back on the key for line two, then six. Nothing. He unplugged them, then stood and stretched. "What are you looking for?"

"An article I saw in last month's publication. It should have been right on top. Did you look through these while I was gone?"

He lifted the chimney from an oil lamp, then drew a match from her safe. "No, ma'am. I sat in that chair the entire time answering everybody's calls."

Pausing in her search, she looked up. "The *entire* time?"

His detour onto the porch flashed to mind. He struck the match against the seat of his pants, lit the lamp, and replaced the chimney. "What happened when you went to town?"

She returned to her stack. "Bettina decided to sell the nest and eggs to Mr. Ottfried — the wealthiest milliner in town."

That was it? That couldn't have caused all the commotion. "What else?"

Resting her hand against the stack of papers, she slowly closed it into a fist. "I saw Mrs. Ottfried."

He set the lantern on the table beside her. "And?"

She turned her face toward the fireplace, even though no fire burned. Her chin quivered. "You should have seen what she was wearing."

Frowning, he lowered himself into the easy chair on her left. "What was she wearing?"

"Bird parts." She choked on the words.

"What kind of bird parts?"

"There was an owl on her hat."

An owl was a bit extreme, but nothing to warrant her reaction.

"Her cape had swallow wings all along the edge." She gestured with her hands, outlining a cape and where the wings had been attached. "Swallows consume billions and trillions of insects. And not just normal insects, but the kind which bite and suck blood. We owe them a great debt. And how do we repay them? By killing them so we can tear off their wings and sew them onto our capes."

He rubbed his mouth. Guess she wouldn't appreciate knowing next to coon hunting, bird hunting was his favorite.

"But that wasn't the worst of it."

Finally. "What was the worst?"

"The finches." She impaled him with her green gaze. "All along the hem of Mrs. Ottfried's gown were dozens of beheaded finches."

He cringed. That was pretty sick. Definitely going overboard on bird fashion. At least he ate the birds he killed. Still, he didn't expect to lose any sleep over beheaded finches. Wouldn't bawl his eyes out, either.

"Are you familiar with finches?" she asked.

"Can't say I could pick them out of a crowd necessarily."

"Finches look like they've been dipped in raspberry juice and left in the sun to fade." She tightened her jaw. "But the ones on Mrs. Ottfried's skirt were yellow. *Yellow*. Not yellow like a goldfinch, but a more saffron color. Do you know what you have to do to turn a purple finch saffron, Mr. Palmer?"

He had no idea what color saffron even was. Clearly, though, it was some shade of yellow. He shook his head.

"Cage it. For *two years.*"

That was the most ridiculous thing he'd ever heard. Where did she come up with this stuff? "You've seen this happen?"

"Of course not. I would never cage a bird. But I've read articles and books and all kinds of publications on them." She swept her hand in a gesture that encompassed the bookshelves. "There are no saffron-colored finches in the wild."

"I see. So someone deduced they turn colors when they're caged. For two years."

"They didn't deduce it, sir. They saw it. With their own eyes."

"Who did?"

She lifted her shoulders. "I can't remember exactly, but I've read it in more than one place."

"But it was one of these societies who want to protect birds which substantiated the claim?"

"Of course."

"Well, in order to confirm it, they would have had to capture the finches and cage them for two years, don't you figure?"

She looked at him, nonplussed. "I hadn't thought about it. I don't know."

He couldn't believe he'd wasted his concern over something so ludicrous as a few dead birds.

"I do know," she continued, "finches sing to us from March to October." Leaning forward, her eyes picked up the lantern's flame. "You should see them when they go a-wooing."

"A-wooing?"

"Yes. The male springs into the air singing to his ladylove while going higher and higher." Clasping her hands, she pressed them against her chest. "That's when his song reaches its highest ecstasy. Why, I've seen him go fifteen — no, twenty feet above his mate before dropping exhausted at her side."

Raising a brow, he lowered his voice. "And did he get what he was going after?"

She gave a soft smile. "He certainly did, Mr. Palmer. He most certainly did."

Blinking, he rubbed his hands against his pant legs. "Right. Well. So what is it again you're looking for?"

She handed him a stack of her papers. "The February issue."

He began flipping and found it almost immediately, but before handing it over, he skimmed it. An Audubon Club in Massachusetts run by a bunch of women had taken up the cause of bird conservation the way suffragettes had taken up temperance.

Determined to eliminate the wholesale slaughter of birds for millinery, they raised a hue and cry to all women members, imploring them to form Plumage Leagues. These leagues solicited signed pledges from ladies in their own communities who must vow to never wear or purchase bird-bedecked hats.

Suppressing a sigh, he pulled the publication free and handed it to her. "Is this the one?"

She put her stack aside. "Oh, it is. Yes. Thank you so much. Excellent."

Standing, he helped gather the other publications and return them to her shelf. She reached up to tuck a few more on top, stretching her shirtwaist against her and calling attention to an hourglass figure no man could fail to notice.

All that magnificence, he thought, wasted on a woman who had no more sense than a grasshopper. A woman who cried over a few dead birds, but had no qualms about knocking around a tomcat. A woman he had to put up with for the entire spring and summer, possibly more.

Retrieving his hat, he bid her good night and let himself out. He'd go crazy if it took that long. He needed to find Comer and his gang. Now.

CHAPTER SEVEN

Luke pulled up on the reins. A long line of naked telephone poles bordered the farm road, disrupting the serene countryside. Pecan, elm, and oak trees shouldered each other for a spot closest to the road, but the redbud's early pink blooms drew all the attention.

Birds of every variety welcomed the morning. He tried to discern the nuances of each, but there were too many to separate. He wondered if Miss Gail knew which was which. A brown bird darted from an elm to a grassy opening. It raced a few steps, stopped, and raced a few more before hammering the ground in search of food. Swallowing its prize, it flew atop a wire tacked to the trunk of an oak.

He followed the path of the wire as it stretched from tree to tree. The thought of voices traveling along that thing was hard to comprehend. After manning the switchboard, though, he realized just how inferior the wire was. The buzz on the line made it almost impossible to hear sometimes. Of course, much of that was the result of too many folks listening in. But even still, the galvanized wire he had in the cart ought to help tremendously.

Shaking the reins, he turned the cart so it sat parallel to the poles, then jumped down. The sooner he started, the sooner he'd be done. The sooner he was done, the sooner he could begin the real work — ingratiating himself with farmers under the auspice of selling phones.

Still, he hoped the stringing wouldn't be a total waste. It should give him plenty of opportunity to comb the area for hideouts without raising suspicion. Cinching a belt around his waist, he buckled it tight, then grasped a wire from the nine-hundred-pound spool mounted inside the cart. He tied it to the back of his belt and started walking, straining forward like a plow horse.

Bit by bit the wire unfurled, but he was only able to make it past two poles before it refused to budge any further. Untying it, he left it on the ground, walked back to the spool, and cut that end.

Digging in a side compartment of the cart, he removed a pair of steel J-shaped climbers with a spike poking out of each. He placed his boot over the curve of the J, then secured it at his ankle and calf with buckle straps. Flexing his leg, he recalled seeing a child once in braces not too different from these.

A deep canvas bag held his wire cutters, splicing clamp, and insulator. He secured it to a rope, then pulled on his gloves. A surge of energy sluiced through him. This was going to be fun.

The live white cedar pole had been peeled and the knots trimmed close. He ran a gloved hand up and down her, then tipped back the brim of his hat and looked up the pole's length.

The thing had to be thirty feet tall. His pulse quickened. Anxious to get to the top, he tied the rope and galvanized wire to the back of his belt, left them to dangle, then reviewed in his mind the instructions from his manual.

Placing both hands on the pole, he sank his right climber into the wood. Lifting himself up onto it, he adjusted to the feel of it, then stabbed the left one into the pole, raising himself even higher. Shimmying his hands, he took step after step watching each stab to be sure it gripped the pole.

It took him a good two minutes, but he

finally reached the top. His chest rose and fell from exertion. The entire countryside spread out before him. He'd climbed plenty of trees in his day, but those had branches and leaves blocking his view. Up here, there was nothing. Just him, God, and the land.

The surrounding prairie stretched in every direction, broken by pockets of dense forest. In another couple of weeks all this would be covered with wildflowers and he'd have the best seat in the house.

A bird glided by, its tail twice as long as its body. The discordant clanging of a cowbell far away reminded him of the Comer Gang posing as farmers. Wolves in sheep's clothing who deceived people into thinking they were harmless and evil was okay.

He scanned the landscape for potential hideouts, but nothing looked promising. What he saw instead were miles of telephone poles like never-ending clotheslines waiting to be strung with wire. He took a deep breath. The manual had been adamant about leaning away from the pole. If he stood too straight, his spikes would cut out and he'd fall thirty feet.

Still, it'd be tricky to wrap his leg around the pole without sliding. Tightening his grip with his hands, he carefully removed his right climber from the wood and hooked his calf around the pole. Slowly, carefully, he relaxed his handhold and looked down, his heart knocking.

Lean back. Lean back.

He leaned back, secured only by his leg. Sweat beaded his forehead. Reaching blindly behind him, he grabbed the rope tied to his belt and began pulling up his bag, hand over hand. Once he had it, he fished inside for the insulator, then hooked the bag over one of two brackets secured to the top of the pole.

His leg began to burn, but he ignored it and fit the insulator on the remaining bracket. By the time he laid the galvanized wire against the insulator and secured it with a tie wire, his leg was numb.

Still, he made five complete wraps with the tie wire just like the illustration in his manual. Sweat dripped down the side of his face. Wiping it with his shoulder, he finished off the tie, grasped the pole with his hands, and unhooked his leg.

Resting his weight on one climber, he allowed his right leg to dangle. Blood flowed into it, stabbing him with needlelike sensations. When he had sufficient feeling back, he jammed it into the pole.

Step-by-step he made his way down. When he finally reached the ground, he took off his hat and wiped his forehead with his sleeve. Take the deuce, but it was going to be a long day.

Georgie put down her pen and flexed her fingers. She had written forty-six invitations for her inaugural meeting of the Brenham Ladies' Plumage League. Only eight to go.

Ding. Capping her pen, she placed her writing box on the floor and answered the call. "Hello, Central."

"What's playin' at the opry house, Georgie?"

"Gilbert and Sullivan's *H.M.S. Pinafore.* Show times are Friday and Saturday night at eight o'clock. Are you and the new Mrs. Bittle planning to attend?"

" 'Course we are. Who's playin' Josephine?"

"Lydia Jones."

"And Ralph?"

"The Zeintiks' oldest boy is playing Ralph."

"Why, he ain't good enough fer Miss Lydia."

"Party lines, Mr. Bittle. Anyone can hear. And it's just a play. The two aren't actually courting."

A bluebird winged into the yard, landing on Georgie's starch-box-turned-birdhouse.

She held her breath. Bluebirds were among the first to nest in the spring and she'd hosted three separate hatchings last year. This particular male had gone in and out of the house numerous times throughout the day, singing to his mate in an appeal for her opinion and stamp of approval.

He jumped across the roof, peering down at the entry hole below, then whistled *cheer, cheer, cheerful, charming . . . cheer, cheer, cheerful, charming.*

Seconds later his female settled on the perch and slipped through the entrance inspecting the home's interior. The hole was small, just roomy enough for a bluebird or sparrow to fit through. But not big enough for starlings or large birds to sneak in and abscond with the eggs or attack the babies.

The female emerged from the house and flew off. The male soon followed. Georgie's spirits soared at the prospect of filling her starch box so soon.

Returning her attention to the switchboard, she realized Mr. Bittle had long since hung up. Unplugging the cable, she reached again for her writing box.

Bettina clomped across the porch and pulled open the screen door. "What's that smell?"

"Pea soup," Georgie answered, dipping

her pen in the inkwell. "I have a pot simmering on the stove. You're welcome to take your supper with me if you like."

"Can't. I caught me a shell cracker in Hog Branch River and I'm frying it up fer me and Pa."

Georgie kept her expression carefully blank. Even though she was only nine, Bettina cooked supper most every night, but Mr. von S chiller rarely shared it with her. Instead, he wore his boot soles out on the brass rail at Charlie's. "Well, if you change your mind, you're always welcome here." She indicated the tin in the girl's hand. "What do you have there?"

"Mrs. Chadaz gave me some cookies fer bringing her a phone message. These ones are fer you."

Smiling, Georgie pointed her toward the office desk. "What kind are they?"

"Molasses." Bettina set the tin on the desk, then leaned against the switchboard.

"Did you tell her thank you?"

"Sure did, but she still made me wash up 'fore I ate." She gave her head a vigorous scratch, loosening her braid.

"Speaking of which, I thought we'd do a hair wash tonight after supper."

Bettina began to back away. "My hair ain't dirty. I done washed it three weeks ago."

"Hair washing is a weekly affair, at the very least."

"Well, I don't rightly know if I'll be able to come over after supper. I got things to do, ya know." She eyed the stack of finished invitations. "Ya want me to start deliverin' some of those?"

Allowing the change of subject, Georgie bit her lip. "They're not really phone business, but I can't get Mr. Crump to answer his line and I was hoping you'd run out to the depot to see if anyone came in on today's train. Maybe you could drop off a few of these on your way?"

"Yes, ma'am."

Georgie sorted through her stack, picking out the households Bettina would pass. "When you deliver Mrs. Kendall's, tell her Mrs. Krauss was asking if she'd finished reading *Tempest and Sunshine.* It's this month's book for the reading circle and she was hoping to have it next."

"Yes, ma'am. I'll tell her." The girl scooped up the envelopes and banged out the door.

Georgie didn't know what she'd do without Bettina. The girl delivered messages to those who didn't have phones and returned with happenings from town. Yet the townsfolk either looked through her or, worse, looked down on her. All because of her father. Very few of them took the time to thank her the way Mrs. Chadaz did.

Her gaze veered to the tin of cookies. Molasses were her favorite. Being tethered to the phone all day didn't allow much time for baking. Still, she'd need to do something for her Plumage League meeting. Most everyone would bring a dish, but the hostess was expected to lead the way.

She wondered how many women would come, mentally counting the number of chairs she owned. If she utilized every seat, including the ones on the veranda, she should have enough. The question was where to set them all.

Ding. "Hello, Central."

"Clover didn't come home for her milking, Georgie. Can you make a general call asking folks to look out for her?"

"I sure will, Mr. Kapp. And don't you worry. She'll show up."

Plugging in all her lines, she whirled the crank for six long rings. Receiver after receiver lifted. When most everyone answered, she explained Mr. Kapp's cow had gone missing and to give her a call if they found it. An hour hadn't passed before Mr. Folschinski phoned in. Clover was grazing in the meadow behind his barn.

She spent the rest of the afternoon finishing her invitations in between phone calls. At five o'clock she took off her earpiece, stood and stretched. The bluebirds hadn't come back, but she had high hopes they would. Still, she'd freshen her birdbath as an extra incentive.

Snitching a cookie from the tin, she opened the kitchen door and slid a stopper underneath. The smell of pea soup filled the room. Nibbling on the cookie, she lifted the soup lid. A puff of condensation billowed up, then parted to reveal a thick green soup ready for eating.

The birdbath would have to wait until she skinned the meat off the hambone. Shoving the rest of the cookie in her mouth, she tied a blue gingham apron around her waist, adjusted the damper, and fished out the bone — a gift from Mattieleene's mother.

Because Georgie's job kept her from traditional chores, subscribers were quick to thank her with hambones, eggs, and all sorts of items. She never knew from day to day what treat she'd receive, but they were always welcome.

Except for the time Mr. Scobey gave her a goat. She smiled at the memory. It had taken some delicate talking to refuse it without offending. Still, his gesture had meant an awful lot.

Skimming the last of the meat, she dumped it into the creamy mixture, gave it a stir, and replaced the lid. If she let it simmer for thirty more minutes, she'd have just enough time to clean the birdbath.

She stuffed one more cookie in her mouth, her cheeks puffing out, when someone knocked.

"Miss Gail?"

It was the troubleman. Pressing a hand to her mouth, she chewed as fast as she could.

"Miss Gail?" The screen squeaked open. "It's Luke Palmer."

Chew. Swallow. Chew. Swallow. But the cookie seemed to multiply in her mouth.

Heavy footfalls approached. He peered around the corner. Dirt streaked across his face, grime coated his overalls, and his eyes drooped in exhaustion . . . or was it pain?

Lifting the body of her apron, she covered her mouth and continued to chew.

He drew his brows together. "What are you doing?"

Swallowing the last of it, she wiped the corners of her lips and lowered the apron. "Nothing. Just . . . testing supper." She twirled a hand toward the stove.

He glanced at the pot, then back at her. "Smells good."

She smiled. "Pea soup."

Nodding, he pointed to his teeth, making a circular motion. "You have something right . . ."

"Oh!" She lifted her apron again, scrubbing her teeth with her tongue and loosening a sliver of cookie. Heat rushed to her face.

"Lemme see," he said.

"What?" She released her apron, allowing it to float down against her skirt.

He bared his teeth. "Let me see. I'll tell you if you got it."

She propped a fist against her waist. "Was there something you wanted?"

His gaze swept across her kitchen, touching briefly on the tiny basswood table shoved against one wall, the sink and drainboard with a window overlooking her garden, the worktable by the stove, and the apron tied about her waist. "Is it after five already?"

"Just."

"I'm sorry to intrude, then."

She softened a bit. "It's all right. Did you need something?"

He shifted his weight. "I was wondering if you had any tweezers."

The request was so unexpected, it took her a moment to comprehend it. What in the world would a strapping man like him need with tweezers? "Yes, I do. What do you need them for?"

"A splinter."

Her gaze flew to his hands. "You have a splinter? Weren't you wearing gloves?"

"I was wearing gloves."

She took a step forward and held out her hand. "Show me."

"It's not on my hand."

"Where is it?"

After a slight hesitation, he released the cuff of his shirt and pulled up his sleeve. Sweet heavens above. The inside of his arm was filled with ugly splinters.

"What happened?" Grasping his hand, she rotated his arm for a better look.

He took in a quick breath.

She immediately loosened her hold. "Did I hurt you?"

"No, I'm just a little sore."

"From the splinters?"

"From climbing poles all day."

Frowning, she cocked her head. "But you do that all the time."

"Stringing new wire involves a lot more climbing than normal day-to-day mainte-nance." He withdrew his arm and began to pull down his sleeve. "Listen, forget I mentioned it. I'll just head on out and let you get to your supper."

"No, no." She pulled out a cane-seat chair from the table. "Sit. I'll get my tweezers."

"That's all right. I didn't mean you had to do it. I just meant to borrow them, is all."

"Honestly, you're as bad as Bettina." She repositioned the chair, thumping it against the wood floor. "Sit, Mr. Palmer. I'll be right back."

Without waiting for an answer, she swept past him and to her bedroom for a pair of tweezers.

CHAPTER EIGHT

Luke lowered himself into the proffered chair, his muscles aching. In his line of work, he'd spent months on the trail under all kinds of adverse conditions. He'd slept on the ground, climbed steep, treacherous terrain, and swum in freezing water for long periods of time. Still, it had been a good while since he'd been this sore.

His arms throbbed, his shoulders ached, his legs were like jelly, and his shins just downright hurt. He started to rub one, but the minute he leaned over, his arms and shoulders screamed in protest.

A tin of molasses cookies caught his eye. Never in his life had he seen a woman stuff a whole cookie in her mouth. But then, Miss Gail wasn't your average woman. Propping his elbows on his knees, he rested his face in his hands and closed his eyes.

He heard her coming and going, banging things around, but kept his eyes closed until a peculiar odor rose from her frying pan. Opening his eyes, he looked for the source of the smell. A crushed root lay on the drainboard, with mortar and pestle nearby.

She glanced over her shoulder. "Almost done." With one more stir of her spoon, she tilted the pan and scraped her concoction into a bowl. "I thought a little elder root and seed of Jamestown weed would help draw out those splinters."

It had been a long time since anyone had fussed over him. He decided to relax and enjoy it. No telling how long it would be before it happened again. Her kitchen was simpler than most, but it still had all the trimmings — white lacy curtains, dish towels with the days of the week stitched across their hems, speckled enamelware, and a woman in a blue gingham apron.

Placing her chair face-to-face with his, she scooted up right in between his knees, the elder root smelling like a wet dog. "Now, let's see those splinters."

He rolled up his sleeve and held out his forearm, exposing its underside. She grasped his wrist with one hand and smoothed on the warm poultice with her other, her touch tentative.

"It's all right," he said. "You're not hurting me."

She didn't change a thing, just kept spreading with the barest amount of pressure. After covering up the last splinter, she held her free hand in the air, looking around for something to wipe it on. She began to scoot back, but he stalled her.

"Just use the legs of my overalls."

She frowned. "I can't do that. It'll stain them." The sunlight behind her shrank her pupils to tiny dots, leaving nothing but green.

"They're pretty scuffed up already," he said. "It won't matter any."

After a moment of indecisiveness, she wiped each finger across his leg, rolling them to get them clean. He tensed, completely unprepared for the sizzle which licked up his leg. She, however, seemed completely unaffected.

As soon as she finished, she cupped his elbow, taking the weight of his forearm in hers, and sat back. The motion pulled his wrist toward her, bringing his knuckles within grazing distance of her rib cage.

He relaxed his fingers, allowing them to curl down toward his palm. But if he unfurled them, they'd reach the top of her corset. Swallowing, he moved his attention to the window. A bluebird landed on the starch box in her yard, a tiny twig in its mouth.

She blew on his arm. He jumped, the recoil pulling his arm back, then forward, straight into her. His hand opened instinctively, before he immediately closed it.

"Oh!" Her eyes widened.

"I'm sorry."

"No, I am. Did that sting or something?" Her face filled with concern.

He searched her expression. Had she not noticed? How could she not notice?

"No, ma'am." He cleared his throat. "I was just looking out the window and wasn't, I didn't . . ." He took a deep breath. "No, ma'am. Didn't sting. I'm sorry to have jumped."

"It's almost ready. Just another minute or so." She tapped the edges of the mixture and blew on it again.

He slammed his eyes shut, but it only heightened his other senses. What the blazes was he doing, letting this woman tend to his needs as if he was some drugstore cowboy? He should have known better.

"I'm going to remove it now," she warned.

Opening his eyes, he nodded, but she was already peeling the concoction back. She smashed it up into a clump, dropped it on the table, and picked up the tweezers.

The elder root had done its job and drew the splinters out so she could grab hold of them. Bending over, she brought her face close to his arm, her breath tickling it. Her rib cage pressed against his curled hand. The fasteners running down the front of her corset were easily identifiable through the lawn of her shirtwaist, their tiny metal housings digging into his fingers.

With her tongue caught between her teeth, she extracted one splinter after another. To distract himself from where his hand lay, he focused on the little mole beneath her lip.

"How on earth did you get all these?" she asked.

"I fell."

She whipped her head up, coming this close to knocking his lower jaw clear to Kingdom Come. "You fell?"

"Yes, ma'am."

"From a telephone pole?"

"Yes, ma'am."

"How far?"

He shrugged. "Fifteen feet?"

She collapsed against the back of her chair, giving his hand a reprieve. Though having it against her had been no hardship.

"What happened?"

He twisted his mouth in disgust. "I got a

little cocky coming down and missed a step."

"What did you fall on? Your head? Your back?"

"My feet, fortunately. I pretty much hugged the thing all the way down and this was my reward." He indicated his arm.

"Well, for heaven's sake. You're supposed to push away from the pole when you start to fall, not hug it. Any seasoned lineman knows that."

He lifted a brow. "What would you do? Push away or grab the pole?"

Her face softened, revealing a hint of laugh lines around her mouth. "I'd probably grab the pole." Bending back over, she continued her work.

He lowered his chin, trying to catch a whiff of shampoo paste. It was something flowery with cinnamon mixed in somehow.

Finally, she finished. "There. Let's have the other one now."

He shook his head. "No, ma'am. You've done enough. I can take care of the rest."

"Don't be silly. The poultice will be useless if you wait until you get back to the boardinghouse." She grabbed his other wrist, released the cuff, and pushed up his sleeve. "This one doesn't look as bad as the other. I'll have it fixed up in no time."

She touched his skin in a couple of spots, then dug the rest of the poultice out and began to spread it. It had cooled and wasn't as malleable as before. Slipping her arm underneath his, she continued to work the doughy substance. The longer she did, the slower she went. Finally, she stopped altogether, her fingers resting against his pulse. It was beating much faster than it ought.

A tiny shiver ricocheted through her. She shifted in her chair, flattening herself against it. But no matter which way she moved, his hand was firmly ensconced against her torso.

Red blossomed onto her cheeks.

Finally, he thought, his ego somewhat soothed. He tried to pull back, but this arm didn't have the wiggle room his other did. The chair had him on one end, her body on the other.

"You can let go," he said. "I'll peel it when it's ready."

She lifted her gaze and his gut clenched. Confusion, wonder, and awe played across her face in slow succession. No artifice. No coyness. Just open, honest expressions.

"How old are you?" she asked.

Too old. Maybe not in years, but certainly in life experiences. "Twenty-six."

He didn't need to ask how old she was. He already knew. She was twenty. Her widowed mother was married to a mean drunk. She'd attended Baylor Female College before having to drop out for lack of funds. She worked at the SWT&T exchange in Dallas for two years. They sent her to Brenham as the town operator last year and she'd been here ever since.

But his Ranger report had plenty of holes in it. He'd had no idea about the birds. Nor Nellie Bly. Nor her unofficial hiring of the town drunk's daughter. Nor the fact she paid Bettina out of her own pocket — which had become abundantly clear his first day when he went over the books.

The largest hole, though, had been its exclusion of her unusual eyes. Her Nordic-blond hair. Her gut-twisting smile. And that teeny mole.

He tried to push back his chair, but between her, the table, and the wall, he was boxed in. "I think I better leave."

"Why?" she breathed.

You know why. "Let me up, Georgie."

"But this is your right arm." As if that explained everything.

He didn't respond.

"You'd have to use your left hand to get the splinters out," she said. "The poultice is ready to come off anyway. It'll only take a minute."

Without waiting for his permission, she bent her head. Several hairpins had partially worked themselves out, as if her hair was too full and luxurious to be contained. Half of him wanted to push them back in. The other half wanted to pull them out.

He gripped the arm of his chair with his free hand.

She looked up. "Does this hurt?"

Her face was close. Very close. Flecks of gold he hadn't noticed before dusted her eyes. Thick lashes swept over them, then opened again. She catalogued his features, her gaze touching his eyebrows, his nose, his cheeks, his mouth.

His finger ached to trace her extended neck and pull her the last few inches separating them. His hand stayed where it was.

She lowered her chin and finished her work. When the last splinter had been removed, she sat, head bent, hands still. He opened his mouth to thank her, to offer assistance cleaning up, anything to get her to move. Before he could, she leaned in ever so slightly, pressing herself against him even more to pull down his shirt sleeve, then shifted to do the same to the other sleeve, causing his knuckles to caress her rib cage.

Heat spread through his body. It took every ounce of control he had not to enhance the caress. But to do so would jeopardize everything. And not just his job.

"Georgie." His voice a warning.

She pushed back her chair.

He immediately stood and skirted around her, putting a good five feet between them.

She stayed where she was, head bent, refusing to meet his eyes.

"Georgie?"

She gathered the supplies and took them to the drainboard.

He'd known her two days. *Two.* He wasn't a telephone repairman in the market for a wife, no matter how delectable she might be. He was a Texas Ranger on official business and he needed to keep his eye on the prize.

To her, however, he was a normal, red-blooded male. And a normal, red-blooded male wouldn't walk away without a by-your-leave. He lifted the water reservoir's lid on the stove, filled a wash pail with hot water, and carried it to her.

"Thank you," she whispered.

"I have to go."

"Would you like some pea soup?"

"Mrs. Sealsfield is expecting me at the boardinghouse."

She bit her lip, the mole coming close to her teeth. "All right."

"Can I have one of those molasses cookies?"

She nodded. "Of course."

"Thanks. And one more thing."

She lifted her chin, her gaze searching. Questioning. Inviting.

"Can I take the tweezers with me?"

She blinked. "Did I miss one?"

"No, it's just, well, my overalls protected my stomach, but my chest . . ."

Her gaze dropped to the area above his bib. His chambray shirt hid the splinters from view, but they were certainly there. Allowing her to remove them was out of the question. And they both knew it.

"It'll only take a minute to whip up another poultice," she said. "You could take it with you."

"No, ma'am. It's all right. If I could just borrow the tweezers."

"Yes. Certainly." She flitted to the table, then held out the tweezers.

It was probably the only opportunity he'd have to touch her. Unable to resist, he enfolded her hand, allowing his thumb to outline hers, before exploring the base of her palm and finally claiming the tweezers.

The pupils which had been so tiny before

now dilated.

He backed up. "Thank you. I'll . . . I'll see you tomorrow." Turning, he went through the living room and out the front door. He completely forgot to grab a cookie.

CHAPTER NINE

The aroma of coffee soothed Georgie's nerves. She'd expected a good turnout for her Plumage League, but not this good. She should have, though. If there was one thing she'd learned about Germans since moving here, it was they loved an excuse to gather — and they never did anything on a small scale.

Her tiny cottage could barely contain the standing-room-only crowd. She knew her walls and tabletops were bare and lacking the typical parlor accessories, but she spent every extra penny she earned on her garden and birds.

Women's voices, some speaking English, some German, filled the room like heat in a teakettle. And no one had come empty-handed. There was coconut pie, *Streusselkuchen,* coffee cakes, potato cakes, *Zwieback,* cabbage loaves, and *Kochkäse.* If more guests arrived, she'd have to move everyone to her backyard.

She'd been very deliberate with the planning of the meeting, right down to what she wore. A sprig of hawthorn nestled in her hair, complementing her pearl-colored percale shirtwaist. Since Easter was in a few more weeks, she had no qualms about wearing her blue-and-white polka dot skirt. It reminded her of bluebirds and spring and never failed to draw admiration.

Checking her watch pin, she picked up her earpiece, plugged in all cables, and gave six long rings. When those still home picked up, she had to shout into the mouthpiece as she reminded them the switchboard would be unavailable for the next two hours.

Those nearest to her quieted, always curious to watch her at work. Taking advantage of their attention, she clapped her hands and called the meeting to order. "If those of you in the kitchen would tell the ladies on the back porch to come in, Miss Gladstone is going to start us off with a song."

Jana Gladstone, a vision of loveliness in a ruffled peach lawn dress, stepped in front of the unlit fireplace. Georgie had chosen her for the recital not only because her voice was clear and true, but because she'd caught the eye of the preacher's son and much speculation had been generated because of it.

The ladies shushed each other, anxious for the opportunity to scrutinize Miss Gladstone without being rude. Georgie wished she had a piano. Music was second only to beer in this town, but as soon as Jana began to sing, her concerns lifted. The girl really did have an extraordinary warm alto voice.

Softly on a summer's eve the cuckoo
    calls its mate,
I linger list'ning to the sound until the hour
    grows late.

The women began to sway to the one-two-three beat, some tapping gloved hands to the rhythm, others keeping it with nods of their heads.

It has for me a magic charm, I love it best
    of all,
When weary at the close of day to hear
    the cuckoo's call.

"The Cuckoo's Call" was not a familiar tune, and Georgie had looked forward to her guests' reactions when they heard the chorus.

Cuckoooooo, cuckooooo, I know you are
    calling,
Yoo-hoo-lee-i-hoo-lee, Yoo-hoo-lee-i,
You always sing when dew drops are
    falling,
Yoo-hoo-lee-i-hoo-lee-i.

As Georgie suspected, the yodel captivated every woman present. Their excitement as Jana sang the second verse was palpable. The moment she finished, the entire company joined her for the chorus. Their ear for music was as much a part of them as their hearty laughs. By the third chorus, they were singing in harmony.

Georgie tried not to gloat, but she knew the catchy waltz would be yodeled in their homes for several weeks to come, reminding them what a treasure the cuckoo bird was. Cuckoos which filled Brenham's trees and yards.

Jana flushed with pleasure in response to the robust round of applause.

Thanking her, Georgie stepped to the front. "Bird life is disappearing from the United States."

A hush fell over the room.

"Our songbirds, plumage birds, tropical birds, and waterfowl are shot in cold blood for no other reason than the barbaric purpose of decorating women's hats."

She looked around, glad to see the women had heeded the instructions in her invitation: No clothing or hats with bird parts were to be worn to the meeting, though many of the women owned such garments.

"I have stood in our own churchyard and heard many bemoan the mistreatment of a horse or dog. Yet the deliverer or sympathetic listener of this woe stood wearing the wings, plumes, heads — if not the entire carcass — of innocent birds. Our birds. The birds of popular song."

Some lowered their eyes. Others wielded their fans, partially shielding their faces.

She continued giving examples, statistics, then anecdotes about her backyard birds. Finally, she called for action.

"I propose we wage a war against the businesses who profit from wholesale bird slaughter, starting with Mr. Ottfried's millinery." She picked up a piece of paper. "This is a pledge to cease wearing bird-bedecked hats. If everyone signs this vow, it will cripple, if not completely end, our milliner's need for the carnage of birds."

Mrs. Oodson, a frail-looking woman with the busiest tongue in town, pinched her lips together. "But Norma Ottfried is a member of *Kaffeklatsch.* To wage war against Ottfried

Millinery is to wage war against Norma."

A murmur rippled through the room. *Kaffeklatsch* had started out as time to share coffee and gossip. And though it had developed into an official ladies' society where fashion, literature, and recipes were discussed, its primary function was to gossip. Mrs. Oodson had been reigning chairwoman for an unprecedented three years.

"I'm not trying to put Mr. Ottfried out of business," Georgie assured. "I'm simply trying to eradicate bird parts from his inventory."

"Nevertheless, if we must choose between losing a few birds or offending one of our own, I'm afraid we've no choice but to sacrifice the birds."

Georgie forced herself to use a gentle tone. "We aren't sacrificing the birds, Mrs. Oodson, we're slaughtering them, murdering them, blotting them completely out of existence."

Mrs. Whitchurst, a full-bodied woman in her fifties, *tsked.* "Now, Georgie. There's no such thing as murdering a bird. God gave us dominion over all the animals to do with as we see fit. And that includes putting an animal down when the situation calls for it."

"Our songbirds are not in need of being

put down."

Mrs. Dimple raised her hand. Her husband ran the local poultry farm. And though Georgie had heard pet owners often resembled their animals, she hadn't seen it firsthand until meeting Mrs. Dimple. Her eyes bugged out, her nose hooked, and loose folds hung from her chin. "Tell me, dear. Do you ever eat chicken? Or eggs? Or use eggs in your recipes?"

Georgie released a huff of breath. "Chickens are not birds."

A murmur of laughter scattered throughout the room.

She closed her eyes and took a deep breath. "I mean, of course they're birds, but they aren't being massacred so fashion-conscious women can parade them about on their heads."

"No, that's true. But they are being slaughtered every day in order to supply sustenance for our bodies, and eggs are whisked from mothers' nests morning after morning. As I consider this pledge, I'm wondering if you might someday ask the ladies of Brenham to sign a similar vow about chickens. And if they did, what would happen to me, Myron, and our passel of little ones?"

"And what about our menfolk?" All attention turned to Mrs. Blesinger, whose husband owned the gun shop and sponsored several hunting expeditions throughout the year. "Are you planning to invite the Gun Club to your home and lecture them? Ask them to give up their trapshooting and their annual quail hunts, dove hunts, and duck hunts? To quit buying guns from Ludwig's shop?"

"I think the entire thing is a waste of time." The sheriff's wife, Corda Nussbaum, had a weak spot for hats. The more outrageous the better. Georgie had been concerned she might not even have one without bird parts, but today's toque sported a profusion of silk poppies in vivid cerise, trimmed with black velvet ribbon. No bird parts. "Even if we were to sign your pledge and the men quit hunting, the birds we saved would simply fly north during winter migration and be killed by Yankees."

"Yankees?" Mrs. von Goethe was nearing her ninetieth birthday and had lost a husband and a son during the Civil War. "Are the Yankees coming? *Schnell!* Hide *die Kinder.*"

Corda patted her grandmother's hand. "The Yankees aren't coming, Oma. The children are safe."

Georgie felt as if she stood in front of a

firing squad, a volley of bullets jerking her body with each subsequent hit. But if they thought she'd fall down and die, they were mistaken.

Still, she'd only been here a year, and if the community had thoroughly embraced her, it wasn't on her own merits but because of her position as switchboard operator. She'd been foolish to think the ladies would support her. Unprepared for the fierceness of their opposition, she swallowed the lump forming in her throat. "What you say is true, Corda, but all of us have to do our part. What if our Plumage League collected the most pledges in the entire country? Why, a member of Mr. Audubon's family might come to personally thank us."

"Who is Audubon?" Mrs. von Goethe looked to her granddaughter. "Is he the Yankee the Cummings girl married? Imagine. Marrying a Yankee. *Skandalös!*"

Corda held a finger to her lips. "Hush, Oma."

The doctor's wife stood. Though her figure was a bit thick in the middle, her corset pushed plenty of excess to the top and the rest to the bottom, giving her an attractive hourglass figure.

As one of the wealthiest women in town, she set the standard for social behavior and fashion. The first time Georgie stepped into their home, she'd gawked at its lush furnishings. Mrs. von Hardenberg's exquisite taste in clothing compelled her to turn to Chicago and New York for her apparel. If she spoke out against Georgie's cause, it would be the final nail in the coffin.

Georgie held her breath.

"I had no idea our birds were in such danger." From her Gainsborough hat to her champagne wool gown, she looked as if she'd stepped out of a *Harper's Bazaar* fashion plate. "God has indeed given us dominion over the animals. And when much is given, much is expected. I vow not to wear any more hats with bird parts. Pass me the pledge, please."

The room burst into chatter, and though Georgie never officially adjourned the meeting, the ladies rose. Some signed the pledge, some ate the food, and a great many left with polite but strained good-byes.

When Georgie closed the door behind her final guest, she had one dozen signatures. Among them the doctor's wife, the banker's wife, and the mayor's wife.

She tried to convince herself their signatures should count double, even triple, but truth was, it would take more than a dozen pledges to put an end to Ottfried's offer and the selling of bird parts. She needed a new battle plan. For her enemy was not only the milliner, but the women in town who had more to lose than a fancy hat.

CHAPTER TEN

The Gun Club met at the fairgrounds every Sunday afternoon. This one couldn't have been a more perfect day for it. The balmy temperature, smattering of clouds, and absence of wind would eliminate the usual excuses for inaccurate shooting.

Luke tied Honey Dew to a hitching rail beside several other horses. A group of men milled about the edge of the racetrack, most with a beer in one hand, a rifle in the other. About two hundred yards out, a tin plate dangled from a hangman's scaffold.

Removing his Winchester from its scabbard, Luke dropped several cartridges in his pocket and ambled toward the group, wondering if any of them were members of Comer's gang. Of the two dozen gathered, he was the only one in overalls and the only one who did physical labor for a living. He hoped his presence would be accepted. Gun clubs were for the affluent. Typical farmers

— and telephone repairmen — couldn't afford the premium prices target rifles claimed, though his .30-40 Krag wasn't out of the realm of possibilities.

Doc von Hardenberg caught sight of him and headed his way. As was the fashion, he'd fastened the first button of his jacket, leaving the rest to gape open over a well-fed belly. His salt-and-pepper mustache was so full it encroached upon his lower lip, giving him a walrus-like appearance when he smiled. Luke rubbed his own upper lip, missing the mustache he'd worn for years. At least these last couple of weeks climbing poles had added color to the virgin skin.

He grasped the doc's hand. They'd met earlier in the week while Luke had been stringing wire and the doc had been heading home after a call.

"Fancy seeing you, Palmer." Doc eyed Luke's rifle. "Didn't know you shot."

"Oh, I don't have much time for targets, but I enjoy hunting when I can."

"What do you hunt?"

"Coons and birds are my favorite, but not with my .30-40, of course."

Doc raised his brows. "Does Georgie know you hunt birds?"

"No, sir. Don't reckon it's ever come up."

"You'd be smart to keep it that way. She's

awful funny about birds."

"So I've heard." He hadn't returned to Georgie's place since she'd removed his splinters. Instead, he'd had Bettina return the tweezers, he'd worked six days a week stringing line, and he'd stayed away from Georgie at church. He wouldn't be able to put off seeing her much longer, though. The new wire was close to being done and the ledgers needed attention.

Doc introduced him to several members whom he'd seen at church but had never actually met.

"And this here's our sheriff," Doc said. "Franz, have you met our new trouble-man?"

Franz Nussbaum looked more like a college professor than a sheriff. Pretty face. No sideburns. Pomaded hair. Oval glasses. And a trim brown mustache. According to Luke's Ranger report, Comer had plenty of influentials in his back pocket. Luke wondered if Nussbaum was one of them. At least the sheriff had a decent weapon.

"You a shooter, Palmer?" the sheriff asked, offering a limp handshake.

Luke hated that. "I can bring down a bird or two."

The sheriff smirked. "Well, we'll see how you do with a target at two hundred."

Luke smiled and looked at the silver plate on the other side of the racetrack. He could hit it square on, but he wouldn't. He'd nick it a few times to gain the respect of the men. Then he'd miss it a few times to keep from being a threat.

Doc clapped Luke on the shoulder. "Go get you a beer, son. We're about to start."

The men lined up watching as the judge stretched prone on the ground and fired, hitting the target dead to rights with a loud *ping*. The steel disc swung back and forth.

A murmur of admiration rippled through the group. Those closest to the judge pulled him to his feet. The man grinned, his natty goatee reaching clear down to the vee in his waistcoat.

The milliner stepped up next, a hard, wiry man with a pitch-black mustache. He loaded his Krag with factory ammunition. The members exchanged knowing looks. Factory cartridges were usually four or five grains off. That might be fine for sporting, but not for precision shooting where every little variance made a difference.

Luke had carefully measured his powder and packed his cartridges before arriving. That way, the only variance he had was the wind, the outside temperature, and himself.

"You aimin' for the plate there, Ottfried?"

the banker asked.

"Yeah," he mumbled.

"Well, pull down on it just a little; it's about two or three —"

Bang. He completely overshot the target.

Cocking the action lever, Ottfried shot again and again, never allowing his muzzle to cool and only nicking the target once. Swearing, he pushed to his feet, grabbed a beer, and tilted it straight up toward the sky, downing half the bottle.

"Look who's here, fellas," Doc said.

The men turned. A tall man with a commanding physique swaggered toward them. His overalls were in worse shape than Luke's, if that were possible, and his boots had seen some hard living. The 1895 Winchester .30-40 Krag he carried was the exact model Luke and the milliner used. In the hands of a competent shooter, it would stand up to any of the expensive, single-shot target rifles the other men carried.

"Arnold Necker, where you been?"

"Necker, you devil, you haven't been to church in a month of Sundays."

"Finally, I'm gonna get some competition." This from the judge.

Necker smiled, giving a fancy bow. "Somebody's gotta work around here. Cain't be leaving the farm ever' week just to hear the preacher tell me 'bout something I done already read three times over."

The men laughed, put a beer in his hand, and walked him to the front of the line.

Stopping along the way, he looked at Luke. "Who're you?"

"Luke Palmer, the new troubleman."

Necker nodded, recognition touching his eyes. "I seen you stringing wire out near my place the other day. I nearly shot you fer a monkey." He turned to the judge. "You oughta see this feller climb a pole. He's up that thing quicker'n a flea hopping outta danger."

In the two weeks Luke had been stringing line, his pole-climbing skills had improved a hundredfold. So if Necker had seen him at ease with the task, the man farmed north of town. It also meant he hadn't shown himself when he'd observed Luke. A bit peculiar for such an amiable fellow.

"You know how to use that Krag?" Necker asked him.

Luke lifted his hat, then resettled it on his head. "I'm not the marksman some of these fellows are, but I get by."

Necker handed him his beer. "Well, let me show you how it's done, then."

Luke held the bottle while Necker stepped to the front. Had Teddy Roosevelt joined the group, the men couldn't have been more energized. Smiles were exchanged, elbows were nudged, and eyes were alight.

Necker didn't lie down, nor even sit, but braced his legs like a sea captain and took the Winchester to his shoulder. He cocked the hammer, squeezed one eye shut, aligned the sights, and pulled the trigger.

Dinnnng. Click-click.
Dinnnng. Click-click.
Dinnnng. Click-click.
Dinnnng. Click-click.
Dinnnng.

The men roared, surrounding Necker, pounding his back, exclaiming over both the speed with which he shot, and the target still swinging like a pendulum gone berserk.

Necker laughed and took his due, then returned to Luke for his beer.

"That's some of the best shooting I've ever seen," Luke said, handing him the bottle.

Necker took a swig. "There are plenty better than me."

"Who?"

A slight smile tugged at the man's mouth. "Well, them papers say Lucious Landrum is ranked as the best all-round rapid-fire marksman in the state."

The men guffawed. Luke tensed. Did they

know? Had he somehow slipped up? But the members were completely focused on Necker.

"Cain't believe everything you read, now, boy."

"Goes to show you how much them papers know."

"That's only 'cause they hadn't seen you shoot."

Necker chuckled. "You know who I'm talkin' about?" he asked Luke.

"I've heard of him. He's one of them Texas Rangers."

"That's right."

The sheriff slung his arm across Necker's shoulders. "If Landrum is so all-fired great, why is it Comer slips through his net every time?"

"Well, Sheriff, I cain't rightly say."

"I can." Joe Lee, the local lawyer, rested the butt of his rifle on the ground. "Landrum may be a fast draw, but he couldn't track an elephant in ten feet of snow."

"Now, boys. You're being awfully hard on poor old Landrum." Doc shook his head. "Not a one of us has ever met him. Ever even seen him shoot. 'Sides, you're forgetting Comer's a man who's all heart above the waist and all guts below. He'd rattle any lawman's think box."

Ottfried rolled his eyes. "Landrum has nothing but hair under his hat and I, for one, don't fancy talking about him all day. Whose turn is it?"

Luke had made a career of keeping calm in the face of his enemy, but this was different. The men weren't trying to get his goat. They honestly believed Landrum — *him* — to be a buffoon and Comer to be a saint. Even the doc.

He tried to convince himself it was nothing personal, but no matter which way he looked at it, it was personal. Very personal.

The men reordered themselves and continued shooting. The longer the beer flowed, the more vocal the gallery became. Necker offered pointers, encouragement, and ribald jokes. When it was Luke's turn, the farmer smiled and indicated the ground in front of him with the sweep of his hand. "Let's see what you got, Palmer."

Never had Luke wanted so badly to shoot standing up. But if Necker wasn't one of Comer's gang, then he'd be mighty surprised. The opportunity to curry favor with the man was much more important than soothing his own pride.

He stretched out on the ground, braced himself and his gun, then aimed a bit right.

"A little to the left," Necker offered.

Luke moved the rifle left.

"That's it, give her a shot."

He pulled the trigger, slightly lifting his muzzle at the last second. The cartridge whizzed above the target.

"Ooooh, almost."

"Just missed her, Palmer."

"A little too high."

"Keep her steady to the end."

Luke cocked his action lever, pulled the hammer back, looked down the sights again, shot, and winged the northeast corner of the target.

"That's it."

"Better, better."

"You're still up and to the right."

On his final shot, he aimed high and right once more, then pulled to bull's-eye at the last second, hammering the steel plate dead center.

The men hollered their approval, grabbing him by the back of his overalls and hoisting him to his feet with congratulatory words and rounds of pounding. Necker gave him a nod, but Luke knew the man thought it dumb luck.

Luke shook his head. "I'm a birdman myself and more comfortable with my shotgun."

Necker rocked on his heels. "Well, Brenham is hosting the Texas State Tournament at the end of the month. A bunch of us'll be practicing trap next week. Would ya like ta join us?"

"Oh, I'm not good enough to enter any tournament, but I'd still like to join you for practice."

"Next week, then."

Luke slid a hand into his pocket. "Would it be all right, in the meanwhile, if I did some target practice with you next time I'm out your way? Get a few pointers?"

"Anytime, Palmer. Come out anytime."

An unusual answer for a farmer during springtime. Didn't he have corn to plant?

Excitement zipped through Luke. He'd picked up his first scent. Smiling full out, he turned to the men and expressed his anticipation about the upcoming tournament, all the while formulating ways he could become better acquainted with Arnold Necker.

Chapter Eleven

Georgie couldn't do anything right. She'd flip-flopped the preacher's number in her head and connected him to the synagogue instead of the church. She'd disconnected Birdie and Fred by mistake. She'd tried to complete a call with two incoming cable lines. And she'd used two longs and one short for the Whitchursts.

Winding the cord of her earpiece around her finger, she slanted a glance toward Mr. Palmer. He hunched over the desk, reconciling bills and writing up collection statements. His overall bib buckled forward, leaving a gaping view of his broad chest and trim waist underneath a chambray shirt.

She hadn't seen him in over two weeks. Not since the removal of his splinters. Not since his hand had been flattened against her waist. Not since her stomach had fluttered like hummingbird wings when she'd thought he was going to kiss her.

It was just as well he hadn't. She'd known him for such a short time. Still, it had taken her half the night to fall asleep and then she'd dreamed of him. She'd dressed with extra care the next day. And the next. And even the next.

But he never came. Until now. Smack-dab in the middle of the day. Unannounced and in a foul mood. Strode in, gave a terse hello, sat down at the desk, and began to work.

The longer he sat in silence, the more unraveled she became. The more unraveled she became, the more mistakes she made. The more mistakes she made, the more her irritation rose.

Where had he been? Why hadn't he checked in? Why had he sent the tweezers back with Bettina? Tapping a finger on the switchboard, Georgie crossed her legs and glanced at her watch pin. Half past four. Thirty more minutes.

Pulling back on a key, she checked Fred and Birdie's connection. The couple still talked, but the crackle on the line was deafening. In the background, a cuckoo clock sounded the half hour. Only one person in all of Washington County had a cuckoo clock.

She threw the key forward. "Excuse me for interrupting, Fred, Birdie, but we need those of you listening in to hang up. This is a private conversation."

Several clicks indicated the hanging up of receivers, but the cuckoos were still singing.

"Mrs. Oodson, I'll have to ask you to hang up, please."

Birdie giggled, but there was no click.

"We're waiting, Mrs. Oodson."

The cuckoos suddenly cut off.

"I'm sorry, Fred, Birdie. You may continue."

"Thank you, Miss Gail," Fred answered.

"Certainly." She returned the key to neutral and tried not to feel too smug about calling Mrs. Oodson by name, but truth was, it felt wonderful.

Ever since the Plumage League meeting, Georgie had taken great delight in thwarting the woman's efforts to obtain gossip for *Kaffeklatsch*. Her clock sounded every fifteen minutes. The first quarter, the cuckoos sang four long notes. At the half, eight. At the third quarter, twelve. And on the hour, they offered a complete concert. Georgie felt certain the woman had no idea what gave her away.

Bettina sailed through the door, newspaper in hand, the screen slapping shut behind her. "The milliner's havin' a fullblown contest." She gave the troubleman a

150

quick look. "Howdy, Mr. Palmer."

He smiled. "Howdy, Miss Bettina."

His smile disappeared as quickly as it came and back to work he went. Not so much as a glance at Georgie.

She accepted the girl's newspaper. "What kind of contest?"

"The person who brings in the most bird parts will win a new Easter bonnet."

"What?"

Bettina pointed to the ad. A lovely woman wearing a capote hat with a puffed brim and folded velvet crown smiled at the reader. Two blackbirds, wings spread, perched amidst the ribbon. Georgie quickly read the caption: *"Two exquisite tropical birds display-ing all the iridescent hues of a peacock are lightly poised atop this lovely Easter bonnet. It is to be awarded to the person who delivers to Ottfried Millinery the highest number of bird wings, bird plumes, bird heads, bird eggs, bird nests, and whole birds between this day and Good Friday."*

Whipping off her earpiece, Georgie surged to her feet. "This is outrageous. He can't do this."

"Already did." Bettina hooked her thumbs in the bib of her smock. "That there hat's sittin' in his front window."

Georgie looked at Luke. He bent further

over his desk, pretending deafness.

Anger shot through her. If she were a man, she'd call out Ottfried, then satisfy herself with a rousing round of fisticuffs. As refreshing as that might be, she wasn't a man. It didn't mean she had to sit still for this, though. Snapping on her earpiece, she plopped into her chair, plugged in line ten, and turned her crank for three long rings.

"How do you do? This is Ernst Ottfried with Ottfried's Millinery."

"What is the meaning of this ad, Mr. Ott-fried?"

A pause. "Miss Gail?"

"You know good and well it's me." She leaned toward the mouthpiece. "I want to know just who you think you are, running an ad like this."

"I do not have to explain myself to you or anyone else. Now if you'll —"

"Oh yes, you do. You'll be explaining it to Almighty God one day. But before you do, you'll answer my question. I live in this town, just like our birds do. You have no right to send an entire county on a hunting expedition just so you can line your purse."

"Miss Gail, I have never in my life hung up on anyone, much less a lady. But if you do not desist, then I'll —"

The cuckoo clock struck the third-quarter hour.

"Mrs. Oodson?" Georgie grabbed the arm of her chair to keep from trembling. "Get. Off. Your. Phone."

The woman gasped. "Well, I never."

"Now, see here, Miss Gail," Mr. Ottfried interjected. "Don't raise your voice to —"

"Off!" Georgie screeched.

The cuckoos cut out.

"Now answer my question, Mr. Ottfried."

Nothing.

"Mr. Ottfried?" She jiggled the jack. "Mr. Ottfried?"

Jerking the cable out, she fell back in her chair and turned to Luke.

He sat frozen at his desk, pencil poised, eyes riveted on her.

"He hung up on me." She still couldn't believe it.

"You were a bit rough on him."

"Rough?" She jerked her earpiece off and rose slowly to her feet. "Rough?"

Bettina scrambled out the door, running down the steps and through the gate.

Luke scowled. "You shouldn't lose your temper in front of her. She has a scary enough time at home. She doesn't need you loaded to muzzle."

"Don't you lecture me, Mr. Palmer."

"I see." He put his pencil down and indicated her aborted call with a nod of his head. "What's good for the goose isn't good for the gander?"

"Get out."

He narrowed his eyes. "You're mighty bossy today. In the last fifteen minutes you've commanded me to leave my own office, Mrs. Oodson to hang up her own phone, and Mr. Ottfried to explain his own business decisions. Don't you think you need to settle down a bit?"

That did it. He was asking for a fight.

She flew at him. He spun his chair toward her, knees open, arms up. Big mistake. She grabbed two fistfuls of chambray shirt and jerked up.

He didn't budge.

"Get up, mister. We're taking this outside."

Amusement lit his eyes.

She gave him a shake. "Don't you laugh, Luke. I mean it. I'm going to take you outside and fold you up like a purse."

He laughed. Head back, chin up, Adam's apple bobbing.

Her throat closed. "Don't. Don't."

With an effort, he reined in his mirth.

She tightened her hold on his shirt. "Have you seen that ad? He's calling for an all-out war against my birds. It's springtime. *Spring-*

time. They're flying in by the thousands. Building nests. Laying eggs. Fledging their young. And he wants to shoot them down and wire them to hats."

She tasted salt on her tongue. She hadn't even realized she was crying. Still, she made no move to wipe her face. Instead, she stayed bent over him, nose to nose, crinkling his shirt.

He cupped her cheek and swiped a tear with his thumb. "Ah, Georgie. Don't cry."

Her lips parted. She'd expected him to engage in a struggle of some kind. At the very least, she'd assumed he would remove the hold she had on his shirt. But he hadn't. He'd returned her attack with kindness.

Her resolve wavering, she willed her eyes to dry and released his shirt, dismayed at the wrinkles she'd created. Smoothing them out with her palm, she tucked the folds back beneath his bib.

He stilled. She spread her hand flat, marveling at how different he felt compared to her.

Threading his hand with hers, he gave a gentle tug, his knees widening as he pulled her closer.

"Where have you been?" she whispered. "Why didn't you come back?"

"I was afraid you'd get the wrong impression."

"And what impression would that be?"

"That I was looking for a wife."

A whiff of shaving soap touched her nose. "I thought all men were looking for a wife."

"Not all of them."

"Why not?"

"I'm only here temporarily. Just long enough to put up the lines and sell some phones. I —" He cocked an ear, then spun her about and pushed. "Someone's coming. Quick, put on your earpiece and sit down."

"But it's after five. I —"

"Sit." He gave her another nudge, then spun back to his desk and figures.

Jamming on the earpiece, she sat down and pinched her cheeks. The loud knock made her jump.

"Come in," she said, turning around, then froze.

Ernst Ottfried, his face florid, stepped inside, strode to Luke's desk, and slapped down a piece of paper. "I hereby end my subscription with SWT&T. I'm also lodging a formal complaint against our operator, Miss Georgina Gail." His dark eyes bore into Luke's. "I'm assuming you'll take care of this for me?"

"Yes, sir."

Georgie jumped to her feet. "I'm right here, Mr. Ottfried. No need to talk around me."

He whirled on her. Luke immediately rose.

"I have no intention of talking to the likes of you, Miss Gail." He stabbed his finger in the air, punctuating his words. "Not here, not about town, and certainly not on the telephone." He marched to the door, pushed opened the screen, then paused and turned to Luke. "Thank you. I'll see you at the trap shoot next weekend."

Luke gave a slight nod. The screen door slammed behind the man.

Gasping, Georgie stared at Luke. "Trap shoot? Have you . . . have you joined the Gun Club?"

But the truth was in his eyes. Unable to catch a breath, she gripped the switchboard, the wood biting into her fingers. "The Gun Club shoots birds for fun."

Luke dragged a hand down his face. "It's business. I'm trying to create goodwill with the men so I can sell phones."

"The members of the Gun Club already have phones."

He fingered Ottfried's cancellation. "Not all of them."

Why, Lord? Why didn't you make me a man?

Unwilling to attack him again or try to

throw him out, she crossed to her bedroom and shut herself inside. Leaning her back against the door, she slid down, propped her head against her knees, and waited for him to leave.

CHAPTER TWELVE

Setting his elbows on the desk, Luke rested his head in his hands. He was being undone by a mere wisp of a girl.

Though his work usually had him dealing with men, he'd certainly had to interact with women. Of course, they weren't often the respectable kind and rarely captured his attention. If they had, he'd managed to walk away without much trouble. But Georgie was different. And this was no brief encounter. He would be in close proximity to her until the end of summer.

So he'd stayed away for two weeks and shored up his defenses. Yet within the space of three hours, his resolve had cratered.

It had to stop. He couldn't do his job and court a woman at the same time. He couldn't court a woman at all. Not with his lifestyle. He called to mind Rangers who were married. Who went home between jobs and stayed just long enough to propagate more offspring before hitting the trail once again.

He rubbed his eyes. That might work well and good for them, but not for him. He knew firsthand what it was like to grow up without a father. He wasn't interested in putting his kids or his wife through that. Not when he was alive and well.

So what did that mean? He'd never marry? Never settle down? Never have kids? Looking out the window, he watched a bluebird bring food to its mate nesting inside Georgie's starch box. All afternoon the male had flown to and from the nest feeding her, singing to her, protecting her, pampering her. What if someone killed the father bird and turned it over to Ottfried? What would the mother bird do?

The question brought back unpleasant memories. His widowed mother gathering up him and Alec, leaving all they knew and moving to a new county to live with his uncle. A man who saw Luke and Alec as free labor. A man who loved nothing and no one but himself.

Georgie's door opened. She'd changed into a simple white shirtwaist and brown walking skirt. Its hem, shortened to accommodate her stride in case she were to set a brisk pace, revealed tiny black boots the size of a child's. Her ankles couldn't be much bigger than his wrist.

He rose, but she whisked by him and into the kitchen, closing the door firmly behind her. It was after hours. He needed to leave. But he hadn't completed half of what he'd intended. Not while she'd been six feet away, flustered and stealing glances at him. He couldn't sit through another afternoon of that. Not with the way he was feeling.

Nor could he stay when the workday was over. Sighing, he lowered himself into his chair. He only had five collection notices left. He'd finish those, then leave. Hopefully, she'd stay in the kitchen.

He hadn't even finished two when the clinking and clanking of plates and utensils coming from the other side of the door ceased. A screen squeaked open and closed. Looking up, he watched her walk out back to a bench set among pink columbine and clusters of a spikelike plant which looked like a dozen red-handled sabers stabbed into the ground.

Arranging her apron and skirts, she dug into a pocket, pulled out a broken roll or cake of some kind, then stretched out her hand. She sat completely still, a living statue in her garden. Moments passed. Surely John Singer Sargent had never had a model so patient and unmoving.

Her arm had to be burning. No one could suspend it in the air for that amount of time without its weight doubling. Yet she didn't so much as sway.

He dared not look at his watch or even rustle the papers on his desk, for the window was open and he didn't want to disturb her. Nor did he want her to know he was watching.

A tiny gray bird with a black head flew close to her hand, then swerved away at the last second.

Fee-bee-bay-bee. Fee-bee-bay-bee.

It swooped down again, landing on the ground in front of her. Two short hops forward. Three to the side. Away it flew again.

The third time it landed on her apron, cocked its head, then fluttered to her hand. Luke held his breath. The bird nipped a piece of cake and whisked away. She never moved a muscle. Die and be blamed, but she was beautiful. The breeze ruffling her hair, blooms trimming her silhouetted figure, birds eating out of her hand. He swallowed. He needed to get out of here.

The bird returned and remained on her hand for several seconds, nipping bites of cake before flying away. On its heels a woodpecker descended for a sample. Luke rose instinctively. Those birds pecked holes through tree trunks. What was she doing letting one land on her soft, supple hand?

He bumped his chair. The woodpecker darted away. Georgie slid her eyes toward the window, locking her gaze with his.

She was furious. And not only because he'd frightened the woodpecker, but because he planned to shoot pigeons out of the sky for sport. He remained frozen, unable to turn from her. Finally, through sheer force of will, he broke eye contact and began to stack the items on his desk. The collection notices would have to wait.

The woodpecker never returned, nor did the gray bird. With a huff of exasperation, she rose and marched toward the back door, arms swinging, fist crumbling the cake.

His stomach jumped. If she grabbed his shirt again, she'd get more than she bargained for.

She jerked the kitchen door open. "What are you still doing here?"

"The children are the key," he said, taking a step back to put some distance between them.

She blinked. "What?"

"To Ottfried's ad. It won't be men and women hunting down your birds. They won't have the time or the inclination. But the ladies are going to want that Easter bonnet, so they'll send their boys out to find bird parts."

She stepped into the room, the door bumping her backside. "That doesn't diminish the call to battle. If anything, boys will be more persistent and ruthless than the adults."

"I agree. That's why you have to win them over."

She pressed two fingers against her forehead. "What are you talking about, Luke?"

"You want to save your birds?"

"Of course."

"Then start up a Plumage League for the kids. Acquaint them with the birds who frequent your backyard. Show them how to feed them out of their hands. If you can make them care about birds the way you do, they won't hunt them. They'll be the birds' fiercest protectors."

She considered him. "And who's going to protect the pigeons from the Gun Club?"

He tightened his jaw. "I told you. That's business."

"And I asked you, what are you still doing here?"

Her gingham apron cinched her tiny waist. Her chest rose and fell with deep breaths. Her lips, even in anger, were full. Lush. Inviting. He took a step forward.

She stumbled back, the door blocking her way.

Reaching around her, he picked up the collection bills he'd completed. "I'm going to deliver these tomorrow, then start selling phones to the areas where new wire is strung."

"What about the areas still waiting on wire?"

He reached again. She plastered herself against the door, banging the back of her head.

He picked up Ottfried's complaint. "As long as you don't interfere with my work, this document will remain in my possession. The minute you stick your nose in my business, I'll post it to Dallas."

Her lips parted.

He folded the complaint and tucked it in his pocket. "Good night, Miss Gail."

Grabbing his hat off the stand, he let himself out.

Tugging on the reins, Luke squeezed his thighs and directed Honey Dew off the road. He'd left his installer's cart in town, though he still wore his overalls and packed a few tools so as not to raise suspicion.

Today's work, however, would not be for SWT&T. He'd had a good look at the territory from the top of his poles and there were a few areas he wanted to scout. He'd spent the morning exploring two of them but had found nothing of interest. It would take the rest of the afternoon to search this third section.

He inhaled deeply, relishing the smell of new growth. After trailing Comer throughout the winter, Luke had promised himself to take particular note of spring's debut. He made a mental checklist, deriving pleasure from each item added. Cherry laurels filled their branches with an abundance of white blooms. Spring peepers woke from their long winter's nap. Deciduous trees sprouted green buds. And the temperatures hovered in a range heaven must surely duplicate.

Slowing his horse, he scanned the forested area, parts of it level, parts of it rough. Most outlaws built dugouts or cabins, and though Comer's boys might live in the open, he couldn't imagine Frank Comer doing the same. He had to have a refuge of some kind.

Sliding off his horse, Luke secured Honey Dew, deciding to make the rest of his search on foot. He checked concealed areas amid trees, brush, and tall grasses, stopping often to listen and ask himself where he would hide if he were on the run.

After two hours of fruitless searching, he veered into a less dense area, then paused. Voices in hushed tones approached from the southwest. The trees hadn't leafed out enough to conceal him, so he crouched behind a dense, shrubby section of ligustrum.

The talking stopped and from the sound of the footfalls, there were at least four or five of them.

"What's that?" a voice whispered.

All movement ceased. Luke held his breath. A bird yodeled, pausing between each phrase.

"That's a wood thrush," the hushed response. "He's much more shy than his cousin the robin."

Georgie's voice produced a sense of panic in him. What the blazes was she doing out here?

"Sounds like he's saying, 'Here I am. Here I am.' " A young voice.

"That's right. Can you find him? His back and wings are a rich cinnamon brown with brown polka dots on his white chest."

Pit. Pit. Pit.

"What's that one?"

"Same wood thrush," she responded. "If you strike two small stones together, you can imitate it."

"How come he sounds mad all o' sudden?"

"We're a little closer than he deems safe."

"I see him! I see him!" No whisper here, but an out-and-out yell.

A bird took wing, but Luke didn't look. Just prayed they wouldn't come to this side of the giant shrub. How in all that was holy would he explain what he was doing?

She was supposed to hold her Junior Bird meeting in her backyard. There must not have been enough activity to suit.

They tromped closer. Taking advantage of their noise, he went belly-down and slithered beneath the hedge. They passed him by. Four sets of feet belonging to girls. Eight to boys. And Georgie.

"Lookit there."

Luke tensed, but from the direction of their feet, they were looking away from him.

"Oh, a robin," Georgie exclaimed. "Next month they'll search high and low for a place which has a roof. And when they find one, they'll build a nest."

"They can come to my house. We have a roof."

"They'd love that, Eugene. But they can't trust us. A shame, isn't it?"

"Why don't it trust me? I didn't do nothing."

Turning around, she paused, then headed straight toward Luke, the toes of her black boots pointing like accusing fingers. A yard away, she stopped beside an old log and settled onto it, sweeping her arm to indicate the children should join her.

They gathered around, some on the log, most on the ground. A blond girl with long curls banded by a bright pink ribbon arranged her calico dress and bibbed pinafore over drawn-up knees. Several boys in short pants plopped to the ground on the opposite side from the girls, other than Bettina. She sat cross-legged among them, her dress a lackluster brown and without a pinafore. He could make out the faces of those sitting cross-legged, but not the ones resting on their heels.

The number of boys in her group surprised him. From what he could see, they weren't bookish types, but as rascally as they came. The two facing him elbowed each other, their freckled grins up to no good. Much as he wanted to shrink further beneath the shrub, he didn't move.

The brown-haired boy picked up a pebble and flicked it over the heads of those around them. It landed softly on the blond girl. She brushed at her hair and glanced up before dismissing it and returning her attention to Georgie.

"The robins used to trust us," Georgie said, her voice soft. "On the first Christmas morning, one visited Baby Jesus in His manger. That was before the robin had its orange underbelly."

The boys had lobbed two more pebbles, but Georgie's statement captured their attention.

"The night was wrapped in a bitter chill, and Jesus had grown cold in that drafty stable. Mary called to Joseph, asking him to stoke their little fire, but it had been a long night and he slept deeply. So she caught the eye of a nearby oxen. 'My son grows cold,' she said. 'Could you blow on the embers?' But the ox was locked behind a stall and couldn't stir from its place."

A rock underneath Luke gouged into his leg. In an effort to ignore it, he concentrated on Georgie's retelling of the old legend.

"Mary asked the donkey, but it was asleep and didn't hear her call. Nor did the horse or the sheep."

Cheerily, cheer up, cheer up, cheerily, cheer up.

They all looked toward the sound.

"There it is!" A redheaded boy pointed.

The children began talking at once. "I see it!"

"Where? Where is it?"

"There. Look there."

Luke imagined the orange-breasted bird. Another early sign of spring. He had heard its song on many occasions, but he hadn't realized it belonged to the robin.

The children quieted.

Georgie pressed her feet together, resting linked hands atop her knees. "A little brown bird in the rafters of the stable noticed the dwindling fire and Mary's distress. It flew down and fluttered its wings, rekindling the ashes. Hopping about the stable, it gathered sticks and hay with its beak, then dropped them into the fire. Suddenly, a flame shot up, touching the little bird's chest and turning it orange."

The boys' eyes grew wide.

"Did it hurt?" the blond girl asked.

"A little," Georgie admitted. "But the robin continued to fan the flames with its wings. The blazes grew, the stable warmed, and Jesus slept soundly. Instead of returning to the rafters, the bird tended the fire all night long. At dawn, Mary lifted her hand. The tired but faithful robin landed on her fingers. 'From this day forward,' she said, 'may your red breast be a blessed reminder of the great charity you have done for Baby Jesus.' And as you can see, the robin's orange underbelly still covers its noble heart."

The children sat quietly, absorbing the tale.

Bettina scrunched up her nose. "Do ya think the robin knew who Jesus was?"

"Perhaps," Georgie answered. "But because of the beauty of their orange chests, women want to use robins as decorations on their hats and cloaks."

The black-haired boy scratched the back of his head. "But what if we only killed one? That won't hurt none."

"It seems that way, Eugene. But look what happened to our friendly beavers. We had millions and millions and millions of them until they were harvested for hats and coats. And the impossible happened. Animals which could not run out, ran out. We barely have a few thousand left in our entire country."

Eugene rocked back and forth on his backside, eyeing Georgie with speculation.

"Deer, bison, pigeons, Carolina parakeets," she continued. "All once numbered in the millions. And all have been hunted to near extinction."

Luke wished he could see her face. Whatever shone on it had captivated her audience.

"Tomorrow, I want you to pay close attention every time you hear a bird," she said. "Every time you see a hat or cloak or skirt with bird parts on it. For every bird part you see, some innocent mama or daddy bird had to die. Then, when you close your eyes tomorrow night, try to imagine a day without birdsong, without seeing a friendly winged creature out your back window, because that's what it will be like when you are a grown-up if we don't stop killing our birds."

"What if it's already dead?" A boy out of Luke's line of vision asked the question.

"Then put it in a box and bring it to our next meeting and we will give it a burial."

Eugene and his friend looked at each other. The thought of a bird funeral clearly captured their imagination.

"In the meanwhile, share your new knowledge about birds with your mothers and fathers." She stood, dusting her hands together. "Next meeting, I will teach you a bird call. Listen."

The piercing whistle he'd heard the first time he saw her rent the air. If she hadn't won the boys over before, this wiped out all hesitation. Their faces lit with awe and excitement.

"That was a Northern Cardinal," she said. "I learned it when I wasn't much older than you. Would you like me to teach it to you?"

They jumped to their feet, shouting their yeses with enthusiasm.

"Then you'd best not miss our next meeting. But it's getting late; we need to head back."

Groans of disappointment followed. Luke smiled. Nothing like leaving on a high note — literally. He watched the battalion of feet head back the way they'd come, some running ahead, some lagging behind, several hovering about Georgie. He stayed hidden until the sound of their voices and footfalls had long since passed.

Finally, he slithered out from under the shrub, wincing as he pushed himself to his feet. No sense in continuing his search for Comer. The day was almost over.

Returning to Honey Dew, he praised her for her patience, then swung atop her. He contemplated all he'd learned from listening to Georgie, admitting to himself she was right. Killing birds for no other reason than to decorate hats was not worth the price of depleting the species.

The question he didn't want to face, but

could not ignore, was if killing birds for sport was worth the price.

CHAPTER THIRTEEN

Now that the ladies of the newly formed Plumage League had voted in their officers, Georgie decided her first duty as president would be to disrupt the milliner's contest.

Her gaze wandered about Mrs. Zach's parlor. They'd moved their meetings to the mayor's home since the Zachs not only had more space, but Mrs. Zach and her daughter, Rachel, were both members. The sitting room stretched almost the entire length of the house, opening onto a grand veranda outside.

Georgie rubbed a hand along the cheerful blue-and-apricot sofa with dolphin arms, its rich upholstery echoed in the wallpaper and drapes. The pièce de résistance, however, was a colorful needlework rug with bouquets of various flowers. She couldn't imagine the patience it must have taken to stitch such a large and intricate piece. Seemed sacrilegious to set her boots on it.

Crossing her ankles so only her left toe touched the carpet, she made a mental note of the ladies assembled in a half dozen chairs, two easy chairs and two divans. They were a cross-section from the crème of society to the very humble. From the elderly to the young. From the doers to the followers.

Resting her cup and saucer on her knee, Georgie cleared her throat. "I was wondering, have any of you read about Mr. Ottfried's Easter bonnet contest?"

The idle chatter fizzled as the ladies turned their attention to her.

"Read about it?" Vicki Lee asked. Her husband, Joe, was the local lawyer and a member of the Gun Club. His court performances were so theatrical, folks would drive from miles around to hear him argue a case. Much of his reflected glory fell onto his wife, making her as much a star as he. "That's all anyone is talking about."

"His motives were less than honorable, you know." Mrs. Yoakum patted the corners of her mouth with a hanky. The judge's wife had slicked her dark hair back into a top-knot, accentuating her receding hairline. "Mrs. Oodson ran to him straightaway after your first meeting. If you ask me, his contest is nothing short of a call to arms."

"Well, I say we answer with a battle cry so loud, that fella won't know what hit him." Kathy Patrick had a big smile, a big heart, and big ideas. There wasn't a soul in town who didn't love her. She chaired the Ladies' Reading Circle and had taught Bettina to read.

"What did you have in mind?" Georgie asked her.

She scrunched up her mouth. "Well, he's chosen his weapon — a contest. All we need to do is come up with one bigger, better, and more enticing."

"What could possibly be more enticing than a new Easter bonnet?" Heather Martin was not native to Brenham but was well respected, having married the town's banker. "And with Easter right around the corner, we don't have time for a contest of our own."

"What if we had ours during Maifest?" Miss Gladstone, her voice melodious even when she wasn't singing, had been last year's Maifest Queen.

Excited murmurs whisked through the group. The German tradition of celebrating spring's arrival had been observed in Brenham since 1874, making this their twenty-ninth festival. Along with the usual eating, drinking, and singing, the fair offered a

Maypole, a parade with elaborate floats, and the coronation of a Maifest Queen.

"Perhaps we could hold a hat-making contest," Mrs. Zach suggested, refilling Georgie's coffee.

Georgie held her cup steady, watching the rich dark liquid pour from the silver spout, its aroma filling the room. "We'd have to make a rule stating the hat can't have any bird parts on it."

"But what would the prize be?" Miss Rachel asked, her wavy hair tucked up with fancy combs. The mayor's daughter had been voted secretary of the Plumage League and held her pencil in readiness.

Mrs. Patrick straightened. "What if the new Maifest Queen is crowned with the winning hat?"

"That's a marvelous idea," Georgie exclaimed. "Mrs. Abney? Would you mind asking the fire department if we could do that?"

Mrs. Abney wore her Sunday best, though the blue woolsey had faded from multiple washings. Her husband was a member of the fire brigade, and since Maifest was put on by them, she'd have a good chance of smoothing their way.

"I'm sure they won't mind," she said. "With businesses squawking about the cost of sponsorship this year, I know the boys could use a show of support."

"We should also have a float." The doctor's wife sat tall and elegant in a cutaway bodice fitted over a beaded blouse. "I'll ask Friedrich if we can use the basket phaeton."

Exclaiming, the ladies applauded with gloved hands. The basket phaeton was a sleek carriage used mostly for parks and beaches. The doctor was the only man in town who owned one, and Georgie could hardly contain her excitement.

"Let's decorate it to look like a bird," Mrs. Patrick suggested. "It could have wings and everything."

Georgie couldn't imagine how to turn a basket phaeton into a bird, but if anyone could do it, Mrs. Patrick could.

"Do I have a motion for Mrs. Patrick to be float chair?" Georgie asked.

"I so move."

"I second."

"All in favor?" Georgie asked.

The vote was unanimous. Smiling, Mrs. Patrick ran the rest of the meeting, forming committees, assigning jobs, and setting deadlines.

"We need someplace to hide all the hat entries," Mrs. Lee said. "Someplace which doesn't have children."

"Georgie?" Mrs. Patrick asked. "Your cottage would be perfect, with you all by yourself over there."

Though Georgie's home was tiny, it was the envy of many in town. A woman with a job and her own place was as rare as hen's teeth.

"Of course," she heard herself saying. "I'll store them in my bedroom where none can see."

Miss Rachel recorded their decisions along with the rest of the minutes. Sitting back, Georgie sipped the last of her coffee, pleased with the afternoon's work.

The only signs of life at the run-down, board-and-batten farmhouse were chickens strutting about a fenced-in hen yard. No smoke drifted from the chimney, no woman washed linen in a cauldron, not even a dog barked in greeting.

The von Wredes were first in a long line of families Luke planned to visit over the next several weeks. He'd pored over Georgie's ledgers and the county's land registration books in an effort to familiarize himself with all outlying farms.

Tying Honey Dew to a tree, he surveyed the pared-down array of outbuildings. The barn looked more like a child's playhouse than a structure for housing animals. Four hogs slept soundly in a mule pen. And a once cone-shaped potato bank sat deflated beneath a giant elm.

Testing each board before putting his weight on it, Luke climbed the steps to the porch and front door. "Hello? Anybody home?"

Nothing stirred. The place didn't look like anything a train robber would own, nor a place which could afford phone service. And deserted as it was, he figured the entire family, including women and children, were in the field weeding and cultivating as much corn as possible before cotton planting began.

Returning to his horse, Luke decided to cross the von Wredes from his list. The men he was looking for would be living higher on the hog. He couldn't help but wonder, though, how many von Wrede children were in the fields and how old they were.

His uncle's farmhouse had looked a lot like this one. When they'd moved to Rusk County, Luke had been ten, with Alec only eleven months behind him in age, but a foot behind him in size. Their uncle made a special cut-down hoe for Alec and demanded a man's work from them both. The dawn-to-dusk, backbreaking labor was a far cry from the hunting, shooting, fishing, and swimming they'd done with their father.

Shaking off the memories, he guided Honey Dew toward the next farm. A hint of breeze teased the leaves on the trees like an invisible finger running along a line of fringe. A woodpecker *rata-tat-tatted* in the distance. Luke scanned the area, spotting the bird at the top of a dead tree hammering the final touches on its oval nest. He hoped the woodpecker's chicks could fly on their first try. Otherwise, it would be an awfully big drop.

He studied the bird's markings: black-and-white body with a brilliant scarlet head. He'd seen plenty of them over his lifetime but never gave them much more than a glance. He took note now, though, of both the bird and where he was so he could tell Georgie in case she wanted to bring out her students.

Much as he hated to admit it, the lesson she'd given the children had fascinated him and made him more sympathetic to the birds' plight. That didn't make hunting a sin, though. Especially if he ate what he killed.

Even for next week's tournament, the local restaurants would pick up the shot-down birds and serve them to the spectators. Either way, he didn't think God would be too upset. The Bible said He'd caused so many quail to fall dead from the sky, the Israelites ate them until they literally came out their noses. And even then, they couldn't finish them all.

No, there was no sin in shooting a few birds. And the tournament would bring enthusiasts from all over the state. He'd bet money every one of Comer's gang would be there. Maybe even Frank Comer himself.

Problem was, Luke didn't know what they looked like. Between the neckerchiefs they covered their faces with and the citizens unwilling to point fingers, the gang remained unidentified. But he knew they could shoot. Especially Comer. Surely the hundreds of dollars worth of cash prizes would be more than they could resist.

Winding his way between two fields, he couldn't help but be impressed with von Wrede's work. The farmer might only have seventy-five acres, but all Luke had passed had been plowed and planted with corn. Nary an acre was left open for cotton. He must have grown cotton last year and was rotating out. That would explain, to some extent, the disrepair of his house and outbuildings. The year 1902 had not been a good one for cotton.

Finally, he crossed into Peter Finkel's

land. Unlike von Wrede, Finkel had close to four hundred acres, yet field after field lay fallow. No cornfields. No plowing or preparation for cotton planting. Just neglected, overgrown ground.

Honey Dew gave a long, blustery exhale, as if disgusted by the waste of fertile soil. Luke had to agree and began to despair of finding any cultivated fields. But a few acres from the farmhouse a good amount of red-top cane had been planted for feed, along with several rows of molasses cane, a half-acre potato patch, and a full-acre garden.

He smelled the cow pasture before he saw it, then rounded the corner to find a giant, fenced-in grazing area. Even though there was room a'plenty to spread out, the black cows plastered themselves shoulder to shoulder in tight clusters beneath a smattering of shade trees.

At the top of the rise a typical one-story house with a front porch faced southward. A flock of guineas in his path scattered, squawking an alarm and pumping their heads like rocker arms on a locomotive wheel.

A young girl in braids and calico scattered shelled corn from her hand to a gaggle of turkeys, chickens, and geese gathering about her feet. She paused and looked his way, shading her eyes from the bright sun. "*Mutti,* somebody's coming."

A boy in a straw hat and overalls churned butter on the porch, his eyes tracking Luke all the way to the yard. The old hound at his feet lifted its head, then thought better of it and lowered it back down.

Pulling Honey Dew to a stop, Luke touched his hat. "Howdy."

The boy switched hands, then continued churning, the *swish, swish, swish* letting Luke know he hadn't been at it very long.

The girl smiled, her two front teeth missing. "I'm Dewiller."

"Pleased to meet you, Miss Dewiller. I'm Mr. Palmer. Your ma or pa around?"

A woman in a brown dress stepped onto the porch, drying her hands with the serviceable black apron about her waist. Though her face still hinted of youth and her eyes sparked with interest, her posture was bent and her blond hair didn't have near the luster Georgie's did.

"*Hallo.*" She scanned the area behind him. "Vhere's *der Wagen?*"

Dismounting, he touched his hat. "Mrs. Finkel?"

She nodded.

"I'm Luke Palmer, the troubleman for Southwestern Telegraph and Telephone."

The tiny bit of animation in her eyes receded. "You're not *der* Peddler?"

"I'm afraid not."

Nodding, she indicated a set of rockers to her left. "Haf a chair, Herr Palmer, and I'll get my *Mann*."

Luke schooled his features, offering no reaction to the fact her husband was home in the middle of the day, during planting season, no less. Tying Honey Dew to a scrub bush, he smiled at the girl, who'd ceased feeding the chickens.

Her large brown eyes took a thorough survey of him. "I haven't seen you before. Are you new to *die Gemeinde?*"

He pushed his hat back. "Reckon I am. New to Washington County, anyway. I guess you must know just about everybody around here."

Her smile grew. "I *reckon*."

The boy on the porch glared at his sister. *"Mutti wird bald Hilfe mit dem Bügeln brauchen."*

Luke didn't speak much German, but he recognized *business, mother,* and *help.*

Rule #5: *Go about your business cheerfully and quietly. When you enter a residence don't overlook the foot mat. If requested to go around to the back door, don't consider yourself insulted. Say "good morning" or "evening."* It doesn't cost anything and shows you started out right at home.

Before he could smooth the boy's feathers, a burly man in his early thirties stepped onto the porch. Brown hair, brown eyes, brown mustache, brown suspenders, brown pants.

He gave Luke the same once-over his daughter had. "You on your way to town for *das* Gun Tournament? You're a bit early."

Luke stretched out his arm. "No, sir. I'm Luke Palmer with SWT&T. Sure is an impressive place you have here."

"SWT&T?" He accepted Luke's hand. "You must be lost. Ve don't have *das Telefon.* Nearest one to us is over at *die* Vampler place." He nodded his head toward the east. "About twelve farms ofer."

Luke whistled. "That'd be a pretty good stretch if you had a hankering to talk to somebody mighty quick."

Finkel raised a brow. "Vell, I'm not often in a hurry."

Pushing the screen open with her back, the missus held a tray with two steaming cups. *"Möchten Sie einen Kaffee,* Herr Palmer?"

"Thank you, ma'am." Luke accepted the coffee, its aroma teasing his senses. As a rule, he didn't drink stimulants, but if he didn't take this, they'd most likely offer him a beer.

Settling into a rocker, Finkel accepted the second cup on the tray and indicated the chair next to him. "You come from town, then?"

"Sure did," Luke said, joining him.

"How are *die* Roads?"

"Good and dry. So if the rain holds off, there shouldn't be any slowdowns for the folks coming next week." He paused, expecting the man to offer up an opinion. As far as farmers were concerned, rainwater for their corn was much more important than the condition of the roads. But Finkel said nothing.

Luke cleared his throat. "The manager of the shooting tournament thinks this year's competition will be the biggest gathering of shooters ever seen in these parts. Claims he's even expecting folks from outside the state." He blew on his coffee. "You planning to go?"

Finkel leaned his rocker back. "I plan on being in it."

Luke whistled. The man hadn't been to Gun Club practice. Wasn't even a member as best he could tell. "You must be mighty good. I hear Winchester's sending their professional."

"F.M. Faroute has a lot of followers, but I can gif him a run for his money. Vhat about you? Are you going?"

"I'll be there all right. I'm helping with the pigeon crates. I wouldn't stand a chance in the competition, though. Anybody else around here signing up?"

Shrugging, Finkel spit to the side. "Von't really know until opening day, I guess."

Luke wondered if he knew about Necker, the judge, and the gun shop owner participating, or if he was simply keeping his cards close to his chest.

The rhythmic swishing of the butter churn changed in tone as the cream thickened. Luke glanced over. The boy switched arms and kept his head down, but Luke knew he was listening to every word — assuming he understood English.

Swiveling his cup, Luke watched the liquid within it swirl. "You know, if you had a telephone, you'd be able to find out right now which of your neighbors were competing."

Finkel harrumphed. "I'm not *die* one all curious about it. You are."

Smiling, Luke propped an ankle on his knee. "I guess I am. But don't you think having a telephone might come in handy? You could discover the conditions of the

190

road anytime you wanted. You'd be able to keep abreast of the coming elections. You'd know the minute the new cotton mill is up and running. You'd know Hodde has a car of white corn on track for cheap. You'd know Thornhill's planted ninety acres." He paused. "But most important, if there was some kind of emergency and you had to talk to somebody quick, why, you could just call them right up."

Finkel stretched out his legs, crossing them at the ankles. "Thornhill's planted *neunzig* already?"

"He has. And twenty-five of it is up."

"How did he get the plowing done vhile the ground vas still vet?"

Luke shrugged. "I don't know, but if you had a telephone, we could call and ask him."

"I doubt that. The vay I hear it, those lines are alvays breaking down."

"Not anymore. I strung brand-new wire right along the road out there. And it runs straight to Miss Gail in town. If you were to give her a ring, she could patch you through to anybody you want."

He scratched his jaw. "Thornhill has *das Telefon?*"

"Yes, sir. A three-box magneto wall set. Would you like to see an illustration? I have one in my saddlebag."

Slapping his hands on his knees, Finkel pushed himself to his feet. "No, no need for that. I haf to head out to the vest forty and see how the planting is coming."

Luke followed him off the porch. "I saw the fields on the east side were laying fallow."

"They have root rot. I had acres of thriving cotton on them year before last, then quick as a blink they died. I averaged about two bales out of every twelve acres." Shaking his head in disgust, he squinted that direction. "The only sure vay to get rid of it is to let it go to clover for a few years. So that's vhat I'm doing."

A few years? Luke had heard of farmers leaving fields with dead soil unplanted for one year. But a few? Not too many could afford that.

He extended his hand. "Well, I wish you luck with it. Guess I'll see you at the tournament."

"*Ja,* you will."

Swinging onto Honey Dew, he looked again at the neatly kept farmhouse, the children wearing clothes made from bolted fabric instead of seed sacks, and the abundance of animals. For somebody who only used the west forty, he was doing mighty good.

By the close of day Luke had stopped at six farms. Of the six, only Finkel had been home and only Finkel was taking time away from his farming to attend the shooting tournament.

Tomorrow, Luke would head north to visit Necker and the farms out that way. Then, on Sunday, he'd find himself a secluded place, strap on his gun belt, and do a little leather slapping. He might not be entering the tournament, but he needed to keep his skills sharp just the same.

CHAPTER FOURTEEN

Picking up the *Brenham Banner* off Georgie's porch, Luke glanced through her screen door. A stack of hatboxes lined the wall between the kitchen and the bedroom. Beyond that, she balanced on tiptoes atop her chair while both arms delved inside the opened lid of the switchboard hutch. Her backside pointed out, her skirt hiked up, her ankles wobbled.

But it was her stockings that captured his full attention. Red polka dots decorated her black hosiery. He followed the line of her legs, imagining their shape, then imagining them ensconced with polka dots. His mouth went dry.

Pulling open the screen door, he tossed the paper onto his desk. "What are you doing?"

Startled, she jumped, thrusting the rolling chair out from under her. He leaped forward, jerking her to him and away from the array of cable-plugs housed like a bed of nails on the key-shelf below her.

She grabbed the top of the hutch with her fingertips, leaving her bent at a ninety-degree angle — her upper body parallel to the floor, her backend smashed against his chest, his right arm locked about her legs.

"Oh!" She looked over her shoulder, eyes wide. "Oh, my goodness."

He couldn't release her or she'd land on the spiked cables. Placing his free hand against her torso, he spread his fingers wide. "Let go. I've got you."

Her cheeks filled with color, but her eyes held fear.

He gave her a slight nod. "It's okay. I won't let you fall, but you have to let go."

She swung her left hand from the hutch to his wrist, squeezing him with a respectable amount of strength.

"That's it. I've got you. Now when you let go with the other hand, go ahead and straighten up. Ready?"

She glanced at him again, her eyes frantic as a spooked horse.

"It's okay. I won't let you fall. Now, on the count of three. Ready?"

She didn't answer.

"One . . . two . . . three." He pushed against her midriff.

She released the hutch and straightened.

"That'a way." He allowed her to slide down him, shifting his hands to her waist. Her skirt bunched up. Swallowing, he kept his eyes forward.

As soon as her feet touched the floor, she jerked her dress into place, then spun around, his hands still on her waist. He looked down.

Mussed hair. Rosy cheeks. Full lips.

"You scared me," she whispered. "I didn't hear you come in."

"I'm sorry." He needed to let go, put some distance between them. He stayed where he was. "I thought you were mad at the milliner."

"I am."

"Then why'd you buy all those hats?" He indicated the stack of boxes by her bedroom.

"I didn't. They're entries for the Plumage League's hat contest."

He nodded, scraping the hem of her bodice with his nail.

"I'm still mad at you, too," she said, but she didn't look mad. She looked soft as a rose petal.

He breathed in the touch of cinnamon that always hovered when she came close and suddenly had an irrepressible yearning to taste of it. He wondered how long it had been since he'd kissed a woman. How long it had been since he'd found one even worth kissing.

Too long, he decided. And all rationales, all wisdom, all thoughts — but one — flew from his brain. Slowly, giving her time to pull back, he lowered his head. Her eyes widened, then drifted shut.

She tasted of cinnamon, and peaches, and something indefinable. Sliding his arms around her, he pulled her close and explored her lips, her jaw, her ear.

She tilted her head back, a tiny sigh at the back of her throat. Without hesitation, he partook of the newly exposed skin. It was his own groan which brought him to his senses.

Resting his lips against the crook between her neck and collar, he kept his eyes closed, knowing he needed to release her, but lingering for just a moment more. His hands rode up her back, then down to her waist, learning, memorizing, relishing.

She turned her face to his, searching for his lips. He allowed her to find them, but when desire began to override good sense, he reluctantly pulled back.

She stood still as a marble column but warm as sunshine. Eyes closed, head back, throat exposed, she took rapid breaths. Cupping her neck, he ran a thumb from the tip of her chin to the indentation between her collarbones.

She opened her eyes. "Now I know why cats purr."

His reaction was swift and immediate. Releasing her, he stepped back. "You hate cats."

She gave him a lazy smile. "Only when they're after my birds."

He waited, knowing it wouldn't be long.

Sure enough, her brows crinkled and she straightened. "Are you still going to the tournament?"

Lifting a tendril of hair resting against her shoulder, he rubbed it between his fingers. "I am, but I'm not entering."

Pleasure touched her face.

"Not because I don't want to," he clarified. "I do. Very much. But I've decided it's too costly."

"For the birds?"

"For my pocket."

Disappointment replaced the pleasure. She pulled back, her hair slipping from his fingers.

"The switchboard is down." She waved a hand toward it. "I don't know what's wrong, but no calls are coming in."

"Maybe everybody's headed to the tournament."

"No. There's something wrong. There are drops down, but I can't answer anyone."

Skirting around her, he looked into the bowels of the machine. A jumble of wires overlapped each other like a pot of spaghetti noodles.

He had no idea how the thing worked, but there were a couple of exposed wires coming up from the bottom. He glanced at her.

She quickly looked away and unfolded the *Brenham Banner.* He had no business trifling with her. Without family to advise and protect her, she was more vulnerable than most. His disregard for her susceptibility didn't sit well with him. But somehow the *wanna-dos* were overriding the *should-dos.*

He turned his attention to the switchboard. "Anything interesting in the news?"

"Not really." She fingered the edge of the first page. "The tournament is taking up the whole thing."

"Not the whole thing, surely."

"Well . . . it does say Grayson and Camp counties went dry after a local option election on Saturday."

Opening his pocketknife, he carefully cut the paraffin and insulation around one wire.

"Helen Keller is appealing to the Massachusetts legislative committee for relief of the adult blind."

"That ought to be effective."

"One would hope." She turned the page. "Listen to this: 'Ottfried Millinery has prepared a feast of style and price lowness that will gladden the hearts of all callers. Miss Julia Wilson has just returned from a two-week trip selecting all the very newest and most correct up-to-date millinery. Come examine the styles. Be sure to bring bird parts for a chance to win an exquisite Easter bonnet.' " A low rumble sounded in her throat.

He started on the next wire.

Snapping the page over, she continued scanning. "Oh, my goodness. Over a thousand dollars in diamonds were stolen in Brownsville."

He looked up. Brownsville was over four hundred miles from here. Surely he'd have gotten wind of it if Comer had traveled all that way. "Does it say anything else?"

"They're calling in the Rangers."

"Does it mention which one?"

She snorted. "Lucious Landrum."

He hesitated. Headquarters must have given out misinformation. They did that occasionally. Rumor that he was on his way often caused a gang of culprits to panic and flee, thus making them easy to track. Comer wasn't one to panic, but if he were still in Washington County, he'd gain a false sense of security from thinking his pursuer had been sent to the southern tip of Texas.

He forced his attention back to the wire. "Read the whole thing."

"That's all it says. 'Diamonds valued at twelve to fifteen hundred dollars were taken in a Brownsville, Texas, burglary. Captain Cecil Heywood of the Texas Rangers intimated Ranger Lucious Landrum, a man of nerve, would be in pursuit.' " She scoffed. " 'Man of nerve.' Those aren't the words I'd have used to describe him."

He stalled again but kept his head down. "You've met him?"

"He interrupted the robbery of a train I was on."

Slowly straightening, he gave up all pretense. "You were robbed on a train?"

Her face lit. "Yes. By Frank Comer himself. He knew I had money, too, but he let me keep it. He actually gave some coins to a widow and a poor boy. It was terribly exciting."

She must have been on that train from Dallas. He tried to recall seeing her but couldn't. "You got a pretty good look at Comer, then?"

"I did, though a neckerchief and hat covered everything but his eyes." She looked out the window, her face softening. "They were blue. Not a subtle blue, like robins' eggs, but a vibrant blue, like the feathers of a blue jay."

His eyes were blue, too. He wondered if she'd noticed. Stuffing down his irritation, he shifted his weight onto one foot. "So what happened?"

"Hm?" She turned to him, then shook herself. "Oh, that ridiculous Lucious Landrum came charging in on his horse, barking orders, shooting his gun, and scaring everyone half to death."

"Yet you wouldn't describe him as a 'man of nerve'?"

Her lips thinned. "He was pompous, arrogant, abrupt, and even tried to take that poor widow's coins from her. Can you imagine?"

He hadn't been taking money *away* from the woman. It wasn't ever hers to begin with. It belonged to the Texas & Pacific. She had, in essence, robbed the railroad same as Comer.

Georgie propped a fist on her waist. "So here's a bandit giving money to the widows and poor, while a lawman tries to take it away." She rolled her eyes. "And the Rangers wonder why no one will help them. They're nothing but a bunch of idiots, if you ask me."

A thousand justifications stacked up in his throat, not the least of which was the Rangers kept her and every other Texan safe. Folks normally revered them. Held them in awe. But Comer had muddied folks' perceptions.

Instead of voicing his thoughts, he lowered his attention to the switchboard. Picking up the two wires, he touched them together. A sizzling sound but no sparks.

"Did you know he named his pistols?" she asked.

He felt his jaw begin to tick and immediately forced himself to relax. "I think I've read that before."

"Well, I just read it recently. As if having a boy pistol and a girl pistol wasn't bad enough, he goes and names them. Odysseus and Penelope." She laughed. A full-throated, from-the-belly laugh. "But what can you expect from somebody named *Lucious?*"

Over his four years as a Ranger, he'd traveled seventy-four thousand miles, made two hundred scouts, and one hundred eighty-two arrests. He'd endured cold, hunger, and fatigue without a murmur. He'd been said to have the eyes of a fox, the ears of a wolf, and the ability to follow scent like a hound. Yet this tiny bit of fluff could throw him off-kilter like no other.

He counted to ten. "What's wrong with the name Lucious?"

She looked at him, incredulous. "What's wrong with Lucious? It's . . . it's . . . I don't know . . . silly, don't you think? Sounds like *luscious.*"

He was named after his father. The father whose life had been senselessly snuffed out by Mother Nature. Carrying his dad's name was a great privilege and a source of pride for Luke. How dare she make fun of it.

Anger simmering, he twisted the wires together and forced himself to respond as if he had nothing personal at stake. "Don't guess I ever thought about it. Can't say the name's ever bothered me, though."

"That's probably because it isn't yours. I'm sure if it were, you'd think differently."

"Maybe so." Picking up a cloth on the switchboard, he wiped his hands. "Did you get a look at this Lucious fellow?"

"I did."

He raised a brow. "And was he luscious?"

"Ha!" Folding the paper, she tossed it on the desk. "Hardly. If anybody was luscious, it was Frank Comer."

Sobering, he snapped the towel over his

shoulder. "I've reconnected a couple of wires. Plug something in and see if it works."

She gave a sharp glance at his tone; then her mouth formed a tiny circle, as if just realizing what she'd said to the man who'd kissed her thoroughly not half an hour ago. At least it gave him an excuse to show his irritation.

Putting on the earpiece, she slid into her chair, pushed the drops back in place, and waited for the phone to ring. The silence in the cottage thickened.

She fiddled with cables, wiggling them into place, though they didn't need it. Finally, she peeked at him through her lashes. "I didn't mean that like it sounded."

"Exactly how did you mean it? He wasn't luscious, after all? You just remembered it wrong?"

Moistening her lips, she clasped her hands. "I only saw his eyes."

"Eyes the color of blue jays' feathers?"

She swallowed. "I think it's his reputation more than anything. You know, all those pulp fiction stories. All the daring escapes he's made. All the good things he's done for folks."

He choked. "Good things? You mean, like robbing people at gunpoint? Stealing from a company who has laid out a great deal of money to bring railroad tracks through this very town? A town which would be dead, just like Burton, if it weren't for those tracks? Those kinds of good things?"

Ding.

She quickly plugged in a cable. "Hello, Central . . . I had a bit of trouble with the switchboard, but Mr. Palmer has it up and running for me now." Her eyes connected with his.

He lowered the lid on the hutch.

Her gaze shot to the cable she'd plugged in, her eyes stormy.

He hesitated.

"Yes, Judge. Five live birds is three dollars entrance, including birds. Twenty live birds is fifteen dollars entrance, which also includes the birds." She pressed her lips together. "You're welcome." She snatched the cable from the jack. "I hate this. I'll have to answer these stupid questions and report on this awful shoot for days."

"The switchboard's working, then?" he asked.

"Yes."

Dropping the cloth on his desk, he made his way to the screen and looked out. The town's librarian let herself through the gate and hurried up the walk carrying a hatbox.

"Luke?" Georgie's voice held a quiver.

"There's someone here to see you." Opening the screen door, he stepped onto the porch. "Good morning, Mrs. Crutcher."

"Mr. Palmer."

Georgie rose. "Come in, Wendy. You have a hat for our contest?"

"I do," she replied, her smile infectious.

Tugging his brim, he nodded to the women. He could see Georgie's distress, but he hardened his heart. "I'll call you with the results of the events as they happen. I'm sure folks will be wanting to know."

Letting the screen slap shut behind him, he nursed his irritation. Better that than the softer, more dangerous emotions she evoked.

CHAPTER FIFTEEN

Crates filled with one thousand fluttering pigeons surrounded Luke, their throaty coos an unceasing clamor, their musky smell overpowering his senses. Reaching into a wooden cage, he grabbed one, its tail feathers fanning.

"Here you go," he said, handing it to Duane Pfeuffer, the son of the feed store owner.

Skinny as a darning needle, the young man tucked the bird under his arm and jogged to the pigeon ring several yards away. A barricade stretching around the ring in a half circle held back a sea of men in their Sunday best vying for position. It appeared to Luke as if every rancher and townsman in the state had turned out for the 26th Annual Texas State Sportsmen's Tournament. A raucous mixture of English and German voices and the exchanges of last-minute bets added to the chaos.

Situated in the center of the half circle and immediately in front of the grandstands was the shooting box, a small wooden platform made specifically for this week's event. A fence of netting fifty yards out marked the boundary the bird had to reach without being shot. If it didn't make it, the shooter was awarded a point.

Contestants, sponsors, referees, and scorers filed into the holding area and took their seats beneath a blue-and-white-striped canopy. Luke picked out Necker, Finkel, and Judge Yoakum, along with F.M. Faurote, Winchester's circuit shooter. Faurote was the reigning state champion out of Dallas and had a contingent of followers in the stands. Sheriff Nussbaum spoke with the referee and shooters, then moved along the barricade, pushing back those who tried to encroach.

A wind from the west whipped the straps of Luke's overalls and rattled the fasteners. Pulling his hat brim low, he looked toward the shooting box. A row of five traps, each several steps away from the next, sat thirty yards from the firing point. All contained a pigeon except the last.

Squatting beside the empty trap, Duane pushed a spring-loaded plunger down to ground level, placed the pigeon on top of it, then folded up four triangular sides, forming a pyramid around the bird.

A distant train whistle signaled the arrival of the 10:55 out of Austin. Luke checked his pocket watch. Right on time. Five more minutes and the competition would begin.

Duane attached a stout cord to the trap's spring. The rope ran from the spring to the hands of Ludwig Blesinger, the gun shop owner, who stood at the other end of the platform and behind the firing point. Each of the five traps had a pull cord. Each cord's end was held by Blesinger.

He'd dressed smartly in a navy one-button cutaway and derby. His responsibility in the tournament was enormous. Unlike the tournaments up north, there was no miniature roulette wheel to determine which trap was released. Instead, Blesinger could trigger whichever one he wished.

Standing, Duane jogged back to the pigeon crates.

"I got butterflies in my stomach," he said, touching his belly.

Luke smiled, but before he could respond, the referee's voice boomed across the noise. "Anson Albert Anthony, toe the mark."

The crowd quieted as Anthony rose from his chair and removed his jacket. Picking up his Remington 12-gauge, he hooked the open shotgun across his forearm.

Luke glanced at the flag above the tent. Its lone star flapped toward the east making it likely the bird would travel to the right when hurled out of the trap.

Anthony stepped onto the platform and placed his left toe against the score line. The onlookers ceased all conversation, but the pigeons were not so courteous. Their cooing continued to fill the air.

Reaching into his pocket, Anthony removed a shotshell, loaded it into the chamber, snapped the gun shut, and mounted it against his shoulder. He aimed it straight ahead toward Trap Three.

"Puller ready?" His voice rang loud and strong.

Blesinger, behind the shooter's shoulder and out of his peripheral vision, continued to hold all five cords in his left hand. Leaning forward, he grasped an individual one with his right. "Ready."

Anthony looked down the barrel. "Pull!"

Blesinger immediately yanked on his cord. Trap Two sprung open and the plunger catapulted a pigeon into the air. The bird had barely taken wing when Anthony's shot rent the air.

The pigeon plummeted to the ground, well within the fenced boundary.

Anthony quickly broke open his gun and ejected the empty shell, black smoke forming a filmy cloud around him. A boy sprinted onto the field and whipped up the bird. He wrung its neck with a flick of his wrist, for if the bird had been merely wounded and managed to hobble beyond the boundary, the shooter would not receive a point.

"Dead bird!" the referee shouted.

The crowd roared its approval and the scorer marked a one beside Anthony's name. Leaving his gun open, Anthony made eye contact with someone in the crowd, smiled, and returned to the tent.

"J.B. Wyrick, toe the mark."

Throughout the next twenty minutes, shooter after shooter approached the box until all contestants had a turn and the referee declared the end of the first inning. With nineteen innings to go, the crowd began to settle in.

Luke pried open a new box with a crossbar, the pigeons uttering short grunts in reaction to the manhandling.

"Arnold Necker," the referee called. "Toe the mark."

A fierce cheering erupted from the crowd as the hometown favorite approached the firing point. Gone were the overalls he'd worn to Gun Club practice. In their place was a fine gray suit, though he'd removed his jacket. The bright red vest he wore underneath made him easy to spot.

Luke rested his elbow atop two stacked crates. He enjoyed the idiosyncrasies of each player. Anthony's habit was to plant his left foot on the mark, lift his right heel behind him, then mount his gun. Judge Yoakum looked down at his feet, shifting back and forth between them. Finkel tended to dig his left toe into the ground as if he were smashing a cigarette.

But Necker did nothing. Just walked up, shouldered his gun, and said, "Ready?"

He was a man used to shooting on the fly.

Blesinger leaned forward and grabbed a cord. "Ready."

Necker didn't so much as hesitate. "Pull."

Blesinger released Trap Three. The bird shot straight up. Necker grassed him immediately, leaving blue feathers behind to twirl on the wind. And though the spectators hollered with approval, Luke was disappointed.

Trap Three was the easiest of them all. With it being dead ahead of the firing point, the shooter was already aiming at it. Then for the pigeon to be a towerer — another easy shot — it plain took all the sport out of it for Luke.

But a dead bird was a dead bird and Necker was two for two.

As the afternoon progressed, five contestants broke away from the rest, including Necker, Finkel, and the reigning state champion, F.M. Faurote. Judge Yoakum had made some fine kills, but he was no match for those in the lead.

"Peter Finkel," the referee called. "Toe the mark."

Finkel, in loose-fitting pants and vest, stepped to the scoring line, rotated his lead toe in his smash-the-cigarette motion, then mounted his gun. "Puller ready?"

Blesinger leaned forward. "Ready."

"Pull!"

Trap One sprang open, the plunger shooting up, but the pigeon merely bounced off the plunger and onto the wooden platform. Finkel kept his Greener trained on the target. The crowd quieted.

Tucking its head under its wing, the bird gave itself a scratch, then began walking toward Finkel.

"No bird!" the referee shouted.

Finkel broke open his gun and the boy retrieving birds took off for the field.

Duane spun toward Luke. "That's the third duffer in a row. Which crate did it come from?"

Grabbing another pigeon, Luke indicated a box to his right. "That one."

"Blast. You weren't supposed to use that one." Duane snatched the new bird and hurried to the ring.

Luke held himself in check until Duane was busy setting the trap; then he squatted down to inspect the crate to his right. The musky odor within intensified as he leaned close.

At first glance it looked the same as all the rest. Yet when he reread the pigeon catcher's stamp on the side, he realized the F on WULFF & SON had been changed to E, so it read WULFE & SON.

His pulse began to drum. A good pigeon catcher knew the good birds from the bad. Those that were easy to catch and slow to react were your duffers. If he had placed all of those in a special bin, or if this particular set of birds had been overfed these last few days to make them lethargic . . .

Completing his task, Duane hurried from the ring. Luke stepped back to where he'd been.

Finkel snapped his gun shut, went through his ritual, then yelled, "Pull." The bird flew this time, but straight at him. Taking quick aim, Finkel fired and missed.

"Lost bird!" the referee called.

Finkel shot an angry look toward Duane, but Luke was already handing the young man a replacement pigeon.

Faurote followed, shooting a right driver, which started straight from the box, then veered to the east.

"Dead bird!"

Faurote's followers cheered. Money switched hands. New bets were placed.

"Arnold Necker," the referee called. "Toe the mark."

The wind increased in velocity, threatening to blow Luke's hat from his head. The crosscurrent would work in the pigeons' favor no matter which trap was pulled. But anything from Trap Five would be nearly impossible to down before the wind assisted its bird over the boundary.

Necker stepped up onto the platform, rocked forward and back once on his feet, then mounted his gun.

Luke stiffened. Necker didn't have a ritual. He just went up and shot.

"Pull."

Blesinger released Trap Five. Necker emptied his gun before the bird had gone ten feet. The pigeon retriever raced into the ring and snapped the bird's neck.

"Dead bird!"

The men in the stands whooped. The retriever gave a huge smile. Luke sucked in his breath. Bettina?

It couldn't be. Gathering pigeons was a huge honor for a kid. No one would award it to a girl, much less during a state match. He couldn't believe the other boys in town hadn't kicked up a ruckus. Surely they'd have strung her up by her toes if they'd known.

He had to be mistaken. He studied the child. She looked nothing like a girl. Not in manner, attire, or the handling of the birds. Yet the longer he watched, the more convinced he became. Bettina von Schiller, posing as a boy, had been appointed official retriever.

"Bryan Heard, toe the mark."

Not waiting for Luke, Duane grabbed a new bird and raced to the ring. It was several seconds before Luke shook himself from his reverie and several more before he realized Duane had grabbed a pigeon from the duffer crate.

A tall man in his fifties stepped up to the score line, shifting his weight as he waited for Duane to finish.

Kneeling beside Trap Five, Duane stuck the bird under his arm, fiddled with one of the sides, then loaded the trap.

Luke glanced between Duane and the puller. No eye contact had been made, but out of all twelve innings, not once had a shooter been made to wait on Duane. And not once had the young man fooled with the equipment. Finally, he stood and returned to the crates.

Heard loaded his Colt and crouched into a bent-knee stance. "Puller ready?"

"Ready," Blesinger answered.

"Pull."

Trap Five. Same one Duane had just loaded.

The plunger ejected the duffer up a few feet, but instead of taking wing, it arced back down to the ground. Too experienced to shoot too early and lose a point, Heard waited, aim steady. But the pigeon merely sat, blinking at its sudden release.

"No bird!" the referee shouted.

Sighing, Heard broke open his gun.

Luke started to reach for a bird from one of the "good" crates, then paused and looked at Duane, brows raised in question.

The corner of his mouth lifted. "That box'll do."

Luke handed him a bird.

Bryan Heard was a crack shot out of Houston and tied for the lead, but the pressure was tremendous and the stakes high.

Having to wait on Duane to load the trap only to have the bird be a duffer was enough to disconcert any player. Now he had to wait again.

But Duane was quick and efficient.

Heard took his stance. "Pull."

Blesinger waited a fraction of a second before triggering a trap. It proved to be the last straw. Heard missed the pigeon completely.

"Lost bird!"

Heard whirled toward the referee, pointing at Blesinger, his angry words obscured by his fans yelling for blood. But the referee sent him to the tent and announced the next shooter.

Duane smiled. "Well, of all the Heard luck."

Forcing a chuckle, Luke handed him the next pigeon.

Things settled down for the rest of the inning, but by the end of the next, Luke's suspicions were confirmed. Duane, Blesinger, and Necker had rigged the shoot.

Chapter Sixteen

Luke kept a sharp eye on the three cheaters. This time when Bryan Heard took aim, Blesinger pulled the cord slowly, the clatter of the trap frightening the bird and causing it to dart out quickly. With Anthony, he gave an infinitesimal tug on one rope to make a trap move. Just as Anthony turned his head toward it, Blesinger triggered a different trap.

The gun shop owner then took advantage of the wind by pulling traps Four and Five for those he wanted to eliminate, One and Two for those he wanted to advance.

But it wasn't just Blesinger. When Necker stepped up to the score line, he would on occasion signal the puller. Rocking once back and forth meant Trap Five. Giving his right pant leg a tiny shake meant Trap Four. Blowing out a deep breath meant Trap Three.

If Duane loaded a duffer, he alerted

Blesinger in some tiny way. With the last bird, Duane turned his back to partially shield it from Luke, then plucked feathers from its wing. But Luke made sure the boy knew he'd seen, then made a point of not alerting the officials. When the pigeon was released from its trap, it flew erratically, causing Heard to miss his shot.

Duane gave Luke a sideways look. Luke responded with a sly grin. The boy's shoulders relaxed. Luke only hoped it would establish a bond of trust on which he could continue to build.

At least Bettina wasn't cheating. But appointing her the retriever certainly made sense. A boy with experience in shooting might have picked up on what was happening. Then again, maybe not.

Had Luke not been looking for Comer's gang so intently, had he not had the clear vantage point he did from the sidelines, had Duane not let it slip about the duffers, he might not have caught it, either.

Putting his disgust and anger aside, he continued to ingratiate himself with Duane. The closer he moved to these men, the closer he moved to Comer.

The race came down to Necker and Faurote. Tied for the lead, with only two birds to go, Faurote approached the shooting box.

An extremely well-dressed and vocal supporter of Faurote's cupped his hands around his mouth. "I bet one thousand dollars Faurote takes the championship. What Necker fan has the gumption to match me?"

Whirling around, Faurote gaped at the man.

Silence descended. Keeping his gun hand free, Sheriff Nussbaum headed toward the gambler.

Luke shifted his focus to Blesinger. But the gun store owner looked as shocked as the rest.

"Can we have a recess, ref?" A member of the Brenham Hook & Ladder squad pushed toward the edge of the stands. "The lunch shed's done shut down and I'm feeling a powerful hunger comin' on."

The referee hesitated, then turned to Faurote. "Do you have any objection?"

Faurote shook his head.

One by one, the official gained permission from each contestant. But the fireman didn't wait for an answer. Jumping off the side of the stands, he began to gather the men of Washington County together.

"Thirty-minute recess!" the referee announced.

Pandemonium erupted from the crowd.

"Who was that?" Luke asked Duane.

"Ed Abney. He lives over on Quitman Street."

"No, I mean the man who made the bet."

Duane put his hands on his waist and arched his back, stretching. "I dunno. Never seen him round here before."

Luke settled onto an empty crate. "You think Abney can get one thousand together in half an hour?"

"I wouldn't be surprised. Ever'body loves Necker. And with the way he's shooting today, it'd be a pretty sure thing."

The two exchanged knowing looks.

"You betting?" Luke asked.

Duane smiled. "Why, that'd be cheating. Ever'body knows the trapper cain't be makin' any bets."

Luke returned his smile. "I reckon not. It's sure a lot of money, though."

"More'n I ever seed at once."

A circle of folks surrounded the sheriff and the man who'd made the challenge. Luke wondered if he was a plant. But that didn't make sense. If Necker was planning to win by fair means or foul, he wouldn't bet against himself.

On the other hand, if Comer had instigated the wager and the town of Brenham matched it, then one thousand dollars would be here for the taking.

Luke checked his pocket watch. He didn't have time to fetch his gun. If Comer showed up, he'd just have to improvise.

Necker and the other contestants remained within the tent. Blesinger visited with the referee. Bettina was nowhere in sight.

Twenty-eight minutes into the half hour, Abney returned with a bulging satchel. The stands quieted as the local fireman approached the finely dressed instigator.

"What's yer name, mister?" Abney asked.

"Hurless Swanning of Cut 'N Shoot, Texas."

Plopping the bag down in front of the other man, he squared off. "Well, the town of Brenham is taking you on, Swanning. Put up your money."

He reached inside his pocket.

Luke tensed, but instead of a gun, the man withdrew a wallet, opened it for Abney and the sheriff to see, then laid it atop the satchel.

"Here, Sheriff." Abney handed him the money. "You hold these 'til the race is over."

The referee cleared his throat. "F.M. Faurote, toe the mark."

Luke forced the tension from his shoulders. He needed to stay loose. He checked the area as if he were a camera taking pictures. The faces in the crowd were tense, but none were out of place. Swanning and Abney stood shoulder to shoulder, the money lying on the other side of the barricade, the sheriff's boot on top of it. The shooters leaned forward in their chairs. The cheaters did nothing to give themselves away. Bettina crept back to her spot. The outlying area lay calm.

Faurote mounted his shotgun to his shoulder. "Puller ready?"

Blesinger grasped a cord. "Ready."

"Pull."

Trap Two sprung open, the wind lifting a pigeon high and right before it took wing.

The report of the gun had barely registered when the bird plummeted like a wet rag.

Faurote supporters roared. Swanning's lips twitched, but stopped short of forming a smile.

Racing onto the field, Bettina whipped up the bird.

"Dead bird!"

The referee's voice was lost in the crowd's jubilation. Luke handed Duane a pigeon, then continued to scan the area. Nothing looked amiss.

Duane trapped the bird with efficiency and returned to the crates.

"Arnold Necker, toe the mark."

Silence again descended. With only a few crates of pigeons left, their cooing took on a subdued quality.

Necker stepped up to the line. He didn't make any extraneous motions, but simply mounted his gun against his shoulder.

"Puller ready?"

"Ready."

"Pull."

The bird inside Trap Four flew up and to the right. As Necker squeezed the trigger, the pigeon unexpectedly dove twenty feet in its flight. The charge of Necker's shot clipped its wing.

Throwing open his gun, Necker ejected his empty shell. Bettina sprinted to the ring. But the wind assisted the wounded, fluttering bird across the fence before she could reach it.

"Lost bird!"

Faurote fans raised fisted hands, screaming with elation. Abney paled. Brenham's townsmen shifted their weight, darting their eyes from each other to Abney to the shooting box.

Necker turned. Upon seeing his distress, they rallied to his aid, yelling encouragement and support.

Though the championship would be decided between Necker and Faurote, the others' tallies still counted toward average scores and each took their final turn.

Luke doled out pigeons, constantly on alert. Comer made no appearance. Perhaps the bet was legitimate and neither Comer nor anyone else had staged it.

With Necker down by one, all Faurote had to do was kill his next bird and he'd not only retain the championship, he'd be the winner of what was sure to be the most talked about competition in the country.

Toeing the score line, Faurote wedged his gun into his shoulder. "Puller ready?"

"Ready."

"Pull!"

The pigeon in Trap Four needed no plunger to help it rise into the air — it came out flying swift and strong. Between its strength, the trap's boost, and the wind, Faurote didn't have a chance.

"Lost bird!"

The men of Brenham whooped in ecstasy, throwing up hats, clapping each other on the back, shaking their fists in exhilaration.

Swanning showed no reaction but stood stoically and without expression.

"Arnold Necker, toe the mark."

Abney slipped his hands in his pockets, rocking from side to side. Others crossed and uncrossed their arms. Several bowed their heads in prayer.

One last scan. Still no sign of Comer.

In typical Necker style, the farmer walked to the line and mounted his gun without any shilly-shally. If he grassed the bird, he and Faurote would go into a shootout. If he missed, Faurote would win.

With a championship, prize money, and a thousand dollars at stake, Blesinger would be a fool to try anything.

"Puller ready?" Necker asked.

"Ready," Blesinger responded.

"Pull."

Trap Two flung a pigeon into the air, its flight erratic before it found its wings. Necker fired. The bird dropped, but not until it lay outside the fence.

"Lost bird!"

Roaring, Faurote's fans leapt over the barricade, storming the shooter's tent and hoisting the 1903 Texas State Champion onto their shoulders.

Swanning picked up the winnings, shook Abney's hand, then quickly gathered his men around him, making his way to his carriage.

"Can you handle things without me?" Luke asked Duane.

The young man stepped back, stunned

and openmouthed. Luke assumed Necker and Blesinger were the same, but he couldn't see them over the crush.

So much for all their efforts to cheat. Without waiting for further permission, Luke quickly followed Swanning. If anything would bring Comer out of hiding, it would be a man traveling by train with two thousand dollars in his possession.

Dropping all pretense, Luke ran to his room. He needed his guns. No matter how far he went or how long he was gone, he planned to follow Mr. Hurless Swanning and hope for the best.

CHAPTER SEVENTEEN

Instead of taking the train, Swanning immediately róde his carriage out of town. Keeping well out of sight, Luke trailed him for a few miles, then pulled Honey Dew to a stop. He studied the road. Partially covered tracks indicated a man had alighted from the vehicle and made his way into the woods.

Tempted as Luke was to see if Comer went after the carriage, his gut told him to follow the money. And if he didn't miss his guess, the money was now on foot.

Urging his mare into the copse, he discovered fresh tracks of a horse who'd been tied and waiting for its rider. No attempt had been made to cover these, nor was the rider in any hurry.

Luke frowned. The rider was either planning to lead any followers on a merry chase, or he was too arrogant to realize a decent tracker would know he'd left the carriage.

Whatever the case, Luke had expected him to put as much distance as possible between Brenham and himself, not mosey along at an unhurried pace.

Keeping well behind the man, Luke ignored the smell of fowl still clinging to him. He'd exchanged his overalls for trousers, but hadn't taken the time to change shirts. It felt good to have Odysseus and Penelope strapped about his hips, though. He'd missed them.

As if having a boy pistol and a girl pistol wasn't bad enough, he goes and names them. Odysseus and Penelope. But then, what can you expect from somebody named Lucious?

He shifted in his saddle. She didn't understand. He didn't have family to speak of. He didn't have a place to call home. He didn't have anything but his horse, his saddle, his guns, and the clothes on his back. So he lavished them with all the attention others lavished onto their dwelling places.

When he wasn't undercover, his clothes were the best money could buy. His boots were custom made and ornate. His saddle, the same. His horse he'd broken himself. But his guns — his guns were his pride and joy. A pair of Colt automatics with carved bone handles and inlaid steelwork clear down to the muzzle.

They were one of a kind, had served him well, and were worthy of being named. She could laugh all she wanted, but they'd helped protect the very lifestyle she took for granted.

A deer galloped across his path in three graceful bounds followed by a leap high into the air, its white tail up, its head held high. He yanked on his reins. White-tailed deer needed only to hear a rustle in the under-brush to zip away as fast as their legs could carry them.

If the deer had been fleeing from him, it wouldn't have run across his path. He scanned the area. Anything could have startled it — a rabbit, a wild turkey, a fox, or a man with two thousand dollars. Sliding off his horse, he studied the tracks. Several yards up, the rider's horse had pawed the ground, stood for a moment, then veered deeper into the thicket.

Luke walked Honey Dew behind him, moving with caution. The sun dipped to treetop level, its welcome rays peeking through a handful of branches yet to leaf out. The sound of water trickling over rocks and brushing up against banks came from the northwest.

A long double whinny answered by a

distant whinny brought Luke up short. Two horses? Guiding Honey Dew to a hedge of shrubs and brush, he tied her off, muzzled her, and checked his guns.

"Sit tight, girl," he whispered, patting her neck. "I'll be back in just a bit."

Keeping himself hidden, he followed the tracks, his step light, his senses alert. The sound of the creek increased in volume. Half a mile down, a riderless buckskin swished its tail.

Luke pressed against a tree, ears attuned to every nuance. He filtered out the cicadas, the twittering conversations of birds preparing to roost, the croaking frogs, the incessant crickets, and focused on the quiet rumble of two men due west.

He peeked around the trunk, spotting two faint outlines at the creek's bank. Staying upwind, he darted from tree to tree until he dared not move any closer. Removing a spyglass from his pocket, he crouched behind some shrubs and brought the men into focus.

Necker. Necker and Swanning dividing the money from the fireman's pouch. Their words were lost to him, but their movements were those of close friends comfortable in the presence of the other.

So Necker had lost on purpose. Had

cheated in order to ensure himself a top position in the competition. Did Duane and Blesinger know? Or had Necker swindled them along with the town of Brenham?

Luke scrutinized the two men more carefully. Neither was Frank Comer. The outlaw had a bit more brawn and was of a shorter stature. The question was which one to follow.

If Swanning was in cahoots with Comer and had planned on seeing him, he'd have most likely taken the money straight to him. Which made Luke suspect Necker as being one of Comer's more trusted members.

Sweeping his spyglass across the area, he spotted a second horse. If he was going to follow Necker, he'd need to reposition himself. Tucking the glass into his pocket, he picked his way back to Honey Dew.

"Where have you been?" Georgie stared at Luke. His clothes were clean and his hair wet from a recent washing, but his eyes held deep circles.

"I sold phone service to Bailey Quade," he said.

"Bailey Quade? What were you doing way out there? I thought you were helping with the state tournament."

"I was. I did. Was there something you

needed?" He jerked open a drawer in his desk and rifled through the papers.

She sighed. "Are you still angry with me?"

"For what?"

She decided not to remind him of her fascination with Frank Comer.

He looked up. "You mean about Lucious Landrum?"

Sort of. "Yes."

"Think whatever you want. I could care less." Pulling some papers from the drawer, he plopped down and began to read through them, checking them against his ledger.

The desk always seemed so big until he sat at it, his long legs cramped inside the knee space, his hunched shoulders hovering over the desktop.

"I can't think when you're watching me." He didn't even look up.

Heat rushed to her cheeks. She moved her attention to the window. The daddy bluebird flew to the starch box, bringing the nesting mama a snack. She'd laid five powder-blue eggs, all of which should hatch by the end of next week. But it would all take place behind the walls of the starch box.

Much as Georgie loved watching them come and go, her gaze returned to the man on her left. He was upset about something. And she didn't think it had anything to do with her regard for Frank Comer.

"Did you lose money on Mr. Necker?" she asked.

Placing one finger on a column in his ledger, he glanced between it and a piece of paper on his desk. "No, fortunately. Pigeon handlers aren't allowed to bet." He looked up. "I haven't seen Duane Pfeuffer, though. Do you know if he lost anything?"

"From what I can surmise, every man in town lost money. I haven't heard anything about Duane in particular, though."

"Has Necker shown his face, yet?"

"No. A bunch of men finally went out about an hour ago to get him up at his place." She shook her head. "Evidently he's inconsolable."

Luke leaned back. "Where are they taking him?"

"To Charlie's Saloon."

"A bit early for that, don't you think?"

"Is there ever a good time?"

He ignored the question. "All's forgiven, then?"

"Of course. How could anyone stay angry with Mr. Necker? He's such a nice, likeable man, and it's not like he missed his shots on purpose."

Luke nodded. "Who are his closest friends, do you know?"

"I don't. If he had a phone, I'd know exactly who he talked with the most. But he's never subscribed."

"Maybe I should go pay him a visit."

"You may as well; you're going to have to go out that direction anyway."

He raised a brow. "What for?"

"Something's wrong with the line north of town." She indicated the switchboard with the wave of her hand. "Drops fifteen through twenty-five only work intermittently. Those are all on the new wire you strung to the north. That's why I've been wondering where you were. Folks have been without full service since the tournament started."

He returned to his notes. "I'll go out there as soon as I finish this."

Angling her head, she watched him scribble a note on a piece of paper. "Where have you been?"

"Trying to sell phone service."

"Well, I'd appreciate it if you'd check in with me. Even Bettina didn't know where you'd gotten off to."

"Somebody's coming."

She blinked. "What?"

"Somebody's coming up the walk."

Removing her earpiece, she crossed to the screen door. Sure enough, Torie Cutler and

Tarrah Montgomery approached with hat-boxes. How did he do that? She hadn't heard a thing.

Pushing open the screen, she waved them forward. "Good morning, girls."

The sisters could have been twins, though they weren't. Both had piles of lovely blond hair, brown eyes, and identical smiles.

"We made some hats for the contest," Tarrah said, handing her box to Georgie.

"Oh, I'm so glad." She propped their entries on top of the others, causing the stack to sway. She needed to move them into her bedroom before they toppled over.

"Look at all those," Torie exclaimed. "And Maifest is still a month away."

"I know. The competition is going to be fierce, I'm afraid." Georgie smiled. "Can I offer you some coffee?"

"No, no." Tarrah tugged on her gloves. "We're on our way to the Reading Circle. We're discussing *Tempest and Sunshine,* by Mrs. Mary J. Holmes."

"Well, say hello to the group for me."

"We will." They hurried back the way they'd come, their suits the very latest in spring fashions.

Georgie envied them their ability to come and go at will. She'd never left her switchboard for more than a few minutes until

Mr. Ottfried started his abominable Easter challenge. Since that time she'd shut the board down for three Plumage League meetings and two Junior Audubon sessions.

She'd received complaints about it, too. Her customers paid for service five days a week. Mr. Lockett from the livery had even requested a partial refund. And Mr. Ottfried, of course, had canceled his subscription completely.

A cardinal landed on her front porch railing, hopped three times, then flew off again. She strengthened her resolve. Even if she had to issue refunds out of her own money, it was the least she could do for her birds.

Turning, she began to transfer the hatboxes to her bedroom.

After two trips, Luke strode in, arms full. "Where do you want these?"

Too stunned to speak, she scrambled out of the way and pointed to the corner.

He skirted her bed, the boxes on top teetering.

Ding.

She hesitated. No one had ever been in here but her.

"Go on," he said. "I've got them."

Ding.

Suppressing a groan, she returned to the switchboard. "Hello, Central."

"My battery's about dead, Georgie. Can you send Luke over with a new one?"

"I'll be glad to, Mr. Schmid. He's working on a line north of town today, though. Would it be all right if he stops by tomorrow?"

Luke stepped back into the living room and gathered up the last of the entries.

"Could it be first thing in the morning, then?" The wire crackled, distorting the mercantile owner's voice. "I'm not sure it'll last much longer than that. 'Course, it lasted longer than Leatherman's."

"Oh?" She kept her eyes on her bedroom door.

"Yep. We were having us a contest to see whose would last the longest."

She shifted her weight. Why hadn't Luke come out yet? "I'm assuming Mr. Palmer needs to bring a battery to Mr. Leatherman, then?"

"Yep. But bring mine first."

"I'll let Mr. Palmer know." Removing the plug, she allowed its cord to retract, then hurried to her room.

Luke stood beside her washstand, fingering a hand towel on its rung. Her bedroom had never been big, but his presence dwarfed it even further.

He lifted his gaze, his fingers still pinching

the cloth. "My mother used to do this to her towels."

"Huck toweling?"

"Yes." His finger grazed the blue stitches woven into the thin fabric. "Did you do this?"

"I did."

"It's nice."

She looked at the towel. It was nothing out of the ordinary. Just a huck towel she used to dry her hands and face. "Thank you. And thank you for helping me with the boxes."

"You're welcome." His voice was quiet, still lost on some distant memory.

"Do you see your mother very often?"

"Not since I left home."

"Me neither."

His eyes connected with hers. So blue. So very blue.

After a moment, she widened the door. "You should probably come on out."

He snatched his hand back and took a quick glance at her bed, as if just realizing where he was.

"Excuse me." He strode from the room.

She closed the door behind them, its soft click loud in the quiet of the cottage.

"I'm sorry." He stood in the center of the room like a chastised child. "I didn't mean to offend."

"You didn't."

"I don't know what I was thinking — I wasn't. I'm sorry."

"It's all right. And I do appreciate your help."

He swallowed. "Right. Well. I guess I better go."

"Schmid Brothers Mercantile needs a new battery for their wall unit, as does Mr. Leatherman over on West Street."

"Yes. I heard. If I can't get to it today, I'll do it first thing in the morning."

"Thank you."

"You're welcome." Clearing his throat, he grabbed his hat and pushed through the screen.

She caught the door with her hand, guiding it shut. She never knew what to expect when she saw him. One minute he'd be grouchy, the next just the opposite. But no matter his mood or hers, the tension between them remained constant.

She watched through the tightly woven mesh of the door as he strode to his horse and unbuckled its breast collar. The pinto turned her head toward him, the reins holding her to the hitching post. He stroked her neck and murmured something, his tone deep, gentle.

Unsaddling a horse was as everyday as washing one's face, yet seeing him undo the flank strap, toss up the stirrup, and release the cinch fascinated her. Each movement sure, fluid, and economic. She pressed a hand against her midriff, but it did little to settle the commotion within.

He grabbed both ends of the saddle blanket and tugged. His back and shoulder muscles bunched as saddle, pads, and bags slid off the horse and into his hands. With a shortened stride, he hauled his burden to her side-yard shed, disappearing inside.

Moments later, he reappeared with the cart harness. His pinto perked her ears and swished her white tail. It was a beautiful horse. Deep brown head, neck, and shoulders. White mane, tail, girth, and legs from the hocks down. Georgie still couldn't believe he'd named it after a brand of chewing tobacco.

Did he chew? she wondered. If he did, she'd never seen him, nor did he ever reek of it.

He sorted out the tangle of leather straps in his arms. Attaching a cart harness was every bit as complicated as attiring a woman for a night at the ball. He buckled the breast collar onto Honey Dew, smoothed out the backstrap, arranged the breeching strap, and tightened her belly band.

In between each step, his large hands stroked, patted, and checked for a tight but comfortable fit. Georgie wished she could hear what he was saying to the mare, for he kept up a steady stream of dialog.

He slipped a bridle with blinders over the horse's nose and ears, fluffing the forelock as if it were a woman's coiffure. Georgie smoothed the back of her hair, tucking loose tendrils into her twist.

Honey Dew bumped Luke with her muzzle. He leaned in and whispered. The horse gave a long, blustery sigh, flicking her ears. Luke chuckled, the deep tenor of it causing Georgie's stomach to drop.

Releasing Honey Dew from the hitching post, he led her to the side of the house where he stored his installer's cart. Georgie couldn't see them, but she could hear the creak of the wheels, the looping of straps, the undertone of Luke's voice. Finally, he walked Honey Dew to the street and climbed onto the green driver's seat. Picking up the reins, he turned his head toward Georgie, his eyes connecting with hers, his gaze intense.

She fell back and out of sight, her breath lodged in her throat. He'd known. He'd known she stood there and ogled him. She pressed her hands against her cheeks.

After a moment, he clicked his tongue, signaling his horse. Georgie stayed in the shadows of her living room until the jangle of harness and creak of wheel had long since faded.

CHAPTER EIGHTEEN

"Hello, Central."

"It's me," Luke said.

A slight intake of breath. "Oh. Well, um, hello. Did you want to connect to someone?"

"No. I'm at the Oodsons'. In order to isolate the trouble, I'm going to stop at each farm or ranch on this line and ring back to you until I find one that doesn't work properly."

"All right."

"Everything's good here, sounds like."

"Yes. I believe the earth would have stopped spinning had Mrs. Oodson's line been down."

He smiled. "Party lines, Miss Gail. Anyone can hear."

A soft snort carried over the wire. "I guess she isn't there, since the Reading Circle's meeting at Mrs. Patrick's right now?"

"No, she isn't here. I let myself in."

"You're off to the Klebergs' next?"

"Yes."

"I'll talk to you in a bit, then."

"All right."

Neither hung up.

He pictured her as he'd left her, standing at the screen door, watching his every move. Why did she do that? But he knew why. And try as he might, he couldn't deny his fascination with her, either.

She'd looked like a living sunset in a dress he'd not seen before. High yellow collar, fawn-colored yoke, deep maroon gown, all trimmed with golden fringe which quivered at the tiniest encouragement. He'd wanted to trace the fringe with his finger, follow it from epaulets to the vee of her yoke.

"Is that a new dress you're wearing?" he asked.

"No. Yes. A little."

He propped a shoulder against the wall. "It's nice. I like it."

A pause. "Thank you."

"What's going on in your backyard?"

He heard her chair creak. "Mr. Bluebird's nowhere in sight. He must be out hunting for food. Mrs. Bluebird is incubating her eggs."

"They're married?"

"Of course."

"How do you know?"

"Because . . . they're, you know, they're having a family."

"Did Audubon's publication tell you birds who nest are married?"

"I'll have you know, sir, bluebirds mate for life."

"They do?"

"They do."

"Well, then. I stand corrected." Across the room a pair of carved cuckoo birds in an ornate clock poked out to announce the quarter hour. "Are cuckoo birds monogamous?"

"Mostly."

"In that case, Mr. and Mrs. Cuckoo say hello."

She chuckled.

He pushed away from the wall. "Listen, I better go. I'll talk to you in a bit."

"All right." This time, she pulled the plug.

"Hello, Central."

"It's me."

"Hello." Her voice dropped to an intimate level.

Slipping a hand into his pocket, he looked down. Mud caked the toe of his left boot. He'd have to be careful not to leave a mess in Mrs. Dobbing's hallway. "Sounds like this line is working, too."

"Yes. What took you so long to get there?"

"I stopped by the Grants'. And guess what? They bought a subscription."

"They did? Congratulations."

"Thanks." He jingled the coins in his pocket. "Mrs. Grant was telling me about Maifest. She says it's the biggest event of the year."

"I suppose it is."

"She said fellas secretly place Mai trees in front of the windows of their sweethearts."

"Yes. The phone lines are always buzzing the next morning."

He wondered if anyone had ever left one for her. "She told me about a parade. Plus a greased pig chase and a Maypole dance."

"I've only been to last year's, but they had all that and a merry-go-round, too."

"Yeah?" He lifted his brows. "I've never seen a merry-go-round."

"It was my first, as well. From what I hear, they aren't bringing it in again. It was evidently quite expensive."

"That's too bad." He cleared his throat. "Are you going with anyone in particular this year?"

A slight pause. "No, I'm not."

"Oh."

"Are you?" she asked.

"Um, no."

Silence.

"Well." He shifted his weight onto one foot. "I guess I'll head on to the next phone."

"That would be the Halls."

"The Halls. Okay. I'll call you from there."

"I'll be right here."

"Talk to you in a bit, then." This time, he hung up first.

"Hello, Central."

"It's me." He plugged up one ear. "Are you there?"

"Yes." She raised her voice.

"Can you hear me okay? The Halls have a passel of kids and I can't hear a thing."

"You're coming through loud and clear."

"Okay. I'm gonna keep going." He hung up without waiting for a response.

"Hello, Central."

"Hi."

"Hi." Her voice dropped again, doing strange things to his stomach.

"This is much better," he said. "Much quieter."

"You're at the Tanskes'?"

"Yes. They're out in the fields."

"Did you stop somewhere on the way?"

"I tried to sell Mr. Büchner a subscription, but he wouldn't have anything to do with it. Mrs. Büchner fed me lunch, though."

"What did you have?"

"Barbeque and some kind of potato dish I can't pronounce, but it was really good. What about you? What did you have for lunch?"

"I didn't eat."

"Why not?"

"I wanted to make some sugar water for the hummingbirds."

He frowned. "You do that a lot, don't you? Skip lunch, I mean."

"I don't know if I'd say a lot, but sometimes."

"You're going to be the size of those hummingbirds if you're not careful."

"I doubt that." He could hear the smile in her voice.

"You know what you need?"

"What?" she asked.

"An ice cream."

"What?"

"An ice cream." He pictured the new ice cream parlor next door to the post office. "Hodde & Kruse opened up today. They're going to dispense cream, soda, and soft drinks all through the summer."

"Oh my."

"You want some?"

"Well, I . . . do you?"

"Why, sure. Don't you?"

"I, yes. I love ice cream."

"Then, let's go get some. Right after work."

"Today?" she squeaked.

"Why not?"

Every alarm bell in his system rang in earnest. He ignored them all. He was a man. She was a woman. He was interested in her. She was interested in him. He'd told her he wasn't looking for a wife. She'd not pressed for an explanation.

"Well . . . all right," she said. "After work?"

Suddenly, he couldn't finish fast enough. "Five o'clock. I'll pick you up."

"Someone's ringing in," she said.

"I'll let you go, then. Call you at the next stop." Hanging up, he hurried out to Honey Dew, anxious to find the trouble so he could return to town in time to clean up.

"Hello, Central."

"Can you hear me now?" Luke asked.

"Yes. Was that you trying to call earlier?"

"Yeah, but I couldn't get through."

"What happened?"

He shook his head. "Mrs. Ragston had

grounded out the circuit by wrapping a hairpin around the line and the ground posts of the phone."

"Good heavens."

"I know. I've fixed it, though."

"You're all done, then?"

"I am. It'll be quitting time when I get back to town. So would you let Schmid know I'll bring him his battery first thing in the morning?"

"Of course."

"Thanks." He wound the cord of the receiver around his thumb. "I can't be by for you right at five. Not if I clean up first."

"That's fine. I want to eat a little supper anyway."

"Okay, but don't fill up."

"I won't."

"Georgie?" He touched the unit, willing her to hear him before she pulled the plug.

"Yes?"

He let out his breath. "Don't change. I like that dress."

"All right."

He dropped his hand. "Bye."

"Bye."

She hesitated before finally disconnecting them.

CHAPTER NINETEEN

Luke hadn't been nervous when he'd disarmed a cold-eyed gunslinger in an El Paso saloon. Nor when he'd charged the hideout of the notorious Miller Gang. Nor when he'd single-handedly subdued a mob.

But as he tied Honey Dew to Georgie's hitching post, his hands shook, his forehead beaded with sweat, and his mouth went dry. He blew out a long breath. It was just a woman. And she was tiny as a cricket bug.

He wiped his hands on his legs. When he'd changed out of his work clothes, he'd automatically put on another pair of overalls. What would she think when she saw him? That he held so little regard for her, he wouldn't even don a pair of trousers?

But the loose overalls provided him an edge of anonymity — maybe not for someone who knew him well, but certainly for those who might have seen him from afar. Lucious Landrum dressed in top-quality clothing made to exact specifications. If someone in town had ever glimpsed him, they wouldn't reconcile that man with Brenham's overall-clad telephone man.

But were he to wear pants and shirt, it might be just enough to spark recognition. That was a chance he couldn't take. Even for Georgie.

He let himself through the gate half expecting to see her waiting for him at the screen door. But not only was she nowhere in sight, the front door was shut. He couldn't remember it ever being closed before.

And it was blue. Between it, her yellow siding, green bench, and red swing, she had most every color in the rainbow up there. Taking a deep breath, he opened the screen and knocked.

The door opened immediately. A burst of cinnamon wafted about them. Her face held no smile, no dimples, no laugh lines. Only wide eyes and a delectable mole. He followed the line of her jaw. A black lace ruffle lining her yellow collar tickled her chin.

He stuck both hands in his pockets. "You ready for some ice cream?"

"Let me grab my wrap."

"Are you cold?"

"No."

"Then I wish you wouldn't. I'd rather you not cover up your dress."

She turned to face him, one hand on her hip, head slanted to the side. "What is it about this dress you like so much?"

It makes your cheeks pink. Your lips lush. Your curves prominent. And the fringe on its yoke moves every time you take a breath.

"I don't know. I just like it, I guess."

"Well, let me at least put on my hat."

"You wear hats?"

"Of course."

"I've never seen you in a hat."

"That's because of my earpiece." She slipped inside her bedroom, then returned a couple minutes later wearing a straw hat with a filmy covering and clusters of yellow and maroon blossoms.

It completely changed her looks. Not better or worse, just different. Her eyes seemed larger, her lips fuller, her mole smaller.

"I'm sorry about my overalls," he said. "It's all I have."

She tugged on her gloves. "I know."

"You do?"

"I'm the telephone operator. I know everything."

He offered her his arm. "God checks in with you, does He?"

"We talk all the time."

Chuckling, he assisted her down the steps and out to the street. A nondescript brown bird winged past them.

"What was that?" he asked.

"A mockingbird."

He gave her a sharp glance. "You can't know that."

"They have a white band on the end of their wings making them easy to spot."

He looked the direction it had gone, but it was nowhere in sight. "How long have you been a birdwatcher?"

She shrugged. "Oh, I don't know. Since I was fourteen, I think?"

"What made you take it up? A nest of hatchlings outside your window? A maidenly aunt taking you on a birding expedition?"

"Nothing that lovely, I'm afraid." The golden fringe along her epaulets and yoke rocked with each step. "My mother married a man with a wicked temper. The forest was my refuge. It was there I discovered birds." Her voice was matter-of-fact. No emotion. No inflection.

"Is that why you've never returned home to see her?"

"Yes. That and my job."

"She's alive, then?"

"Yes. What about you? You said you'd not

seen your mother, either. Is your mother alive?"

"She is."

"What about your father?"

He took a deep breath. "He died when I was ten."

She stopped, her eyes round. "Me too."

Plenty of emotion that time.

"You were ten?"

"Thirteen. And the farm we'd lived and worked on our entire lives was taken from us because Mama wasn't allowed to keep it without a husband."

He nodded. "A hurricane hit our house. The lanterns inside were lit and the house burnt to the ground with my dad inside. So we didn't have anything, either. We moved four hundred miles to my uncle's place."

"Was he a good man?"

"Not as good as my dad." He tucked her arm back under his, keeping his hand atop it as they turned onto Sycamore, passing house after house.

The more traditional were T- or L-shaped, but the two- and three-story Victorians postured in bright colors and gingerbread trim. All sported large verandas with rocking chairs along the front. The occupants of the chairs called out to Georgie, looking with interest at Luke.

At Market Street, they exchanged homes, picket fences, and sprawling trees for commercial buildings with two-story fronts and awning-covered entrances. Horses, wagons, carts, and carriages jockeyed for position, churning up a constant swirl of dust. He guided Georgie to the side opposite Ottfried's Millinery, giving the place a wide berth. Still, she never took her eyes from its entrance, noting who was going in and who was coming out.

"Did you have time to eat supper?" he asked.

Her attention remained focused on her nemesis. "Did I tell you Mr. Ottfried's son is a member of my Junior Audubon Society?"

He lifted his brows. "You didn't."

"Well, he is. I think initially, Fritz joined in order to find out where the birds were and how to call them so he could kill them for his father."

Luke tipped his hat to a man, woman, and two boys dressed in their Sunday best. The man returned Luke's nod, then opened the door of Winkelmann's Photography Studio.

"It backfired, though." Georgie's eyes dropped to half-mast. Her smile turned smug. "Fritz is my biggest proponent for bird conservation and has tripled the size of our society."

"What does his father say about that?"

"I don't know, but ads for his contest and spring collection continue to appear in every edition of the paper."

Three tiers of beer bottles clinked inside a bottler's wagon, temporarily blocking the millinery from view and diverting her attention.

"What's the word on his contest?" he asked.

"It's not doing too well. My Plumage League has secured a great number of pledges, even though our membership is still quite small."

"You planning on running him out of town?"

She looked up in surprise. "Goodness, no. We just want him to stop using bird parts."

Two women exited Schleider Furniture Company, intent on their conversation. Executing the intricate dance of walking without jostling others, Luke pulled Georgie closer to his side, skirting the preoccupied ladies. A few more steps and they reached the ice cream parlor.

Men, women, and children of all ages filled bent-wire tables and chairs, raising their voices to be heard over a player piano's rendition of "Daisy Bell." Luke took a deep breath, inhaling a melange of sweet smells. A white marble counter as fancy as any he'd ever seen stretched the entire length of one wall, swivel stools marking its length.

Two men in white coats and a woman in a low-bibbed black apron worked frantically behind the bar. Rows of flavored syrups lined their shelves like hard liquor in a fancy saloon.

Luke immediately spotted Peter Finkel across the room. The farmer's side part, high forehead, and curled-over ears gave him more the look of an untried boy than a train-robbery suspect. Yet after Necker collected his purse, he'd made two stops on his way home. One was at Finkel's, the other was at the home of a new telephone customer named Ragston. Luke had pushed both men to the top of his suspect list along with Necker, Duane, and Blesinger.

Georgie tapped Luke's arm and pointed to a display of toothache gum and digestive tablets. "I hope that isn't a portent of a fate to come."

Chuckling, he asked what her favorite flavor was, then inched his way to the counter and ordered two helpings of tutti-frutti. Balancing a bowl in each hand, he returned to find she'd secured them a table in the corner.

"Looks wonderful," she said, lifting a cherry from the top of her serving, placing it in her mouth, and plucking off its stem. "I can't remember the last time I had ice cream."

They sat in silence, savoring each bite until they'd satisfied their initial cravings.

"So what do you do at night after work?" he asked, tilting his bowl forward to scoop up the last few bites. "Once it's too dark to be outside with your birds, that is."

She shrugged. "Different things. I do a lot of my cooking and cleaning at night, since I'm not able to do much during the day. Lately, tasks for the Plumage League have kept me busy. And I read most every night just before I put out the lantern. What about you?"

"There's not a lot to do at a boarding-house. So I meet up with friends when I can."

She smiled. "Who are your friends?"

"Duane Pfeuffer is my closest friend."

Her smile lost some of its luster. "Duane Pfeuffer? From the Pfeuffer Feed Store?"

"You know him?"

"Not really. I've heard he's a bit wild."

"Duane?" He pretended surprise. "What else have you heard?"

"That he spends a lot of his time at

262

Charlie's Saloon."

Luke nodded. "Well, I can't deny that."

She touched the corners of her mouth with her napkin. "Is that where you spend your evenings? At the saloon?"

"Sometimes, but more for a game of billiards than anything else."

She pushed the cream around in her bowl. "Who else do you spend time with?"

"Duane and I are going hunting with Arnold Necker on Sunday."

Taking a bite, she looked at everything but him.

"You told me you liked Arnold," he reminded her.

"I do." She gave him a false smile. "What will the three of you be hunting?"

He didn't answer.

She set down her spoon. The bouncy tune on the Pianola contrasted with her tight-lipped disapproval.

Sighing, he placed his forearms on either side of his bowl. "We're not shooting songbirds, Georgie."

"Well, I should hope not." Her words were soft, barely audible.

"You know, slaughtering a cute little mild-eyed lamb isn't nearly as pleasant to contemplate as eating spring lamb and mint sauce. But it's done all the time."

She tucked her chin. "I know."

"Every November families all across our country put a turkey on the block and chop off its head."

She folded, then refolded the napkin in her lap, refusing to look up.

"Every bird we down will be eaten. There is absolutely nothing wrong with enjoying a wholesome outdoor sport when we'd otherwise have to single them out of a cote and wring their necks."

She pushed out her chair. "I'd like to go home now."

He looked at her bowl. "You haven't finished."

"Oh, I'm finished. I'm definitely finished."

"You're being unreasonable."

"Because I want to go home?"

"Because you begrudge me my bird hunting."

"You can do whatever you like, Luke. Just like I can. And I'd like to go home." She stood.

Shaking his head, he pushed in their chairs and offered his arm. She hesitated, but was too polite to refuse it.

Street traffic had slowed considerably with only an occasional dray rumbling by. He checked the sun's descent, noting the long shadows it cast along the street. He kept at a leisurely pace, though Georgie held herself stiff beside him.

A shop boy stepped onto the boardwalk to sweep the landing in front of Seelhorst Tin Shop before closing up for the evening.

As soon as the boy was out of earshot, Luke cleared his throat. "Georgie —"

"I don't want to talk about it, Luke."

He debated pressing her, then decided against it. He'd had no business stepping out with her in the first place. Even if she knew who he really was, it wouldn't change the fact he loved to bird hunt. And he had no intention of giving it up. Not for her. Not for anybody.

CHAPTER TWENTY

Pulling a dressing sacque over her night-gown, Georgie shoved her feet into fleece-lined slippers, then dragged the wool blanket off her bed. A pair of cardinals had chosen her backyard as their breeding ground. Repeatedly the male had seen his reflection in her window, mistaken it for another male cardinal, and slammed into the glass over and over in an effort to protect his territory.

She'd finally covered the spot with newspaper, only for his mate to see herself in the opposite window and do the same thing. Still, Georgie had never had cardinals nest in her yard, and she wanted to get to know them before they did. It was an hour yet to sunrise and they'd awaken soon, so she'd best hurry.

Wrapping the green blanket around her, she pulled her braid free and tiptoed out the back door. The air smelled of dew and had a slight nip to it.

She settled onto a chair, tucking the blanket under her, and held as still as she could. Nothing but darkness greeted her. She allowed her mind to wander.

After her confrontation with Luke, she'd redoubled her efforts to save the birds. She presented Mistrot Bros., Ottfried's local competitor, with literature documenting forty thousand sandpipers killed on the North Carolina coast for millinery purposes. The mercantile owner added the first and only male signature to the Plumage League's pledge and announced he would solely stock hats that excluded bird parts.

Filled with a sense of victory, she immediately asked him to judge the Plumage League's Maifest hat competition. He not only accepted her request, but also offered to place the top five hats up for sale in his shop.

His announcement doubled the number of hats entered, completely upstaging Ottfried's showcase and contest. Easter came and went with the lion's share of women sporting bonnets without a hint of birds upon them.

Cheo.

She caught her breath, her gaze swiveling toward the sound. The cardinal was somewhere on the east side of the yard, but it was too dark to determine its exact spot. Dawn was a good forty-five minutes away and none of the other birds had even awakened.

Cheo cheo.

So loud. But he was slow to get going. Like an old man creaking out of bed one joint at a time.

Cheo cheo.

A few more seconds passed, as if he was yawning and stretching before his next verse.

Wheet wheet wheet wheet wheet wheet wheet wheet.

She smiled at the familiar tune. He started his song over from the beginning, this time with a little more liveliness, until finally, he was singing the entire thing with total abandon. On and on he went, sometimes with a single *cheo,* sometimes with two. Sometimes *fortissimo,* sometimes *pianissimo.* Sometimes with pauses between, sometimes without stopping.

She closed her eyes, amazed at how a tiny thing could produce such a powerful sound. As far as she knew, only two species on God's green earth could sing. Men and birds.

There was no comparison. The grandest

virtuoso would be no match for her feathered friend.

His concert awoke a robin, prompting it to go through its repertoire. A bobwhite stirred, then introduced himself by name. A warbler fluttered to a tree nearby, with a *sweet sweet sweet sweet sweet sweetersweeter.*

The cardinal, not to be outdone, switched to a new song. *Whooett . . . whoo-ett whooett . . . whoo-ett whoo-ett tuer tuer tuer tuer.*

The sky lightened to gray; the moon began to fade. A plethora of robins joined the fray, along with blue jays, chickadees, whippoorwills, and thrashers. And then she heard it. A soft echo of the cardinal's *whoo-ett whooett tuer.*

Her male heard it, too. He held his song and was rewarded with another muted *whoo-ett whoo-ett tuer.*

Georgie searched the garden, squinting through the cusp-of-dawn light. The female had to be in the buttonbush across the yard.

Their conversation continued, her songs brief and ladylike, his manly and loud. Showing off, he introduced yet another new song.

Instead of echoing, she responded with the *whoo-ett-tuer* of before.

It took him aback. He sang his new one

again, a little gentler this time. Then again. And again, each verse gaining volume.

Whoo-ett, the female replied.

Georgie smiled. The female liked that first song. But her mate was relentless, singing the new melody over and over until finally she matched him.

In a blur, he dashed across the yard, landing in the top of an elm, looking down his bill at his woman. She was definitely in the buttonbush.

The sun peeked over the horizon, gilding the edges of the cardinal's brilliant plumage. He hopped across the branch, then spread his wings and glided down to the buttonbush.

He slipped into its crooked branches, the leaves rustling behind him and offering the couple privacy as he gave her a proper good morning. Cardinals mated for life and Georgie knew they spent each day together, foraging for food and nesting material, then looking for the perfect place to raise their young.

She pulled her legs up underneath her. Would Luke repeat his song until she capitulated? What would happen if the female cardinal never sang the male's song? Would they still be mates for life?

Closing her eyes, she rested her head

against her knees and tried not to wish she was the one receiving a proper good morning.

The further into April they went, the more the town emptied as farmers spent all waking hours in their fields. Not to be outdone, Mother Nature dressed the county for Maifest, blanketing the hills and meadows in a kaleidoscope of wildflowers.

On the eve of the festival, Georgie's switchboard buzzed with excited chatter, and if ever she needed Bettina, it was now, but the girl hadn't shown her face for over a week. The milliner's son, Fritz Ottfried, had stopped by to help when he could, but he too had disappeared of late. As a result, messages to nonsubscribers were delayed or not sent at all.

The jangle of harnesses signaled Luke's return from the field. Placing her earpiece on the switchboard table, she poked her head out the screen door. "Have you seen Bettina?"

Unwinding the breeching from the cart shaft, he shook his head. "I haven't. She still hasn't come by?"

She stepped onto the porch, the screen bouncing shut behind her. "No, and I'm beginning to worry. Are you still visiting the saloons in the evenings?"

His head whipped up, his hands stilling.

She crossed her arms, belatedly realizing the personal nature of the question. They'd spoken little over the past month, and when they had it was of nothing but business. "I was asking because I wondered if Bettina's father was still being served."

"What do you mean?"

"You know, after the election and all."

He frowned, then comprehension dawned. "You mean because of the passing of the habitual drunkard bill?"

"Yes." The bill had made it illegal for liquor to be sold to any person who habitually drank.

Resting a hand on Honey Dew's back, he looked into the distance, searching his memory. "You know, now that you mention it, I haven't seen him."

"Well, that's good. I just . . . I can't help thinking it might have something to do with her absence. It's simply not like her."

He returned his attention to her. "You want me to check on her?"

"Would you mind?"

"No. I'll go over there tonight."

He didn't continue unhitching the cart, but remained with his hand resting on Honey Dew, his hat pushed back, his gaze intense. With an effort, she lowered her eyes and turned toward the door.

"Miss Georgie!" Her gate opened, then slammed shut.

She whirled around. "Bettina. For heaven's sake, we were just talking about you. Where on earth have you —" She gasped. The girl's left jaw was swollen and her eye black and purple. "What happened?"

"I fell out of a tree, but that's not why I'm here." She glanced Luke's direction, then ran the last few feet to Georgie. "Something bad is fixin' to happen."

Georgie squatted down, resting her hands on the girl's bony shoulders. "What is it?"

"I heard tell somebody's gonna do somethin' to yer float."

"My float?" Georgie's eyes widened. The von Hardenbergs had delivered the Plumage League's flower-bedecked Maifest float not an hour earlier and parked it behind her cottage. "Somebody said something?"

"Fritz."

"Fritz Ottfried?"

"Yeah. He said some of them fellers is mad about the ruckus you and them other ladies have caused about shooting birds. So they've decided to teach you a lesson."

Her heart began to accelerate. "Who's 'they'?"

"I dunno. That's all he told me, but I think we oughter keep watch tonight. You can take the first shift. That's the easiest one. I'll take the second."

"That won't be necessary," Luke said.

Startled, Georgie looked up. She hadn't heard him approach.

He loomed large, his expression fierce. "I'll see to the float. Who did that to your face?"

Bettina's expression grew guarded. "I done said already, I fell out of a tree."

Georgie hooked a piece of hair behind the girl's ear. "Does it hurt?"

"Nothing like it did at first." She leaned close. "I'm not sure we should trust him, Miss Georgie. He's one of the ones who likes to shoot birds."

"Not for hats," he said. "And I'd never do anything to Miss Georgie's float."

Georgie nodded. "I believe him, Bettina. He may like to shoot pigeons, but he wouldn't harm me or you or sabotage our float."

Bettina took his measure.

He lowered onto one knee. "She's right, but you need to tell us everything Fritz said. Word for word."

"I already did. Fritz heard some fellers talking, then he came out to my shack and pitched a few rocks at my window. He needn't have, though. Pa was sleeping it off. Nothing can wake him when he's booze blind."

"Why didn't Fritz tell Miss Georgie?" Luke asked.

She gave Georgie a side glance before answering. "His pa's forbidden him to come out here anymore. Not even fer our bird meetings."

Georgie stiffened.

"I'm not surprised," he said. "I'd expected him to put a stop to it long ago."

"He didn't know nothing 'bout it 'til yesterdee. Fritz got in a whole passel o' trouble."

Luke nodded. "Do you know where he is?"

"I could prob'ly find him."

"Go ask him for names. I need the names of the men he overheard."

Standing, Georgie held out her hand. "First you come inside and let me put something on your face."

"I'm fine."

She crooked her fingers. "Come on, it won't sting."

Bettina began to back up. "Sorry, Miss Georgie. If I'm gonna find Fritz, I'd best get goin'." Spinning around, she raced out the gate and clomped down the street in her oversized boots.

Georgie followed her with her eyes. "She didn't fall out of a tree."

"No, ma'am." Luke pushed himself up. "I don't believe she did."

"I'd like to take Mr. von Schiller and —"

"Where's the float?" he asked.

Blinking, she turned toward him. "It's round back."

"Show me." Extending a hand in front of him, he indicated she should lead the way.

He walked around the decorated carriage amazed at the ingenuity of the women. The shaft and wheels were covered with green leaves and moss simulating shrubbery. The body of the two-seater was wrapped in dried brown leaves and twigs simulating a bird's nest. Then, attached to a pole extending high over the vehicle was a huge cardinal in flight.

Chin up, wings outstretched, tail down, the wire structure had been carpeted with red roses, their heady aroma bringing women and romance to mind. Shaking his head, he peeked inside the carriage. Even the interior had been cloaked with nesting material. "I've never seen anything like it. How long did it take to make?"

"The ladies have been working on it for weeks. Just wait until tomorrow. I've heard the floats get more elaborate with each year." She beamed at their creation like a proud mama. "The Patricks will be driving ours."

"It's very impressive, Georgie."

"Thanks." She fingered one of the leaves on the wheel. "Do you really think someone would try to do it harm?"

He'd seen firsthand what men were capable of and nothing surprised him anymore. "If someone were mad enough, anything's possible."

"I probably ought to hide it, then. Can I borrow your horse?"

"Where would you take it?"

She worried her lip, considering. "I could park it behind the Campbellite church."

He glanced at the church down the street, its steeple peeking above the treetops. "Too close."

"What about the cemetery? No one would think to look there."

"Too wide open. They'd be able to see it from the road." He rubbed his mouth. "What about that abandoned place about a mile north of here?"

She furrowed her brows. "The old Langkwitz place?"

277

"I don't know. It's a run-down, two-story with a giant birch too close to the house."

She nodded. "I know exactly where you mean. That road dead-ends now. Nobody even lives that direction anymore. If I pulled the float behind their house, it would be completely hidden."

"That's as good a spot as any, I guess."

She smiled. "I can borrow your horse, then?"

"No."

She blinked.

"I'll take the float out there myself," he said. "No woman should be driving a carriage, much less one all decked out like this. No telling what Honey Dew's reaction is going to be."

She stiffened. "Being a woman has nothing to do with whether or not I can drive a carriage."

"It has everything to do with it."

Narrowing her eyes, she opened her mouth to protest.

He held his hand up in a stop position. "Don't get yourself in a snit. It's my horse, and if anyone drives her anywhere, it's going to be me. Besides, it can't be moved until after dark or your secret would be up. I'm not about to let you take this thing out in the dark."

She released a huff of breath. "Fine. You drive. But I'm going with you."

"No."

"Yes."

"No."

She took a step toward him, her head jutting forward. "Either I go with you or I borrow someone else's horse and do it myself."

He didn't want her going to anyone else. Not until he knew whom to trust and whom not to. But if she went with him, she'd hinder the operation. He rubbed his forehead. He'd just have to make the best of it. "I'll pick you up around ten."

"Ten? Don't you think that's a bit late?"

"If anyone decides to do anything, they won't venture out until after midnight when the town is well and good asleep." He raked his gaze over her white shirtwaist and blue polka dot skirt. "You'll need to wear black."

She gave him a curt nod. "I'll be ready."

CHAPTER TWENTY-ONE

Georgie sat on her back porch steps, broom in hand. She'd followed her normal evening routine, but instead of donning her night-dress, she'd wrapped her bosom, then pulled on a simple black shirtwaist and a pair of boy's britches, leggings, and boots. She shifted, trying to find a more comfortable position. It had been years since she'd dressed like a boy and the trousers were a bit tight.

Trapping the broom handle between her knees, she adjusted the stocking cap on her head, its tassel tickling her cheek. She'd had no trouble locating the pants at the back of her bottom drawer, but she couldn't find her old cap anywhere and had used the only thing available — a night stocking her mother had knitted when Papa was still alive. Though Georgie's head wasn't much bigger than it used to be, she had a great deal more hair, and the base of the cap kept creeping up.

Tugging it into place, she settled against the porch railing and listened to the night sounds. Her birds had long since turned in, but the crickets and cicadas kept up a steady conversation. A coyote far away let out a long, sorrowful howl.

Placing the broom across her lap, she gripped its handle, closed her eyes, and concentrated on anything out of the ordinary — a snapping twig or a lull in the katydids' banter.

A few minutes later, her head bobbed. She jerked awake. Nothing but blackness stretched before her. Stifling a yawn, she wished she could check the time. Tomorrow was sure to be a full day and she had no wish to be up all night. Hopefully, Luke would arrive soon.

It took Luke a moment to realize the boy curled up on the porch was, in fact, Georgie. What the blazes was she doing in britches?

Treading quietly, he almost had Honey Dew hitched up when Georgie stirred.

"Who goes there?" Though her voice was scratchy with sleep, it held a warning.

"It's me," he whispered. "Keep your voice down."

He went around the float, then stopped.

"What are you doing?"

Crouched on the porch, she held a broom like a baseball bat, bottom side up, then slowly lowered it. "I wasn't sure it was you."

"And you thought to do in whoever it was with a broom?"

"I didn't have anything else."

Rolling his eyes, he snatched the broom from her hand and tossed it to the ground. "Go to bed, Georgie. I'll do this."

"No, no. I need to come." She rubbed an eye with her fist, looking like the child she'd dressed to be.

"I mean it." He turned her toward the door. "Go on."

She locked her knees. "I'm going with you, Luke."

His eyes had long since adjusted to the dark, but even still he squinted. "Are you wearing a nightcap?"

Straightening the stocking on her head, she circled round him, then climbed up into the float. She might think she wore a clever disguise, but no boy he'd ever seen moved like that. He slammed his eyes shut. The woman was crazy as popcorn on a hot skillet.

Drawing on the calm he was known for, he joined her on the float, released the brake, and slapped the reins.

"Watch out for my dewberries," she said.

He was tempted to run them over as punishment for her stubbornness, but refrained. Shifting, he tried to find some elbow room. The basket phaeton was cozy in the best of times, but the decorations along the seat's sides forced the two of them even closer.

The carriage hit a rut, jostling them from side to side. Without the normal layers of skirts and petticoats between them, he found himself very aware of the feminine leg plastered against his.

"What are you wearing?" he asked.

She tugged on her stocking cap. "You told me to wear black."

"You have black skirts."

"Well, I couldn't very well wear those. If someone were to see us riding out at this time of night to the place sparking couples go when they don't want to be discovered, why, my reputation would be ruined."

Yanking the carriage to a halt, he looked at her aghast. "Langkwitz's place is Lovers' Walk?" He couldn't believe he hadn't learned of it earlier. What was the matter with him?

"So?"

"You chose to hide the float in the one place sure to have nighttime visitors."

He couldn't see her expression, but he felt her bristle.

"Not tonight, it won't be." Her voice held a defensive edge. "Not only is it way too late for sparking, our young men are spending tonight chopping down birch trees, decorating them with streamers, and delivering them to their sweethearts."

The Mai tree tradition. He'd forgotten about that. Still, there were always exceptions. "We can't take it there."

"There's nowhere else."

Removing his hat, he dragged a hand through his hair. "I can't believe you didn't tell me about this." An unsettling thought occurred to him. "How do you know it's Lovers' Walk?"

She flipped the pom-pom on the end of her stocking as if it were a swath of hair. "I'm the telephone operator, Luke. I'm privy to all sorts of things."

"No one's ever taken you there?"

"Of course not."

"Then how did you know what the place looked like when I described it to you?"

She folded her hands in her lap, prim as a Sunday school teacher. "I've done some birding over there."

He couldn't decide if she was telling the truth or not, but even if she weren't, it wasn't his business. Still, he didn't like the idea of it one iota.

Slamming his hat back on, he shook the reins. "We'd best get a move on, then. If a bunch of fellows are combing the area for trees, I need to get this blame thing hidden and return you home. If you're seen in that getup, there'll be the devil to pay."

"If I'm seen in this 'getup,' no one will recognize me."

"I wouldn't be so sure. So, if we run across anyone, you pull that cap down and let me do the talking."

But luck was with them, and they made it to Langkwitz's without mishap. He checked the likely spots couples would go for privacy, but none were occupied. Pulling the float behind the house, the two of them un-hitched Honey Dew and carefully stored her harnesses in the boot box of the carriage.

"That's it. Let's move." He cupped his hands together and made a stirrup, Honey Dew's hide smelling like a warm barn. "You'll have to straddle her and go without saddle, but don't worry. Just hang on to her mane and I'll walk us back."

"I know how to ride bareback."

He slowly straightened. "And how in the blazes do you know how to do that?"

The moon had come out from behind the clouds, offering plenty of light to see her shrug. "My brother, the only boy in our family, died when I was eleven. My father was inconsolable. Told me he wished I were a boy. So I vowed I would be. Then I set out to do everything LaVerne had."

He pursed his lips. That explained a lot. "And LaVerne rode bareback?"

"LaVerne did a lot of things."

He made another stirrup with his hands. "Well, come on, then. Up you go."

She glanced at the float. "We're just going to leave it here?"

Sighing, he straightened again. "What did you think we were going to do?"

"I don't know. Guard it?"

"Nobody's guarding anything. Whoever was wanting to sabotage your float — if there even was anyone — will check your place and maybe the immediate vicinity before getting discouraged and giving up. No one will come looking for it out here. Now, come on."

She nibbled her lip. "What if they happen upon it by accident?"

"Georgie." He heard the strain in his voice.

"I can't just leave it out here." She tugged her cap down. "Maybe we should make some scarecrows."

"Scarecrows."

"Yes. Then if someone does poke around, they'll think the thing is being guarded and won't bother it."

"You have nothing to make them with. No hay. No poles. No men's clothing."

"Then I'll stand guard myself."

He fisted his hands. "With what? You don't have your broom."

"Then take me home and I'll get my broom."

Over my dead body, he thought.

She fit her boot into his hand and swung on. Blustering, Honey Dew shied at the feel of a saddleless rider.

Shushing the animal, she leaned over and stroked its neck. "Hand me the reins, please."

"Not likely," he mumbled, and began leading the horse toward home.

Though the soft grassy ground absorbed Honey Dew's clomps, it didn't completely silence them.

"You can't go back there, Georgie."

She said nothing.

"I mean it. If someone wants to retaliate for the trouble you've caused over the birds, and they catch you out at night alone, no telling what would happen."

"They don't frighten me."

"They should." He wondered at her father's admonition she be a boy. What a great bunch of foolishness. He glanced over his shoulder. She appeared to be relaxed atop the horse, but being walked while astride was a great deal different than riding bareback.

"So what else did LaVerne do?" he asked.

She sighed. "Well, he climbed trees. He studied Latin, Greek, and mathematics. He jumped hurdles with his horse. He rafted across rivers. All kinds of things."

He shook his head. "You telling me you've done all those things, too?"

"Once or twice."

"Yet you plan to defend the float with a broomstick."

"It's the only thing I have."

"What about a gun?"

"LaVerne didn't shoot guns."

He scanned the area in front of them. He'd never heard of a boy who didn't shoot guns. "You're from Texas, right?"

"All my life."

"Then why didn't your brother shoot?"

"He just didn't care for the sport, I guess. I don't know."

He thought about her living in that cottage all by herself with nothing but a broomstick for protection. "When Maifest is over, I'm teaching you to shoot a gun."

"No, thank you. I don't care to —"

"Shhh." He pulled up short, cocking an ear. "Somebody's coming."

"I don't hear —"

Tossing the reins over Honey Dew's head, he swung up behind Georgie. "Hang on."

He dug into the horse's sides. It was probably a group of kids with their Mai trees in tow, but even still, he had no wish to be caught with a female in britches. If they recognized her, not only would her reputation be in shreds, she'd lose her job. SWT&T held high standards for their employees — particularly the women.

Clinging to the shadows as best he could, he kept them at a trot and on the road. The last thing he wanted was for Honey Dew to twist an ankle. With each of the mare's strides, he and Georgie bounced, rising and descending at different times.

He slipped his arm around her and pulled her close to keep them in unison. Even so, the tassel on her hat slapped him with each bound. Reluctantly, he had to admit she hadn't been lying when she said she could ride without a saddle. She kept her back straight, her body in tune with the horse.

In another minute, he'd slow them down.

But for now, he enjoyed the feel of her in his arms. He wished he could see her costume in daylight. He felt sure she wouldn't fool anyone. With their positions as such, he could tell she'd bound her chest. Why go to all that trouble only to wear a lady's shirtwaist? And that stocking cap was about to drive him —

The cap flew from her head, releasing a bounty of hair and a burst of cinnamon.

She whipped her face around. "My hat!"

A thick braid, loosened from the cap's constant agitation, began to swiftly unravel.

He tightened his grip on her. "I'll go back for it later. First, we get you home."

"But my mother —"

"Shush."

Reaching around her neck, she grabbed the remains of her braid and pulled it over her shoulder, holding it tight against her collarbone.

Instead of slowing them, he continued at a trot, bouncing as one atop the horse. Finally, when the cottage came into sight, he slowed to a walk, but kept his arm where it was.

She plaited the ends of her braid with quick, efficient movements. "My mother made me that cap."

"I'll go get it."

"I don't know why we couldn't have just stopped."

He guided Honey Dew to the backyard, slid off, then took Georgie by the waist and pulled her to the ground. "You can't go back."

She took a quick step away from him, breaking their contact. "Thank you for helping with the float. I could have done it, but it was nice to have some help."

"You can't go back."

"I can and will do whatever I please."

He felt his jaw begin to tick. "Then you leave me no choice."

"What's that supposed to mean?"

"I'm taking Honey Dew and I'm moving the float. You won't be able to guard it because you won't know where it is."

She gasped. "You wouldn't dare."

He strode to Honey Dew. "I'll pick your cap up on my way and bring it back to you in the morning."

Racing after him, she tried to grab his shirt, but he swung astride before she could.

"Where will you take it? There aren't any other good hiding places."

"There are plenty of places." He spied the broomstick he'd thrown down earlier. "Take your weapon with you to your bedroom and lock the door behind you."

"I never lock my door."

He turned Honey Dew toward the Langkwitzs'. "Well, lock it tonight and I'll see you in the morning." Tapping his heels into the horse's flanks, he rode from her yard.

"Luke! Don't you do this!"

Instead of stopping, he spurred his mare on.

CHAPTER TWENTY-TWO

Luke headed toward the Langkwitzs', hoping Georgie would have sense enough to stay put. Slowing Honey Dew, he scanned the area for her cap. The moonlight made a shadow of a bump in the road, tricking him into thinking he'd found it, but it was only a clump of debris.

Voices of young men filled with bluster came from just ahead.

"You'll spoil her, Fred."

"It's only a Mai tree."

"Only a Mai tree, he says."

A round of masculine laughter.

Luke squinted. Silhouettes of five men carrying a twenty-foot tree emerged at the bend in the road. Adjusting his hat, he moved Honey Dew into the light so as not to startle them.

"Hello!" he shouted.

The boys, armed with axes and a pull-wagon full of empty beer bottles, waved.

"Hallo."

"Who's the lucky girl?" Luke asked.

They stopped next to him, one of them stroking Honey Dew's nose.

"Fred's gal." A young man indicated another with the nod of his head.

Of the five, Fred seemed to be the only sober one of the bunch.

"What about you?" Fred asked. "You're getting a late start."

Luke nodded, allowing them to misinterpret his reason for being out. "I'm fairly new to town. Any particular spot you recommend?"

All talking at once, the boys offered locations for the best crop of Mai trees — each contradicting the other.

"Who're you leaving a tree for?" Fred asked.

"Georgie Gail," Luke answered, without hesitation.

The boy whistled. "Best of luck with her. She's not one to give her favor easily."

"That a fact?" Honey Dew shifted her weight beneath him.

"Yep." Fred removed his hat, revealing a severely receded hairline for one so young. "Plenty tried when she first arrived last year, but she rebuffed every-a-one of 'em."

Several yards back, two more men came

around the bend, the glow of a cigarette briefly flashing. Neither had a tree.

Luke tipped his hat to the boys. "I guess I better get started, then. Sounds like I've got my work cut out for me."

"Don't ya need an ax?" the boy pulling the wagon asked.

Luke looked at his empty hands. "I guess I do."

Fred offered his. "Hall's the name. I live on Jackson Street."

"Luke Palmer and I'm much obliged. I'll return it first thing."

"Take your time."

Tipping his hat, Luke lay the ax across his lap and nudged Honey Dew forward.

The boys continued on, the discarded bottles clinking in their wake. It took only a moment for Luke to recognize Duane's skinny silhouette and Necker's more muscular one.

"There ya are," Duane said. "We been lookin' all over fer ya."

Over the past month, Luke had spent every spare moment available with them, hunting, fishing, and visiting the saloons. In order to avoid drinking, he'd splattered himself with gin before going out and carried his own flask filled with water.

"Well, I've been looking for you, too." A

waft of cigarette smoke touched Luke's nose. "You scouting around for Mai trees?"

Necker shook his head. "I got me a wife now. No need to deliver dead trees decorated with a bunch of paper streamers to her."

Grinning, Duane took a swig from a beer in his hand. "Did I hear right, Luke? Ya thinkin' ta put a Mai tree at the switchboard operator's window?"

Honey Dew gave a quiet nicker.

Luke stroked her neck. "I'm thinking on it."

"Well, ain't that a coincidence?" Sliding a hand in his pocket, Duane rocked on his heels.

"Coincidence?" Luke kept his voice casual.

"Why, sure. Miss Georgie's place is where we're headed, too."

Honey Dew stepped backward in reaction to Luke's sudden tensing. He pulled her still. "You fellows plan on giving me a little competition?"

"Nah," Duane said. "We ain't leaving somethin', so much as we are takin' somethin'. Ain't that right, Necker?"

Necker kept his own counsel.

"What're you taking?" Luke asked.

Duane looked at his feet, then over at Necker.

After one last pull, Necker flicked the cigarette to the ground. "The float them bird ladies made fer tomorrow's parade."

"Why?"

Duane took a long drink, then scraped his sleeve across his mouth. "Some of us don't like the uproar she's causing over our birds. Heard tell she's sending our women's signatures to that bird society she belongs to. The same society what instigated them new bird laws in Tennessee."

Luke adjusted the ax on his lap. "I hadn't heard that."

"Well, it's true and I don't know why you'd wanna be with a woman like that."

Necker tipped his hat back. "Now, Duane, you've seen our little operator. I don't think it takes much imagination to figure what Palmer here wants with her."

Duane gave a low laugh. "Yeah, I guess even I could forget about her birds long enough to amuse myself with her."

Throwing his leg over the horse, Luke dismounted, gripping the ax. "I don't like sharing, Duane."

Duane tapped his beer bottle against his leg. "That a fact? Well, maybe when you're done with her, ya can let me know."

Luke ground his teeth. "I wouldn't count on it."

With a bark of laughter, Duane clapped him on the back. "Oh, ya got it bad, brother, ain't ya?"

Before he could respond, Duane pointed to Honey Dew with his beer bottle. "Hey, Neck, if we use his horse, we won't have to go round up one of our own."

"I'm not sure he'd be interested in comin' along, Duane, him making claims on Miss Georgie and all."

Luke forced himself to shrug. He was unsure of what their reaction would be when they discovered the float missing, but whatever it was, he wanted to be there when it happened. "I'm not opposed to playing a prank now and then."

The more time he spent with Duane and Necker, the more they took him into their confidence. Never, however, had they involved him in their escapades or betrayed their involvement with Comer.

Pursing his lips, Necker nodded. "Let's go, then."

Luke grabbed Honey Dew's reins and the three headed toward Cottonwood Lane. He hoped Georgie had gone to bed like he'd told her. If she was on that porch with her broom, he just might strangle her pretty little neck.

A few minutes later, the outline of her picket fence and tiny cottage came into view. They circled round to the back, but of course the decorated carriage was missing.

"What the devil?" Duane turned in a circle, scratching the back of his head and knocking his hat askew. "It was here earlier. I helped the doc deliver it myself."

"You know anything about this, Palmer?" Necker asked, his voice low.

Nodding, he propped the ax against a tree. "Georgie was fretting about the float when I returned from repairing a line on Main Street. I didn't pay much attention, though."

Finishing off his beer, Duane flung it into the foliage. "Had yer mind on other things, huh?"

Luke shrugged. "Maybe."

Necker sighed. "Well, come on. She couldn't have taken it far. Let's spread out."

They searched for thirty minutes, looking behind every house and shed, down every alley within easy walking distance, but of course didn't find it. As Luke had predicted, they weren't willing to extend their search any further than the immediate area.

"What're we gonna do?" Duane asked, the three joining up at the corner of Georgie's property.

Necker pulled his lips into a thin line. "I'm thinking."

Duane picked something off his tongue, then wiped it on his trousers. "What if we go inside and give her a little scare?"

Luke tensed. Exactly what constituted "a little scare"? he wondered.

"Those weren't the instructions," Necker replied. "We're to destroy the float."

"But the float ain't here."

Much as Luke wanted to ask whose instructions they were following, he kept quiet.

Necker sighed. "Scaring her won't do any good if she don't know why."

"What about them hats?" Duane asked. "We could burn up them hats all those ladies made."

Luke stilled.

Necker lifted one corner of his mouth. "We could at that." He looked at Luke. "Where does she keep the hats?"

"Inside," he answered.

"Where?"

He hesitated. "Her bedroom."

Duane cackled, rubbing his chest. "Well, ain't that a pretty thought."

Luke grabbed him by the shirt and yanked him forward. "She's mine, Duane. And until I say otherwise, nobody goes into her bedroom unless it's me."

Duane snarled. "Listen, Palmer, we only included you 'cause we needed your horse. We don't need ya no more, though."

Necker gave Luke a speculative look. "Ya willing to burn those hats, Palmer?"

He wasn't about to leave Georgie at their mercy, even if it meant burning the hats himself. "I am."

"Well, let go o' Duane, then."

He released the boy.

Duane stumbled back, catching himself before falling. "What about me? What if I wanna burn 'em? What if I wanna go into her bedroom?"

"You ain't man enough to handle her," Necker said, dismissing the sputtering boy. He pinned Luke with his gaze. "Every last one of 'em has to be burned."

"That'll take a while," Luke said. "There's more than you can count."

"He just wants to linger in her bedroom," Duane complained.

Luke refused to let himself be riled. He needed to protect Georgie. If that meant putting up with Duane and demolishing Georgie's pet project, then that's what he'd do.

"Children, children," Necker crooned.

"Well, I don't wanna stand out here twiddlin' my thumbs while he has all the fun."

"No, I don't suppose ya do." Taking a bandana out of his pocket, he began to tie it around his nose. "And neither do I. We all go in."

Luke kept his voice level. "I need to borrow your belt and jacket."

Necker paused. "Belt?"

"For my overalls. If I belt them and cover them with a jacket, she won't recognize them for what they are. But if I simply put a neckerchief over my face, she'll know me the moment she sees my clothes."

Necker pulled his belt through his loops, then handed it and his jacket to Luke.

Luke cinched his waist. "Hats, too. We need to exchange hats."

"Change out with Duane, then," Necker said. "No chance of her mistakin' him fer you."

When all was ready, Necker made a follow-me motion, and the three slipped through her unlocked back door.

CHAPTER TWENTY-THREE

Georgie woke with a start. A large, looming man glided toward her, his body fluid. Terror crushed her voice box, cutting off the scream at the back of her throat.

The sound of footsteps, quick and fast, reached her ears, yet the man had stopped to hover at the edge of her bed.

There's more than one.

She tried to turn her head, to throw up her arms, but her body wouldn't move. Paralyzed, eyes wide, she couldn't think. The Twenty-third Psalm jumped into her head.

The Lord is my shepherd; I shall not want.

A second man appeared beside the first, this one skinnier, smaller than the other. He reached out as if to touch her, his action freeing her scream, the sound high and shrill, as if it came from someone other than her.

Both men jumped. The larger one reached

for her head. She came alive, flying to her knees, swinging her arms. Screaming. Screaming.

But the man didn't touch her. Instead he jerked up her pillow and whisked off the pillow slip.

"Shut her up." A third man. This one arranging wood in her fireplace.

She surged to her feet on the bed, scrambling toward the foot of it.

The smaller one grabbed her ankle and pulled. She fell facedown onto the mattress, then flipped over, her nightdress twisting about her legs. She kicked with her other foot, landing a solid hit.

Letting out a grunt, the man cursed and reached for her again.

She screamed, pressing herself against the wall.

"Shut her up!"

Gripping her cheeks, he squeezed her mouth open. She yanked at his arm, but even skinny, he was much stronger than she. He stuffed a handkerchief into her mouth. She bit him.

Howling, he lifted his hand as though to strike her.

The larger one grasped him by the scruff of the neck and the seat of his pants, then hurled him aside. Windmilling his arms, he collided into her commode, the bowl and pitcher crashing to the floor.

He cursed again.

"Shut up and help me with this," the third man said.

A spark. They were lighting a fire in the fireplace. Her breath froze. Were they wanting to watch as they did their wicked deeds?

He makes me to lie down in green pastures; He leads me beside the still waters. He restores my soul.

She yanked the handkerchief from her mouth. Before she could scream again, the large one clapped a hand across her mouth and pushed her back onto the mattress. She struggled and fought. Kicked and flailed.

He easily overpowered her, yet without hurting her the way the other man had. He poked the handkerchief back into her mouth before she had a chance to bite again. Placing a knee against her torso, he pinned her to the bed while he secured the pillow slip to the wrought-iron headboard.

She struggled anew, shoving, bucking, squirming, beating.

He didn't budge.

He leads me in the paths of righteousness for His name's sake.

Capturing her wrist, he secured it to the pillow slip. He was tying her to the bed. She renewed her struggles, pounding him with her free hand. Pushing him with her legs. He acted as if she were no more than a pesky fly.

The moment the knot was secure, he released her and moved to her chest of drawers. She yanked the handkerchief from her mouth, but held back her scream. No one would hear and it would only serve to make them angry. Instead, she concentrated on the knot. It was tight and secure.

The fire took hold, the smell of wood smoke filling the room. The fire maker continued to feed the flame. The small man touched his chin beneath the neckerchief, then looked at his fingers.

They'd all hidden their faces behind bandanas, their hair beneath hats. Yet the large one sparked a familiar chord. She'd seen him before. She was sure.

He pulled open drawer after drawer until he found her night wrap and stockings. In two strides, he returned to her side, tossed her braid behind her, and put the wrap on her backward, threading its left sleeve up her right arm, then draping its back across her front and tucking it about her.

Though she was still completely indecent, the extra layer of nainsook was far better than the translucent cotton of her nightdress. He reached for her free arm.

"No." She pressed it against her back. "Please."

The skinny one lifted the edge of his neckerchief and spit on her floor. "Tie her up good. Then maybe if we have time, we can have us a little extra fun."

In a move so fast she'd have missed it had she blinked, the large man laid a fist across his jaw. The recipient skidded across the floor and into the wall of hatboxes. Boxes shot in all directions, hats tumbling out. The man crumbled to a lifeless heap.

Hands and body trembling, she clawed at the pillow slip.

The fire maker sighed, flames filling the room with light. "Was that really necessary?"

Though she'd made a career of listening to voices over the phone, she always knew in advance who was on the line according to what number dropped. Still, she'd swear these men didn't have phone service. If they had, she felt sure she'd have recognized them.

The large one returned to her side.

She scrambled onto the bed, crouching into a ball and pressing her back against the headboard. "Please, please. Don't do this."

He looked at her full on. His eyes filled

with concern and remorse.

She sucked in her breath. They were blue. Blue with thick brows above each. Recognition shot through her like an electrical shock.

It was Frank Comer. The same man who'd robbed their train. The same man who'd let her keep her money. The same man who'd been so generous with the widow.

The pillow slip securing her to the headboard chafed at her skin. Her eyes filled. How could she have ever thought him to be a kind, benevolent man? "Why are you doing this?"

Alarm briefly touched his eyes. Had he guessed she knew who he was?

Reaching behind her, he withdrew her other hand.

"No, no!" She yanked and kicked, but nothing fazed him.

"Either shut her up or I will." The fire maker's sharp command sliced through the air, cutting off her cries and her struggles.

Yea, though I walk through the valley of the shadow of death, I will fear no evil; For You are with me. Your rod and Your staff, they comfort me.

Releasing her wrist, her captor picked up the handkerchief and held it in front of her, a question in his eyes.

She pressed her lips together.

Relaxing his shoulders, he tossed the handkerchief aside, then reached for her hand again.

She shook her head, pressing it against her back.

Please, she mouthed, tears spilling down her cheeks.

But he wasn't looking at her. Instead he found her wrist and secured it to her other with the pillow slip, then clamped her ankles together and tied them with one of the stockings.

With a penetrating gaze, he touched his finger to his neckerchief in the vicinity of his lips. *Be silent.*

Swallowing, she nodded. He squatted down next to the skinny man, slapping him awake. She shifted her attention to the fire maker and gasped. He'd not used wood to stoke the fire, but hats. The hats women all over the county had labored over and submitted for tomorrow's Maifest contest. The hats which were to raise money for the Audubon Society. The hats which were to help preserve the lives of countless birds.

Someone let out a long keen.

Scowling, the large man looked over his shoulder and touched a finger to his mouth again.

Then she realized, it had been she who'd moaned. With renewed determination, she struggled against the bindings. Yet the more she struggled, the tighter they became.

Leaning over, she picked at the knots with her teeth. But they were too secure.

Finally, sinking to the edge of the mattress, she watched through silent, blurry tears as the men tore open box after box and tossed the beloved hats into the fire. She had always loved the smell of burning logs. Straw, fabric, and tissue, however, gave off a completely different odor. A harsh, astringent one.

She tried to convince herself they were only things. But they weren't. It was as if they took her dreams and threw them into the fire.

With a deep, gripping ache in her heart, she finished reciting the Twenty-third Psalm. She moved to the Lord's Prayer, then every memory verse she knew about fear, courage, grief, heartache, and vengeance.

Luke shut off the part of him which ached to respond to Georgie's distress. First and foremost, he must do whatever it took to protect her from a fate much worse than being bound at wrists and ankles.

He felt sure Necker's intent was to impair

the Plumage League, not bring harm to Georgie. Duane, however, was another matter. The boy had had too much to drink and, from what Luke could tell, had allowed his mind to wander.

Still, Luke would need to make amends with Duane once the boy sobered up. He didn't want tonight's rough handling to sabotage his chances of getting into Comer's gang.

He tossed a hat into the fire. The frilly confection burned like corn husks and produced an abundance of smoke. Flames high, heat stifled the room. Sweat beaded along his forehead and neck.

Moaning, Duane finally pushed himself to his feet.

"You finish up in here," Necker murmured to Luke. "I want every last one of 'em destroyed."

He nodded. Necker looked at Duane, signaling him to follow. The two left the room.

Tempted as he was to check on Georgie, he concentrated on his task. But that didn't keep him from picturing her in his mind. Her thick blond braid reached clear down to her waist, and her white nightdress looked nothing like his mother's.

His mother's had always reminded him of

a flour sack with sleeves and a bow at the throat. But Georgie's was light as a feather, had a scoop-necked, lacy yoke, and a tiny ribbon gathering up the gown just below her breasts. Its sleeves tied below her elbows, trimming them with a ruffle of lace.

When she'd struggled with Duane, her gown had twisted and hiked up, exposing not only delicate ankles and well-formed feet, but a good portion of shapely calf.

He hated knowing the other men had seen her so tousled. Were probably picturing her in their minds, as well. At least he'd managed to cover her up some with the wrap. Still, the suppleness of her ankles and the high arches of her feet as he tied them seared his brain. He swallowed. The less interaction he had with her the better.

For a moment, he'd thought she'd recognized him. But if she had, she never called him by name.

A giant crash came from the living area. He glanced at the door, but couldn't see anything beyond a chair and the bookshelf. Kicking empty boxes out of the way, he found the last dozen and started on them.

"Why are you doing this?" she asked, her voice soft enough to keep from being overheard by the others.

He threw in a hat, shoving it to the back

with a poker.

"You have a reputation to uphold," she continued. "Why would you mar it over a bunch of women's hats?"

He frowned. A reputation? What was she talking about?

"I know who you are."

He stiffened.

"You're Frank Comer."

He wheeled around, startled.

"You needn't act so surprised. I was on the train you robbed in February. The switchboard operator. Remember?"

Instead of answering, he pulled a lid off the next box and snatched the hat from packing tissue.

"I've followed every article they've written on you. Read the pulp fiction novels about you. Sang your praises to my friends and neighbors." She wiped a tear with her shoulder. "I just don't understand. This isn't like you at all."

He gave her his back and continued his task. But her words confused him. He knew Comer was broad of shoulder and had blue eyes, but he was well under six feet. Could she be mistaken about having met him? But no, if she'd been on that train from Dallas, she'd definitely met the man.

"I can't feel my feet and my wrists are

313

bleeding."

He hesitated. Her wrists shouldn't be bleeding. Tossing the hat in the fire, he approached her and pulled back the bindings. Sure enough, her skin had been scraped raw. Clearly, she'd been trying to work herself free.

The sooner they left the better. Hardening his heart, he returned to the task at hand. Only four more hats to go.

Duane stepped to the threshold and leaned against the doorframe. He didn't speak, but eyed Georgie with interest. Luke opened the last of the boxes, stuffed the hat in the fire, then nudged Duane into the living area.

The switchboard lay on its side, severed wires coming out its back. Necker was nowhere in sight.

"Ya finished?" Duane asked, his voice low.

Luke nodded.

"Then let's go."

Returning to Georgie's room, Luke assured himself the fire was safe, then checked her bindings. They were tight, but not dangerously so.

Her chest rose and fell. Her eyes darkened with fury and loathing.

He picked up her pillow and wedged it between her head and the headboard. He wasn't sure how long it would be before he could return for her. Hopefully, the pillow would allow her to rest a bit more comfortably until then.

"If you think this puny gesture will make up for how you've behaved tonight, then you greatly overestimate your charm." She set her jaw. "You're a rogue and a scoundrel. And I'll make sure everyone in the county knows it the moment I'm free."

Irritation flicked through him. What was she thinking to threaten the man she believed to be Frank Comer? Had she no sense at all?

He swiped up the handkerchief, wadding it in his fist and holding it in front of her lips. She tightened them and turned her head to the side.

He stood in indecision, wanting to impress upon her the danger of her bravado, but unwilling to gag her.

Duane stepped into the room, grabbed the hanky, and tossed it on the bed. "Let's go."

After a slight hesitation, Luke turned and followed Duane from her bedroom, then out the back door.

CHAPTER TWENTY-FOUR

Grabbing the ax and Honey Dew, the three men headed out. After putting some distance between themselves and Georgie's lot, Necker glanced at Luke. "You leave her tied up?"

He nodded.

Necker tightened his lips. "The boss won't like that. He's particular about the ladies."

"I can still fetch a Mai tree for her," he offered. "Then make enough noise to wake the dead when I deliver it. I'm sure she'll cry out. That'll be all the excuse I need to go in and free her."

"Duane, you help him find one, then. I don't wanna leave her like that any longer than I have to."

"Where ya goin'?" Duane asked.

"I'm gonna report in."

Luke suppressed his frustration. If Duane weren't to accompany him, he could follow Necker and see whom he was working for, then go free Georgie.

Stopping, Necker ran a gaze over Luke. "Gimme my jacket and belt."

Now that the imminent danger for Georgie had passed, Luke realized his participation in tonight's activities might have inadvertently strengthened his position with Necker. It was a small consolation.

He returned all articles of clothing to their rightful owners and secured Honey Dew to a tree just inside a copse. Necker continued north while Duane joined Luke and the two moved into the woods.

He glanced at his companion, unable to see much of the young man from the little bit of moonlight filtering through the trees. "I'm sorry about all that back there. Your face all right?"

"It hurts like the dickens. What'd ya go and hit me fer?"

"I told you. I have feelings for her. Weren't you listening?"

Duane rubbed his jaw. "Not good enough, I guess."

"You didn't lose any teeth, did you?"

"Nah. Just my pride."

Luke slapped him on the shoulder. "Well, I'm sorry, friend. I guess I'm a little touchy when it comes to females. I don't like to see them ill-treated. Particularly that one."

Duane grunted, but he wasn't the type to hold a grudge. Much as Luke would have preferred to talk of something else, Duane relived the excitement of the evening, taking out each moment and recounting it for pleasure's sake. "What happened while I was out cold?"

"Not much. I finished tying her up, then woke you."

"Is her skin as soft as it looks?"

Luke growled.

The boy held up his hands, pale swatches of flesh in the darkness. "Come on, have pity. Cain't ya tell me nothin'?"

"I took no pleasure in tying her up, Duane, or manhandling her."

"Ya sound like Frank."

He slanted the boy a quick glance. "Frank? Is that who Necker's going to see?"

They moved into a clearing, allowing enough moonlight for Luke to see Duane flip up his collar. "I'm not supposed to say nothing."

Halting, Luke pretended surprise. "You don't mean Frank Comer, do you? That fellow who robs trains and shares his loot with the poor?"

"He don't share near as much as them papers say." Duane strode to a twelve-foot tree on the edge of the clearing and looked up. "This one oughta do."

"You've seen Frank Comer?" Luke infused his voice with awe and admiration. "Talked to him?"

Duane straightened his shoulders, hooking a thumb in his waistband. "That ain't the half of it."

"Tell me."

The boy cocked a hip. "I'm in his gang."

"You aren't."

"I am."

"You've robbed a train?" He widened his eyes.

"Shore. Plenty o' times."

He whistled. "How'd you get in with Comer?"

"Necker introduced us."

"Does he need anybody else? Can I join? You've seen me, I'm good with a gun."

Duane considered him. "I'll ask. I know Necker thought ya done good tonight and word is Frank's thinkin' about another train job. But don't say nothin' 'til I talk to Necker."

A rush of energy sluiced through him. "Another train? When?"

"Don't know."

Luke forced a grin. "That'd be something. I guess I can't write home about it, though."

Chuckling, Duane stepped away from the

tree. "No, you cain't write home. Cain't tell nobody. Folks round here like Comer well enough, but things is kinda uneasy right now." He pointed to the tree. "You start. I'll spell ya when ya get winded."

Bracing his legs, Luke swung the ax, biting into the wood, then alternated between uppercut and undercut. Chips scattered with each slice. After several minutes, he paused to catch his breath.

"Ya quitting already?"

He shook his head. "I still can't get over you knowing Comer. What's he like?"

"Nothing like those pulp fiction novels, I can tell ya that."

"Really?"

"Oh, he puts on a show fer folks when he's out and about, but truth is, he's meaner 'n a bitin' boar."

Luke wiped his forehead with his sleeve. "Then, why do you run with him?"

"The money. The excitement. You shoulda been at this last robbery. Who-wee, this Ranger come outta nowhere. I thought we was caught fer sure."

"What happened?"

"We split up. Gave him the slip. It was close, though."

"Must have set your heart to thumping."

"Shore 'nough."

Returning his attention to the tree, Luke circled around it, chopping his way to its core. He noted Duane didn't mention the six men Luke had captured.

He wanted to push for more information — what did Comer look like, was he anybody Luke knew, where was he hiding out, who else was in the gang — but he refrained. Too many questions would look suspicious. Best to extract the particulars a little at a time.

"Watch out," Luke said, backing up. "Here she goes."

The birch fell to the ground with a thump, stirring up a tiny puff of dirt. Positioning themselves at separate ends, they picked it up and carried it to Honey Dew.

"Where's yer saddle?" Duane asked.

"Didn't think I was going to need one."

"Well, leave the mare here, then, and I'll help ya tote it the rest of the way."

Luke put his end down. "No, I need to wash in the creek and then change. I smell like smoke from all those hats. I'll saddle up before I come back, then drag it with a rope."

"Ya sure?"

"Yeah." He extended his hand. "Thanks for your help and again, I'm sorry about your jaw."

Shaking hands, Duane crooked up a corner of his mouth. "It's all right. Though I may think different tomorry when the beer's worn off."

A twinge of remorse flickered through Luke. He hadn't meant to hit him quite so hard. "Where you off to?"

"Home. Watchin' you chop down that tree plumb wore me out."

Chuckling, Luke lifted himself onto Honey Dew. "I'll see you tomorrow, then. Don't sleep through the festivities."

"I wouldn't miss 'em."

Touching his heels to the horse's flank, Luke hurried toward Mrs. Sealsfield's boardinghouse for a clean set of clothes.

A thump outside jarred Georgie awake, sending tremors of pain to her wrists and ankles. Had they come back? Terror overrode the burning sensation in her limbs. She forced herself to sit still.

In between grunts and thuds, someone whistled a popular love song. Upon reaching the chorus, his baritone voice broke into song.

Her eyes don't shine like diamonds,
She has no golden hair.

I know she loves me dearly,
Then what more need I care.

Frowning, she squinted, trying to see out
the open window overlooking the porch, but
her fire still burned, making it impossible.

With a smile she always greets me,
From her I ne'er will part.

He paused, letting out a grunt as if he
were lifting something, followed by a
whoosh of air. A loud thud signaled the
dropping of something against her cottage.

For lads, I love my mother,
And she's my sweeeeeet-heart.

He began to whistle again.

Mustering up her courage, she drew in a
breath. "Who's there?"

All sound and movement ceased.

Her heart began to hammer. "Who's
there?" she asked, raising her voice even
more.

"Georgie?"

Relief welled up inside her. "Luke?"

Heavy footfalls clomped up the steps and
to her window. "I'm sorry. I didn't mean to
wake you."

"What are you doing?"

His shadowy form was obscured by her lace curtains. "I'm leaving you a Mai tree. But it was a surprise. You're supposed to be asleep."

Tears sprang to her eyes. "Help me, Luke. Someone broke in."

"What?"

"Someone broke in." Her voice cracked. "I'm tied up. Please. I need you to —"

She never finished her sentence. He burst into her bedroom, took one look at her, checked behind her door, then rushed out to check the rest of the house. The fire highlighted a multitude of empty hatboxes and lids strewn about her floor. The lingering smell of burnt fabric stirred her emotions.

"They're gone," she called, choking on the last word. "They've been gone for some time."

He returned, kneeling before her and slicing her pillow slip with a knife from his pocket. "What happened?"

Pain flared through her wrists and spread to her fingers as blood rushed back in. She tried to choke back her cry, but couldn't completely muffle it.

He sawed through the stocking around her ankles. "What the blazes happened? Are you all right?" He whipped up his head. "Did they —"

"They burned the hats." The horror she'd been holding inside spilled over, bringing an ocean of tears.

He spared no glance for the boxes strewn about the room, but kept his attention solely on her. "Did they hurt you?"

"A little. When I fought. But mostly it's my hands and feet that hurt."

Grimacing, he lifted her into his arms and carried her to the living area. The switchboard lay on its side, a sad hulk in the darkness. "No! Oh, Luke. Look what they did."

"Shhhh. I'll fix it." He set her on the couch, then disappeared inside her bedroom, returning with her coverlet. He tucked it around her body, his movements swift but gentle. "Tell me everything."

With broken sentences, she told him all that happened. The more she talked, the more her body began to tremble. It refused to stop shaking. She looked at it as if it were not her own.

Scooping her up, he pulled her to his lap, blanket and all, then tucked her head beneath his chin. He smelled of soap and rainwater.

"It's okay." He wrapped his arms around her as if he could will her shakes away.

"They're gone now. You're safe."

Both his words and his embrace brought warmth and relief, triggering fresh tears. Not only for herself, but for her hats and all they represented.

She still couldn't make sense of it. Why would Frank Comer burn her hats? Why would he act so dishonorably toward a woman? What on earth did he have to gain?

She knew of only one person who would benefit from the destruction of her hats. Ernst Ottfried. Had the milliner put Comer up to this?

Luke kissed her scalp, rubbed her arms and legs through the blanket, and rocked her like a baby, his touches bringing comfort and reassurance. Still the tears fell.

"I'm sorry," he whispered, over and over.

Her cries turned into hiccups. She wiped her face and nose with a corner of the blanket.

"We need to tell the sheriff," he said.

She burrowed closer, drawing up her knees. "Not yet. Please. I don't want to be alone."

"He needs to know."

"Then, take me with you. But don't leave me by myself." The tears started again.

He rested his cheek against her head. "I'll be back quick as a wink."

"No." She wrapped a fist around his overall strap. "No."

He acquiesced, making no move to leave the couch.

Her breathing leveled. Her tears slowed. "You brought me a Mai tree?"

Running a hand over her hair, he kissed her head. "Yes."

She lifted her chin. "Why?"

He traced her jawline with a finger, its roughness abrading her skin and sending tingles along its path. "I don't know."

"No one's ever brought me a Mai tree before."

"Then the men of this town are idiots."

Snaking a hand out from the blanket, she drove her fingers into his thick, rich hair. "Your hair's wet."

"I was hot after chopping down the tree and jumped in the creek to cool off."

"It must have been freezing."

"It was."

She wished she could see his eyes, but there was no fire lit in this room. She applied the slightest pressure to his head with her fingers. It was all the coaxing he needed. Bringing his lips to hers, he kissed her with a tenderness so sweet, her body turned to liquid.

He rode a hand down the length of her

arm, then stalled, stroking, stroking, before continuing to her waist, dragging the blanket with it.

She shivered.

He pulled back. "You need to get dressed."

With all that had happened, she'd totally forgotten she was in her nightdress. And though she should be embarrassed, shocked, she felt neither. Not anywhere close.

He gently pushed her knees from his lap and lifted her to her feet. "Go on, now."

Her legs wobbled.

He held her waist until she steadied.

"You won't leave?" she whispered.

"I'll be right here."

Tugging the blanket back up to her shoulders, she padded to her room and clicked the door softly behind her.

CHAPTER TWENTY-FIVE

Georgie stepped back into the living room, her hair up and her chemise, corset, petticoat, stockings, shoes, and gown in place. Somehow, completing her toilette caused her to be starkly aware of how disheveled she'd been before. A delayed sense of embarrassment and shame swept through her.

A fire blazed behind the grate. The switchboard sat upright. Luke crouched behind it, only his elbows and knees visible. At the sound of her door opening, he slowly stood, his gaze traveling from her coif clear down to her boots.

Her cheeks burned.

"You all right?" he asked.

"I'd like to apologize."

Frowning, he laid a pair of pliers on top of the switchboard's hutch. "Apologize? For what?"

She lowered her chin. "For not repairing

myself immediately. For . . ." She twirled her hand toward the couch. "For crying all over you while I wore no more than . . . than my nightclothes." She choked. "I'm so sorry. You must be mortified."

A log in the fire popped.

He approached, his footsteps loud against the plank flooring. With an index finger, he tilted up her face. "Mortification isn't exactly the word I'd have used."

His eyes were penetrating. His lower lip full. His whiskers dark.

The blackness beyond the windows reminded her she stood alone, in her home, at two in the morning, with an unmarried man.

"I think you're right," she whispered. "You'd best go get the sheriff."

"There's no need. I fixed the board and called him already. He'll be here any minute."

She slid her eyes shut. Her reputation would be ruined. It hadn't even occurred to her until this moment. But no one would believe she was still chaste after being set upon by three men. And even if they did, an unmarried man had been the one to rescue her.

"Are you sure that was wise?" she asked.

He drew his brows together. "You think

your attackers might retaliate?"

"I think my reputation will be in shreds come morning."

His entire face paled. "But nothing happened."

"Not with the intruders." She glanced at the couch. "I can't say the same about us."

He scowled. "Nothing happened between us, either."

"I'm not sure the good ladies of Brenham would agree."

"Then the good ladies of Brenham can be d—"

She touched a finger to his lips. "There's a reason society has rules about unmarried women being alone with unmarried men. And what happened between us on the couch is a perfect example."

He wrapped his hand around hers. "Nothing happened on that couch. We kissed. Nothing more."

"I was in my nightdress," she whispered, humiliation clogging her throat. "On your lap."

"If anyone is to blame, it's me. I'm the one who carried you out here. I'm the one who pulled you onto my lap. But truth is, under the circumstances, I'd do it again."

"You're justifying."

"So I am. Nothing happened."

Outside, Honey Dew gave an expectant whinny and received a distant one in reply.

"The sheriff's almost here," he said. "When he arrives, you tell him about the men who broke in. What happened after I found you is between you and me."

She pulled away from him and headed to the kitchen. "Doesn't matter. I'm ruined anyway."

"You're not ruined."

"I am." She propped open the door. "And, as such, I won't be able to stay."

"Won't be able to stay?"

"In Brenham."

His jaw began to tick. "Did those men touch you, other than to tie you up?"

"Doesn't matter."

"Oh, yes it does." He followed her into the kitchen. She felt him closing in, his footsteps stopping right behind her.

She fit a small muslin bag into a coffeepot. "Thank you for stocking the stove and putting some water on to boil."

Grasping her arm, he spun her around. "Did those men touch you, other than to tie you up? Yes or no?"

"No."

"Then you are not ruined." His eyes were ablaze, his tone fierce.

She sighed. "Please let go. I'm tired of being treated roughly."

He dropped her arm as if he'd been singed and fell back. "I'm sorry. I didn't mean to hurt you."

She pulled the coffee canister from a cupboard, her eyes filling at the thought of leaving her job, her cottage, her birds, her friends.

"What if you marry me?" he asked.

Letting out a short huff of air, she scooped two tablespoons of coffee into the muslin bag. "Don't be ridiculous."

"I'm dead serious."

"But you don't love me."

"I'm thinking we'll get along just fine."

She looked at him and saw he was, in fact, serious. The overwhelming generosity of his gesture filled her with warmth. "I can't let you do that, Luke. But thank you. Thank you for being willing."

"Georgie?" The sheriff pounded on her door. "Open up. It's me. Nussbaum."

She set down the spoon and moved toward the door.

Luke grabbed her hand.

She winced, her wrists still tender.

"Marry me," he repeated.

"Georgie?" The sheriff again.

"I'm coming!" she called, then tugged on her hand, but he wouldn't free it. "No,

Luke. I appreciate the offer. I really do. But I'm not going to marry you."

"Then, will you go to Maifest with me?"

She tugged again. "Let go."

"Answer me."

"Georgie?" More hammering. "What in tarnation is going on in there? Open up or I'm bustin' in."

"Coming!"

"Answer me." Jaw set, his eyes impaled her.

"Fine," she hissed. "Now *let go.*"

He released her. She flew to the door.

The sheriff's brown hair was mussed, his glasses cockeyed, his mustache flat. He looked like an untried boy with pasted-on facial hair. "What took so long? You all right? Palmer said you had some trouble. What's he doing over here at this hour?"

"I was leaving a Mai tree at her window." Luke crossed the room, extending a hand. "She called for help when she heard me. I busted in and found her tied up."

"Tied up?" He shook Luke's hand, then gave her a once-over.

"Show him your wrists, Georgie," Luke said.

She pushed up a sleeve, revealing rings of raw, scraped skin.

The sheriff furrowed his brows. "Better

tell me everything."

Taking a breath, she tugged her sleeve back into place. "I've just put some coffee on. Would you care to join me in the kitchen? We can talk in there."

Without waiting for an answer, she headed to the kitchen. Both men followed in her wake.

Luke and Nussbaum hadn't been gone for more than thirty minutes when Kathy Patrick arrived. She swept into the cottage and wrapped Georgie in a bear hug. "The sheriff came by and had Jay wake me up. He thought you might not want to be alone."

Having grown up in a home where every ounce of her mother's energy had been used to survive, Georgie was nearly brought to her knees by the unexpected comfort and support of Mrs. Patrick. The two of them clung together, strength from the Plumage League Float Chairwoman funneling into Georgie.

"Did they hurt you?" Mrs. Patrick cushioned Georgie against her breadth, providing an unflappable refuge.

"No," she said, her voice muffled in the folds of Mrs. Patrick's embrace. "The skin on my wrists is broken, but that was mostly from me struggling against the bindings." Georgie pulled away, her lip trembling. "I'm ruined, though. I can't stay here anymore."

Mrs. Patrick sucked in her breath. "I thought you said they didn't hurt you."

"They didn't. But that doesn't change the fact three men were here, in the dead of night, and me in nothing but my night-clothes."

Mrs. Patrick's face hardened. "I don't know what the women were like where you come from, Georgie, but the women of Brenham will not pass judgment over you for something that was not your doing. You have my word on it."

Georgie had seen that look before and knew it meant business. She swallowed. "They burnt the hats." She choked. "All of them."

"A rather small sacrifice, all things considered."

Georgie swiped her eyes. "But the women spent hours making them. And what about all the money we were to have raised for Audubon? What will the Maifest Queen be crowned with?"

Mrs. Patrick slipped her hand into Georgie's and squeezed. "You let me worry about that. Did they do anything to the float?"

"I don't think so. I hid it behind Langkwitz's house. Luke went to check on it when he left here. He said if anything had happened, he'd come back and tell me. Since he hasn't returned, I'm assuming all's well."

She let out a soft sigh. "Well, that's a piece of good news, anyway. Did you recognize the men who broke in?"

She nodded. "One of them was Frank Comer."

"Frank Comer?" Mrs. Patrick pulled in her chin. "Why, he'd never be involved with something of this sort. What makes you think it was him?"

"I spoke with him while my train was robbed in February. Remember?"

She tilted her head. "I remember you saying you thought it was him, but you can't be sure."

"Who else would it have been? And one of the men tonight had his eyes. I'm sure of it."

"But what possible reason would Comer have for burning the hats? Because clearly that's what they came to do. If it was you they were after, things would have gone much differently."

"That's what the sheriff said, too." In an attempt to relieve her headache, Georgie rubbed her temples. "I told him the only person I knew of who would benefit from destroying the hats was Mr. Ottfried."

Mrs. Patrick herded her toward the kitchen. "Well, I wouldn't rush to any conclusions. Let's wait and see what Nussbaum says once he's had a chance to look into things. For now, I want to make a poultice for those wrists of yours."

"I can do it."

"Nonsense. You sit and let me pamper you."

Georgie pointed to the cupboard where she kept her powdered resin and clean rags.

Mrs. Patrick retrieved them, then sifted the resin onto Georgie's wrists. "I saw someone brought you a nice big Mai tree."

"It's big? I haven't been out there yet."

"Plenty big. And filled with streamers."

She bit her lip. "It was Luke. He made a terrible racket when he delivered it. As soon as I realized it was him, I called out. He's the one who found me."

"I think it's probably best if you keep as much of the particulars to yourself as you can." Setting the resin aside, Mrs. Patrick blew on the raw skin.

Tenderness for her welled up within Georgie. "Thank you."

"Don't you worry another minute." Finished, she sat back in her chair. "Have you had any sleep at all?"

"A few snatches here and there."

She helped Georgie to her feet. "Well, let's get you to bed, then. But first, I need you to show me how to operate that switchboard out there."

Georgie paused. "The switchboard? Why?"

"I told Jay I was staying the night, and while I'm here, there are a few phone calls I want to make."

Yawning, she allowed Mrs. Patrick to guide her into the living area. She explained the basics, then fell into bed — corset, boots, and all. Memories immediately bombarded her. She forced aside the thought of being tied to the bed. Of being threatened. Of being freed from it. For now, all she wanted was to escape into blessed oblivion.

CHAPTER TWENTY-SIX

A yelp of fright escaped Georgie as a booming cannon awoke her.

Mrs. Patrick hurried into her bedroom. "It's all right, little one. That's just the Brenham Field Artillery announcing the opening of Maifest."

The events of the night filled her again as thoroughly as sunlight filled her bedroom. She placed an arm over her eyes. "What time is it?"

"Almost nine. Luke's been by once already with the float. I told him to take it to my house so Jay could hitch it up to our horse. But he'll be back for you right soon. So get on up now and I'll help you with your toilette."

Pushing herself to a sitting position, Georgie immediately noted the empty hatboxes had been removed. On the door of her wardrobe hung Luke's favorite gown of maroon with the epaulets and beaded fringe.

"Come on." Mrs. Patrick helped her to her feet. "Let's get you dressed."

At some point, the woman had found time to change into a gold silk festival gown and to adorn her dark red hair with a stunning hat of tulle.

"You look gorgeous," Georgie said, admiring the hat's beaded net overlay with intricate embroidery.

"Thank you, dear."

For the next forty minutes, Mrs. Patrick fussed over Georgie, helping her remove her wrinkled linsey-woolsey and underclothes, then replace them with fresh underpinnings before changing her bandages.

"Luke specifically requested you wear this." Mrs. Patrick shook out the gown's freshly brushed skirt. "It's just the thing, I think. Its long sleeves and lace trim will keep your bandages well hidden."

Without protest, Georgie allowed herself to be dressed, then guided to a chair Mrs. Patrick had brought in from the kitchen.

Laying her hands in her lap, Georgie closed her eyes, relishing the feel of having someone comb out her hair. She felt like a princess with a lady-in-waiting.

Humming a soft tune, Mrs. Patrick clamped some celluloid pins in her mouth.

"What hat do you usually wear with this dress?"

Moisture filled her eyes. "They burned it."

Mrs. Patrick paused, her gaze meeting Georgie's in the mirror. "They burned it?"

"Yes. Every hat in the room was thrown into the fire."

Sorrow tugged at her lips. "Well, I'll fix your hair especially nice, then."

She was as good as her word, arranging Georgie's hair in an artful profusion of tucked-in curls. Stepping back, she admired her work. "Lovely. Now come outside. I have something to show you."

Georgie assumed she wanted her to see the Mai tree, but Mrs. Patrick led her to the back porch instead of the front. The unmistakable chirping of baby birds pulled Georgie's gaze to the starch box. Mr. Bluebird slipped inside just as the missus slipped out.

Euphoria filled her. The second set of eggs had hatched. She scanned the trees. The cardinals had yet to build their nest, but they were never very far. She could hear their vibrant, musical voices, but could only spot a flycatcher and two thrushes. A monarch butterfly lifted from the yellow buds of her sumac bush. It flitted to the side yard, passing an old farmer's wagon, its bed filled with hatboxes.

She slipped her hand into Mrs. Patrick's and squeezed. "You didn't have to have a wagon brought around. I would've found some way to dispose of the boxes."

A smile played at Mrs. Patrick's lips. "Go look inside them."

"What?"

"Go on." She shooed Georgie with her hands. "Open them."

She hesitated. Truth was, she didn't want to. She had no desire to touch anything those men had. But after everything Mrs. Patrick had done, she wasn't about to refuse her request.

Weaving around Turk's cap and coneflower, images of the night before replayed themselves in her mind. The man at the fireplace rumbling orders. The skinny man crashing into the boxes and scattering them to all corners. Mr. Comer tearing lids from boxes and tossing hat after hat into the blaze.

She clenched her teeth and stopped at the back of the wagon, glancing toward Mrs. Patrick.

The woman nodded her encouragement. "Go ahead."

Georgie reached for a round white box with thin golden stripes, her hand trembling.

A ropey handle lay across its gold-colored lid. Tucking the handle to the side, she removed the top.

A high, curved hat decorated with lush mauve silk and velvet roses sat amidst tissues. She looked at Mrs. Patrick. "They missed some?"

"No." She shook her head. "Those boxes were empty when I carted them out here. Look in another one."

Sliding the gold-striped box aside, she reached for an octagonal one the color of robins' eggs. A sapphire blue hat with a dipping brim, net veil, and frothy bows filled its interior. Picking up speed, she threw open box after box like a child on Christmas morning. Each contained a hat, some extravagant, some wonderfully simple.

After the seventh or eighth box, she stopped. "I don't understand. Where did these come from?"

Mrs. Patrick joined her and began to replace the lids. "Some are from members of the Plumage League. But the majority are from the women of Washington County."

Georgie restacked each box, trying to assimilate what Mrs. Patrick was saying.

"But how?" she asked. "When would they have had time to make these, much less deliver them?"

"I made a general call."

"A general call?" She looked toward the window where her switchboard sat. "To everyone?"

"To everyone."

"When?"

"As soon as you fell asleep."

"I didn't fall asleep until almost three in the morning."

Mrs. Patrick said nothing.

Georgie surveyed the turrets of boxes. "But I still don't . . ."

"They signed our pledge, too. Counting the signatures we had before, we now have a hundred six women who have vowed not to wear or purchase hats with bird parts."

"One hundred six," Georgie breathed, unable to fathom such a number.

Mrs. Patrick gestured toward the boxes. "Many of these are hats the ladies already had. They just removed the bird parts and rearranged the trim."

Her lips parted. "They donated hats from their personal collections?"

"They did." Pausing, Mrs. Patrick smoothed a hand across the top of a box. "For some, I'd say it was the only hat they owned."

She touched the brooch at her collar. "Why? Why would they do that?"

Capturing Georgie's gaze, Mrs. Patrick tilted her head. "Because there isn't a woman in this county who doesn't admire and respect you for supporting yourself and having your own place." A soft breeze picked up a dark red curl, fanning it along her neck. "We may not be able to vote. We may not be able to hold office. We may not be able to wear trousers. But make no mistake, we're not powerless."

Emotion clogged Georgie's throat. "I don't know what to say."

She sighed. "Well, it won't all be smooth going. There'll be some who'll whisper behind their fans. But don't you give them a thought. You just hold your head high and meet every gaze square on. Remember: you're only a victim if you choose to be a victim."

Such simple words, yet it had never occurred to her she had a choice. The more she thought about it, the more emboldened she felt.

Those men might have overpowered her and burned up all the hats, but it didn't mean she had to cower or be ashamed or cry defeat. Quite the contrary.

A huge weight lifted. She surveyed her garden. The starch box housing precious new chicks. Bumblebees sipping nectar from pink columbine. Chickadees rejoicing over the buds on her Virginia creeper.

It was May first. A day set aside to celebrate a new season. New life. New beginnings.

Stretching onto tiptoes, she wrapped her arms about Mrs. Patrick's neck and hugged her. "Thank you. Thank you for everything."

Mrs. Patrick returned the embrace. "No need to thank me, dear. Now look smart. I think your man's coming up the street."

Letting go, she whirled around and bit her cheeks. He was wearing overalls, but they were starched and shiny, accentuating the broadness of his shoulders underneath.

She touched a hand to the back of her hair, thankful she wasn't wearing a hat after all. Next to his overalls, it would have been out of place.

The closer he came, the more handsome he looked. His tenderness and his proposal of the night before filled her, tugging at her heart. Thinking of his touches made her body respond as if they had just occurred. Still, his defense of last night's kissing had been imprudent.

She lifted her chin. In the future, she'd be extremely careful not to betray the trust the women had placed in her. Mrs. Patrick was right. Her position was unique and with it came a responsibility. A responsibility to prove a woman could be independent without falling victim to questionable behavior.

He reached the corner of her property and looked up. It was then she saw the fistful of red roses he carried at his side.

She took an involuntary step forward. Every bone in her body wanted to run to him and pitch herself into his arms, drown herself in his kisses. She took a tumultuous breath.

Lord, help me. For though her intentions were good, she'd need His very strength if she were to stick to them.

He stepped inside the gate, absorbing the sight of Georgie lifting her skirts and rushing toward him in a skip-hop-scurry combination. She'd piled her hair in a mess of curls atop her head, her spectacular smile giving no indication of the trauma she'd suffered just a few hours earlier.

She skidded to a halt in front of him, her eyes lit from within. She pressed her hands against her waist. "Good morning."

A wealth of feelings for this woman assaulted him, leaving him tongue-tied and off-balance.

Her gaze moved to the flowers he held at his side. "Are those for me?"

He looked at them as if he couldn't quite remember where they'd come from, then handed them to her. She scooped them up, gently hugging them to her breast, and buried her nose against the soft red petals.

Closing her eyes, she inhaled their potent perfume. He marveled at the extraordinary length of her lashes as they rested against flawless white cheeks. How could something so simple cause such a ruckus within his chest?

"They're lovely, Luke. Thank you." Opening her eyes, she tilted her head. "Everything all right?"

"Can I kiss you?"

A spark of fire touched her eyes before she immediately squelched it. "I think it's a little early for kissing, Mr. Palmer." But her whisper was more flirty than admonishing.

He zeroed in on the mole beneath her lips. "When, then?"

Pink touched her cheeks. "I'd best go put these in some water." She turned around, then froze. "Oh. Oh my. Would you look at that?"

He followed her gaze to the Mai tree he'd left her. In the light of day it looked even more pitiful than he'd imagined it would. Mrs. Sealsfield had left a large bowl of crepe decorations in the boardinghouse parlor. By the time he got to them, though, only the dregs were left.

After walking through town this morning and seeing the trees other fellows had left their lady-loves, embarrassment crept up his neck. His birch was shorter than most and had but a handful of limp yellow streamers.

"You're just now seeing it for the first time?" he asked.

With slow, tentative steps she moved toward it as if she were approaching the Holy Grail. "I fell asleep. Mrs. Patrick just woke me."

She didn't look as if she'd just woken. She looked fresh and pretty as a basket of daises.

"It's not as grand as most of the others," he said.

"I love it." She studied its branches, her chin raised, her jaw exposed. "Thank you."

At his lack of response, she peeked at him over her shoulder. "Flowers, Mai tree, rescuing me in my hour of need. You certainly know how to sweep a lady off her feet, don't you?"

Guilt pressed against his conscience. He shoved it away. He'd been doing his job. Had he not been there to intervene, no telling what Duane would have done.

Her gaze lowered to his lips. She unconsciously brushed hers against the soft petals of the blooms in her arms.

"Good morning, Luke." Mrs. Patrick rounded the corner, causing them both to jump.

With gloves and fan in hand, she looked as pretty as one of Georgie's songbirds in her golden gown, striking red hair, and elaborate hat.

"Good morning, Mrs. Patrick. I didn't realize you were still here."

"I'm just finishing up." Clipping the fan in her hand to Georgie's chatelaine, she exuded an aura of pride. "Isn't our girl just about the sweetest thing you ever did see?"

"Breathtaking," he answered.

The woman's smile widened, her attention still on Georgie. "Here, let me have those flowers, dear. I'll take care of them and the hats while you two run on."

"Are you sure?" But even as Georgie asked, she relinquished the bouquet to Mrs. Patrick in exchange for her gloves.

"Of course. Go on, now. You're going to have to hurry if you want a good spot for the parade."

Georgie shook out a glove, but Luke stalled her. "Wait. Not yet." Capturing her fingers, he tucked them into the crook of his elbow. "Thank you, Mrs. Patrick. We'll see you there."

He took a step toward the gate, but Georgie gently broke free, retracing her steps to give the woman a peck on the cheek. "Thank you."

"*Pshaw.* It was nothing. Now, quit your dallying. A man doesn't like to be kept waiting, you know."

Smiling, Georgie extended her naked hand toward him. His heart swelled and this time, instead of placing it on his arm, he entwined his fingers with hers and they headed to Main Street hand-in-hand.

CHAPTER TWENTY-SEVEN

Georgie loved Maifest. It wasn't a holiday her hometown had celebrated, nor had Dallas when she'd worked the switchboard in SWT&T's large exchange. But here in Brenham it was the biggest festival of the year.

Farmers ignored their crops. Men ignored their businesses. Women ignored their chores. And for one blessed day everyone devoted themselves to renewing old friendships, forming new ones, and breathing the air of heaven.

At the moment, however, heaven's air was riddled with dust from a multitude of wagons. They entered the county seat from every direction. A freckle-faced boy hung off the edge of a green one, pointing to red, white, and blue bunting draped across residences and businesses. A tiny dog barked, weaving between horses' hooves and nipping at the wheels of a buckboard.

Georgie smiled. "Wonder what he'd do if he actually caught the thing."

Before Luke could respond, an automobile squawked its horn like a loud, angry goose.

The horse pulling the green wagon whinnied and bucked, tossing the freckled boy inside its bed into the oncoming traffic.

Georgie screamed, her shriek underscored by a dozen more. Luke dove into the street like a baseball player reaching for a low flying ball. Scooping the boy into his arms, he adroitly rolled out of harm's way, barely missing the hooves of an oncoming team.

It happened so fast, Georgie hadn't time to react. But realization quickly crashed down upon her. Her heart jumped to her throat. Both the boy and Luke could have been killed.

Traffic came to a standstill. The farmer guiding the boy's wagon surged to his feet, his face florid. Shaking his fist, he cursed the driver of the automobile.

Men from every wagon in the vicinity jumped to the ground like corn popping from a pan. The automobile driver swung open his door, accidentally cutting off an approaching couple on a bicycle-built-for-two.

They swerved, their bike teetering. Wrestling the handlebars, the rider at the back put out one trousered leg and then the other, kicking up dirt. In front of him, the woman rider screeched, slapping a hand onto her hat while desperately hanging on with the other.

Georgie held her breath. The man somehow righted the bicycle and continued on his way. Releasing a whoosh of air, she turned her attention back to Luke. A large press of bodies blocked her view.

She tried to push through, but they were too compressed. Standing on tiptoes, she hopped. It was no use. She couldn't see a thing.

When the crowd finally broke, the boy had been returned to his mother, his eyes bright with excitement. Men shook Luke's hand, pounded his back, and offered to buy him a beer when they reached the pavilion.

He made light of his actions, as if they were nothing out of the ordinary. His freshly laundered and ironed overalls were caked with dirt. His hair mussed. His hat crushed.

In that moment, as she stood on the periphery watching him slap the dust from his pant leg, punch his hat back into shape, and chuckle at something someone said, it hit her. She was falling in love with him. And it had nothing to do with his devastating good looks and intoxicating kisses.

It had to do with his uncanny ability to always be there when she needed him. With his willingness to serve others and repair their phone lines no matter what the hour. With his willingness to respect her views, yet not be manipulated by them. With his tenderness toward Bettina, Fritz, and the other children in her Junior Audubon Society. With his capacity for acting quickly and decisively in times of danger.

He glanced her way, his eyes stalling. Though vehicles still rolled by and men still shouted and horses still whinnied, for her all sounds receded. All movement ceased. All of time stood still.

Glancing neither left nor right, he walked toward her. Men parted like a curtain on opening night. And then he was there. Something about his eyes unsettled her, but a curl slipped down against his forehead, distracting her.

She reached up, pushing the curl back into place. "You could have been killed."

"I'm fine. I was never in any danger. I saw the other team coming. I knew I had time to get the boy out of the way."

"You saw all that in the split second before you hurled yourself into the middle of this mess?"

"Yes."

"I don't know how." She bit her cheeks. "You scared me, Luke."

"I'm sorry."

A wave of vulnerability swept over her. The what-ifs, the what-could-have-beens, the what-could-bes. "You may kiss me now."

He swept his gaze across the panorama just above and behind her. A mixture of chagrin and amusement touched his lips. "Much as I hate to pass up such a sweet offer, I think I'd better take a rain check. I'm not sure now's a good time, exactly."

She blinked. The sounds slowly returned. Creaking wheels. Jingling harnesses. Merry voices. She looked around.

The crowd had dispersed and she was no longer standing in the middle of the street, but on the edge of the boardwalk. She had no recollection of getting there.

"You all right?" he asked.

No. "Just a little too much excitement, I think."

"You want me to take you home?"

Shaking herself, she took a deep breath. "No, no. I'll be fine. I'm just . . ."

What? she thought. *In love with you?*

She swallowed. "The parade should be starting soon. I don't want to miss the Patricks in our float."

"You sure you're okay?"

"Yes." She gave him a small smile. "I'm fine."

"You're awfully pale."

"Am I?" Touching her cheeks, she realized she still wasn't wearing gloves. She removed them from the hidden pocket of her skirt and quickly pulled them on. "Well, I'm sure it's nothing a walk downtown won't cure."

If he wasn't completely convinced, he at least didn't argue. Placing a hand beneath her elbow, he fell in step with others on the sidewalk and guided her toward Main.

In his line of work, Luke didn't have much opportunity for play and absolutely none for festivals. He'd attended a boxing match a couple of years ago, but for crowd control, not pleasure.

Today, however, he had full license to enjoy Brenham's Maifest. He'd still do some work. He'd keep an eye out for his primary suspects — Necker, Duane, Blesinger, and the two farmers Finkel and Ragston. He'd see whom they interacted with. See if they were bold enough to join one other. See if he could discover a connection between them and the milliner — if there even was one. He'd also be interested to see if the betting man from the shooting tournament

— Hurless Swanning — made an appearance.

For the most part, though, he could enjoy examining the stock exhibits, listening to orations, watching the Maypole dance, attending a Texas A&M College baseball game, and best of all, taking Georgie to tonight's dance. He glanced at her, his eyes drawn for the umpteenth time to her animated expression, her wide smile, and the tiny mole beneath her lips.

Her color had much improved since his rescue of the boy. He'd tried to play it down, hoping word would not get around with so much else going on. But already several townsfolk had approached him, saying they'd been told of his efforts and wanted to thank him.

He sighed. Being undercover was not one of his strong suits. He often acted first and thought later. But what else could he have done? He couldn't exactly leave the boy to his own devices.

Still, his actions could undermine the impression he was trying to give. An ordinary telephone repairman wouldn't be expected to jump in front of an oncoming team. He hoped word of his swift reaction wouldn't get back to Necker.

Georgie pointed to the Maifest Queen's

float pulled by high-stepping iron-grays with white tasseled trappings draped across their backs. Luke admired the driver as he kept his horses in perfect time to the music of the marching band.

This year's theme was the lily, the violet, and the rose. The milliner's daughter, Lillie Ottfried, had been elected reigning queen and sat in white splendor, clutching a lily in one hand and waving with the other.

White, purple, and red flowers festooned her carriage's frame while evergreens and arbor vines wreathed the supports of its canopy. The finest decoration by far, however, was the collection of little girls sitting at Miss Ottfried's feet. Crowns of dainty white flowers rested upon heads of golden curls, their frothy white dresses poofing about them. A more lovely group of train bearers he'd never seen.

Miss Ottfried's gaze traveled across the crowd, snagging on Georgie. The girl's smile stiffened. Switching her flowers to the other hand, she turned to the opposite side of the street and began to wave again.

Georgie looked down, her teeth catching her lower lip.

Reaching for her hand, he tucked it in his elbow and gave it a squeeze.

Two carriages containing the queen's

maids of honor followed, with the speakers' wagonette next, the Hook and Ladder Company, the Bellville brass band, and finally, the decorated wagons and floats representing German mythology, German history, local businesses, and social societies.

Luke recalled his hometown's parades on the Fourth of July. One year, instead of wrapping his little wooden wagon with bunting, he'd painted its sides red with big white stars. When he was done, the stars looked more like giant circles, but he'd never forgotten the pride he felt pulling his little brother behind him in such a finely turned-out cart.

This parade, however, was nothing like home's. He couldn't imagine New York City itself putting out a finer, more elaborate show. A two-seated surrey with a yellow-and-black scheme passed by. A single white horse drew a creation in pink chrysanthemums. And then Georgie's float, its red-rose cardinal flying high over the procession.

Ladies ooohed, gentleman hooted, children pointed. From inside the carriage, Mr. and Mrs. Patrick saw the two of them, their smiles widening, their waves more insistent. Laughing, Georgie used her entire arm to wave back, jumping up and down like a schoolgirl.

A well of protectiveness bubbled up inside him. She was so young. So naïve. And she had no idea he wasn't a telephone repairman.

His impromptu marriage proposal flashed through his mind. Never once had he thought the break-in might jeopardize her reputation. He'd been too long on the move. Too out of touch with what it was like to live in a town where everybody knew everybody else's business.

Had he known what it would come down to, he'd have led Necker and Duane to the float. But he hadn't known. He should have, though. He should have.

Georgie clasped her hands together, resting them against her lips as she regarded the back of the Plumage League's carriage. Thanks to the Patricks, it appeared as if her reputation would remain intact.

And though he was grateful, he was also, strangely enough, disappointed there'd be no need for a wedding. He found himself wondering what changes he'd have made if she'd said yes.

Would he quit his job? Two months ago the thought would have been ludicrous. Now, however, when he lay down at night, instead of dwelling on lawbreakers and hideouts and desperados, he dwelt on Georgie.

Georgie wearing a blue gingham apron in a bright, sunny kitchen. Clamping her tongue between her teeth when she withdrew his splinters. Laughing when he said something which somehow amused her. Frowning when he refused to capitulate or agree with her.

Even during the days she'd haunt his thoughts. His duties as troubleman required time on lonely roads and quiet hillsides. More and more he'd catch himself ruminating like a lovesick swain.

He'd picture her feeding birds out of her hand. Protecting them by beating off cats, educating children, or spearheading a countywide campaign. He'd picture her at the switchboard looking out her window with opera glasses and exclaiming over every species that visited her fiefdom.

And now, he pictured her squaring up to her intruders, determined to protect those hats without thought to her own safety. His blood turned cold. Thank the good Lord he'd been there. No telling what would've happened.

A bystander jostled her, momentarily bumping her into his side. Brief as the contact was, desire flared within him.

She looked up, her face suddenly solemn and mirroring his inner turmoil.

He placed a hand against her waist, under the guise of steadying her, though she'd already righted herself. "Careful. You all right?"

She zigzagged her gaze, as if she couldn't decide which of his eyes would give her a glimpse into his soul. He grazed his knuckles along the buttons running up her back, the urge to kiss her overwhelming.

Tearing his eyes away, he looked around for an alley, an alcove — anything that would give them a moment's privacy. But there was nothing. Just wall-to-wall people.

Another jostle. Another bump. This time, he splayed his hand wide, holding her against him for the briefest of moments.

I'm not who you think I am. I'm Lucious Landrum. Texas Ranger of Company "A" and, God help me, but I think I'm in love with you.

Her lips tilted up. Her lashes swept down.

His stomach clenched. Had he said that out loud?

But no, she returned to her own two feet and tugged her gloves into place as if his world had not come crashing down around him.

"You want to head to the pavilion?" She shook out her skirt. "The queen's corona-

364

tion will start as soon as the last of the floats arrive."

He extended his arm. "I wouldn't miss it."

With her tiny hand tucked inside his elbow, they turned onto North Street and headed to Firemen's Park. If his arm skimmed her side or her skirts brushed his leg, neither tried to correct it. But both tried to ignore it.

CHAPTER TWENTY-EIGHT

"I planted *die* Cotton pretty thick," Finkel said. He'd exchanged his overalls for a fancy plaid suit. " 'One for *den* Cutworm, one for *die* Crow, one for *den* Blackbird, and one to grow.' "

Luke chuckled at the German rendition of the old saying, but Georgie tuned out his response.

The sun splashed warmth onto her cheeks, the sky looking as if heaven had been swept clean with a broom. A vast lawn of emerald grass provided a cushion for ladies in wide-brimmed hats and high-necked bodices, their bustlines covered with pouty fronts. Behind them, skirts and trains flowed over ample hips, giving them the popular S-silhouette.

A young man who'd outgrown the length of his trousers removed his hat and bowed deeply to a group of ladies close to Georgie's age. All but one giggled behind their fans.

The sober member was younger than the rest, her heart clearly on her sleeve. She'd yet to receive her womanly curves and sought to help nature along with rows of frills inside her bodice, achieving a rather unnatural ripple effect.

As the girl passed the tall Maypole erected for the day's festivities, she grasped one of its long, trailing ribbons, allowing it to slither through her fingers. But the boy never noticed. He had eyes for another.

A scissortailed flycatcher, twice as long in tail as in body, swooped over some buttonbush, catching insects on the wing and drawing Georgie's attention to the plethora of exhibits lining the perimeter of the park and beyond.

Women manning vegetable booths set out trays of beans, peas, okra, cucumbers, and squash. A roped-off area held a stack of burlap sacks and a sign for races. Men crouched over a long log and soaped it with bars of lye.

The squeal of a pig caused many to turn toward a fenced-in area. One man held the animal by the head while another greased it up.

It was then she saw Mr. Ottfried's exhibit. He'd brought hats of every color and style. Some chic, some dainty, some somber. All held flagrant bird parts. Attached to the roof of his tent, a painted sign with curlicues and fancy lettering swung in the breeze. *Today Only . . . 2-for-1.*

She wondered again if he had anything to do with the break-in. He hadn't been one of the intruders, of that she was certain. Still, he stood to gain the most from her troubles.

Scanning the area for the Plumage League's location, she whispered an "Excuse me" to Luke, then released his arm. On the opposite side of the park, their exhibit spanned two booths. One for the hats, another for the hat walk.

She veered toward it, stunned at the entries crowding every surface. High, puffy toques, tricornes with wavy brims, and stylish short-back sailors congested the tables. In the corner, summer leghorn hats spilled out of a chiffonier's open drawers. Opposite it, an open steamer trunk sat on its end, box turbans and shepherdess-style hats stacked inside its compartments.

None had bird parts.

She stopped in front of the booth, unable to comprehend where such abundance had come from.

The mayor's daughter, Rachel Zach, lovely in a white lingerie dress and matching Gainsborough hat, caught her eye and smiled. "Can you believe it? We've even more under the tables."

Robbi Bittle, a recently wed League member, moved beside Rachel and pointed to an oak parlor stand. Atop it lay a ledger, pen, and inkwell. "Wait until you see our pledge sheets."

Georgie angled the booklet toward her. Signature after signature filled its columns. She flipped back a page. More signatures. She turned back another and another.

Mrs. Bittle clasped her hands in front of her. "Three hundred thirty-seven so far."

Georgie shook her head. "I don't understand. How . . . ?"

"It's all Mrs. Patrick's doing," Rachel said. "You know how she is when she's on a mission. There isn't a person on God's green earth who can say no to her."

Mrs. Bittle pointed toward the grandstand. "The winning hats — the ones Mr. Mistrot will sell in his store — are over there."

She turned. A large pavilion with fresh robes of white sat amidst a wooded grove. Beneath its roof a thousand chairs provided ample room for those in attendance. To the right of the stage, a display of five hats rested on a cloth-covered table.

"Whose hat won?" Georgie asked.

"Janice Spuhler's."

She spun around. "Mrs. Spuhler? Really?"

At Mrs. Bittle's affirmative nod, Georgie ran her gaze across the crowd, hoping to spot the unassuming widow who didn't say much but had a sparkle in her eye and never missed a thing.

"She was late finishing it," Rachel said, "and didn't have time to bring it by your house yesterday."

Georgie bit her lip. "So it wasn't burned."

"No. And it's absolutely divine. It's the one in the center on the highest hat form."

Before she could look, Luke caught her attention.

Heading toward her, his strides were long and unwavering. The straps of his overalls divided wide shoulders clad in a white chambray shirt. The denim bib was small compared to the breadth of his chest.

Reaching them, he glanced at the women manning the booth and touched the brim of his hat. "Good morning, ladies. You're looking lovely, as usual."

"Mr. Palmer."

He held his arm out to Georgie, his eyes conveying pleasure and admiration. "The band's taken their seats on the rostrum. Should we head to the pavilion?"

Nodding, she thanked the girls, then hooked her hand in his elbow. She'd never been escorted to a festival before. Much like the young girl she'd seen earlier, she'd always been on the outside looking in.

But today, she was with the handsomest man in attendance. And his overalls were growing on her by the minute.

"As president of the Plumage League, I'll be crowning the Maifest Queen," she said. "They've reserved us seats up front."

He changed course, heading toward the royal procession, which had parked just outside the pavilion. Courtiers laid a red carpet walk for Her Royal Highness. Squires stood ready to escort her when the signal was given.

Luke and Georgie slipped into their seats just as the band played "God Save the Queen."

"That's my cue," Georgie whispered. She had no trouble discerning which hat Mrs. Spuhler had made. Lilies-of-the-valley trimmed its brim. A collection of white silk loops covered its bandeau, while streamers of polka dot netting held the confection in place.

She fell in line behind the little Montgomery and Cutler cousins proudly carrying their queen's train. After all were assembled on stage, the band concluded their song, the crowd quieted.

Judge Yoakum presented Miss Ottfried with her regal insignia of rank and the scepter of sovereignty. The girl smiled her thanks, then turned to Georgie, her eyes frosting.

For the first time, Georgie realized this honor would be bestowed upon the girl not only by her father's nemesis, but with a crown in direct protest to her father's very livelihood.

Georgie's step faltered. The election by popular ballot for Maifest Queen hadn't been held until this morning. It never occurred to her the recipient would be Miss Ottfried.

Still, the winning hat was deliciously stylish. Would be the envy of any woman.

Swallowing, she lifted her arms and settled it on Miss Ottfried's head, carefully securing it with a hatpin. She smoothed a streamer of netting underneath the girl's chin, up the other side, and began to tie the ends together.

Of the same height, they stood toe to toe, nose to nose. Georgie lowered her gaze. The girl had the loveliest eyes she'd ever seen. A light, light brown surrounded by a dark brown ring.

"You look beautiful," Georgie whispered. And she meant it.

In a lily-white moiré silk dress with bead trimmings and pearl ornaments, Lillie bore herself with dignity. "Thank you."

Georgie finished the bow, fluffed it, then stepped back and made a low curtsy. The applauding crowd cheered. Miss Ottfried stepped forward to make her acceptance speech while Georgie slipped off the platform and back to her seat.

Luke surreptitiously squeezed her hand, but she didn't dare look at him. Her feelings were too jumbled. Too confused. Not just about him, but about the Ottfrieds.

She'd thought of the milliner as an object, an obstruction, a hindrance to her birds. Not as a father with a beautiful and gracious daughter.

Behind that thought came the realization he'd had to sit in the audience and watch. Watch the bane of his existence crown his most treasured possession with a hat representing a cause he diametrically opposed. A crown his daughter would be required to wear the entire day.

Heat moved from Georgie's neck clear up to her hairline. She forced the blush away, refusing to feel guilty about campaigning for her birds. Nor would she feel guilty about the hat. It was stunning. Gorgeous. And his daughter looked every inch the queen.

The ledger at their booth with three hundred thirty-seven signatures flashed through her mind. Three hundred thirty-seven women had pledged not to wear or purchase hats with bird parts on them. Even hats on special, 2-for-1.

She took a deep breath. Before the day was through, more would certainly add their names to the list. Had Mr. Ottfried brought any non-bird hats to sell? What if the women misunderstood and thought they had to quit frequenting shops which *carried* hats with bird parts? What would happen to his business? His wife? Lillie Ottfried?

On stage, Lillie took a seat upon her throne, her train bearers arranging her gown amidst lilies, violets, and roses. The fire chief stepped to the podium, delivering a history of Brenham and Washington County, recounting incidents and legends that had been passed down since Richard Fox Brenham arrived at Washington on the Brazos in 1836.

Georgie pictured the hats on Ottfried's tables. For every one an innocent bird had died. She searched the wooded copse beyond the stage. Somewhere in there a waxwing might be sitting politely digesting a meal of berries without disturbing a thing around it. An oriole might be weaving grasses with far more precision than any basket a person could make. A whippoor-will might be ridding the town of mosquitoes, gnats, June bugs, and katydids.

No. She would not feel sorry for Mr. Ottfried. Especially when there were things he could do to compensate. He had only to look to Mr. Mistrot's example for ways to cleverly construct artificial birds, feathers, and quills.

She had nothing personal against Mr. Ottfried, nor his family. And if he mended his ways, she would quit her campaign against his millinery. Until then, however, she would stand firm and continue to do all she could to save the birds.

CHAPTER TWENTY-NINE

Though it wasn't oppressively warm, many patrons, including Luke's suspects, sampled the beer imported clear from St. Louis at Thirsty Man's booth. Necker, Duane, Finkel, and Ragston had spent part of the day with their families, and a good deal more of it with each other.

If Frank Comer was in attendance, he was keeping well away from them, though an out-of-town fellow by the name of Prysborski received an overly warm welcome from the suspects. Luke had briefly visited with him and each of the others, met their families, then sat with the men during the baseball game while Georgie took a turn manning the Plumage League's booth.

He picked up no new information. Still, the more time he spent with them, the more they would grow to trust him. No mention was made of their foray into Georgie's home, nor of any upcoming train job.

But there was plenty of talk about Hurless Swanning, the man from the shooting tournament. Seemed he'd lost his life in a runaway carriage down in Cut 'N Shoot. While Blesinger and Duane shared what details they'd heard, Necker, Finkel, and Ragston remained strangely quiet.

After the game, Luke and Georgie waited for the sun to completely set and the evening's dance to begin. They wandered through the pleasure grounds, listened to the fiddlers' contest, and visited with the townsfolk.

Though the hobby-horse man still collected two pennies from anxious boys and girls, the line to his rocking steed was beginning to wane. Georgie pointed to one of her students as he was awarded a prize for catching the greased pig, then smiled over the fact he'd ruined his suit accomplishing the feat. In the center of the park, twelve charming little girls wove ribbons around the Maypole.

He noted Bettina watching the dancers when she thought no one was looking. Steering Georgie that direction, he pretended surprise when they happened upon her.

"Good evening, Bettina." He tipped his hat.

"Howdy, Mr. Luke. Miss Georgie." Her braids had long since come unraveled, her chin had an angry scuff, and more filth than usual coated her sack dress. But the swelling in her jaw had subsided some.

"I haven't seen you much today," Georgie said, reaching out to repair the girl's hair.

She immediately drew back. "I been busy."

Georgie let her hands drop. "Doing what?"

"Played me a game o' ball with the fellers. Shot Mr. Weiss's mules with my slingshot. Put a lizard down Birdie Jones's dress. And helped Pa home 'cause he done forgot how to walk."

Blinking, Georgie's lips parted. "You mustn't put lizards down young ladies' necks — down anyone's neck."

Bettina squared her shoulders. "Weren't my idea. Fred Hall paid me a penny to do it."

"Fred Hall? Why, he wouldn't do that. He adores Birdie."

A sly grin lifted one side of the girl's mouth. "I reckon that's why he spent so much time comfortin' her afterwards."

Georgie choked.

"What'd you do with your penny?" Luke asked, chuckling.

"Got me some rock candy."

He reached into his pocket. "Well, I can't

help but notice Miss Georgie's about the only gal out here who doesn't have a hat. Would you take this nickel over to the Plumage League's booth and try the hat walk for her?"

Bettina tried to act nonchalant, but the spark in her eyes was unmistakable. "If ya want me to."

"I'd very much appreciate it."

Spinning, she raced to get in line. There'd been a steady stream of players all day. He figured the ladies had raised quite a bit of money for their cause.

"That was thoughtful of you, Luke."

"She's a good kid." He guided her toward the booth. "I'm not sure she's had anything to eat other than that rock candy, though."

"Probably not."

"Well, it's almost suppertime. Why don't we take her with us when we stop at the Ladies' Restaurant booth?"

"That'd be lovely, though I can't imagine her eating a whole meal. What if she and I shared?"

He nodded. "We'll see."

They walked in comfortable silence, feeling no need to fill in the gap. The smell of pig, flowers, food, and beer floated on the breeze, its breath ruffling the fringe on Georgie's yoke. Children laughed, vendors hawked their wares, and mothers called for their little ones.

As Luke and Georgie neared the hat walk, she peeked up at him. "Does it bother you that I'm not wearing a hat?"

He lifted his brows. "Not at all. I was just using it as an excuse to let her play the game."

"Good. I'm glad."

"You don't like hats?"

"I love hats."

"Then, why didn't you wear one?"

"They were burned up along with the rest."

He stopped short. "What do you mean?"

"I guess the culprits couldn't tell the difference between my hats and the contest entries. So they burned them all."

Exhaling quickly through his teeth, he dragged a hand across his mouth. It never occurred to him her personal hats would be in with the others. "Were they stored in the same place?"

"No, no. Mine were in the corner by my wardrobe." She shrugged. "I imagine to a man, a hatbox is a hatbox."

He scoured his memory, vaguely remembering a set of hats in the spot she mentioned. But, as she said, he never gave it a thought. He hadn't wanted to give Necker

380

any reason to hurt her.

Sighing, he slid his hand down to hers. "I'm sorry."

"Me too," she whispered. "It takes me a long time to save for a hat."

He looked at Bettina filing in for her turn at the game. "Come on. Maybe it's your lucky day."

Inside the roped-off area, twenty crate lids lay in a circle on the ground, each with a number painted on it. Females of all ages stood on a lid, along with one scowling baseball player from Texas A&M. He'd donned a cadet uniform and slicked down his hair, but Luke remembered his three-run homer, which gave A&M the victory.

A group of hecklers around the perimeter offered advice to their out-of-place teammate. Luke bit his cheek. Clearly, the boy had lost a dare of some kind.

When all were in position, a member of the Men's Glee Club played "Old Heel Fly" on his banjo.

As long as the music played, the participants stepped from lid to lid. At the end of the chorus, the music stopped, the players stopped, and a number was drawn.

Standing on the eighteenth lid, Bettina searched the crowd until she found Luke and Georgie. Luke held up crossed fingers, and she responded in kind.

Mrs. Lee, the lawyer's wife, drew a number from a decorated basket. "Four!"

The A&M cadet had already begun to leave the circle when he whipped his head around. His buddies howled, grabbing their stomachs and doubling over with laughter.

"Woo! You got you a winner this time, Mrs. Lee!" one of them shouted.

"Pick out a right purty one for Daniel, here. He's especially fond o' the ones with lots o' ribbons."

Smiling gamely, Mrs. Lee handed the cadet a hat that looked like a giant mushroom with braid, satin, and lace. The young man flushed with embarrassment until he took in the expressions of his lady competitors. Even Bettina was besotted with the confection.

A slow smile formed on his face as he tucked his military cap into the back of his waistband and replaced it with the feminine piece of frippery, securing the ties beneath his chin. His buddies roared.

"Well, I've got me a fine hat for tonight's dance, fellas," he boomed. "But what I don't have is a gal I can give it to." He paused, giving meaningful looks to the girls he favored. "But if'n I could persuade one of these lovely ladies to accompany me tonight,

I might be talked into lettin' her take my prize home for safekeepin'.'"

Bettina immediately stepped forward. "I'll go with ya. But I don't want yer hat. You can give it ta my friend, Miss Georgie."

Daniel's teammates broke into another round of hilarity, but the cadet was not to be put off. Tweaking Bettina's cheek, he winked. "That's a mighty tempting offer, miss, but I'm afraid you're a bit too short to serve as a suitable dancing partner." He ran his gaze over a young woman closer to his age. "Might there be another interested party?"

The entire group of spectators held their breath. Taking him up on his offer would be nothing short of scandalous, but the hat looked ridiculous on him and sang a siren's song to the girls.

Shrugging, Daniel turned to Mrs. Lee. "Well, looks like it'll be me and my hat going to the ball. Such a shame, too, for —"

"I'll go."

Daniel spun around, the hat a second behind and falling to the side. The young lady stepped forward, a vision in her white frilly dress and dark brown hair.

As Daniel pushed the hat up into place, his Adam's apple bobbed. His friends stared in stunned silence.

Still, it didn't take long for the cadet to recover. Straightening, he untied the hat, placed it on the lady's head, tied it in a tight boy's bow, then stepped back. "Miss Grant, would you care to join me at the dance?"

"It would be my pleasure, Mr. August." Joheather Grant, the daughter of a new phone subscriber west of town, laid her hand on his arm.

All parted to let them through. Just before clearing the crowd, he slanted a victorious glance at his friends, all with comical expressions of shock.

Georgie sighed. Luke flashed her a glance. What a romantic she was. Again, he felt a pang of guilt about her hats. Some way or another, he'd have to make it up to her.

"Sorry, Mr. Luke," Bettina barked, her legs straddled, arms akimbo. "I done tried."

"And it was a valiant try, missy. Thank you." He placed a hand on his stomach. "Did you hear that? My stomach is growling something fierce. Where's the best place to find supper, do you think?"

"Them ladies over yonder been cookin' up a storm all day. I'd go there if'n I was you."

Frowning, he nodded. "I thought about that, but I've noticed Miss Georgie doesn't clean her plate the way she ought."

Bettina's eyes widened. "She don't?"

"Nope. And I don't like wasting good coin on food which doesn't get eaten."

The girl scratched her jaw. "Well, that's a problem, then."

"I have an idea," Georgie said. "What if Bettina and I shared a plate?"

"Well, now. There's an idea." He looked at Bettina. "You think you could help me out again? It'd only be through supper; then you'd be free to go back and do whatever it is you had planned."

Slipping her hands in her pockets, she pretended to consider it. "Well, I reckon I could. But after supper you're gonna be on yer own. I can't be holdin' yer hand all night, you know."

He bit back a smile. "I understand." He extended a hand in an after-you gesture. "Lead the way."

The girl marched toward the concession booth, arms swinging, hair bouncing.

Georgie slipped her hand through his elbow, leaned into his arm, and mouthed a *thank you.*

Smiling, he followed Bettina at a more sedate pace.

CHAPTER THIRTY

Instead of reviving her, supper made Georgie sleepier than ever. She'd only snatched a bit of slumber the night before. Surely Luke couldn't be much better off.

But if he were tired, he gave no sign of it.

The pavilion had been cleared of its chairs, leaving its polished and waxed floor open for the two hundred couples who'd followed the queen and her escort in during the Grand March.

Whisking Georgie around the floor to "Hannah Go Hide Your Bloomers," Luke led her with a confident hand and steady step. After the last note, the assembly applauded. Luke and some of the others let out loud whistles.

Stifling a yawn, she swayed.

"You all right?" he asked, leading her from the floor.

"I'm having a marvelous time, Luke, but last night's beginning to catch up with me."

His expression softened. "You tired?"

"I am."

"Well, come on, then. I'll walk you home."

"Can we rest a minute first?"

"Of course." But there wasn't an empty bench or chair to be found. "How about a piggyback ride?"

She gave a small huff of laughter.

Pulling her hand further into his arm, he tightened his hold. "Let's head on home. We can always stop along the way for a rest."

She nodded her response and they meandered through the park, finally reaching North Street. A jam of buckboards with heavy-eyed children and content parents crawled along the road. Crickets competed with the faint strains of "In the Good Ol' Summer Time" coming from the now distant pavilion.

A cart full of Texas A&M baseball players pulled alongside them, waiting in line behind the other wagons. The young men lounged against its sides, talking softly and swaying in time to the music.

At the chorus, one of them began to sing along in a clear tenor voice.

In the good ol' summer time,
In the good ol' summer time,

Strolling thro' the shady lanes,
With your baby mine;

Luke slid Georgie's hand down to his,
then intertwined their fingers. One by one,
the other baseball players added their voices
to the tenor's. Not in a boisterous manner,
but in harmony as pleasing as any barber-
shop quartet she'd ever heard.

You hold her hand and she holds yours,
And that's a very good sign,
That she's your tootsey wootsey, in
The good ol' summer time.

A soft breeze lifted a tendril from her
neck, some of her curls loosening after the
long day's activities. Ahead of them, a
couple in a spring-top buggy lent their
voices as well.

To swim in the pool, you'd play hooky
    from school,
Good old summer time;
You'd play ring-a-rosie with Jim, Kate and
    Josie,
Good old summer time.

She smiled, thinking of the days when she,
her brother, and her little sister thought
nothing of running barefoot, climbing trees,

and gigging frogs. More and more voices from surrounding wagons joined in.

> Those days full of pleasure we now
>   fondly treasure,
> When we never thought it a crime,
> To go stealing cherries, with face brown
>   as berries,
> Good old summer time.

Luke slid his arm around her waist, tucking her against him and keeping his strides slow and small to match hers. Closing her eyes, she rested her head on his shoulder, trusting him to steer her.

> In the good ol' summer time,
> In the good ol' summer time,
> Strolling thro' the shady lanes,
> With your baby mine;
> You hold her hand and she holds yours,
> And that's a very good sign,
> That she's your tootsey wootsey, in
> The good ol' summer time.

The silence at the end of the song was full of kinship and belonging. The Bible might say faith, hope, and love, with the greatest being love. But Georgie had discovered in a German community like Brenham, it was cards, dominoes, and singing, with the greatest being singing.

Luke turned a corner. She fluttered her eyes open but left her head against him. He was cutting down Academy Street instead of staying on North the whole way.

"Do you have brothers and sisters?" she asked.

Cicadas kept up a thrum as steady as her heartbeat.

"I had a brother growing up."

"Me too. And a sister."

He said nothing.

"Did the two of you steal cherries?" she asked, referring to the song.

"Not cherries. But we got into plenty of trouble."

She smiled. "I miss those days."

"I miss my brother."

"You don't see him much?"

"He's dead."

A distant dog barked. She lifted her head a bit to look up at him. "When did he die?"

"In ninety-six."

Sighing, she closed her eyes again. 1896. Her brother had died in '95 of a cold which moved into his chest. "What happened to him?"

"He was shot and killed."

Jerking straight, her eyes flew open. "What?"

He stared into the distance, his face slackening. "It's a long story."

"How old was he?"

"Nineteen."

Her chest tightened. "Oh, Luke. I'm so sorry."

"Not as sorry as I am."

Something about his tone gave her pause. His remark didn't express grief so much as it did self-reproach.

"Tell me." The words were out before she could collect them. But he'd taken her so off guard.

Heaving a sigh, he slowly continued down Academy. This time, he didn't take her hand. "I was fifteen, Alec just eleven months behind me in age. But he always seemed a lot younger. Maybe because he was so much smaller than me. I don't know. But this particular year, I considered myself a full-grown man."

She didn't know if it was the moonlight, this day they'd spent together, or the experience they'd shared the night before, but on some primal level she knew this was not something he talked about often — if ever. Unclipping the fan from her chatelaine, she opened it and stirred up a gentle draft.

"I did a man's part on our farm. I cut and hauled wood to town for money. I spent my nights hunting raccoons in the dark woods with my hounds. I called on the young ladies." He took a deep breath. "And I developed a taste for whiskey."

A light in the window of a home up ahead was snuffed out, plunging that side of the house into darkness. A few seconds later, the light in the room next to it went out as well.

He slid his hands in his pockets. "One night, I took Alec with me to the still-house and we tasted a bit more than we should've."

She glanced down. Her brother had only been thirteen when he died. Not nearly old enough to have sown any wild oats. But she knew well the effect liquor could have on a man who imbibed too much. Her stepfather was living proof of that.

"On our way home," Luke continued, "I talked him into racing down Main Street and shooting out the windows of businesses closed up for the night. I'd do one side, he'd do the other, then we'd compare to see who shot the most the fastest." He shook his head. "Alec and I were both crack shots, even then. But he was no match for me. I'd already made it to the other end of Main, when the sheriff caught Alec only halfway finished."

The sidewalk ended. He cupped her elbow, assisting her with the transition from board to dirt, then let his hand drop. "Before I could organize a rescue party, the sheriff whisked Alec away to the state prison, where he served for three years."

She closed her fan, pressing it against her waist. Three years? For shooting out windows? "That seems an awfully severe punishment for a boyhood prank."

"It was because of me. The sheriff and I had had many collisions. I was hotheaded, wiry, and fearless, and had yet to develop any moral principles. My Achilles' heel, though, was my brother. And Sheriff Glaser knew it. He had connections with the boys over at State. All he had to do was throw out some trumped-up charges and Alec's fate was sealed."

She reattached her fan, then pulled off her gloves one finger at a time before slipping them into her hidden pocket. "So he was eighteen when he got out?"

"We both were. I went to meet him and bring him home, but when I arrived I found out he'd been released three days earlier." He shook his head. "I tracked him for weeks on end, catching a trail, then losing it, then catching it again until it finally went cold."

"Did he know you were looking for him?"

"He knew, but he didn't have much use for a brother who turned tail and ran instead of coming back to rescue him from the sheriff."

"Did he know you'd planned to go back for him, once you had some help?"

"I wrote to him. Told him. But he never responded or acknowledged any of my letters."

At Cottonwood Street, they turned right. Her cottage was two lots down. "What happened to him?"

"He joined up with a gang of ne'er-do-wells. I tried off and on to find him and several times thought I'd come close. But I could only be away from my job for so long."

She bit her lip. "He was killed while running from the law, then?"

"I don't exactly know. All I know is out of the blue one day, Ma received a farewell letter from him along with a photograph. It was of Alec laid out in a long pine box."

Her heart constricted. Reaching over, she clasped his hand.

He squeezed it. "He'd evidently given instructions to his comrades to send the letter home if anything were to ever happen to him. At the time, I was a grocer in a neighboring town."

She blinked. A grocer?

"I went home immediately and verified the letter had been written in Alec's hand. In it, he confessed to an endless list of crimes. Everything from stealing bread when he was hungry to robbing stagecoaches."

She sucked in her breath, grappling for something to say. "Well, at least he confessed. That's a good thing."

Glancing at her, he shook his head. "He wasn't apologizing. As a matter of fact, he didn't show any remorse whatsoever."

"None? Are you sure?"

"Positive. I never did find out who he was running with, but ever since, I've had a strong distaste for men who play outside the law."

She immediately thought of Frank Comer, the man adored by citizens all across the state. She recalled her thrill at coming face-to-face with him during the train robbery. Her defense of him to Luke and his fierce reaction. Her realization last night that Comer was not at all a man to esteem.

They'd reached her home. The Mai tree still leaned against her porch. Had it only been last night when Luke delivered it?

He opened the gate for her.

Instead of walking through, she turned to face him. "I'm sorry I revered Frank

Comer."

He looked at her sharply.

"I know I was somewhat enamored of him. But that was before last night. Before I realized he's nothing more than an unprincipled man who preys on those weaker than himself. And I'm sorry."

Clearing his throat, he looked at everything but her. She frowned. Instead of soothing him, her apology seemed to have discomfited him. Perhaps he regretted sharing his brother's story with her.

She stepped toward him and placed a hand on his cheek.

He stilled, finally making eye contact with her.

"Thank you. Thank you for today. Thank you for helping me last night. Thank you for the Mai tree. And thank you for telling me about your brother." Stretching onto tiptoes, she kissed his cheek. "Good night."

She slipped through the gate.

He grasped her wrist. "Wait. I want to check your house first."

The raw skin beneath her cuff stung at his grasp, but it wasn't nearly as disturbing as the thought of someone waiting inside for her. "Surely you don't think they'll come back? Maifest is over."

He released her. "I think it highly unlikely

they'll bother you again, but I still want to check. I'll go around back and enter from that direction. You wait here. If something happens or if I don't come out, go to the nearest neighbor and send for the sheriff."

Nodding, she hugged herself, a crawly sensation skittering up her arms and neck. He disappeared down the left side of the cottage.

Every sound intensified. The cicadas increased in volume. A gurgling armadillo rooting somewhere close by caused a shiver to pass through her body.

With short, tentative steps, she tiptoed toward the bench beneath the oak in her yard. A rustling in its branches made her jump back. Muffling a squeal, she pressed her knuckles against her lips, searching its boughs. Nothing moved.

Still, she decided to wait where she was. Light had yet to appear behind her windows. Was he checking it in the dark? Her fingers brushed the fan hanging from her waist. She closed her fist around it. What was taking so long?

At a rustling to her right, she spun around. A large rodent-looking animal scurried between two bushes. Unable to contain a startled cry, she scrambled backward into

the fence, grasping its planks and squeezing.

It's only a possum. Calm down.

But her heartbeat refused to obey, threatening to fly right out of her chest. Glancing
at the cottage, she took a deep breath. How
long should she wait before going for help?
A flare of light sparked inside the living
area, then settled into a glow. She tracked
its progress from the main room to her
bedroom.

She swallowed, trying to remember if
she'd made her bed or cleaned up after Mrs.
Patrick did her hair, but she couldn't
remember. Had she even put her nightdress
away?

Her cheeks heated. The light moved back
into the living area, then to the kitchen.
Finally, he returned to the front and opened
the door, stepping onto the porch.

"It's fine. You can come in." His voice was
soft, low.

She tried to approach with as much com-
posure as she could, but found herself lifting her skirts and scuttling to him.

He widened the screen. Memories of the
passionate moments they'd shared on her
couch flashed through her mind. "I think
we'd best say our good-nights out here."

The lantern cast shadows on his face,

making it impossible to read his expression. Finally, he stepped away from the door and closed the screen.

They stood several feet apart, the streamers on the Mai tree whispering in the breeze. Lowering the wick, he doused the flame, making the darkness deeper after being in the light. "Come here."

She didn't hesitate, but stepped into him, wrapping her arms about his neck, stretching up to meet his descending mouth. His kisses were fierce, possessive, and full of all the things they wanted to say aloud but had not.

He slanted his head the opposite way, kissing her again, cinching her to him, his hands reaching clear around to her sides. She went further up on her tiptoes, tightening her hold, giving back as much as she received.

I love you. But she couldn't say the words first. Must wait until they came from him.

He wrenched his mouth from hers, dragging it across her jaw, nibbling at her ear, nuzzling her neck. Fire sang through her veins.

Say it, Luke. Say it.

But he did not and finally, she loosened her hold, running her hands from his neck to his shoulders to his chest. "We must stop," she whispered.

He hesitated, then rested his forehead against her shoulder, his breaths deep. He moved his hands to her sides, squeezing her waist.

Say it.

Nothing.

Bracketing his cheeks, she lifted him from her, placed a heartfelt kiss upon his forehead, and stepped back. His fingers lingered at her waist, as if he couldn't quite let her go.

"Good night, Luke. Thank you for today. Thank you for everything." She retrieved the lantern, breaking the connection between them, then opened the screen.

"Georgie?"

She paused inside the threshold, hope filling her.

"Lock your doors."

Swallowing, she nodded, pushed the door closed, and, for the first time in her life, locked it.

Chapter Thirty-One

"Hello, Central."

"Good morning, Georgie. I have to say I still can't get over what Mr. Ottfried did to you and your hats."

Giving Luke a sidelong glance, Georgie traced the outline of a lever with her finger. "We don't know who exactly burned the hats, Mrs. Kleberg."

"Well, who else could it be? In any event, refusing to frequent his millinery isn't enough. I've decided I want to plant a bird garden, too. But I haven't the slightest idea where to start."

Georgie pictured Mr. Ottfried's Maifest booth with hardly a customer all day while the Plumage League's booth was never without a line. "Signing a pledge doesn't mean you can't frequent his shop. It just means you won't buy or wear hats with bird parts."

"Yes, yes. But with Mistrot Brothers right

there on Douglas Street, I don't see any reason to go to Ottfried's shop. Now, about that bird garden?"

Georgie hesitated. She still couldn't imagine what anyone other than Mr. Ottfried would gain from burning the hats and in her heart of hearts, she believed he was the one responsible. She just found it strange Frank Comer would do his bidding.

"Hello? Georgie? Are you there?"

"Yes, Mrs. Kleberg." She cleared her throat. "As for your garden, if you would but put a fresh pan of water out daily, why, you'd be surprised at the number of birds you'll attract."

"Oh, splendid!"

"Just be sure it's in the shade and up off the ground. Birds can't fly far with wet feathers, and you don't want them to be caught by a cat or something."

"Goodness. I'll make sure it's elevated, then. Thank you, dear."

Ding.

"Hello, Central."

"Hello, Georgie. It's me."

"How's the baby, Mrs. Bargus?"

"Still keeping me up at all hours, I'm afraid. But listen, Mart said he'd build me a birdhouse. I couldn't believe it when I heard what happened to you. Imagine Mr. Ottfried doing such a thing. But don't you worry, Georgie. Us women are banding together. We want to send a clear message to anyone who thinks they can take advantage of a woman simply because she lives on her own. Now, I heard you have baby bluebirds in your yard. Is it true they're in a starch box?"

Ding.

With the switchboard alive as it was, she simply answered the question. "Yes, but a short log sawed in two will work just as well. Have Mr. Bargus hollow out the halves and nail them together again. He'll need to include an entrance, of course, on one side of the cavity."

"Yes. I'm writing this down. Excellent."

Ding.

"Did you have anyone you wanted me to connect you with?"

"No, no. I did have another question, though."

Ding.

"One moment, please." She placed the toggle key to neutral, then plugged in number thirty. "Hello, Central."

"I'm lookin' fer Luke. He there?"

She glanced again at the desk. With it being the first of the month, Luke had been preparing invoices all morning.

"He is, Mr. Ragston. Can I give him a message?"

At Mr. Ragston's name, Luke whipped his head up.

"I'm havin' trouble with my telly-phone," the farmer said. "I need him to come out."

She lifted her brows. "But you're on your telephone right now and you're coming through loud and clear. What seems to be the problem?"

Putting down his pen, Luke slowly straightened. The wavy curls on his head scattered in every direction. The bib on his overalls flattened against him.

"How's I supposed to know? Just tell him to get out here."

"That's an awfully long way for him to go if everything is working properly, which it certainly sounds as if it is."

Luke rose. "Let me talk to him."

She lifted a finger.

"Is he there or not?" Mr. Ragston barked. *Ding.*

"He is, but the switchboard is —"

"What's the use o' this thing if'n I can't talk to the fella I'm callin'? Now, put him on."

"One moment, please." Tightening her lips, she flipped the key and looked at Luke. "He wants to talk to you, but the switchboard is going crazy."

Ding.

"Sounds as if they're all calling you, though. This should only take a minute."

"Let me at least answer this, then. It's the doc's house." She plugged in number twelve. "Hello, Central."

"Georgie, it's Julia. Do birds prefer big airy yards or dense, tree-filled yards?"

She drew a deep breath. "They like plenty of open sky for flying and chasing."

"Thanks."

Flipping the switch to neutral, she pulled off her earpiece, handed it to Luke, then rolled out of his way.

He pushed number thirty's key forward, then bent down to talk into the mouthpiece. "Hey, Clem. Georgie said you wanted to talk to me?" He looked at her and winked.

They'd not had a minute to do more than wave across the room at each other. He'd arrived just as the phones began to ring. But instead of coming in, he'd chopped her Mai tree into firewood and stacked it neatly beneath her side windows. Time and again, her attention had strayed to the sight he made sawing the tree into sections, then splitting each log into manageable pieces.

She'd barely had time to thank him, though. With the overwhelming success of the Plumage League's booth yesterday, it seemed every woman who'd signed a pledge now wanted a bird garden.

Her gaze moved to the vase of roses atop her switchboard, their blooms full open, their sweet fragrance perfuming the air. Her pleasure with them and him swept through her again.

"I'll be there as soon as I can." Luke unplugged the cable, allowing it to retract into the table.

"What's wrong with his phone?" she asked. "It sounded fine to me."

Instead of answering, he leaned over and kissed her flush on the lips, making her chair roll backward. He still smelled of the outdoors and tasted of salt.

Ding.

He blindly set the earpiece down, grabbed the arms of her chair, and gave her his full attention. She tunneled her fingers into those thick brown curls, holding him steady.

Ding.

She tugged on his hair. He pulled back slightly.

"I have two people holding —"

He cut off her words with a peck to her lips.

"— and three drops down," she finished between pecks.

He rested his lips against hers. "They can wait two seconds. I've been waiting all day."

Though she knew she should protest, she closed her eyes and gave herself over to the kiss. By the time he finished, she'd lost all train of thought and sense of time.

He touched his forehead to hers. "I could do that all day long."

She smiled, eyes still closed. "Me too."

"What are you doing after work?"

"Tinkering in my garden. With Maifest, I let it slide some. I have some making up to do."

"Need any help?"

"Sure."

"I'll see you after supper, then." He kissed her again, then straightened.

She opened her eyes.

"I'm going to deliver these," he said, scooping up a stack of bills. "While I'm out, I'll swing by Ragston's. He's only had his phone for a couple of weeks. I think I ought to go by, even though nothing's wrong with it."

The fog began to clear. "There is no 'swinging by' the Ragstons' place. It's over an hour each way."

"Doesn't do us much good to string wire out there if we can't service it when they call." Picking his hat up off the rack, he

407

propped it on his head. "See you tonight."

No sooner had he stepped out than Bettina rushed in. "Mr. Prysborski done kicked up his heels. So you'd best be ready when the death bell starts tollin'."

Ding.

Georgie gasped. "But I just met the Prysborski family at Maifest and the father looked to be in good health."

"The undertaker said he was doin' some night huntin' and got shot."

"Shot?"

"Yep. Probably by another hunter who thought he was a coyote or somethin'."

"They don't know who shot him?"

"Nope, but the sheriff says it were an accident."

"Well, of course it was. That's awful."

Ding.

Fumbling for the cable, Georgie pictured Mr. Prysborski's wife and ten children. They lived quite a ways away and she didn't know them at all, but her heart ached for them nonetheless.

She'd no more answered the waiting calls than the church bell began to toll, one ring for every year of Mr. Prysborski's life. Within seconds, every drop on her board fell, the entire town wanting to know who had died.

Luke never made it back to her house after supper. Instead, he'd had to clear Spanish moss off Ragston's line. It, along with all the rest, had been busy with calls about Mr. Prysborski's death. With every call initiated, Luke received a healthy jolt of magneto current.

After the third jolt, he decided to wait until after hours to finish the job. By the time he returned to town, it was well after dark and too late for a social call.

At church this morning, he told her he'd made previous plans with some members of the Gun Club. She squelched her disappointment and put on a bright face for him, but in truth, she was terribly let down.

Refusing to be one of those females who pined away at home while her suitor was otherwise occupied, she put on a serviceable brown dress, slipped her opera glasses over her neck, and gathered up her field notebook. It had been several weeks since she'd gone birding and today was the perfect weather for it.

Crisp breezes compensated for steady sunlight, culminating in the perfect temperature. She headed southwest of town, past the school, the ice factory, the cotton yard, and on toward Industry, the closest town with another switchboard. Of course, theirs was in a saloon and run by a man operator, but it was progress nonetheless.

It took over an hour to reach the spot she was looking for. An old pecan with arms as thick as Paul Bunyan's stretched out over a hushed opening in the thicket. A brown thrasher had visited the tree the last three times she'd been out.

Standing near an oleander, she raised her opera glasses and scanned the pecan. No sign of him.

In a dead elm to her right, a collection of barn swallows decorated its leafless branches like beading on a woman's bodice. She'd first become acquainted with the steel-blue species while playing hide-and-seek in her father's barn and tumbling about the hay in its rafters. As a result, swallows always called to mind happy hours filled with warmth and laughter.

As she waited for her thrasher to appear, grackles, scissortails, blackbirds, and wrens stopped in to say hello. With each visit, she recorded the time, place, species, behavior, and song in her journal.

And then she saw him, dipping in and out of the pecan, circling his territory with a tilting, uneven flight, and singing an aria which captivated and inspired. The thrasher repeated each phrase, as if to make certain she understood him.

I missed you I missed you . . . how are you how are you . . . sing with me sing with me . . .

Tempted as she was to whistle back, she didn't dare. With a flutter of wings, he landed in the very top of the tree, noticeably perched, long tail working like one end of a seesaw. Viewing him through her opera glasses, she couldn't help but smile at the elevated opinion he had of himself, his speckled white breast and rusty back as handsome as any coat and tails seen in the opulent ballrooms of society.

He didn't make her wait long for the opening of his performance. Dropping her glasses, she scribbled the names of the birds he mimicked, tried to tally the number of couplets he sang over a thirty-minute period, and reveled in her front-row seat.

As she began to sketch his foot-long silhouette and long, long tail, a series of gunshots shattered their oasis. The thrasher cut off mid-note and launched from the branches, darting across the grove and out of sight.

Rapid gunshots sounded again.

Pop-pop . . . poppoppoppoppoppop.

Fury drove her toward the sound. Stupid, stupid hunters. How dare they desecrate God's beauty with their accursed weapons? If they were after her birds, so help her, she just might turn a gun onto them and see how they liked it.

She ran through the thicket, opera glasses bouncing, scrub brush snagging her skirt, twigs slapping against her arms and pulling at her hair. Still she ran, following the sound, rage simmering in her veins. It wasn't until the trees began to thin and a distant field came into view that thoughts of Prysborski's accident began to temper her headlong rush.

What if the hunters weren't aiming at the sky? What if they were pursuing game that roamed the earth? She'd purposely dressed to blend in with her environment so as not to scare or distract her birds. What if the men with guns mistook her brown form for something worthy of gutting and putting on a spit?

Another series of rapid shots bounced off her ears, making her jump. She took a deep breath, ready to call out when another thought stopped her. What if they weren't hunters at all? It was well known the Comer Gang claimed Washington County as their home, and though she didn't know exactly

412

where they hid, she knew it had to be close. Especially after Frank Comer's visit on Maifest Eve.

Her chest rose and fell, partly from exertion, partly from fear. She didn't know what to do. If she crept away and they were hunters, she could very well get herself shot. But if she called out and they were outlaws . . . the repercussions didn't bear thinking of.

Slowly, quietly, she set her journal on the ground, lifted her skirt, and crept forward. A twig snapped beneath her foot. Freezing, she scanned the area. No movement. No sound. She didn't so much as shift until the next rush of shots.

The minute they erupted, she lifted her skirt with both hands and sprinted to a tree several yards in the distance, then hid behind it, waiting, waiting. Three times she made her dashes under the cover of gunfire until finally, she was close enough to see the field without exposing herself.

She peeked around the tree. There was only one man in the clearing. He set up a row of bottles on a sawhorse-like contraption, then headed back toward some predetermined spot.

He wasn't overly tall, but he certainly wasn't short. He was powerfully built, though, with wide shoulders and massive chest encased in a white shirt. A gray neckerchief hung loosely at his neck. Tight black pants hugged long, muscular legs. His white Stetson obscured the color of his hair, but he was clean-shaven. His most distinguishing characteristic, however, was the low-riding gun belt strapped across his hips.

He wasn't shooting at birds or game but at beer bottles. Expecting him to find his spot and then take aim, she was taken off guard when he spun around, drew two guns at once, and shot every single bottle before she had time to say jackrabbit. She hadn't even known he had two guns on his belt until he turned around.

Leaning her head against the tree trunk, she closed her eyes. He looked familiar. She knew she'd met him before. Where? Where?

Picking up her opera glasses, she once again leaned ever so slightly around the tree. As he lined up more bottles, she studied him as carefully as she would any specimen she tried to identify.

He didn't have his back fully to her, but the angle kept her from seeing his face. She allowed her glasses to travel down his length and back up again. She swallowed. Very powerfully built indeed.

He turned and she jerked back into hiding, trying to hear his footsteps. But even as quiet as the forest had become, she was too far away to discern his movements.

With extreme caution, she peeked around the tree again and watched him annihilate the newest row of bottles. Bending his head, he reloaded his pistols. Lifting her glasses to her eyes, she trained them on his face.

The brim of his hat camouflaged most of his features, but the profile reminded her of —

Without any warning, he jerked his head up, whipped it to the right, and drilled his steely eyes straight into hers.

Letting out a scream, she stumbled back and dropped her glasses, only then remembering he wasn't as close as he had seemed. But her game was up. Pushing off the trunk, she scrambled toward the safety of the forest. She knew the woods like the back of her hand. If she could just make it to the thicket . . .

Footfalls pounded behind her, gaining, gaining.

Tripping on her skirts, she lurched forward several steps before regaining her footing. She'd taken no more than two steps when she was tackled from behind.

He took the brunt of the fall, then quickly rolled her beneath him, trapping her wrists above her.

She screamed, twisting, bucking, squirming. This couldn't be happening again.

"Georgie! Stop it!"

His voice finally penetrated, and she slowed enough to take a look just as the wind blew a corner of his neckerchief across his mouth.

She froze. For though her mind immediately identified the man as Luke, that brief glimpse of eyes-only brought forth another pair of eyes she'd seen. The eyes of the man who'd robbed her train and the man who'd burned her hats.

A sick feeling began to churn in the pit of her stomach. Luke Palmer was none other than Frank Comer.

CHAPTER THIRTY-TWO

"Get off me." Though her voice was steady, the distress in her expression was evident.

He stayed where he was, her binoculars pressing into his ribs. "What are you doing way out here?"

"Birding. What are you doing? Practicing for your next holdup?"

"We need to talk."

"Get off me, Luke. Or should I say *Frank?*"

He frowned.

"Don't even think about pretending you don't understand. You're Frank Comer and you robbed that train and you . . ." She blinked rapidly, but moisture still collected at the base of her eyes. "You burned my hats."

He watched, helpless, as memory after memory bombarded her.

"You bound my wrists . . . and tied me to the bed . . . and pretended to look for the

417

culprits when you came to my rescue . . . all the while knowing, *knowing,* it was you." Her struggle intensified.

"Georgie —"

She tugged on her hands. "Let me go, you lying, thieving prigster."

He released her wrists but did not get up. "I can explain."

Tears leaked from the corners of her eyes. She pushed against his chest, but even in her fury, her strength was no match for his. "You're despicable. Like the snake in the Garden of Eden, you blinded me with your looks and charm, yet all the while you lied. Worse than lied, you deceived and took advantage and preyed on my feelings."

"I didn't. I never pretended about that. Never. Make no mistake, Georgie, I have feelings for you. Strong feelings."

She pulled her lips back against her teeth. "Perhaps you do, but not the kind which cherish and love. Only the kind which use and take advantage."

"That's not true."

Her nostrils flared. "Did you or did you not tie me to my bed?"

"One has nothing to do with the other."

She gave him an incredulous look. "Are you even listening to yourself?"

"You're the one who's not listening. I'm

trying to —"

"Did you or did you not burn my hats?"

Blast.

She shoved his chest. "Get off. I mean it. Get off me right now, you no good humbugger."

Sighing, he pushed himself up, then reached to assist her.

She swatted his hand away and scrambled to her feet. "I hate you."

She'd taken no more than a step when he grasped her arm and pulled her back around. Her binoculars bounced against her stomach.

"You're not going anywhere until we talk."

"Or what?" She looked from the hand that held her to his face. "You'll tie me up?"

"If I have to."

Her eyes narrowed into slits. "I'd like to see you try."

"Do you doubt me?"

Her chest rose and fell. Her lips trembled. "Say what you have to say."

Looking around, he indicated a large log with a nod of his head. "Do you mind if we sit? This might take a while."

She trembled, her eyes a mixture of rage and disgust. "I will sit, Luke, but not if you touch me. You will take your hand off of me and will never, ever, touch me again. I will have your word."

"I cannot give it."

"Then I will not sit."

Lifting his hat, he settled it back on his head. "All right. I'll release you for now and I won't touch you unless you touch me first —"

"Don't hold your breath."

"— under one condition. You will not leave until I say you can leave."

"I will not make any such promise."

Taking a step forward, he tightened his hand around her arm. "Then let me make you a promise. If you run, I will catch you. If you hide, I will find you. If you reveal my true identity to anyone, I will put you away until I've done what I need to do. Now, sit down."

Her lips curled.

Before she could blink, he captured her wrists in one hand and unbuckled his belt with his other. Her eyes widened as he whipped it from its loops.

"What are you doing?" She tugged at him, her binoculars bouncing, but he held her secure.

With the belt dangling in one hand, he strengthened his resolve. "You have a choice, Georgie. You can either sit on that log tied up, or you can sit on that log without binds.

But you are going to sit on that log for as long as it takes to talk through this thing."

"I'm already finished talking."

"I'm not." He softened his tone but not his hold. "I have no desire to shackle you, but I will. Too much is at stake. So which will it be? With or without the binds?"

Her chest rose and fell. Her eyes clouded. "I will sit without binds, but you'd best say what you have to say and be done with it." Yanking at her wrists, she waited for her freedom, then stormed to the log and plopped down.

He followed, but found himself too agitated to join her. "I'm not Frank Comer."

She rolled her eyes.

"I'm Lucious Landrum. Texas Ranger of Company 'A.' "

Her lips parted before she laughed. Laughed. Though her laugh was without mirth. "Of all the people you could claim to be, I think he would have been waaaaay down on the list. Why on earth would you want to be him?"

He tightened his jaw. "I don't want to be him. I *am* him."

"Really? And you expect me to believe you? Just like that?"

He pinched the bridge of his nose. "It would be nice, yes."

"Well, you'd have had an easier time convincing me you were Santa Claus. Do you forget I was at the train robbery? Do you forget it was Ranger Landrum who gave chase? I met him, Luke . . . Frank. I met him and you are not him."

"I am him. I don't know why you think I'm Comer. Is it because our builds are somewhat similar? Does he have the same color hair? Same color eyes?"

"Not the same color eyes. The *same* eyes. It was you. I know what I saw. Just like I know you were the one to burn my hats."

He rubbed the back of his neck. "I'm sorry about the hats. And about tying you up. It was never my intention, and I only did it to protect you."

She looked at him as if he were daft. "You really must think me an utter and complete fool. Not that you don't have reason, but honestly. The game is up. It's insulting, these stories you're coming up with."

He lowered himself onto the log, careful to keep several feet between them. "I'm Lucious Landrum. I was assigned to find Frank Comer and his gang. We know they're in the area, so they had me go undercover as a troubleman."

Crossing her arms, she drummed her fingers, trapping the binoculars against her.

"Fine. You're Lucious Landrum and I'm Annie Oakley. Can I go now?"

He rested his elbows on his knees. "What do you know about Lucious Landrum — other than he has a 'ridiculous' name?"

With a put-upon sigh, she lifted her face to the sky. "He's a fancy dresser. He's been in vain pursuit of you for over a year. He holds some kind of record for being a fast draw. He carries two bone-handled pistols. A boy carved on one, a girl carved on the other. He's named his pistols after Odysseus and Penelope — the most romantic couple of all time. And he keeps Penelope on his left hip, closest to his heart."

Widening his knees, he rummaged through the brush, then picked up a small brown rock, smooth on one side, rough on the other. "That's because she's known for her faithfulness. Even though she hadn't seen Odysseus for more than twenty years and even though she'd been relentlessly pursued by other suitors, she remained loyal to him."

He waited, but Georgie made no snide comment in response. He looked over. She studied him, her green eyes uncertain.

"I'm going to remove my left gun from my holster."

Her gaze fell to his hip.

"Before I hand it to you, I'm going to take the cartridges out so you don't hurt yourself by accident. All right?"

Biting her lower lip, she nodded, never taking her eyes from his left hip.

He pulled Penelope from his holster, emptied the cartridges into his hand, snapped the cylinder back into place, and extended the pistol, grip first. Her hand dipped, as if she hadn't expected it to be so heavy.

She cradled the Colt with both hands, studying the woman carved into its handle and the steelwork, clear down to the muzzle, which was inlaid with gold in intricate patterns. She ran a finger over the inscription just ahead of the trigger. *Never Draw Me Without Cause or Holster Me With Dishonor.*

"Can I see the other?" she asked, her voice soft, subdued.

He emptied Odysseus, then handed him to her.

Stretching her legs out to make her lap level, she set the pistols against her thighs. "They're lovely."

"Thank you."

"How do I know you haven't simply killed Ranger Landrum and absconded with his guns?"

"I have a Warrant of Authority and a

badge hidden in my room at the boarding-house. I can fetch them if you'd like."

She returned Odysseus. "Also items which could have been stolen."

He placed the cartridges back into Odys-seus's cylinder, then holstered it. "No one but me would know about my brother Alec's past."

"Unless he was part of Frank Comer's gang." She handed him Penelope.

Taking it, he shook his head. "He wasn't. Frank Comer wasn't around back then. Besides, if Lucious Landrum had met with foul play, the papers would be filled with the news."

The forest creatures remained still, but three black-throated birds winged past, cheeping and trilling.

Drawing up her knees, she wrapped her arms around them. "I want to believe you."

"I'm not lying."

"But everything's been a lie."

"Not everything. Not how I feel about you."

She searched his eyes. "How do you feel about me?"

Swallowing, he knew he had no choice but to tell her the absolute truth. Studying her face, he recalled the panic he felt when Necker announced his intent to go inside her cottage. The fury when Duane made offensive innuendos. The easing of his anxiety when he cradled her within his arms. "I love you, Georgie."

Her lips quivered. "I don't even know who you are."

"You do. I'm still me. The only thing that's different is my name and occupation."

"That's not true. Luke Palmer — or Lucious Landrum, for that matter — would never have tied me up and burnt those hats."

"I've sworn to protect. And in order to do my job, sacrifices sometimes have to be made. In this case, there was no contest. Your safety was much more important than the hats."

"You tied me up."

"And you're lucky it was me, because I made sure your circulation wasn't cut off. I also protected you from unwanted advances."

He could see the memories flicker through her mind. Of him tying her to the bedpost, tight enough to impress Necker, but not so tight she'd lose blood flow. Of him tossing Duane across the room when he'd made crude suggestions. Of him covering her nightdress and preserving her modesty.

"Who were they?" she asked.

"I can't tell you."

Her lips parted. "Why not?"

"It would be too hard for you to act like yourself around them."

She gasped. "I know them?"

"Yes."

"Are they part of the Comer Gang?"

"Yes."

She wrapped her hands around her binoculars, as if hanging on to them would somehow give her stability. "Was Mr. Ottfried behind it?"

"No. He had absolutely nothing to do with it."

"But the entire town thinks he did."

"I know." He watched as she absorbed the ramifications of his revelation.

She rubbed her forehead. "What about the train robbery?"

"What about it?"

"Why did you rob it?"

"That wasn't me."

"But your eyes . . ."

"Are blue. Lots of people have blue eyes."

"Not like yours." Her tone held a dreamy note and despite himself, he felt a pang of satisfaction.

"Did you see me when I was questioning the passengers?" he asked.

"I did."

"Then maybe that's what you remember.

It was an awful lot to take in all at once."

Her brows crinkled. "Maybe so." Hugging herself, she rocked back and forth.

Never did he want to take her in his arms so badly as he did now, but he'd promised not to touch her until she touched him first.

"Was the Mai tree a ruse?" she asked.

"A ruse? What do you mean?"

"Did you bring it to me voluntarily, or was that also part of your 'job'?"

"A little bit of both, I guess."

"What does that mean?"

He slipped his belt back through the loops and fastened its buckle. "It wasn't a tradition I was familiar with, not like valentines or something. So it never really occurred to me in advance to bring you one. But if it had, I certainly would've."

"So it was a ruse. An excuse to free me from my binds." It wasn't so much a question as a statement.

"Once I thought of it, I'd have brought it to you whether you were in need of help or not."

Sighing, she rose to her feet. "I'd like to go home now."

He stood in response. "I enjoyed escorting you to Maifest. I can't remember when I've had such a good time. And it had nothing to do with my job. Nothing."

She gave him a sad smile. "It's all very confusing — what's real and what's not." Her nose crinkled. "Am I really going to have to call you Lucious?"

He shook his head. "No one can know who I am. Everything has to appear exactly the same as before."

"I see."

"I'm sorry I'm not going to be able to walk you home, but I'm not in my overalls."

She looked him up and down. "You look much different in normal clothes."

"That's why I wear the overalls."

Nodding, she backed up a step. "Yes. Well."

"I need your word you won't tell anyone who I am or what I'm doing here."

"Does Sheriff Nussbaum know?"

"No one knows."

She wrapped the strap of her opera glasses around her finger. "I'd like to see your badge and paperwork."

"I'll bring it by as soon as I clean up the glass over there and change back into my overalls. Do I have your word?"

Biting her lip, she nodded.

"The entire operation would be jeopardized if anyone suspected."

"Do you know where Comer is?"

"Not yet."

"Are you close to capturing him?"

"Closer than I've ever been."

She looked down. "That isn't saying much, is it?"

He reared back at the slur but said nothing.

"Well, I'll see you in a bit, then." Turning, she headed back the way she'd come, her skirts swaying with each step.

He watched until she disappeared into the thicket. He needed to send word to his captain. Tell him the mission had been compromised. But if he did, Heywood might pull him off the job. And that he could not, would not, allow.

CHAPTER THIRTY-THREE

Arriving home, Georgie latched the hook on her screen door, then dropped her opera glasses and field notebook on the easy chair and fell onto the couch. She didn't change, light a lamp, review her notes, or make supper. She simply sat, staring at the empty fireplace.

Questions swarmed in her head. She tried to go back to her earliest memory of Luke and reconstruct what had happened to see if there were clues she should have seen. But how could she have? Never would it have occurred to her Lucious Landrum was sitting in the desk beside her. Or was it really Ranger Landrum? Perhaps she was right the first time. It was Comer pretending to be Landrum pretending to be Luke.

Her head began to ache. She recalled his splinters that first day he climbed the poles, something a seasoned troubleman would have known how to avoid. She thought of the numerous times he'd heard someone come up her walk well before she did. And then, there was the inordinate amount of time he spent in the field. Was he actually working or spending time with his gang?

Mr. Ragston's call yesterday came to mind. How he'd specifically asked to speak to Luke, even though most folks reported their problems to her and she conveyed them to Luke. How Luke had insisted on going out to the Ragstons', even though nothing was wrong. How he'd waited until after hours to clear the Spanish moss off the lines.

Had there even been any moss, or was it all a ruse? Was Mr. Ragston part of the Comer Gang? The idea seemed preposterous. He had a wife, children, and a farm to run. He had no hair, huge ears, and droopy eyes. Outlaws didn't look like that. She had seen sketches and pulp novels. Why, she'd seen the Comer Gang herself. Not a one of them looked like Mr. Ragston.

But she hadn't seen them all. Only the ones who'd boarded the train or held them at gunpoint. She closed her eyes, conjuring up Comer. His eyes had been blue, no question. And he'd had extremely wide shoulders. But she wasn't certain he was as tall as Luke.

No, he'd only been about a head taller than she was. Hadn't he? And Luke was more like a head and a half. Still, she couldn't be sure.

She called to mind her impressions of Lucious Landrum. None of them had been favorable, but if she pushed those aside and concentrated solely on physical characteristics, would she recognize him as Luke?

Pulling up her legs, she leaned her head on her knees. *Think. Think.*

His silhouette as he talked to the engineer. But it was the engineer who wore overalls, not Landrum.

His scowl as he demanded the widow return the money Comer had given her. But the light had begun to fade and his Stetson had shadowed his face and eyes.

The thick, dark beard had made his features appear round, so different from the sharp, angular lines of Luke's cheeks and jaw.

No, she simply could not reconcile the man called Lucious Landrum with the man she knew as Luke Palmer.

But there was no disputing those pistols. They were Landrum's, all right. That didn't mean it was Landrum who now carried them, though.

She took a deep breath. Luke had certainly

looked different today in shirt and pants. She'd not realized how flat his stomach was, how muscular his legs. She thought of the gun belt riding low on his hips, the exquisite scrollwork on his guns, the motto beneath —

Her head whipped up. The gun belt. Lucious Landrum had worn his exactly the same way, but Frank Comer had his cinched around his waist as if he needed it there to hold up his trousers.

She slowly lowered her legs. If there was one thing a man didn't change, it was the way he wore his guns. In both Comer's and Landrum's line of work, their very lives depended on having those pistols exactly where they expected them to be.

Her body began to tremble. He wasn't Frank Comer pretending to be Lucious Landrum pretending to be Luke Palmer. He really was Lucious Landrum. Texas Ranger.

Covering her mouth, she looked around as if she might find someone in the room who would confirm her realization. But there was no one. Just her, the switchboard, and her birding paraphernalia.

She moved her fingers across her lips. She'd been kissed by Lucious Landrum. *Luscious* Lucious Landrum. Panicky giggles escaped her before horror quickly replaced them.

Good heavens. She'd made fun of his name right in front of him. She pressed two fists against her mouth. What had she said?

She couldn't remember. Something about it being a ridiculous name — which it was — and something about it sounding like luscious — which it did.

What had he said? She slid her eyes closed but couldn't recall the words. She could recall his expression, though. He'd been furious.

The knock at her door startled a squeak out of her. She jumped to her feet and whirled around. It must be Luke. Or Lucious.

She grimaced. She simply could not be in love with a man named Lucious.

I love you, Georgie.

The words he'd said to her in the glade boomeranged inside her head. He loved her. He'd said he loved her.

"Georgie?" Another knock. "Can I come in?"

Her hands flew to her hair. She'd not changed or freshened up or combed her hair.

The screen rattled. There was nothing for it.

"Coming." She scrambled to the door, unhooked it, and swung it open.

Pushing her aside, he rushed in, looking left and right. "Why was the screen latched? Why are all the lamps out? What's the matter?"

She smiled. He was doing his Texas Ranger stuff, except in overalls. How could she not have noticed?

He turned around, the worry on his brow slowly transforming into uncertainty. "What?"

"I love you, too."

He blinked, then utter shock. "What?"

She let the screen close. When had the sun gone down? She must have been sitting on that couch for quite some time. "I said, I love you, too."

"Yes, I heard you. Why did you say it?"

She moved to the lantern and lifted its globe. "Because you said it first. This afternoon while we were talking." She struck a match, touched it to the wick, then shook out the flame. "I can't remember what I said, but I know I didn't tell you —"

One minute she was facing the table, the next she was in his arms, his mouth pressed to hers, his arms crushing her against him. Hmmmm. Luscious.

She giggled.

He pulled back. "Are you laughing? Is something funny?" His voice held a decidedly affronted tone.

"I think you're luscious," she whispered.

"That's not funny."

She giggled again.

"We'll discuss it later." He continued with his kiss.

By the time he was finished, she couldn't think, much less laugh. He appeared satisfied with her reaction. Arrogant man.

As the fog began to clear, her curiosity swelled. She wanted to know everything there was to know about Lucious Landrum. "Do you have your badge and Warrant of Authority?"

Slipping a hand in his pocket, he withdrew a silver five-pointed star, then handed it to her. The cold metal spanned her entire palm. In its center, RANGER had been engraved in large, bold letters. Arced above it, TEXAS. Below it, STATE.

She pressed it against his chest. "Looks kind of silly with overalls, doesn't it?"

He smiled. His eyes patient. Tolerant. And smoldering.

Swallowing, she handed it back to him and exchanged it for a black pocket-size folding case. She smoothed her hand over the soft, well-worn leather, wondering what stories it could tell. Inside she opened a small official-looking document with fancy lettering.

This is to certify the bearer, Lucious Landrum, is a Private in Company "A" Ranger Force, State of Texas, and this is his Warrant of Authority as a Ranger and will be exhibited as his authority to act as a Ranger when called upon for his credentials.

Beneath it was a descriptive list.

Name: *Lucious Landrum*
Age: *23 Years & 8 Days*
Height: *6'*
Hair: *Brown*
Eyes: *Blue*
Complexion: *Light*
Rank: *Private*
Where Born: *Indianola, TX*
Occupation: *Grocer*
Enlisted Where: *Rusk Co*
Enlisted When: *22 Jan 1900*
Enlisted By: *Capt. C. L. Heywood*

It was signed and sealed by the Adjutant General and the Captain of the Ranger Force.

She looked up. "You're twenty-six now?"

He nodded.

"I believed you before you showed me all that," she said, handing it back to him. "I was just curious."

Refolding the document, he tucked it inside the case, then slipped it into the pocket on his bib and snapped it closed.

"Have you eaten?" she asked.

"Mrs. Sealsfield had some sandwiches set aside. I ate one on the way over."

"Well, I haven't. Come into the kitchen while I find me something."

She fried a slice of ham, whipped up some gravy, and asked him about his growing-up years.

Leaning back in a spindly chair, he spoke at length of his father, their hounds, and the deer, fox, and raccoons they'd hunted. She noticed he skipped over any mention of birds.

Over their meal, she told him of her father and his reaction to her ambition of becoming a boy. His pride, as well as her mother's horror, when she won the prize for being best in Greek studies.

Though Luke attended Soule's Commercial College as an adult, he admitted to playing hooky from school as a child, preferring to ride, shoot, swim, and fish.

He shook his head. "I'll never forget the time a bunch of us were at our favorite swimming hole trying to catch fish with our bare hands. We'd muddied the water good with all our thrashing about, making it impossible to see."

They'd moved into the living area where he'd made a small fire. The pleasant odor of burning wood permeated the room. He sat facing her on the couch, his arm hooked across its back, his knee hiked up onto the cushion.

"I plunged my hands into the water and right smack-dab onto a big ol' catch. I was boasting about its size before I ever even swung it up out of the water. Told my friends there wasn't a one of them who'd be able to beat mine."

Leaning against the corner of the couch, she tucked her feet up under her skirt and smoothed its hem over her boots.

Amusement played across his features. "And that certainly ended up being the case, for in my hands was the biggest water moccasin you ever did see."

She sucked in her breath. She'd never personally known anyone who'd been bitten by the deadly snake, but she'd read many accounts of those who had — and died because of it.

"Fortunately," he continued, "I had it good and tight about the neck so it couldn't bite me, but it immediately coiled itself around my arm." He smiled. "You've never seen a bunch of boys move so fast. I waded out of the water calm as you please, though I thought I was dead for sure. I strode up to one after another asking them to unwind it, but none of them would have anything to do with it."

She bit her lip, trying to picture a seven- or eight-year-old Luke. "What did you do?"

He gave her a wry look. "Told Alec I'd beat him to death, cut off his ears, and skin him alive if he didn't unwind that stupid thing."

She curled her knees up closer to her chest. "Did he?"

"He did. His face was awfully gray, but he unwound it. After about a yard or so, he undid the last coil. I flung the thing down and stomped on it good."

"In your bare feet? It didn't bite you?"

"Nah. I'd practically choked it to death already." His smile slowly faded. "I sure do miss him, Georgie. I'd give anything to go back and redo that last night I saw him."

A log on the fire collapsed, popping and throwing sparks.

She reached out a hand. "He could have

said no. Nobody made him race down that street with you."

He hooked his fingers with hers. "He'd have done anything I asked. He idolized me and I knew it."

"Which was also his choice."

He tugged on her hand, but instead of going to him, she looked at the timepiece above her breast. "It's getting late."

"Are you coming over here or not?"

"Not." But she smiled to lessen the refusal.

After a moment, he stood. "I was planning to cover the south side tomorrow. Sales have been kind of slow and I need to find us some new subscribers."

Unfolding herself from the couch, she rose as well. "Does SWT&T know who you are?"

"Only the chairman. Everyone else thinks I'm a troubleman, including our boss."

She tilted her head. "Are you really going to try and sell phones or are you doing your, um, other work?"

He ran the back of his knuckles against her cheek. "Both. I'm always doing both."

Twisting her face to the side, she gave his hand a peck. "You be careful, then."

He slid his hand around the nape of her neck, and gently pulled her toward him. Defenses melting, she let him reel her in as surely as if she were one of his fish.

The kiss was slow, gentle, and devastating.

"If I don't see you tomorrow," he whispered, "I'll see you on Tuesday."

Chest pumping, body tingling, she could only nod.

He gave her one more quick, solid peck and then he was gone.

CHAPTER THIRTY-FOUR

In between calls, Georgie pored over every scrap of information she had on Lucious Landrum. Unfortunately, he'd never been of interest to her before. Frank Comer had. So whatever she found about Lucious was because it had been mentioned as part of an article about Comer.

A sorry state of affairs, she thought, to have glorified the villain instead of the good guy. And not just her, but the entire state of Texas. How demoralizing for Luke and the other Rangers.

She paused on an article about a bank robbery the gang had committed. Lucious had been the Ranger called in to investigate. While in town, he'd walked down the street when a drunken saloon owner emptied a load of buckshot into someone simply because they rode by on a horse.

Lucious stormed into the saloon and came face-to-face with a double-barreled shotgun.

Instead of lifting his hands and backing out, he approached the man and his gun head-on.

"You been having a bit of your own inventory, mister?" he'd asked.

His boldness stunned the bartender, allowing Lucious time to reach him. He shoved the barrel with one hand, collared him with the other, and hauled him to jail.

Georgie set the paper on her lap, trying to picture him doing such a thing. But all her memories — other than yesterday — were of him as a troubleman in overalls. Of course, there was the night of the break-in, but she didn't like to think about that.

She continued scanning the papers, reading a snippet here and a snippet there. When put all together, they formed an impressive picture. A much more worthy subject for a pulp fiction novel than Frank Comer.

She thought of the injustice Mr. Ottfried had suffered. He might sell hats with bird parts on them, but according to Luke, he'd had nothing to do with the break-in. She wanted to exonerate him but couldn't figure out how without revealing Luke's identity. Still, she had to do something.

She glanced out the window. What if she went to his millinery and purchased a hat from him to show she'd let bygones be bygones? Yet she didn't want the men who really did burn her hats to think she wasn't upset. She was.

What if she encouraged the women of the Plumage League to purchase a hat from him? But then what would Mr. Mistrot say? Especially after he'd been so supportive from the very beginning.

"Hey, Miss Georgie." Bettina pulled open the screen, letting it slam behind her. "Whatcha doin'?"

"You really mustn't let the screen bang like that, Bettina. Try to use a little decorum, please."

She scrunched up her nose. "What's got you pullin' at the bit?"

"Nothing. It's just there are some things a lady doesn't do."

"But you always said a gal can do anything a feller can."

"That doesn't mean we have to emulate their bad habits. Only their good ones." She folded her hands. "Did you find Kyle and tell him his mother wants him?"

"I found him. Don't know if he went home, but I done told him."

"That was all which was required. Thank you."

The girl peered over Georgie's shoulder. "You readin' up on Frank, huh?"

"Things were kind of quiet, so I thought I'd thumb through a few of these."

"Which one is that?" She inched closer. "Oh, the bank robbery. That's a good one."

Georgie folded the paper. "You know, Bettina, after looking these over, I'm beginning to wonder just what it is that's so appealing about Mr. Comer."

"What do you mean?" She dug around in her ear.

Georgie grasped her wrist and pulled, giving a gentle shake of her head. "I mean, he preys on the unsuspecting and takes things which aren't his and has even been rumored to kill people."

"Only lawmen." She wiped her finger on her dress. "He ain't never killed no real people."

"Lawmen are real people. Many of them have wives and children. Brothers and sisters. Mamas and daddies. Why, look at Sheriff Nussbaum. What would you think if Comer killed our sheriff?"

Bettina laughed. "Aw, he wouldn't do that. Not to Nussbaum."

She slowly straightened. "Does the sheriff know Frank Comer?"

The girl's eyes darted to the window, then back to Georgie. "Well, I wouldn't know nothin' about that. What I meant was, Nussbaum don't think ill o' Frank any more than you or I do. So Comer pro'bly wouldn't do nothin' to him."

"But that's just it. I am beginning to think ill of Mr. Comer." She patted the papers on her lap. "There are accounts in here of him robbing banks, stagecoaches, trains, and all sorts of things. I just don't see what there is to admire about that."

"He don't mean nothin' by it."

"What he's doing is selfish and harmful to others, and it's against the law. And I, for one, am through being sympathetic toward him."

Bettina scratched her head, loosening her braids. "You're just sore about them hats."

"I am. I'm not only sore, I'm furious. How dare those men do that. Think of all the women who worked so hard on their entries."

"But that's just it." Her eyes lit up. "It worked out even better. If he hadn't burnt 'em all up, none of them other women would've signed yer pledge and brought in all them entries. You made bunches o' money fer them bird folks up north. You oughta be thanking Frank. He done did you a favor."

Georgie held on to her patience. "I know I told you I thought Mr. Comer was there that night, but now I'm not so sure. Still, that's beside the point. The point is, they didn't do me any favors, Bettina. They tied me up and burned my hats."

The girl rolled her eyes. "Well, if'n you don't think it was Frank, then how come yer all mad at him?"

Ding.

"Never mind. We'll talk about this later." She slipped on the earpiece. Before the call was over, Bettina had sidled out the door.

CHAPTER THIRTY-FIVE

Luke rode clear to Industry to mail his report. He couldn't send it directly to his captain or even the headquarters in Alice. So he posted it to a contact in Bentonville who'd make sure it was delivered.

Prysborski's death was no hunting accident. When Luke had gone out to Ragston's Saturday to check on his phone, he'd been told there wasn't a thing wrong with the service. Ragston just wanted him to join a poker game between himself, Necker, Duane, Blesinger, and Finkel.

Luke had excused himself to check the lines anyway, just so he wouldn't have to lie to Georgie, and ended up cleaning off a bit of Spanish moss. Upon his return, the boys' voices filtered through the windows in soft, urgent tones.

Without making a sound, Luke had eased up to the house and crouched beneath the kitchen window. A row of hedges would block him from view should anyone wander by.

"Prysborski's heart wasn't in the last job or the one a'fore that." Ragston's voice. "Had he been one o' the ones Landrum had caught, we'd all be in jail."

"But did you haf to kill him?" Finkel asked.

"Better that than the lot of us rotting in some cell."

"I just don't know why Frank didn't say nothin' to me." Necker's voice.

"What'd you expect?" Ragston asked, his inflection filled with disgust. "He sent ya to strip them gals' float and ya ended up terrorizing the town operator and burnin' hats the whole county had a hand in making."

"That was Duane's idea."

"Since when you takin' orders from a kid?"

"Hey —" Duane's voice. "I ain't no kid."

"It don't matter," Ragston responded. "Frank's worked mighty hard to curry favor with folks. He was spittin' mad about them hats. You're just lucky that milliner's takin' the blame."

"Frank could've at least told me." Necker again. "I didn't find out 'bout Prysborski 'til them church bells started ringing."

"Hush up, all of you." Finkel. "Palmer's

sure to come back any minute. Now, deal the cards."

Luke slipped back to the edge of the yard, then made plenty of noise as he approached. All the while, disappointment and remorse assailed him. Discovering Ragston to be a cold-blooded killer was a great deal worse than suspecting him of train robbery.

Why would he resort to something so grievous? But greed and fear were powerful motivators and ones Luke had seen at work many a time.

The cardinals began building their nest not eight feet from Georgie's corner window. She could not sit still for the excitement. All morning the brownish yellow female with her red underlit wings and orange bill had placed vine stems, small twigs, and bark strips in the tangled, dense interior of Georgie's ligustrum.

Many birds had nested in her yard, but never at eye level and never so close to the house. She could not believe her good fortune. Without ever setting foot outdoors, she'd see everything from the building of the nest to the laying of the eggs, the female's song as she incubated, the hatching of the eggs, the feeding of the young, and the first flight of the fledglings.

Gathering up cotton and wool, hair from her brush, yarn from her sewing basket, straw from her broom, and a beautifully colored ribbon from her drawer, she quietly placed her offerings on the back porch, then retreated inside to watch.

The mother perched in the shrub, looking at her work, then picked up a twig and moved it just so. Puffing herself up, she squatted down and did a fast little twist. Georgie pressed her knuckles to her mouth, already recognizing the bowl-shaped indention the bird created.

Standing behind Georgie, Luke slipped his arms about her waist and pulled her back against him.

She rested her hands on his. "She used my colored ribbon. Do you see it?"

They faced her corner window, watching as the mama cardinal nosed the edges of her nest. It had taken her only three days to build it. The compact bowl was a masterpiece of twigs, rootlets, vines, and strips of bark. Interlaced within its siding was a frivolous piece of yellow-and-orange frippery.

"I do," he said. "Definitely gives it the woman's touch."

She smiled.

He had to admit the process was fascinating. The male had kept a close eye on his mate during construction, but didn't offer any help. He wondered if it contributed at all once copulation had occurred, but wasn't quite sure how to pose the question.

"How long before she lays?" he asked.

"Five or six days."

"Then how long before they hatch?"

"Another twelve, give or take."

He rested his mouth against her hair and inhaled the flowery-cinnamon shampoo paste she used. "You going to name them?"

She angled her head back. "I believe the most romantic couple's names have already been taken."

Unable to resist, he gave her a soft kiss. "There's Romeo and Juliet."

Scrunching her nose, she turned back around. "I don't much care for the ending of that tale."

The female cardinal hopped to the edge of the ligustrum, then darted away in search of food.

"Cleopatra and Caesar?"

"No, I'm through glamorizing people who don't deserve it."

He gave her a quick squeeze. "Then what about Queen Victoria and Prince Albert?"

Her spine straightened. "Oh, I like that.

And with the cardinals' rich beautiful plumage, they deserve royal names."

They watched the last-minute scurrying of the cardinals and other songbirds as the sun began to set and they looked for a place to roost. Their grand finale included more songs than he could count.

He'd not heard back from the captain since sending him a report, but he hadn't really expected to. Much as Luke wanted to avenge Prysborski's death, the intent of the mission was to locate Comer. Everything else was secondary.

He'd been as cryptic as possible in case the letter was intercepted and only hinted he'd had to reveal himself to a third party. He made no mention of it being a woman, only that the party was in his corner.

He needed to decide what to do about her. Them. She'd not asked for a declaration and he'd not offered one, but his actions were those of a man with marriage on his mind. And that wouldn't be far from the truth. It *was* on his mind. The problem was, he hadn't yet decided if he actually wanted to marry her.

He tried to imagine walking away from her when the job was over and never coming back. Impossible. He wouldn't do it. Still, he didn't want to marry her only to see her for snatches at a time in between assignments. Plenty of Rangers did it, but he wasn't willing to. If he was going to settle down, it would be in the most literal sense.

And do what? he thought. *Telephone repair work?*

That was the part which always brought him up short — that and the fact he loved rangering. Still, his prejudice against phones wasn't nearly as bad as it had been. He could actually see some benefits in having one. But there was a big difference between having one and foisting the blame things onto someone else.

The sun disappeared from the horizon, prompting a need for lanterns, but he was reluctant to move just yet.

"So tragic about Mr. Prysborski," Georgie said. "His boys are going to have to grow up mighty fast now. Can you imagine? Fields full of cotton. The price dropping every day. And ten mouths to feed."

The telephone poles had stopped well short of Prysborski's place, which was why Luke had never run across his farm. He'd meant to scout the areas beyond the poles, but he'd always been in a hurry to return to home base at the close of each day. It was no excuse and now a man was dead.

He wondered if Mrs. Prysborski knew of

her husband's involvement with Comer. Tempted as he was to ride out, he didn't want to show his cards by asking too many questions. Not when he was so close to finding his quarry. So he'd keep eyes and ears open, and continue to bide his time.

"Want to play Around the World With Nellie Bly?" Georgie asked.

He cringed. Never had he played a more ridiculous board game. It could be worse, he supposed. It could be All Around Texas With Frank Comer.

"Sure," he said, releasing her. "I'll light the lanterns."

He moved to the match safe, and she fairly flew to the shelves housing her beloved game.

CHAPTER THIRTY-SIX

If anyone had told him being a Ranger would require trapping mice in Mason jars, he wouldn't have believed it.

"Make sure that string's good 'n' tight, now," Duane cautioned, stretching a piece of brown paper over the lid of his jar while simultaneously keeping an eye on Luke.

Luke secured the string around the rim of his, then flicked the paper covering with his middle finger. Tight as a drum.

"Good. Now take yer knife and cut a little x right in the center o' yer paper."

Opening his pocketknife, Luke did as instructed.

"That's it. Now start on the next one."

The two of them sat in the back room of Pfeuffer Feed Store preparing a dozen traps. It was Duane's job to keep the storage area clear of rodents, and he'd been negligent of late. The overwhelming odor of grain and rodent feces made it difficult to breathe.

Luke repositioned the lantern to better see, its moving flame throwing shadows over bags of feed piled in every available corner like hulking ghosts. A selection of new and old cast-iron feed boxes, feed trays, and feed troughs leaned against the south wall.

"I'm gettin' mighty tired of Necker always making excuses ever' time I wanna go night hunting." With a put-upon sigh, Duane shook his head. "Don't ever get hitched, Luke. It done ruins yer life."

Luke had met Necker's new wife for the first time at Maifest. She was a pretty little thing and clearly thought he walked on water. If he felt the same of her, he gave no indication — other than his reluctance to spend too many evenings carousing with the fellas.

"How long they been married?" he asked.

"He doubled up soon as the harvest was in. Said he didn't wanna go through another winter without a gal to snuggle up to."

Luke smiled. "Well, I can appreciate that."

"I can't. I don't want my haunches spurred by no drip-nose of a gal."

"I imagine you'll change your mind one of these days."

"I don't know. They seem like an awful lot o' trouble to me. Besides, you ain't doubled up and yer lots older than me." Duane looked up from the lid he was slicing. "Or are you thinkin' on it now that you got yer eye on our hello girl?"

The last impression Luke wanted to give was one which placed any more importance on Georgie than he already had. "I'm not what you'd call the marrying type."

Tension eased from Duane's shoulders. "Me neither."

After finishing the last jar, they bent pieces of thin wire into J-shapes, turned them upside down, and secured one to each jar. From the tip of the wire, Duane hung a piece of toasted cheese. Though Luke recognized immediately how the trap would work, he allowed the boy to demonstrate.

With eyes alight, Duane cycled his fingers as if they were the mouse. "It'll reach for the bait, see, and fall right through them cuts we made in the paper. Quick as a wink, the paper will flap back into place and wait fer the next mouse to come along."

Luke watched the boy with a pang of grief. He wasn't a bad sort and hadn't done any killing that he knew of, but was simply bored and without direction. From what Luke could tell, his father didn't interact with him much. He went through the same routine every day of opening the feed store, running the feed store, closing the feed store, then going home. He never kept up with Duane's comings and goings. Never asked what he did with his time. Never praised, nor criticized.

It was another reason Luke hated going undercover. Under normal circumstances, he went in, made his arrests, and dropped the men off at jail. They had names, of course, and sometimes even faces, but Luke didn't know them. They were outlaws and scoundrels, not men with parents, wives, children, and a sense of humor.

Duane continued to speak, animated in his excitement over the simple task of catching a few rodents. Luke wanted to interrupt him, talk to him about what he was doing, the direction he was taking, the different choices he had available to him. But his assignment was to become one of them and to cross enemy lines. If he tried to reform Duane or any of the rest of them, he'd never find Frank Comer, much less stop any train robberies.

The constraints left him frustrated and unsettled.

Georgie pushed open the heavy oak door and stepped into Ottfried's Millinery. In the year she'd lived in Brenham, she'd only been inside the shop once. She'd taken one sweeping glance at his inventory, then promptly turned around and left. This time, however, she was determined to stay.

The thick door closed behind her, shutting off sounds from the street. Not another soul was in the room. Lush carpets covered the wooden floor and cushioned her feet. Light-colored walls held drawers with shiny brass knobs, shelves with charming displays, and glass-fronted cabinets packed with merchandise.

Ottfried swept through a curtain in the back, then pulled up short. His face flushed. His breathing grew labored.

"I know you're about to close for the day," Georgie said, taking a tentative step forward, "but I saw your display window and couldn't help but come in."

That wasn't exactly true. She had, of course, seen the window display just now. It held a variety of beautifully decorated hats — not a bird part in sight. But she'd come today because the women of town had told her about it.

"He's completely redone his stock," Mrs. Patrick had said. "Instead of every hat having a bird part on it, none of them do."

Georgie had touched the receiver at her ear, ensuring she'd heard correctly. "None? Not a single one?"

"None," Mrs. Patrick confirmed. "If a woman wants a bird part on her hat, she has to put in a special request."

"But if he has no bird parts, how will he fill the request?"

"He still has the bird parts he's stripped from his hats. So he opens the drawers and lets the customer choose what she wants."

Georgie had collapsed against her chair. "Good heavens."

With such a momentous show of support, and knowing he'd been wrongfully maligned, she could not stay away. "I'd like to buy a hat, please."

"Why?" he asked.

She swallowed. The truth was, she couldn't afford a hat. Especially not one from a place as fine as his. But sometimes, doing the right thing was more important than worrying over the financial implications. "I feel you've been treated unjustly and I'm partly to blame."

He blinked. Clearly, he'd not expected her response. It didn't take long, however, for his expression to sour. "You're entirely to blame."

"Not entirely." She was willing to call a truce, but she wasn't willing to shoulder all the responsibility. "Before now, the majority of your products held bird parts. Still, we live in a country where one is innocent until proven guilty. I know you weren't one of the men who broke into my home. And though I don't know who instructed them to destroy the hats, I find I can't condemn you simply because it's convenient."

His jaw tightened. "A little late, wouldn't you say?"

"I hope not."

He swept his arm to encompass the room. "Do you see how empty this is? It's been this way since Maifest. Since those men burned your hats." He looked her up and down. "I have to admit, I've wondered if *you* weren't the one who hired them simply to tilt the scales in your favor."

She sucked in her breath. "I assure you, I did not."

"No?" He crossed his arms. "Not very pleasant to be wrongly accused, is it, Miss Gail?"

"No, it's not." She cleared her throat. "If you have time, I was hoping to look at some of your toques or maybe something with a straw foundation."

His eyes took on a smug quality. "I understand you place great store on Nellie Bly."

Lips parting, she quickly scanned the shop. "Do you have her hat?"

"Matter of fact, I do. It just came in this

week." Opening a cupboard, he removed a Panama hat on a handsome stand and plunked it on the counter. "Here you are, Miss Gail. A genuine Nellie Bly hat on a straw foundation. Would you like me to point out its features?"

She stepped up to it. A miniature bird poised on its crown. Its body was of pure white, its wings a glossy, radiant purple and black. She didn't know what it was, only that it was tropical. Had Nellie seen the species during her travels around the world?

A wave of sickness swept through her as another idol fell from the pedestal she'd placed it on. First Frank Comer, now Nellie Bly. It wasn't a fair comparison, of course. Comer was a criminal. Bly was a suffragette.

But to Georgie, they'd both been idols. And by their very nature, at some point or another, they always, always disappoint.

Taking a deep breath, she placed her coins on the counter. "Even without the bird, I'm afraid her hat would be out of my range. This is all I have."

He glanced at her money. Without a word, he turned around, opened a drawer, pulled out a bare straw hat, and slapped it on the counter. "Here you are, Miss Gail. Thank you for your business."

Her lips parted. She'd given him seven

dollars. A fortune, especially for her. She knew as well as he the frame of a hat didn't cost seven dollars. More like fifty cents.

She opened her mouth to argue, when a spurt of compassion stopped her. She took another moment before deciding to listen to the prompting of her heart. "Thank you. Would you mind wrapping it for me?"

For the second time, he looked nonplussed before remembering all the ignominy he'd suffered and placed upon her doorstep. With righteous indignation, he wrapped the hat in tissue, then brown paper, and tied it with a string.

Scooping it into her arms, she offered a quiet thank-you and left the building.

The children clamored around Georgie's window, each trying to peek inside the nest.

"I don't see what all the fuss is." Eugene crossed his arms over his overall bib. "She's just sittin' there."

"She has eggs under her, dummy," Bettina snapped. "The eggs won't hatch less'n she sits on 'em."

"I ain't no dummy." He dropped his hands, his chest puffing out.

Good heavens, Georgie thought. Did all males inherit a predisposition to that stance? "Bettina, do not call names. Apologize to

Eugene."

The girl jiggled her leg. "Sorry."

"Listen, Miss Georgie." Belle turned to her, blue eyes wide, blond curls swinging. "She's calling for Prince Albert."

The female cardinal's soft voice floated over the yard.

"So she is."

The group quieted.

"What's she want?" Eugene whispered, his interest captured.

She peered over their heads. "A little snack, I suppose. Or maybe just some company. Try to imagine how you'd feel if you had to sit in one spot for ten days in a row."

A fate worse than death for a lively group such as this.

"How much longer does she have to sit there?" This from Fritz Ottfried.

Georgie had told no one, other than Luke, of her exchange with the milliner. But two days later, Fritz had attended their Junior Audubon meeting and every one since. They'd been having them more frequently because the children were as excited as she about the cardinals.

She wondered if Mr. Ottfried knew she'd have paid much, much more for Fritz's attendance. "Only a couple more days. Three at the most."

"Then they'll hatch?"

"Then they'll hatch."

CHAPTER THIRTY-SEVEN

Duane kicked a rock, sending it skittering down the alley. "If that Necker don't be careful, he's gonna be so henpecked he'll molt twice a year."

The boy had been sulking all night, and Luke could hardly blame him. His position as best friend had been usurped by a woman. As soon as Luke bid Georgie good night each evening, he'd sought out Duane and Necker. And once Necker had assured himself of Luke's availability, the recently wed man often bowed out.

Luke hadn't minded at all. Necker's idea of fun was of a more sordid nature. Duane, however, had yet to fully develop a taste for the unsavory. His pranks were suited to those of a mischievous youth. He was also less guarded than Necker and easier to extract information from.

" 'Lulie don't like ta be left alone,' " Duane imitated in a singsong voice. " 'Lulie ain't feelin' well tonight. Lulie saw a mouse and gots the shivery creeps.' " His lip curled in disgust. "The shivery creeps. I'd like to show her the shivery creeps." He pulled up short.

Luke scanned the alley front and back to see what had startled the boy, but saw nothing. "What?"

Duane's eyes were wide. A slow smile began to form.

A sigh of resignation escaped before Luke could stop it. He'd seen that look before.

"I got an i-deer." Duane took off at a fast clip. "Faller me."

They wound their way through town, avoiding the main thoroughfares, finally ending up at the feed store. Striking a match on his back pocket, Duane opened the door to the storage area and quickly lit a lantern. " 'Member those traps we set?"

Nodding, Luke closed the door behind him.

"Well, they worked real good. And Pa told me I had ta get rid of the mice 'fore they get loose and I have to catch 'em all over again."

They skirted around a large feed cutter and past several sacks of grain. The squeaks and distress calls of mice filled the hemmed-in room, backed by the stench of their droppings.

Duane handed him the lantern. "Hold this." Bending over, he caught hold of a large cage and lifted it from behind a stack of feed troughs.

Four or five dozen mice screeched and crawled over each other like waves cresting and dipping in an ocean.

"Ain't that somethin'?" Duane tilted the cage, sending the lot of them sliding to one side. "I had no i-deer we had so many of these fellers back here."

"That's a mighty big catch, all right."

Duane bent his face close to the cage and clicked his tongue. "It's okay, fellers. It's just me." He tapped his fingernail against the bars. "Pa tol' me to drown 'em last week, but I just can't bring myself to do it again. You have any idea how long it takes to drown a mouse?"

Luke pursed his lips. "Can't say I do."

Duane looked over his shoulder. "A looooong time."

What was this boy doing in Comer's gang? A boy too tenderhearted to drown a mouse was holding up women and children on trains. How was Luke going to haul him off to the calaboose when he reminded him so much of Alec?

"Listen, Duane —"

Straightening, the boy wagged a finger at Luke. "Now, don't tell me yer backin' out 'fore I even tell ya the plan."

"I'm not trying to back out, I'm just —"

He scowled. "Necker done tol' me yer all gurgle and no guts, but I stuck up fer ya. Told him I know ya better than he does. I'm gonna be sorely disappointed if'n you turn out to be full o' butter."

Luke tensed. Necker still had doubts? Was that why he hadn't been invited into the gang? What more did they want? "Lead the way. I'm all in."

Duane clapped him on the back. "That's it. Now grab two of them buckets over yonder and come with me. It's a good hike out to Necker's and we ain't even made it to Charlie's yet — though you stink to high heaven as usual. How 'bout letting me have a swill from yer stash?"

Patting the bib hiding his flask of water, Luke shook his head. "Sorry, Duane. I don't share my coffin varnish with anybody. Not even you."

"Well, come on, then. Let's get this over with, 'cause if I don't get me some neck oil soon, I'm gonna have to prime myself to spit."

Necker slept awfully sound for a man living

on the edge. Between Duane stirring up dust and the mice letting out squeaks, Luke had expected to be on the receiving end of a double-barrel shotgun. But nothing moved inside the little log cabin other than a tiny trickle of smoke from its chimney.

Duane looked at him. "You ready?"

He nodded.

Pointing to a window on the side of the cabin, Duane lowered his voice to a whisper. "That's the one." His smile grew wide. "It's right over the bed."

Luke couldn't help but answer the boy's infectious grin.

"We'll have to move fast," Duane continued. "Them critters aren't gonna like being bounced around. If Necker hears, he'll go straight fer his gun, but he'll go round front 'fore he does any shootin'. So keep going, 'cause his missus'll still be abed. If he catches us 'fore we make cover, he'll know who it is and aim high."

Luke set the empty buckets on the ground, his pulse picking up speed. "I'm ready."

Opening the top of the cage, Duane poured mice into each bucket. Sure enough, the tiny creatures protested. Swooping up the buckets, the two of them raced to the open window and tossed the contents inside.

Horrific screams and a string of curses erupted from the cabin. They sprinted to the thicket, then dove to the ground when the shots started. Duane tried to hold his laughter but couldn't.

"Duane Pfeuffer, you no 'count son of a pig keeper, I'm gonna knock yer ears down so they'll do ya fer wings."

The boy rolled to his back, laughter pouring from his gut. The sound echoed across the landscape and mixed with a woman using words so hot they'd burn her throat. The coarser her curses, the harder Duane laughed. "Who-wee, but that gal sure knows how to air her lungs."

"You out there with him, Palmer, you lily-livered dog?"

"I am," he shouted, then rolled to the right as more gunfire sounded. But he needn't have bothered. Necker was clearly shooting into the sky. "Well, get back here and help me catch these godforsaken things."

Scrambling to his feet, but keeping low, Duane half ran, half crawled in the opposite direction. "Come on," he whispered. "Let's get outta here."

Luke needed no urging. When Necker realized they weren't returning, the gunfire came a bit closer, but they pressed on until they were well out of range.

Three of the four eggs hatched. Georgie named them Edward, Alice, and Leopold. The children filed in and out, checking on the progress of the chicks. They watched Victoria and Albert take turns hunting for food. Grabbed their throats when they saw how far the monarchs inserted their bills when feeding the fledglings. And asked if birds ever ran out of bugs.

From her position at the switchboard, she could see them perfectly, though sometimes she used her opera glasses just to get a close-up look. Today was Day Five, and as soon as quitting time came, she rolled her chair to the corner. Through her glasses she could see a tiny crest on top of Edward's head.

Field book in hand, she sketched him perched on the side of the nest, mouth open and squawking for Mama. A muffled snort behind her caused her to glance over her shoulder.

Luke had arrived at half past four and fallen asleep in the easy chair. Though he never spoke of his Ranger work, she knew it had kept him up late this past week. She assumed he was writing reports. He certainly couldn't be looking for men in the dead of night. But whatever it was, it had worn him out.

Her gaze moved to the hat he'd brought her. A double-faced satin straw with maroon on the outside and yellow underneath its brim. A perfect complement to his favorite dress and a poignant apology for burning her hats by mistake. It had to have cost him a fortune.

With warmth spreading through her, she turned back around, then continued to sketch and make notes until the sun completely set and darkness kept her from seeing anything further. She slowly closed her notebook. Victoria hadn't chosen to nightbrood her nestlings. Georgie sat for thirty more minutes in the darkness, but still the queen did not return to the ligustrum.

She bit her lip. The fledglings were too young to be left alone. They were completely defenseless. Perhaps she should keep watch. At least for tonight. Just to be sure they'd be all right.

"Georgie?" His voice held a scratchy, sleep-induced sound.

"I'm here."

He shifted in his chair. "What are you doing? Why haven't you lit the lantern?"

"I can't see anything but my reflection when I do that."

She heard him stand and move toward her. "You can't see anything but black when you don't."

Sighing, she rose as well. "I know."

He slipped his arms around her and gave her a long kiss. "I'm sorry I fell asleep."

"You're fine. I was making some sketches."

"Can I see them?"

"If you'd like."

He gave her another kiss, then released her and lit a lantern.

She told him of the day's activity. He perused her drawings.

She scrambled them some eggs and fried up a bit of sausage. He sharpened her sketching pencils with his pocketknife.

She read him a chapter out of *The Swiss Family Robinson.* He fell asleep again.

Closing the book, she placed it on her lap and took the opportunity to look her fill. She noted the curl falling onto his forehead. The short brown eyelashes. The sharp line of his nose. The whiskers beginning to shadow his face.

She'd like to wake up every morning of her life looking at that face, but he'd not so much as hinted at anything permanent, and she'd been too afraid of his answer to bring it up herself. She knew once he caught Frank Comer, he'd be given a new assignment. Then what?

Would he leave and chase down the next criminal without a backward glance? And if he were to ask for her hand, would he still leave her behind while he rode across the hills and plains of Texas?

How long would he be gone? He'd arrived here in March and now it was the first of June. Did every job take an entire season?

He opened his eyes.

She lifted the corners of her lips. "Hello."

"Why'd you stop reading?"

"You fell asleep."

"I wasn't asleep. Just resting my eyes."

Quirking a brow, she gave him a skeptical look. "What have you been doing during the nights to make you so exhausted?"

"I'm not exhausted." Locking his hands behind his head, he twisted from side to side. "You know when you check your telephone lines to see if anyone is on them?"

It took her a moment to follow the change in topic. "Yes."

"And if you don't hear anyone talking, you unplug the cables?"

"Yes."

"Well, when you do that — listen in for a couple of seconds — can the people talking tell you're on the line?"

"Not if I pull the lever back, only if I push

it forward."

Lowering his arms, he rested his elbows on his knees. "If I gave you a couple of names, would you listen in on their conversations and tell me what you hear?"

She stared at him as she considered the question. She'd been anticipating it. Had been surprised it hadn't come up earlier. Yet she was no more sure how to answer now than she had been when she first thought of it. "It's against company policy."

"I'm aware of that."

Lacing her fingers together, she kept her tone level. "Are you using me, Luke?"

He jerked up straight. "What?"

"Are you using me? Wooing me and sparking me in order to enlist my help in your search for Frank Comer?"

"No."

"Then, why are you wooing me?"

He shifted in his chair. "I told you. I love you."

"I remember. Yet a month has passed and you haven't said it again, nor have you made your intentions at all clear."

"I love you." He repeated the declaration quickly and with no waver in his voice.

Her heart warmed, but she wondered if just once he'd say it without being prompted.

"I love you, too," she replied, then waited for him to give her the rest of it. The intentions part. When he remained silent, she lowered her gaze to shield her hurt.

"I think about you all the time," he said. "About us. I don't know what to do. My job is — well, it's not very conducive to married life."

She smoothed her hand across the cover of the book in her lap. "So you don't plan to marry?"

"I hadn't. Until I met you. Now I'm not so sure."

"I see." Moistening her lips, she looked up. "And when do you think you'll reach a decision?"

"I don't know." He rubbed his hands against his pant legs. "I guess I was trying to keep my focus on finding Comer. Then, once that was done, I figured I'd cross that bridge."

She wasn't sure she wanted to be an afterthought. "Well, while you're making your decision, I think it best if we not, um, spark, if you will."

A crease formed between his brows. "What exactly does that mean?"

"No more kissing, touching, spooning. That sort of thing."

"But, it's the best part of my day. It's all I

can do to keep my hands to myself as much as I already am. I can't just not touch you."

"I don't like it any better than you, but the more we spark, the more attached I become, and . . . well, I just need to know where this is going. And if it's going no-where, then I need to stop. Immediately."

He scooted to the edge of his chair. "It's not going nowhere. It's going somewhere. I just don't know where yet. I've got to sort it out, is all."

She nodded. "You can sort it without sparking."

"No, I can't."

"Yes, you can."

He ran a hand through his hair, dislodg-ing more curls. "Can't you give me a couple days' warning? So I can adjust to the idea?"

"You mean, spark for two more days and then discontinue?"

"Exactly."

She held back her smile. "I'm afraid not."

"So just like that," he said, snapping his fingers, "you expect me to just . . . stop?"

"Yes."

"What about tonight? Are you going to kiss me good-bye tonight?"

"No."

"Not even one last time?"

"No."

He jumped to his feet. "What are we supposed to do, then? Shake hands?"

"I'm not telling you to quit coming over or quit spending the evenings with me. I'm just saying we need to pull back a little on the . . . other until you decide how you feel."

"Pull back? *Pull back?* You're not pulling back, you're chopping me off at my knees."

She didn't know what to say. She didn't want to stop kissing any more than he did, but she knew on some deeper level she needed to protect herself. The hurt would be devastating enough. No need to compound it further.

And if he decided to marry her . . . well, then they'd have a lifetime to make up for the kisses they'd missed.

He paced in front of her. "Listen, I'm sorry I asked you to eavesdrop on those calls. You don't have to do that. I take it back."

"One has nothing to do with the other."

He stopped. "It does. You think I'm using you. I'm not, but I can see how you'd think that. So forget I asked."

"Give me the names and I'll listen in. I want the Comer Gang caught just as much as you do."

His chest rose and fell. A tic at the back

of his jaw began to beat. "No. It was a bad idea."

Putting the book aside, she rose. "If you change your mind, just let me know."

Hurt flashed in his eyes before it transformed to anger. "I won't be changing my mind. And I'm not sure if I'll make it by tomorrow night or even the next. I've got a lot of work to do right now."

"I see." She clasped her hands to keep them from trembling.

His lips thinned. "I guess I'll see myself out."

Striding to the hat rack, he grabbed his hat, then slammed out the door.

She collapsed onto the couch as if she'd been a marionette and her strings had all been severed. Placing her hands over her face, she curled up and sobbed. She was so confused. What if he decided to quit courting her? It was just a kiss. What harm was there in a kiss?

Drawing in a shuddering breath, she swiped her eyes. There wasn't a thing wrong with a kiss. But if he quit courting her because she held them back, then his reasons for coming around would be pretty clear.

If, however, he continued to seek her out and spend his evenings with her, knowing full well the only "reward" he'd receive for his efforts would be her company, well, that would also be telling.

Sniffling, she drew her knees up more tightly. The longer she lay there, the more peace she had about her decision. She wanted to know if she was enough for him as is. If she was, he'd be back. If she wasn't, then she'd rather know now, before her heart was any more engaged.

CHAPTER THIRTY-EIGHT

Luke couldn't find Duane and Necker. The longer he looked, the angrier he became. What if something were happening tonight? What if the gang decided to rob a train while he was twiddling his thumbs at Georgie's house?

He never should have started calling on her. What had he been thinking? He'd come to Brenham to do a job. *Finish* a job. The captain had made it clear, this was his last chance to collar Comer. If he failed again, he'd be pulled off the hunt and Harvey would take over.

Well, that wasn't going to happen. Luke would find Comer and bring him in, with Duane, Necker, and whoever else was involved. Georgie had made him soft. Distracted. He'd even begun to feel sorry for Duane.

Well, no more. He was done fooling around. He wanted that gang and he wanted them now. And the minute he found Comer, he'd make his arrests, then hightail it out of here.

The thought of never seeing Georgie again tried to make itself known, but he knocked it aside. She was nothing but a Nellie Bly devotee who played typical female games of catch-me-if-you-can.

He checked every saloon in town, the feed store, the ten-cent show, and even the brothels. Now he methodically walked up and down the alleyways, the full moon riding low in the sky and turning everything into tintype gray.

Flies buzzed around heaps of garbage, while rancid odors assaulted his senses. A dog whose skin hugged his ribs saw Luke and skittered off in the opposite direction. A couple of drunks propped themselves up against the brick siding toward the end of the passageway, one gesturing with his bottle in grandiose movements.

Luke slowed his steps. It wasn't just a couple of drunks, it was Duane and Necker.

"Well, lookee here, Duane. Look who's come ta call."

The two of them laughed at Necker's attempt at humor.

Resting his head against the building, Duane squinted. "You look mad enough ta eat the devil with his horns on. Somethin' wrong?"

"I've been looking for you," Luke answered, his tone sharp.

"Now, Duane," Necker slurred, "don't ya be believin' that sorry excuse. You and I both know he usually shows up fair to glowing after his little nightcap with Miss Georgie." Holding the neck of his bottle, he swiped his mouth with his sleeve. "What's the matter, Palmer? She too tired to dance the coochee-coochee fer ya tonight? Have a headache instead?"

Luke snatched the man clear off his feet. The bottle crashed to the ground and shattered. "Keep a civil tongue in your head when you talk about her, Necker."

"Hoo, would ya listen ta that? She sure got yer spurs tangled, don't she?"

Reining in his temper, he set Necker down, cursing himself for letting her interfere with his work yet again. "I guess she does. Sorry about your whiskey. Come on and I'll buy you another one."

Necker clapped him on the shoulder. "Ya can't be lettin' her do that to ya, Palmer. Ya got to be like me. Show her what's what. Then go on about yer business."

Duane harrumphed.

Necker peered over his shoulder. "You got

487

somethin' ta say?"

"Yeah. I'm bored. There's never nothin' ta do in this miserable town."

Holding out a hand, Necker helped Duane to his feet. The action threw him off-balance and nearly sent both back to the ground. Luke reached out a hand to steady them.

"There'll be excitement enough tomorry," Necker said, recovering his footing.

Luke sharpened his gaze. "What happens tomorrow?"

Necker picked his teeth with his tongue. "Nothin' that need concern you."

Slipping his hands in his pockets, Luke rocked on his feet. "I want in."

Faint strains of "Hello, Ma Baby" mixed with a dog barking in the distance. A man falling asleep in the saddle clomped by, his horse knowing the way home by heart.

Duane stepped forward, glass crackling under his boots. "How 'bout it, Neck? The man done said it's up ta you."

Hope kindled inside Luke. Comer must have given his blessing, but as any good leader, he'd delegated a feeling of power to his underling by letting him decide when. If something was happening tomorrow, though, then that *when* needed to be now.

He held Necker's gaze.

The man wasn't in any rush to give up his

control. "I'm still a little sore about them mice."

Duane huffed. "Oh, come on. Ya done laughed yer head off when you's tellin' the boys about it last night."

"That don't mean I enjoyed chasin' after those critters while Lulie plumb wore my ear out. Shoot, they's still popping outta everywhere and making her carry on like the end is comin'."

"Well, why didn't ya say nothin'? I'll lend ya my traps. They work real good." He nudged Necker with his elbow. "What do ya say?"

"I say he's got to do something ta make up fer it. That's what I say."

Duane's face split into a grin. "All righty. Ask him anythin'. He'll do it. Won't ya, Luke?"

"Pretty near." As soon as the words left his mouth, he thought of Georgie and what he'd do if Necker's plan involved her. *Please, Lord. Don't let it involve Georgie. Not again.*

Scratching his jaw, Necker strolled out onto the street, looked up and down its length, then raised his gaze to the roofs of the buildings. "I got somethin', but not here. Too many folks is around. Follow me."

Duane gave Luke an excited glance. They

followed Necker to Main Street. Though streetlamps lined the road, this section was well away from the saloons and bawdy houses. No lights came from inside the buildings. No people walked the board-walks. No horses stood tied to the rail. Nothing but a swirl of dust as a breeze blew down the thoroughfare.

Necker reached inside his jacket and withdrew a gun. Luke froze. Slipping his finger through the trigger guard, Necker spun the pistol around, then caught it, muzzle down, grip toward Luke.

He accepted the weapon, then checked for ammunition. It was loaded.

With his other hand, Necker withdrew a second pistol and repeated the process, except this time the grip faced Duane.

Luke's throat went dry. Was he going to make them duel? He couldn't shoot Duane. Wouldn't. He could wing him, though. But in return, Duane might outright kill him.

Eyes lighting up, Duane took the proffered gun. "I get to do it, too?"

"You too."

Duane let out a whoop, the sound bounc-ing off the storefronts.

"Here's what ya do," Necker began. "Ya see all them telly-phone wires up there?"

Luke glanced at the grid of wires going in

every direction. Down the street, up the street, across the street, and back again. Main connected everyone to everything and had four times as many lines running over it as any other street in the county.

"Well, we're gonna have us a little contest." Necker pointed to the east. "You get that side, Palmer. Duane gets the other. On the count of three, I wanna see who can sever the most lines in one minute's time."

Duane's shoulders slumped. "Is that all? Shoot, I could do that with my eyes closed."

The boy's boast wasn't far from the truth. Luke had hunted with him enough to know he was fast and very accurate. It was, most likely, the quality which afforded him a place in Comer's gang.

Necker gave Luke a steady gaze. "Whoever gets the most, wins."

Duane might not have understood the implication, but Luke did. If he didn't beat Duane, he wouldn't be invited in. And clearly, Necker thought he'd fail.

"You know," Luke said, giving Necker a sardonic look, "I'm going to have to repair every single one of these."

Necker smiled. "I know."

The mice. It was payback for the mice.

Necker drew a starting line in the dirt with his heel, then gave each of them enough cartridges to down every line up there. It was an awful lot of ammunition to be toting around unless he was anticipating trouble.

A sense of unease crept up his spine. He'd stood once before at the end of Main with a boy close to Duane's age. He and his brother might have been shooting out windows and it might have been a different town, but the scenario was exactly the same.

Luke turned to Duane. "You don't have to do this. You can give me your gun and I'll do it."

The boy gave him a knowing smile. " 'Fraid I might show ya up, Palmer?"

"No, I'm afraid the sheriff might come along and haul you to jail."

Duane laughed. "Nussbaum? Shoot, he'd probably make us do it over again so he could watch. Ain't that right, Necker?"

The man didn't say anything. Just stepped to the side. "Shooters ready?"

Duane placed one foot on the line, then crouched down like a runner. "Ready!"

Necker waited. "Palmer?"

Protect him, Lord. Shaking his arm loose, he toed the line. "Ready."

"On the count of three, then. One . . . two . . . *three!*"

Gunfire exploded. Wire popped and snapped, then drooped to the ground like a metal weeping willow.

Luke kept pace with Duane, glancing over his shoulder with every reload to assure himself he wasn't too far ahead. If the sheriff came, he wasn't about to let the boy take all the blame.

But the sheriff didn't come. No one did. And when they reached the ending stretch, Luke surged ahead in order to beat Duane and secure his position in Comer's gang.

"Come on, boys!" Necker shouted, racing up behind them. "I hear the cavalry!"

Distant shouts and footfalls set them to running down back streets, through alleyways, and across backyards, not stopping until they reached the lumberyard on the edge of town.

Hands on his knees, Duane hunched over, breathing hard. "Who won?" he gasped.

Luke fell against a tree, pretending he was winded, then closed his eyes, listening. No one was coming. Whoever had been pursuing them hadn't put up much of a chase.

"Palmer won," Necker said in between breaths. "For a minute there, I thought he was gonna let you win."

"*Let* me win?" Duane was still bent over, but glanced up at this remark.

Luke kept his expression neutral.

Necker studied him with speculation.

"You been holdin' out on us, Palmer?"

He shook his head. "I want in. That's all."

A long moment passed, their wheezes slowing bit by bit.

"I ain't never seen ya shoot like that," Necker said, not willing to let it go.

"It's something about getting caught, I guess." He shrugged, scrambling for a reasonable excuse. "I'm really good when I think someone's coming."

Necker chuckled. "Well, there's always someone a'comin'. So if you can keep yer focus, then yer in."

The first genuine smile of the night formed on Luke's face. "Really?"

"Yep. I think you'll do right nicely."

Duane punched the air. "Woo-hoo! Can I tell him?"

"Go ahead."

The boy looked both ways, then lowered his voice. "We're robbin' the 4:53 to Houston tomorry."

Luke's pulse picked up. "Tomorrow?"

"Yep. It's all decided."

"Whose place are we meeting at?" he asked.

"Nobody's," Necker answered. "Too dangerous. So each of us will leave at different times and ride to the designated spot."

"Sounds good. Tell me when to leave and

where to go, and I'll be there."

Necker shook his head. "You can ride with me. Nobody will think nothing if it's just the two of us. Meet me at my place come noon tomorrow."

Frustration gnawed at Luke. If he could find out where they were to rendezvous, he could get word to the captain and have the whole company waiting.

"He can ride with me and Blesinger." Duane turned to Luke. "We're leavin' first thing in the morning."

"No, he rides with me." Necker gave Luke an admiring look. "That was some fine shootin'. I'll see ya tomorry. You boys better turn in now. We got a big day ahead of us."

Necker jogged north, eventually disappearing from sight.

Duane punched the air again. "I can't believe it. Ya know how hard it is to get in?"

Luke smiled. "I'm not going to be able to sleep at all."

They headed in the direction of Luke's boardinghouse. It was just up the road from the lumberyard.

"So how will it work?" Luke asked.

"I've only been on two, but they did exactly the same thing both times."

Only two. Maybe Luke could talk to the judge. "Tell me."

"Everybody's given a different location. Even me and Necker don't go to the same place. That way, if the lawmen get wind o' somethin', the townsfolk can honestly tell 'em we all went in different directions."

"That's mighty smart."

"Comer don't use up all his kindling gettin' his fire started, that's fer sure."

"So what happens when you reach your destination?"

"I wait around until Finkel gets there, then we go to a different spot and pick up the next feller who's been a waitin' fer us."

"Finkel?"

"Yep, though I didn't recognize him 'til he started talking."

He drew his brows together. "Why didn't you recognize him?"

"Ever'body, including me, is supposed to show up with their neckerchief strapped on. Shoot, I ain't never even seen Comer without a mask."

He pulled up short. "Never?"

"Nope."

"Has Necker?"

Duane gave a quick shrug. "I'm not real sure, but I can tell ya Comer don't show up until the very end."

"What do you mean?"

"Well, Finkel takes us to the spot we're

going to rob the train at. Then, when the train is barreling down on us, Comer rides in so fast his horse is throwing dirt in the eyes of jackrabbits." A tone of awe coated the boy's voice.

"You've never seen him?"

He straightened. "No, but I spoke to him once while we was waitin' fer the train."

Luke tugged his hat lower on his head. "What about afterwards? Do you see Comer then?"

"Nope. We all have different routes fer goin' home. One route if ever'thing's fine. Another route if the lawmen show up. And no two are the same."

"Then how do you get paid?"

"I get mine from Necker. I don't know how ever'body else gets theirs."

What a convoluted mess.

"Who else is in besides you, me, and Necker?" he asked.

"Only ones I know about are the ones at our poker games — Ragston, Finkel, Blesinger, and us three. Prysborski was with us fer a while, but he, uh, had that huntin' accident."

"What about that Hurless Swanning guy from the shooting tournament? Who was he?"

"I dunno. That was the first time I'd ever

seen him. But Necker tol' me later he was tryin' to horn in on Comer's territory, so they got rid of him."

A light inside the window of Mrs. Sealsfield's boardinghouse burned low. Luke paused outside the gate. "You ever have second thoughts, Duane?"

"No, why? You havin' second thoughts?"

"I've just been reading a lot in the papers. The Rangers seem determined to catch Comer."

"They caught us unawares this last time. Like to scare me to death."

"So why not quit?"

"What else would I do?"

"I don't know. Take over the store for your pa. Find you a woman. Have a few kids. Go to church. Just be normal, I guess."

Duane looked off in the distance. "I've thought about it before. But after Prysborski, well, there ain't no gettin' out less'n it's in a coffin."

"Prysborski wasn't an accident?"

Duane pulled in his chin. "You need ta decide if yer in or not, Luke. 'Cause if yer not in all the way, it puts the rest of us at risk."

He wanted to tell Duane he was already at risk, but he couldn't chance the boy going straight to Necker. "I'm just thinking out loud. Trying to think beyond today and consider tomorrow."

"Then what ya oughta do is think about goin' ta bed, 'cause ya won't get much sleep tomorry." He grinned. "But you can earn in a day what would normally take a whole year."

Luke lifted his hat, then resettled it on his head. "If you aren't with Comer when he splits up the money, how do you know you get a fair shake?"

"Comer divvies it up different fer each feller. The ones who have children get the most. Then ones who're married. Then fellers like you and me. I'm purty sure that's why Necker got married. We do most o' our robbin' between harvest and plantin'."

"And Necker married Lulie after the harvest?"

"Yep."

"That still doesn't guarantee the money is split like it should be."

"Aw, ya worry too much. Frank Comer's the best dad-blamed outlaw to ever live. He wouldn't cheat nobody."

Other than the people he robbed, Luke thought. *Or who want out of his gang.*

He placed a hand on Duane's shoulder. "You be careful tomorrow."

"Don't worry. Everything'll be just fine."

Nodding, Luke opened the gate and let himself into the boardinghouse.

CHAPTER THIRTY-NINE

Luke needed to alert his captain. The lines in town were down, but everything originated at Georgie's cottage. So the wires going to rural areas would still be functioning. He waited in his room, allowing Duane time to make it home, then set out.

After these last few months, he knew every shortcut and back alley, especially to Georgie's. He kept well out of sight until he was practically at her door.

Circling to the front, he knocked. "Georgie? It's me. Can you answer? I need you to make a call."

"Luke?" He heard her scramble; then a light came on in the living room.

The moment she opened the door, he pushed inside and closed it behind him. Instead of a nightgown, she wore a calico. What was she doing dressed at two in the morning?

"They came back," she said, distress

etched on her face.

He sucked in his breath. "Necker? He was here? Did he hurt you?"

She took a step backward. "Is that who it was? Arnold Necker?"

His pulse thrummed. "Did he hurt you?"

"No, no. He didn't come in. He stood out front and fired his pistols, making all kinds of racket. It scared me so much, I crawled to the switchboard and tried to phone the sheriff. But the lines won't work." Her body trembled.

Pulling her against him, he rubbed her back. He hadn't had a chance to think much about their argument. Truth was, he understood her position and deep down respected her for it. But the thought of doing without her kisses was not to be borne. Still, now wasn't the time.

"I'm sorry," he said. "The wires in town were shot down, but everything else should be working."

"They aren't. Nothing's working. I tried every single one."

"Blast." He gave her shoulders a squeeze, then released her. "I'll be right back. I need to check something outside."

He didn't have to go more than halfway down the walkway to see every telephone line on the pole had been shot off. He

502

cursed. Necker had made sure there would be no way for anyone to communicate with the outside.

Why had he done that? Did he suspect something? Did he suspect Luke? Was that the real reason for tonight's prank?

Taking the steps two at a time, he darted back inside. "Everything's down. He shot the lines clean in two. There'll be no way to use the telephones or the telegraph. We're completely without communication."

She glanced out the window. "Why would he do that?"

Walking over to his desk, he yanked open a drawer and pulled out schematics for the various lines. "I need to reach my captain. Do you know offhand which line runs out to Industry?"

"The one that leads to the Dobbings' place." She joined him at the desk. "What's wrong? What's happening?"

"I'll be right back." Grabbing the lantern, he hurried out to his tool cart and snatched up his gloves, climbers, splicing pliers, and wire grip. But when he reached the pole, he stood amongst a tangle of wires, having no idea which one went where. It would take sunlight and a great many hours to sort them out.

He returned his tools to the cart, resisting

the urge to vent his frustration. But there was no time.

Georgie met him at the door. "Too dark?"

"And too much of a mess."

"What's happening? What do you need your captain for?"

"Comer's going to rob the 4:53 to Houston."

Her lips parted. "When?"

"Today." He tossed the schematics on the desk, then headed to the back door.

"What are you going to do?"

He stopped, his hand on the knob. "I'm going to round up a posse. Lock your doors."

Georgie resumed her position in front of the window, keeping watch over the fledglings. She'd been there all night and had dozed off until Necker's shooting jerked her awake. Now, knowing Luke had no way to call for help from his Rangers, she was once again wide awake.

She racked her brain for a way to get word to his captain. She could ride to Industry at first light and use their switchboard, but with Brenham's phone lines in the shape they were, the entire town would be in an uproar. Were she to leave during a crisis of this magnitude, SWT&T would be sure to dismiss her.

She supposed she could send Bettina, but it was an awfully long way for the little girl to go. In addition to the fact the switchboard was housed in a saloon.

Mrs. Patrick would have helped her, but she and her husband were in Jefferson visiting relatives. Georgie went through her list of acquaintances and customers. The men would most likely be helping Luke. The women either had children, were too old, too young, or had sympathies for Comer.

In the end, her thoughts circled back to Bettina. It wouldn't be the first time the girl had gone to a bar. Heaven knew she'd had to haul her father home any number of times. And if she dressed like a boy, then perhaps no one would ever be the wiser.

She drummed her fingers. She crossed and uncrossed her legs. She jiggled her chair. Finally, she rose and placed a palm against her cool windowpane. "Sit tight, little ones. I'll be back as quickly as I can."

The von Schillers' shack looked more like a horse shed than a house. Entire pieces of siding had splintered. The right side of the lean-to's roof hung precariously from the eaves. And the porch had been torn completely off.

Georgie had no idea what to do. Should she knock on the door? What if Mr. von Schiller opened it? What if he didn't? She couldn't just walk in and start peeking under bedclothes.

She scanned the dark oblong windows, the gaping holes like yawning entrances to fathomless caves. If she knew which one belonged to Bettina, she'd throw rocks through it. But she didn't, and she couldn't risk guessing wrong.

In the end, she put her fingers in her mouth and did her cardinal call. The high-pitched sound pierced the air as loudly as a train whistle. She held her breath. After a few moments, she positioned her fingers in her mouth again, when a small silhouette raced around the corner.

Relief swept through her. "Over here," she hissed.

"What's happened?" The girl had either taken time to dress or she didn't own a nightgown.

"I've just found out the 4:53 to Houston is going to be robbed today."

Bettina's eyes widened. "You gonna tell the sheriff?"

She shook her head. "He won't do anything. Besides, we mustn't tell anyone other than the Rangers. I tried to alert them by phone, but the lines all across town have been shot down by . . . by some pranksters."

"Don't ya think that's a good thing? 'Cause it's probably Comer who's doin' the holdup, and if word got to the Rangers, they might catch Comer unawares."

Squatting down, she took the girl by the shoulders. "Listen, Bettina. You remember those men who broke into my home and burned up our hats?"

"Why, shore."

"Well, we can never get those back. And that's what Frank Comer does. He takes things which don't belong to him and folks never get it back."

The girl shook her head. "He takes stuff from trains and banks."

"It's not the banks' money, though. Banks store money for their customers. The money belongs to those people. And trains cart money to business owners so they can pay the people who work for them. What if the money on today's train belongs to SWT&T? If Mr. Comer robs it, then SWT&T won't be able to pay us, will they?"

Bettina scratched her head. "Why would SWT&T put money on a train?"

"To send it to you and me, and then on to the next town where SWT&T has workers." She could see the girl waffling. "I need you to take a message to the switchboard operator in Industry. Will you do it? You'll get to dress like a boy."

After a long pause, Bettina nodded. "Well, I reckon. If I get to wear my trousers."

"That's a girl. And you'll need to hide your hair in a hat, as well."

"All right. When ya want me ta leave?"

"Right now. While you get ready, I'll wake up the livery and bring you a mount."

"I don't ride."

"What?"

"I don't ride. Don't know how."

Georgie blinked. She'd assumed Bettina walked everywhere because her father couldn't afford to keep or even rent a horse. It never occurred to her the girl didn't know how. "Oh, dear. That just won't do. You can't walk clear to Industry."

"Shore I can. Me and Pa done it a million times. One o' his favorite drinkin' holes is there. The H.H. Boelsche Saloon."

She straightened. "Why, that's where the switchboard is."

"I know."

"It'll take forever. By the time you get there and send word to Ranger headquarters, it'll be too late for them to send out a company of men."

"Maybe. But they might could get some

on the 4:53. If'n they did that, then they'd catch the fellers red-handed."

Biting her lip, she looked around. "It's the middle of the night."

"So?"

"So you can't just walk to Industry in the middle of the night."

"If I were a boy, would you feel the same way?"

She rubbed her forehead. Truth was, she'd have asked Fritz or one of the other boys in her Junior Audubon Society to go if she thought their parents would let them. But she knew they wouldn't.

"Well? Would ya?" Bettina pressed.

"Probably not," she admitted.

"What about the way yer always tellin' me a gal can do anything a feller can?"

"This is different."

"It ain't. 'Sides, I've made up my mind. I'm goin' whether ya say I can or not. Ain't nothin' you can do ta stop me."

She'd seen that look in the girl's eye on more than one occasion. With a sigh of resignation, she gave Bettina her blessing. "Just remember, you can't tell anyone other than the Industry operator."

Georgie didn't bother returning to her vigil in the corner. Daybreak would be within

509

another hour and the fledglings' parents could take over the task. Falling onto her bed, she closed her eyes, second-guessing herself once again. If she'd had any idea Bettina would have to walk to Industry, she wouldn't have involved her. And now it was too late. Bettina would have long since left. She prayed for the girl's safety, but sleep overtook her before she ever made it to the amen.

Something was wrong. Georgie pushed herself up off the bed and glanced out the window. Dawn had just begun to lighten the sky.

Then she realized. It was quiet. Too quiet. Why weren't the fledglings squalling? Cardinals were early risers.

Swinging her legs over the side of the bed, she rose and padded to the living room window. Even though dawn touched the horizon, it was still too dark to see anything through the glass. Without taking time to grab a blanket, she hurried to the back porch and tiptoed toward the ligustrum.

No sound. No movement.

She edged closer, then pulled back. The fledglings were gone. She looked left and right. No sign of them.

Her heart sped up. She knew good and

well they hadn't been taught to fly in the dead of night.

Hurrying off the porch and into the yard, she scanned the trees. And then she saw Prince Albert, his bright crimson coat a fine jewel against the green of the elm's leaves. He hopped along its branch.

Chit chit chit. A short, sharp cry of distress. Victoria fluttered down, landing beside him, then repeated the staccato notes.

Georgie whirled back around, covering her mouth with both hands. No. *No. Please, Lord.*

But there was no question. Something had snatched up the babies during the night. She saw no sign of disturbance. The ligustrum had no broken branches. The nest wasn't cockeyed. Everything looked perfect. Except the cradle was empty.

For the first time, she realized how bright and noticeable the woven, colorful ribbon was. A sick feeling churned in her stomach.

Was that what alerted the predator? Was she at fault? Letting out a low moan, she dropped to her knees, for whether it had been snake, cat, hawk, or raccoon, one thing was certain. Edward, Alice, and Leopold were dead.

She rocked back and forth, keening, grieving. How could this have happened? She'd watched over them all night.

But that wasn't exactly true. She'd dozed off and on, then been interrupted by Necker and Luke. She'd abandoned them completely to rouse Bettina, only to fall asleep the moment she returned. And at some point, something had grabbed those fledglings.

If only she'd stayed awake. If only she'd never left them. Her watery gaze traveled over the utopia she'd created for her birds. Oaks, cottonwood, and elm. Buttonbush, sumac, and honeysuckle. Columbine, Turk's cap, and coneflower. She'd given them everything they needed. A veritable Garden of Eden.

Yet a serpent had come calling and it had swallowed up the helpless chicks.

No, she wanted to scream. *They were safe with me. I provided for them.*

But they weren't safe. She might groom her garden to help His creatures. She might set out houses and fill up feeders. But ultimately, it was her Father in heaven who clothed them, fed them, and taught them to fly.

Suddenly, Luke's words rang in her head. *I've sworn to protect. And in order to do my job, sacrifices sometimes have to be made.*

Had the fledglings been sacrificed? But

why? She looked around her garden. Perhaps it was because some other of God's creatures needed life. And God in His infinite wisdom had the perfect plan.

She swallowed. It didn't make the hurt go away. It didn't keep her from watching helplessly as Albert and Victoria flew down a branch, confused and upset.

Still, she wasn't God. She couldn't control the universe and all the living things in it. That, she admitted, was something best left up to Him.

Immediately, Bettina's face flashed before her. She'd sent a nine-year-old, in the wee hours of the morning, by herself, to a town sixteen miles away. All because she wanted to help where no help had been requested.

This was much worse than leaving a colorful ribbon out. If anything happened to Bettina, Georgie would never forgive herself.

Scrambling to her feet, she stumbled inside just as a knock sounded. She swung open the door, and there Luke stood, nothing short of a gift straight from heaven.

Chapter Forty

Nussbaum looked even younger than usual, his hair tousled, his glasses missing, his union suit covered by trousers he'd yet to button. Even after a full night's sleep the man didn't have any whiskers to speak of.

"Palmer?" He squinted. "That you?"

Luke pushed inside the sheriff's home. After telling Georgie he was to round up a posse, he'd gone straight to the boarding-house, lifted some loose planks in his floor, then collected a satchel of handcuffs along with his clothes, hat, boots, gun belt, badge, and Warrant of Authority. It felt good to be himself again. "Go get your glasses, Nussbaum."

"Look here, what do you think —"

"Go get your glasses," he barked.

The sheriff fell back, then shuffled down the hallway grumbling. A few minutes later, he returned with glasses and a hastily donned shirt. "If you're comin' about the lines that were shot down, I already know about 'em. You needn't have woken me up."

Luke opened his jacket to reveal his badge, then handed the sheriff his papers. "I'm Lucious Landrum, Texas Ranger of Company 'A'. I need to get a posse together."

"Lucious Landrum?" Nussbaum huffed. "You're no more Lucious Landrum than I'm —"

"Read the warrant. I don't have a lot of time."

The tone somehow penetrated and Nussbaum scanned the document, looked up, then scanned it again. "You're not Luke Palmer?"

"No."

"Then, who's gonna fix them telephone wires?"

He barely checked the impulse to roll his eyes. "I need to make some arrests, but time is of the essence, so I'd appreciate it if you'd help me put together a posse."

"Who ya wanna arrest?"

"Arnold Necker, Peter Finkel, and Clem Ragston." He left out Duane and Blesinger for now. Since they both lived in town, he didn't want word reaching them before the posse was on its way. Still, the names on the list left a bitter taste in his mouth. Comer

515

would not be among those he captured today. With communication cut off, there was simply no way to send for the rest of his company.

He'd considered going with Necker and trying to take Comer alone. But if Duane's story was accurate, then the gang would have their guns out by the time Comer made an appearance. Luke might be able to disarm them if he caught them off guard, but his chances wouldn't be too good with that many men holding loaded pistols in the ready position. Besides, he had an uneasy feeling about Necker. Something just didn't sit right.

Nussbaum returned the warrant. "Do you have any idea who them men really are?"

"Yes."

The sheriff scratched his neck. "Well, if ya get yer Rangers to go along, I might come with ya. But nobody round here'll bring 'em in."

"What about your deputies?"

Nussbaum shook his head. "Not them, neither. Ya don't know them fellers like we do. With the way they're scattered, we might get the drop on one or two, but that'd leave a lot more to get the drop on us. Why, we'd be full o' lead 'fore the sun's even up."

Whipping off his hat, Luke pointed south.

"They're planning a train robbery for later today. People's lives are at stake. If I could do it alone, I would, but we need to hit the houses simultaneously. Surely you can persuade your men to cooperate?"

" 'Fraid not. Nothin' short of a company o' Rangers could go after those men and come out alive."

"We don't have time to wait for my company. I need to round them up within the next few hours."

Nussbaum opened the door. "I'm right sorry, Palmer."

"It's Landrum. Lucious Landrum. And if I had such pitiful deputies, I'd discharge them on the spot."

The sheriff wasn't moved. His fear of the Comer Gang clearly outweighed any pride he had over his deputized crew.

Luke jammed on his hat. "Fine. I'll go out there alone. All I need is one fearless man with nerve enough to drive a hack." He poked Nussbaum with a finger. "You give me the name of that man and I'll come back with a load of criminals."

"You'll come back in a coffin is what you'll come back in. Now, good night — or good morning, or whatever it is."

Barely suppressing his anger, Luke stormed out the door. House by house, he roused men from their beds with his request. One driver, that's all he needed. He asked the doc, the judge, the fire chief, the banker, the blacksmith, the tanner, the livery owner, even the milliner. On each occasion the door was shut in his face.

Time had run out. If he didn't leave within the next half hour, he'd miss Duane, Blesinger, and possibly the others. There was only one person whom he hadn't asked. One person who he knew would face the enemy square on. One person who'd risk everything.

Standing on the familiar porch beside a green bench, rattan rockers, and a porch swing, he opened the screen, then knocked on the bright blue door of Georgie's cottage.

She thought she'd seen him in his Ranger's garb, but clearly she hadn't. His transformation was every bit as dramatic as that of caterpillar to butterfly. His quality Stetson and long-sleeve shirt offered the only bit of white he wore. Everything else was black — leather vest, string tie, trim pants, worn chaps, polished boots.

But it was the row of cartridges in his hand-tooled belt, the enormous emblem-buckle of gold and silver, and the pair of pistols at his hips which drew her attention.

She allowed her gaze to travel back up the length of him until his denim-colored eyes snagged hers.

"Bettina's on her way to Industry," she said, her brain starting to work again. "By herself. I have to go get her. Can I borrow your horse?"

"No, I need it. And I need you."

She shook her head. "But, I —"

"No one would join my posse."

She blinked. "No one? Was it because of their loyalty to Comer?"

"For some. Others — like the sheriff and his deputies — refused out of fear."

"What about the men in your gun club? Did you ask for their help?"

"They all said no."

"Even Mr. Lee?"

"The lawyer and his wife went with the Patricks to Jefferson."

"I'm sure the mayor would help." She shook her head. "No, wait, he's in Austin."

"Believe me, I've asked the butcher, the baker, and the candlestick maker. No one in the entire town is willing."

She nodded. "It'll be all right. You can ride to Industry and intercept Bettina on your way. Once the two of you arrive, you can put a call through to your captain and arrange to have more Rangers brought in."

"There's no time. I'm going to round them up myself, one at a time."

"By yourself?" Her lips parted. "But how?"

He glanced at the horizon. "May I come in?"

"Oh!" She jumped back. "I'm sorry. Of course."

Stepping inside, he shut the door. He'd been in this room a thousand times, but never had he filled it the way he did now. It was as if he'd grown ten feet in the last two hours.

He removed his hat, then combed his fingers through the hair above his left ear. "I can't do it completely alone. I need someone to drive the hack."

"You mean there wasn't one man in the entire town who'd drive a hack for you?"

"Unfortunately, no."

She propped her hands on her hips. "Well, that's ridiculous. Why, anyone could drive a hack. Even me."

His gaze held hers.

Her stomach dropped. "Oh my. Do you, do you want me to drive the hack?"

He shifted his weight. "You wouldn't have to do anything. I'll haul them in and keep them covered between locations. But you'll have to hold them at gunpoint while I go inside each home."

She pressed a hand against her waist, then covered it with the other. "You don't understand. I sent Bettina *by herself* to Industry."

"I heard you and I appreciate it. Hopefully she'll make good time."

"She's nine years old, Luke. She can't walk all the way to Industry."

"And I can't round up Comer's gang without help. You're my last hope, Georgie. If I don't intercept these men now, this minute, innocent lives will be put in danger. And not just men, but women and children. Many children. Children Bettina's age and younger."

She thought of the little girl who'd stood beside her during the robbery back in February. "Comer won't hurt them."

"Don't fool yourself. The only reason no one has been hurt is because no one has challenged him. Putting your trust in his 'good nature' is about as safe as sharing a tree with a grizzly."

"What about Bettina?"

"That girl's about the most resourceful thing I ever did see. Matter of fact, if you don't come with me, I just might go get her to drive the hack."

She paled. "You wouldn't."

"Try me." His blue eyes had turned to points of gray. This was the Lucious Lan-

521

drum she'd read about in the papers. But somewhere in there was also the Luke Palmer she knew and loved.

"The girl needs protecting."

Like the fledglings? The thought seared through her mind with such vehemence she stumbled back two steps.

"The folks on that train need protecting, too," he said.

She swallowed. She couldn't be two places at once, but she knew someone who could. And she'd just have to put her trust in Him. "I won't be able to hold the prisoners at gunpoint. I've never shot a gun in all my life."

"And hopefully you won't have to. I meant to take you out and teach you, but there just hasn't been time." He rotated the hat in his hands. "I think it might work in your favor, though. If the fellows knew you could shoot, they'd figure you wouldn't be able to actually kill one of them if the need arose. But if they discover you don't know how to shoot, they'll be worried you might shoot them by accident — which is a distinct possibility. That alone may keep them from giving you any trouble."

"What if they give me trouble anyway?"

His eyes turned steely again. "Then you point and pull the trigger."

She placed a hand against her throat. "I see. Well."

If she went with him, it would mean leaving Bettina in God's capable hands. It would mean losing her job. It would also mean ridding the state of men who preyed upon others.

She took a deep breath. "When do we leave?"

The tension left his shoulders, his eyes filling with relief and appreciation. For the first time, he looked like the Luke she knew.

Grabbing her hands, he flipped them up and kissed them on the palms. "Thank you. I'd kiss you properly, but I'm not allowed. We need to leave in about twenty minutes. I'll go get a hack and horse from the livery. Meanwhile, put on something which allows you to move as freely as possible." He whipped open the door, then leaned back in. "Not your trousers, though. You hear?"

She nodded, then scurried to her room as soon as the door closed behind him.

CHAPTER FORTY-ONE

Luke drew Honey Dew alongside Georgie at the juncture of Jackson and Fourth. She wore her brown calico, no hat, and a pair of men's driving gloves. He was pleased to see how well she managed the hack and its horse.

"Wait here," he told her.

She glanced at him.

He pointed up the street with a nod of his head. "That's Duane and Blesinger. They're on their way out."

"Duane Pfeuffer? You can't mean Duane and Mr. Blesinger are mixed up in all this."

"Just sit tight. I'll be right back." Nudging Honey Dew, he trotted ahead hoping the men would recognize the horse and let their guard down.

Duane twisted around in his saddle, then grinned. "What in tarnation are you wearin', Palmer? Ya don't need to get all frocked up in fancy doodahs."

Luke caught up to them. "Morning, Duane. Ludwig."

"Look at ya. I didn't even know ya had nothin' other than them overalls."

"What are you doing here?" Blesinger hissed. "You're supposed to ride out with Necker."

Instead of responding, Luke snatched Duane's pistol out of its holster and turned it onto the men. "I'm going to need you to come with me."

Blesinger immediately reached for his gun.

Luke cocked his. "Don't even think about it."

Freezing momentarily, the gun shop owner made a show of keeping his hands wide and high.

Duane's smile faltered. "Are ya funning us? What're ya doin'?"

He flipped his jacket back, revealing his badge. "I'm Lucious Landrum, Texas Ranger of Company 'A.' You're under arrest." In the seconds it took for the men to absorb the shock, the betrayal, then the panic, Luke grabbed Blesinger's pistol, stuffed it in his own waistband, then gathered the reins of both horses. "Get off your mounts and keep those hands in the air."

Duane looked at the Colt in Luke's hand.

"I mean it, Duane. If you've really only

been involved in two of the robberies, I'm hoping the judge will go easy on you. Either way, I'll put in a good word for you."

The boy's body relaxed. "Aw, Judge Yoakum ain't gonna do nothing."

"Then, get on down." He figured they'd find out soon enough Yoakum wasn't the one who'd be making the decisions.

"But we'll miss the robbery."

Clearly, he still hadn't been able to make the jump from Luke to Lucious.

"There is no robbery," Blesinger gritted.

Luke had expected more resistance from the gun shop owner, but the man had a healthy respect for pistols and slowly dismounted.

"I don't understand." Duane slid off his horse, his brown eyes pleading for mercy. For a second chance.

But it wasn't Luke's to give. He just brought them in. The courts decided the rest. He tried not to think of Alec, yet the image of his brother being seized by Sheriff Glaser flashed through his mind. He recalled the trumped-up charges Glaser had heaped onto Alec and the resulting three-year term. But this was different. Duane's crimes were real, not manufactured. Focusing on his task, he jumped to the ground and gave a whistle, signaling Georgie to join them.

"I thought ya were my friend. I trusted ya."

His heart turned at the hurt coating Duane's words. "That's the thing about living outside the law, the men have no honor. You can't trust any of them."

"They ain't the ones pretending to be my friend, all the while knowin' they wasn't. It's the feller *inside* the law what's doin' that."

"I wasn't pretending about that. I like you. I like you a lot. But my orders are to bring in Comer and his gang, regardless of how I feel about them."

"That's the biggest bunch a tripe I ever heard," Blesinger mumbled.

"You know what this is gonna do to my pa?" Duane asked. "I'm the only son he's got."

Georgie arrived with the hack, wind playing with her hair, a look of determination on her face.

"I'm guessing your pa has a pretty good idea already of what you've been up to." Luke nudged the men toward the bed. "All's not lost, though. You've plenty of years left. When you get out, you can start all over. Find you some good, honest

527

friends. A nice God-fearing woman. And this time around, don't let worldly gain rob you of true prosperity."

Blesinger climbed into the hack, Duane behind him. Luke cuffed their hands.

"Do ya have all that?" Duane asked, watching as Luke secured him and Blesinger to a chain bolted inside the cart. "Do ya have good, honest friends? A God-fearin' woman? True prosperity?"

Luke didn't know what to say. Especially since the answer to every question was no. His gaze lifted briefly to Georgie's, her eyes offering sympathy and love.

Swallowing, he returned his attention to Duane. "Truth is, my job doesn't give me much of a chance for all that. I spend my days and nights crisscrossing the state with nothing but my horse, my saddle, and my guns. Folks like to glamorize the life of us Rangers, but it can get awfully lonely."

"Then, why do ya do it?"

"It's an important service, and up to now I've been happy to provide it. But here lately I've been asking myself the same questions you just did."

"Maybe ya need a fresh start, too."

Luke squeezed his shoulder. "Maybe I do, Duane. Maybe I do."

Returning to Honey Dew, he mounted

and glanced at Georgie. "Let's go."

She turned the wagon north. Resting his wrists against the pommel, Luke kept his eyes moving, but nothing seemed amiss. Birds fluttered from tree to tree. Squirrels played tag. A rabbit froze, then bounced out of sight.

The fellows remained quiet, their morose expressions and slumped postures in stark contrast to the quiet beauty of the new dawn.

When they were two hundred yards from Necker's place, he had Georgie pull to a stop. Climbing onto the seat beside her, he retrieved Blesinger's gun, then went through the procedure for loading and firing it.

Blesinger's eyes widened. "She's never used a pistol before?"

" 'Fraid not," Luke said with a shake of his head.

Blesinger swore.

More alarm than Duane had exhibited all morning filled his eyes. "Well, don't let her point it at me!"

"Watch your language, Ludwig," Luke said. Giving Georgie the gun, he fitted his hand over hers and helped her cock it. "It's in firing position now. If they make any attempt to leave, just squeeze this lever. If you feel like you didn't slow them down enough, pull the hammer back and squeeze again. That ought to do it."

She nodded. "I've got it. Hammer back. Squeeze trigger."

"Yep. And it's best if you keep your eyes open."

"For the love of —"

"Language." Luke gave Blesinger another look of warning, then jumped to the ground. "Try to quit trembling, Georgie. Those triggers are pretty sensitive."

She held the gun with both hands. "I'm just a little nervous, is all."

He scratched his neck. "You might not want to make any sudden moves, fellas."

"Ya cain't think to leave her with that thing," Duane pleaded. "What if her nose gets a tickle and she sneezes or somethin'?"

"Then I suggest you duck."

Blesinger clenched his jaw. "At least bring her a couple of pillows when you come back. That gun gets awfully heavy. If she had something to rest her wrists on, she'd be a mite more steady."

"I'll do that."

Luke withdrew his Winchester from the scabbard attached to his saddle. It was early yet and everything was still. He knew from the mouse episode Necker was a sound sleeper, but he didn't linger. At this time of morning, the whinny of the horses might be all it took to rouse him and his wife.

He made a quick sweep of the perimeter to ensure they were in the bedroom, cocked the rifle, then pushed open the door. The bedroom was straight ahead.

Necker's wife, a pretty little thing with huge brown eyes and curly brown hair, sat on the edge of the bed hooking the buttons on her boot. Whipping her head up at his entry, she locked eyes with him.

Luke charged.

"Arnold!" She jumped between Luke and the bed.

Necker reached for a gun lying beneath a pillow. Luke pushed the woman aside and covered him before he could bring it up. "Drop it."

Necker hesitated.

"Drop it or you're dead." He held steady, preparing for the worst.

Necker must have sensed his sincerity. He slowly withdrew his hands and put them in the air. Luke moved forward, stuffed Necker's pistol in his waistband, then handcuffed his prisoner. "I'm Lucious Landrum and you're under arrest."

"I knew somethin' weren't right about ya. I tol' Frank o' my suspicions. You'll never catch him. Never."

"That may be so, but we have you and that's a start." He snatched the pillows off the bed and tossed them to Mrs. Necker.

Eyes wide, she stood with back and arms plastered to the wall, making no attempt to catch the pillows.

Luke swept the gun to indicate she join her husband. He didn't fancy putting his back to her just yet. "Grab those pillows, please, ma'am, and walk us to the hack. I suggest neither one of you make any suspicious movements."

Instead of whistling for Georgie, he walked them the entire two hundred yards. He didn't want the missus running back for a weapon while they were still in range.

Necker and his wife remained silent during their walk to the hack. Luke could see Duane talking away, a smile playing on Georgie's lips as she listened, though her gun never wavered from its mark.

Typical Duane, Luke thought. His natural good humor always took over no matter what the circumstance.

The young man caught sight of them, started to wave, then had the motion cut short by chains. "I was tellin' her the one about the skunk what thinks he's a frog."

Luke chuckled. "That's a good one."

"Mornin', Necker," Duane called. "Can

ya believe it? This whole time it was Lucious Landrum fixin' our telly-phones. I had no i-deer. Even Miss Georgie, here, didn't know. Did ya?"

She smiled. "I certainly didn't. Good morning, Mr. Necker."

"Can she put the gun away now?" Blesinger asked, his voice a bit desperate.

Luke helped Necker into the wagon, then secured his chains. "Let me show her how to ease back on the hammer first."

Necker reared back. "She doesn't know how to use that?"

Luke pursed his lips. "She's a fast learner."

The man swore.

"Watch yer language," Duane said, scowling. "We got us a lady on board."

Necker leaned over and spit but kept his words to himself.

Luke climbed up next to Georgie. "You did real good, honey. Since we're done for now, you just put your thumb here on the hammer and pull back, then ease it forward. Make sure your barrel isn't pointing at anyone when you do it, though." He cocked it again. "Now you try."

She aimed in the direction of his horse.

Luke gently lowered the barrel. "These bullets go far. You don't want to accidentally shoot anything."

Keeping the pistol trained to the ground, she released the hammer, then looked up at him, her green eyes sparkling with pride.

"That's the way," he said. "You can relax now. I'll guard the men while you drive. You needn't be afraid to put your back to them. I'll protect you."

Her eyes softened. "Thank you."

He emptied Necker's pistol, took the pillows from Mrs. Necker, and stashed everything under the wagon seat. "I'll send word about your husband as soon as I can."

Her eyes teared up. "What's going to happen to him?"

"That's not for me to decide, ma'am. But I wouldn't count on him coming back anytime soon."

"We're married, though. And he hardly put in any corn a'tall. What am I supposed to do?" She turned to her husband. "Arnold?"

He kept his head down, refusing to even offer a good-bye.

"Arnold?" Her voice rose an octave.

Luke swung up onto his horse.

Georgie picked up the reins. "You come on by my cottage next time you're in town, Mrs. Necker. We'll make sure you get along."

Her face twisted in anger and hurt. "I

don't want nothin' to do with you and your holier-than-thou kind. I hate you. *Hate you!*"

Georgie blinked, her lips parting.

Clicking his tongue, Luke touched his heels to Honey Dew's sides. "Come on, Georgie. Next stop's a good ways from here."

Biting her lip, she shook the reins. "Hiyyup."

CHAPTER FORTY-TWO

Luke tensed. Peter Finkel stood on his front porch. He raised a hand to block out the rising sun behind Luke's back, then must have smelled trouble. Breaking into an all-out run, he jumped onto a black thoroughbred hitched to a nearby mesquite tree.

"Stay here," Luke shouted to Georgie as he dug in his heels and gave chase.

Finkel headed straight for the brakes, whipping his horse on both sides with his reins. Luke leaned forward along Honey Dew's neck, the pommel of his saddle hitting his stomach.

Looking back, Finkel laid into his horse, goading it with his spurs. His horse accelerated. Dirt clods flew up behind the thoroughbred, pelting Luke and stinging his shoulders, arms, and face with each blow.

Squinting his eyes against the onslaught, he kept his focus on his quarry and prayed there were no gopher holes or loose footing.

A fall at this speed would break Honey Dew's neck and likely his own.

Not for the first time, he wished he had his own horse and saddle. He shouted encouragement to the mare, but Finkel's black continued to pull away.

Luke whipped his reins back and forth. Sweat bubbled along Honey Dew's neck and chest. She stumbled, lurching forward. Tensing, he managed to keep his seat. She recovered her footing and he let out a breath.

The slip had given Finkel an even greater lead. Honey Dew's hoofbeats slowed. He couldn't afford to let the energy drain from her. They still had one more man to round up.

Pulling her to a stop, he grabbed his Winchester, swung to ground, and settled the butt of the rifle into his shoulder. Honey Dew wheezed and blew beside him. The distance between him and Finkel increased exponentially, but he was still well within range.

Looking down the barrel, Luke shot the ground in front of the galloping thoroughbred, knowing full well his bullets came within a hair of Finkel's ears before striking the earth.

He'd long since learned he rarely had to

actually hit his mark. The sound of a bullet singing by usually raised the level of concern enough to bring his man to a halt, for most weren't willing to gamble on where the next one would land.

"Stop!" Luke shouted. "Or I'll shift a little left this time." He followed immediately with a second shot.

Instead of slowing, Finkel spurred his mount to greater speeds.

Hardening his resolve, Luke aimed at the man himself. "Last chance," he hollered and hooked his finger around the trigger.

At this final warning, Finkel brought his horse up so short it rose onto its hind legs before settling. He quickly put his hands in the air.

"Keep them there, get off your horse, and come on in." Heart hammering, he kept his gun trained on the man.

"Who are you?" Finkel asked, drawing close. His horse had not followed but stood where he'd left it. "You certainly aren't *der* Troubleman."

He clamped on the cuffs, anger sluicing through him. "You have any idea how close you were to missing your day in court?"

"Who are you?"

"Lucious Landrum."

"You're supposed to be in South Texas

chasing *die* Diamonds."

"What did you go and run off like that for?" Luke barked. "I thought I was going to have to shoot you."

"Vhy didn't you?"

"I was seconds away from it!" His breathing was as labored as Honey Dew's, his fury palpable.

"Vhy didn't you?" he asked again.

With an effort, Luke brought himself under control. "It's not something I care to do unless I absolutely have to."

Finkel studied him. "Zat de only reason?"

The men faced each other, memories shuffling through their minds. They'd played cards, shared meals, traded jokes, exchanged confidences.

Luke sighed. "Let's get going. We've got one more stop."

They headed toward the hack. "Comer von't let you take us in. You know dat, don't you?"

"This is the end of the rail, Peter. You're going to jail."

The creak of the hack and the clinking of chains drew the man's gaze. He whistled. "You pick up all *dies Männer* this morning?"

"Yep."

"You planning on getting every-von?"

"Yep."

Finkel shook his head. "Comer hates jails. He von't sit by and let you lock us up."

"He let me have six others."

"He vas hopping mad about it, too. Promised us he vouldn't let it happen again." Walking to the back, he climbed into the bed.

Duane perked up. "So how ya likin' that telly-phone Luke sold ya?"

Finkel scowled. "Shut up, Pfeuffer."

"Who-wee, I think he's got a couple o' lines crossed, Luke." Duane leaned in. "What happened to yer ear?"

Luke whipped up his head from securing the chains. A trickle of blood ran down Finkel's ear.

Tightening his lips, Luke finished shackling him. "Well, that was some mighty sorry shooting on my part, Peter. I'm sorry. I aim to miss by about three inches."

"I should haf stopped right avay."

"We couldn't believe it when ya kept going after Luke here gave ya warnin'." Duane shook his head. "We thought ya were dead fer shore, didn't we, boys?"

The men offered their agreement. Duane rehashed what they saw, telling Finkel how each of them had been caught.

Luke checked Honey Dew's flanks. They were covered in a foam of sweat. Her nostrils flared wide as she sucked in air. He wiped her sides and patted her neck. "You did real fine, girl. Real fine."

When Duane wound down, Finkel nodded at Georgie. "*Guten Morgen,* Fräulein Gail. *Das Telefon* isn't vorking."

"Good morning, Mr. Finkel." She gave him a soft smile. "And you're quite right. Seems someone shot down every line we have."

He gave a disgruntled look at Necker. "Vas that your idea? Did you stop and think that now our *Frauen* can't call the next *Mann* and warn him?"

Necker sneered. "Shut up, Finkel."

Georgie exchanged a look with Luke, then faced forward.

Taking Honey Dew's reins, he walked beside the hack and back toward the farmhouse. The gunfire had emptied it of its occupants. Finkel's wife and five stairstep children stood on the porch. Luke picked out the boy who'd churned butter and the girl who'd fed the chickens that first day he stopped by.

The missus ran down the steps. "Peter?"

"Go back in *das Haus, mein Liebling,*" he said, his voice gentle.

She turned to Georgie. "Vat's happening? *Was ist los?*"

"Mrs. Finkel, this is Ranger Landrum. I'm afraid . . ." Georgie looked at him, at a loss for words.

"I'm going to have to take him in, ma'am. I'll get word to you as soon as I can."

"Is this because of Herr Comer?"

"Stille!" Finkel said.

"I'm afraid so," Luke said to the woman.

"But *das Telefon* doesn't vork. How vill I hear?"

The children spilled into the yard like ducklings trailing after their mother.

"We'll get it fixed or send someone out," he said. "Either way, I'll be in touch."

Finkel twisted around, catching his son's eye. "Morgan's out in *die* Pasture. You'll need to get her and cool her down, *ja?*"

"Jawohl."

"That's a good boy. You take care of your *Mutter* now. I'll be back soon as I can."

"When, *Vater?*" The boy's gaze traveled over the occupants of the wagon.

"I don't know, *Sohn.* But not for a long vile. I love you, and *die Mädchen,* too." He glanced at his daughters, then gave his wife a sad smile. "It'll be all right, *Liebling.*"

She brought her apron to her mouth. "*Nein,* Peter. What vill ve do?"

Finkel looked at Luke. "Let's get going."

Heart heavy, Luke swung up onto Honey

Dew, then rode alongside Georgie as she urged the horses in a westwardly direction. The image of the five ragamuffins swirling about their mama's skirt seared his brain. He knew what it was like to lose a father at age ten and to have your ma and siblings to take care of. He wished he could come back, check on them from time to time, see if they needed anything. But if he kept rangering, chances were, he'd never see them again.

He glanced at Georgie. She kept her eyes forward, her throat working. The men in back quieted. Even Duane was subdued.

Clem Ragston was the only one left, but Finkel's words had given Luke a sense of unease. Was Comer in the area? Would he try to get the drop on them? When would he realize his men had not met up at their rendezvous points? And when he did, would Georgie be in harm's way?

But he already knew the answer. She would. And if anything happened to her, he'd never forgive himself. He glanced at her again, her nose and cheeks a muted pink where the sun had touched them. A deep well of love for her sprang from within. So sweet. So brave. And, Lord help him, but he wanted her with him always.

Feeling his regard, she glanced over.

He winked, then returned his attention to the men in the back.

They approached Ragston's house with extreme caution. He'd planned to have Georgie wait for him well away from the house. But if Comer really was out there, he wanted to be within hearing distance. They pulled to a stop just before a bend in the road.

The men quieted. After Finkel, they knew Luke would take them in dead or alive. And they wanted their buddy Ragston alive. So rather than shout a warning, they anxiously awaited Ragston's reaction. Would he run or would he come in peacefully?

He gave each of the men a hard look. "Nothing is to happen to Georgie. If Comer comes, as you expect him to, I want your word you'll protect her."

Necker spit. "That's askin' an awful lot. She's been pointin' a gun at us all day."

"I'll have your word." His voice was short, clipped.

"Ya got mine," Duane offered.

"And mine." This from Finkel, echoed then by Blesinger.

Necker shook his head. "I ain't makin' any promises. If she gets in the way, well . . ." He shrugged.

Dismounting, Luke walked over to Necker

and, with one swing of his fist, put him to sleep.

Necker slumped over. Georgie squeaked.

Duane grimaced. "Who-wee. That hurt yer hand, Luke?"

Blesinger rolled his eyes.

"Get your pistol out," Luke said to Georgie. "If anything happens, and I mean anything, you shoot. You hear me?"

Swallowing, she nodded, the color in her cheeks fading a bit.

"He don't mean shoot us," Duane clarified. "He just means, ya know, shoot up at the sky or somethin'."

Pinning her with his gaze, Luke waved his hand in a circular motion encompassing his own torso. "Aim anywhere in here. I'll be back as soon as I can."

"Aw, come on, Luke," Duane whined. "Ya cain't leave us here. We cain't see nothing. Take us round the corner."

Ignoring him, Luke grabbed his Winchester, then crept toward the house. The morning was well advanced, reducing his chances for success astronomically. The place was awfully quiet for a family the size of Ragston's.

Keeping cover among the shrubs, he darted from tree to tree until he was pressed against the house's whitewashed siding. He stayed where he was, listening.

A man's rumble followed by a child's giggle came from the back window. Luke eased that direction, inclining his ears, but could only make out voices, not actual words. He didn't risk looking inside, but from the sound of it, Ragston had one of his daughters with him.

Where was the missus? The rest of the children?

Creeping toward the kitchen door, he flung it open and pointed the gun, not at Ragston, but at a man playing cards with . . . Bettina.

A pistol sat on the table, a foot from the card-player's hand. Darting a glance at the weapon, the man grabbed for it.

Luke fired the Winchester. The bullet sent the pistol skittering across the room, well out of reach. Bettina dropped to the floor, covering her head with her arms.

Luke cocked his rifle and kept the barrel leveled at the stranger. "Where's Ragston?"

The man made no move to raise his hands, but instead settled into his chair and played a card as if he didn't have a care in the world. He was about Luke's age, brown hair, blue eyes, very familiar looking. Where had he seen him?

"Ragston's not here." The man's voice

sent shock waves through Luke. He knew him. Knew him well. But from where? Where?

He kept his rifle steady but spoke to Bettina. "What are you doing here, girl? You're supposed to be on your way to Industry."

Her eyes wide, she slowly straightened. "Mr. Luke? What happened to yer overalls?"

"My real name's Lucious Landrum."

Her lips parted. "The Ranger?"

"Yes. Now, why are you here?"

She glanced between him and the man. "I didn't go ta Industry. I went and fetched Comer instead."

Euphoria swept through him. This was Comer. Dead to rights at the other end of his barrel. Bettina might have gone to warn him, but instead had delivered him right into his hands. He wondered at Comer's audacity. Had the man become so complacent he thought he couldn't be brought in? Well, he'd find out differently now.

Comer put down another card and drew one from the deck. "I want to thank you for rounding up my men for me. We've a train to rob today." He raised his gaze. "I believe I'll take 'em off your hands now."

"You're not doing anything but putting your own hands in the air."

Comer shook his head. "Still bossy, I see."
Luke frowned.

Setting his cards on the table, Comer nodded toward the door. "Go let the men loose, Bettina."

"You'll do nothing of the kind."

She froze at his sharp command. "You really Lucious Landrum?"

"I am. And, make no mistake, Bettina, as of now, the Comer Gang is no more."

She swallowed, torn between her misplaced loyalty to Comer and what was clearly a fascination with the new Luke.

"Go on." Comer shooed her with his hand. "I'll join you in a minute."

After a slight hesitation, she dashed down the hallway and out the front door. Luke let her go. She didn't have keys for the cuffs and she had no idea Georgie was out there. When she found out, she'd be hard-pressed to betray the woman who'd hired her when no one else would. No, he was much more worried about Ragston than Bettina. He needed to get out there.

"Let's go, Comer."

He leaned back in his chair. "You don't recognize me, do you?"

"I recognize you. I just don't know from where."

Comer lifted a brow. "Well, I'd recognize

you anywhere. You look exactly the same since the last time I saw you. You'd tucked your tail under and run, leaving me high and dry at Glaser's mercy."

CHAPTER FORTY-THREE

The wind left Luke as surely as if he'd received a flattening blow to the gut. He fell back a step. "Alec?"

"In the flesh." He crossed his arms. "So, what do you hear from Ma?"

Luke soaked in the changes the last eleven years had wrought. Alec's face had lengthened and lost its roundness. His cheeks and jaw had taken on sharp angular lines he'd not had before. His nose had lost its gentle slope and instead started high between the brows before coming to a straight point.

But now that he knew who it was, he was able to pick out the familiar. The eyes were the same. The smile. The dimple. The mannerisms.

On the outside, Luke held the Winchester level, but inside he was reeling. Like a bare-knuckle boxer who'd dropped his guard at the wrong moment, the revelations pummeled him one by one. His love for the brother he'd raised cracked his head back like an uppercut. The news he was alive after all these years hit him like a left jab. But the finishing blow, the hard right, was the discovery his beloved brother was none other than the notorious Frank Comer, and this time, instead of watching Alec be arrested, he'd have to do it himself.

He took a shaky breath. "You've changed. You've . . ." *Become a man,* he wanted to say. But the man he'd become wasn't worthy of the name, so he said nothing.

"You may as well put the gun away, Lucious. You aren't going to shoot me."

He adjusted the rifle, securing the stock against his side, aiming the barrel at Alec's heart. But if it came to pulling the trigger, his brother was right. He wouldn't, couldn't do it. It had been a long time, though. Long enough for Alec not to know for certain what Luke would or wouldn't do. He hoped.

"We were told you were dead," Luke said. "Had a photograph, a letter written in your hand, everything."

His brother shrugged. "I was tired of you hunting me down. Seemed like every time I turned around, you were on my trail. Made the fellas I ran with a bit uneasy. So I staged my death." He gave a rueful smile. "Posing in that coffin was a mite uncomfortable, but it sure looked convincing, didn't it?"

"Ma was devastated." He paused. "I was devastated."

"You both managed to carry on."

"A day hasn't gone by where I haven't thought of you. Why didn't you wait for me when you got out? I told you I was coming."

Alec dropped his chair legs on the floor, his eyes turning cold. "I wanted nothing to do with you. Still don't." He gave a sardonic smile. "How'd you like shooting up Main Street? You think of me?"

"You know I did."

He cackled. "That's why I had you do it. And all that stuff to your lady friend, too."

Heartsore, Luke shoved his emotions aside. Now more than ever, he needed to remain calm. "Do Necker and the others know we're brothers?"

Alec harrumphed. "I'd never admit to something like that."

Sorrow shot through Luke like a fiery dart finding the one sure kink in his armor. "I'm sorry I left you with Glaser that night. In my arrogance, I'd planned to go round up a bunch of fellows to bust you out of jail. Never did it occur to me Glaser would hightail it out of there, heap on a bunch of unfounded charges, and have you locked up

in the penitentiary before I knew what happened."

Scooping up the cards, Alec began to
shuffle. "They weren't trumped-up charges.
I'd done every single one of those things."

A hard right cross completely out of
nowhere. "What? But how? Where was I?"

He began to deal a game of solitaire.
"While you were out coon hunting and
chasing the ladies, I had a pretty good
operation going."

Luke sucked in his breath. He'd had no
idea Alec had dealings on the other side of
the law. "When did that start?"

"I dunno. Does it matter?"

Grief warred with shock. "Why didn't you
tell me?"

Alec moved an ace to the foundation pile
and began to build a stack. "I was tired of
being in your shadow. Lucious this, Lucious
that. You're all anyone ever talked about. Yet
all the while, I was the one robbing the
neighbors, peeking in girls' windows when
they thought they were alone. And one time
I snuck in and took more from a gal than
the jewelry on her dresser. But I couldn't
tell nobody nothing."

Luke's gut clenched. He remembered
hearing rumors about one of his school-
mates who'd been packed off to live with

her aunt and uncle in Virginia. Alec, in particular, had spread the worst kind of gossip about her. Claimed he had firsthand knowledge of her. Never had it occurred to Luke his brother had forced himself on her. Bile churned in his stomach.

Alec shifted in his chair. "Everything changed, though, when I went to jail. Those fellows had never heard of Lucious Landrum. Only of Alec Landrum. And I made a name for myself. Everybody looked up to me. Me, not you. When I got out, I just continued on, is all."

Luke didn't know what to do. What to think. He'd sworn an oath. Yet to uphold it, he'd have to sacrifice the very person he'd spent his youth trying to protect. It seemed the ones who needed protecting, though, were their friends and neighbors. "I thought you cared about the people you robbed."

"I needed to win 'em over so my boys could stay hidden. But that's about the extent of it."

How could two brothers be so different? he wondered. Make such different choices? And how could he not have known?

Alec moved a row of black-and-red cards to another spot, then turned over a four of hearts. "I was really sore when you joined the Ranger force after I staged my death and the papers began talking about how you'd been born with a gun in your hand or could pick cherries with your rifle, or how you charged into the last retreat of desperados and brought them out handcuffed — the living ones, anyway." He shook his head in disgust. "Lucious this. Lucious that. I'd just read about you capturing the state title for all-round rapid-fire marksman when I decided to make a name for myself. To turn the tide." He finished off a second foundation stack. "And I did it, too. I'm every bit as famous as you and a lot more popular."

Luke's mind began to spin. All his young life his pa had impressed upon him the importance of family and loyalty. But he'd also spoken of integrity and the sacredness of a man's word. What he'd never mentioned, however, was what to do when family loyalty and personal integrity squared off.

"Don't use me as an excuse for your choices, Alec," he said. "This isn't a competition. Never has been."

Looking up, Alec pushed back the brim of his brown felt Stetson. "No? What about right now? When we leave this room, one of us will be the winner. One will be the loser. Sounds like a competition to me. And one I don't intend to lose."

"I'm the one holding the gun. And make no mistake, I'll use it." It wasn't until that moment he realized it was true. The inscription on his pistols flashed through his mind. *Never Draw Me Without Cause or Holster Me With Dishonor.*

The very best way he could show his love and loyalty to Alec was to stand firm on what was right and what was wrong. Compromising his word would not only be dishonorable, it would do a lot more harm than good. It was his sworn duty and moral obligation to protect innocent lives. If that meant arresting Alec, so be it.

Luke gave a quick upward jerk with his chin. "Put your hands in the air. You're under arrest."

"And if I refuse?" His eyes clouded, making them as opaque as a thick curtain. "You gonna shoot me down in cold blood? Your own kin?"

Luke's pulse hammered so hard he could feel it in his neck. "Get them up."

After a tense moment, Alec lifted his arms and slowly rose, approaching as if he were a deadly cobra preparing to strike. "It's over, Lucious," he snarled. "Ragston's out there. He'll have freed the boys. Threaten me all you want, but you're not leaving here alive."

A shot rang out in the distance. Georgie's

scream pierced the air. Luke jerked toward the sound.

It was all the advantage Alec needed. Lunging forward, he knocked the barrel aside, wrenching the butt away from Luke's torso.

Tightening his grip, Luke took advantage of the rifle's momentum, whipping the stock against the side of Alec's face. The crack of bone sounded loud in the small room. Screaming, Alec staggered back, then charged him again.

Desperate to reach Georgie, Luke hit him once more with the rifle's butt, putting his weight behind the blow. Alec crumbled to the ground.

Snapping a handcuff on his brother's wrist, he hauled him to the stove, locked the other cuff to it, then sprinted out the door and into the brush, weaving his way under its cover and toward the place he'd left Georgie and the hack.

CHAPTER FORTY-FOUR

Even with her hands propped on the pillows, the pistol's weight tested Georgie's strength. As its five pounds grew heavier and heavier, so did her eyes. The warmth of the morning sun wrapped her in its blanket. She'd slept very little and the men's quiet conversations against a backdrop of birdsong beckoned to her like a soft feather bed.

A gunshot exploded from the direction of Ragston's place, jerking her to attention. The men exchanged glances, speculation in their eyes.

"Who ya think it was?" Duane asked. "Luke or Ragston?"

"Sounded like a rifle." Blesinger shifted in the seat, his chains rattling. "But that could mean anything."

Georgie's heart took up a rapid beat. What would she do if something had happened to Luke? Should she try to intervene? Or should she go for help while the men were still shackled?

But who would help? The entire town had already refused to become involved. What if she drove these men all the way to town only to have the sheriff release them? What if Luke was lying on Ragston's floor bleeding to death?

Before she could decide what to do, Finkel whipped his head around. "Some-von is coming."

Her grip on the gun tightened.

Blesinger held up his hands. "Easy, Miss Georgie. Relax your shoulders. You don't want that thing going off by accident, now."

All attention swerved back to her.

After a lifetime of priding herself on doing anything a man could, she suddenly felt very inadequate. Seeing Luke's mastery with guns and horses, hearing the men whisper of his escapades, and watching him single-handedly round up the Comer Gang had been eye-opening. But the thought of finishing this job without him brought everything into immediate perspective.

She couldn't sit a horse the way he did. Couldn't command men the way he did. Couldn't shoot like he did. Couldn't garner the respect he did.

That wasn't to say all women couldn't. Annie Oakley was said to have hit coins flipped into the air, broken marbles on the fly, and shot a cigarette right out of her husband's mouth. But all of a sudden, Georgie was tired of trying to be a man. There were an awful lot of things she liked about being a woman.

She liked garden clubs, reading circles, and being around children. She liked pretty dresses, fancy shoes, even frilly undergarments. Spitting, chewing, cursing, wrestling, and holding men at gunpoint held no appeal whatsoever.

"Bettina-hyena," Duane said. "What're you doin' here?"

Georgie whipped her head around, the gun barrel swinging with her. The men ducked and shoved trying to get out of the line of fire.

"*Bettina.* What on earth? You're supposed to be on your way to Industry." She glanced in the direction of Ragston's place. "Do you know what happened? Who shot the gun? Is Luke all right?"

The girl ground to a halt, just as stunned to see Georgie. "What're you doin' here?"

"Do you know if Luke is all right?"

"Sure. Last I seen him."

"What was that gunshot?"

"Mr. Luke shot Comer's pistol clean off the table."

The men groaned.

Georgie frowned. "Comer? Frank Comer's in there with Luke?"

"Yes'm."

"And no one is hurt?"

"No, ma'am."

"And Luke still has his rifle?"

"Yes'm."

Relief slammed into her so swiftly, she began to tremble.

"Miss Georgie!" Blesinger barked. "Quit shaking."

She gripped the pistol with two hands, but the tremors wouldn't stop.

The men scrambled for cover, limited by their chains.

She scowled. "Would you stop that? I'm being careful."

Duane peeked out from under his arm. "Would ya mind releasing the hammer, at least? We're all chained up. None of us are goin' nowhere." He pointed toward the north. "Point it that'a way when ya do, though."

After a slight hesitation, she pulled back on the hammer, returning it to its normal position. The men visibly relaxed.

She turned her attention back to Bettina. "What are you doing here? Where's your disguise? Did you get lost?"

The girl twirled her finger round and round her braid. "I ain't lost and I didn't go to Industry."

"Why not?"

She looked down, toeing the dirt.

Duane peered around Finkel's shoulder. "What were ya goin' ta Industry fer?"

She shrugged. "I's supposed to call Ranger headquarters and tell him 'bout today's job."

The men exchanged glances.

Clearing his throat, Duane turned to Georgie. "Hyena sorta looks out fer us. Ya know, is one of us."

"One of you!" She pulled back.

"She doesn't go on *die* Jobs vith us," Finkel clarified. "She just delivers messages. Like she does for you."

Blesinger frowned at the girl. "How come ya didn't warn us Landrum was coming?"

"I didn't know he was. Miss Georgie tol' me 'bout the train. She didn't say nothing about Lucious Landrum."

Georgie touched a hand to her forehead. "Wait one minute. Wait just one minute. Do you mean to tell me, Bettina von Schiller, all this time you've known who was in Frank Comer's gang?"

The girl slowly nodded.

Georgie's eyes widened. "And you've

known who Frank Comer was, too?"

She nodded again.

"Good heavens."

"Vhat's going on in *das Haus?*" Finkel asked the girl.

"When I left, Mr. Luke was holdin' a gun on Frank, but Frank didn't look none too worried. He just leaned back in his chair and tol' me to come set you fellers free."

Duane held out his hands. "Then, hop to it, gal."

She scratched her thigh. "Well, I'm not so sure no more."

"About what?" Blesinger growled.

" 'Bout lettin' you fellers go. Mr. Luke, he looked mighty sharp in his Ranger doo-dahs."

Blesinger spit. "Now, isn't that a typical female? Sees a fellow all spruced up and loses her head."

"I ain't, neither."

He rattled the chains. "Then, get over here and let us loose."

Georgie slowly lifted the gun, pointing it at the back of the hack. The men's attention shifted from Bettina to her.

"No one is releasing anyone."

"Now, Miss Georgie." Duane gave her a winning smile. "You ain't gonna shoot Bettina."

"No," she said. "But I might shoot you."

He looked doubtful.

Cocking the gun with one hand, she made a circular motion with her other, indicating her torso. "I believe the instructions were anywhere in this area."

The men froze.

"Bettina?" she called.

"Yes'm?"

"You will not release these men."

The girl let out a sound of distress. "Frank'll be really sore with me."

"He'll be much more upset if I shoot his men. And *I'll* be upset if you force me to. Do you wish to upset me, Bettina, and risk losing your job?"

"Now, that ain't fair," Duane began.

Georgie pointed the muzzle of her gun at him.

"Though I can certainly see," he quickly interjected, "why you'd not want her workin' fer ya if she made ya shoot somebody." He sliced a look at Bettina. "Ya prob'ly shouldn't make her shoot nobody, Hyena."

Georgie narrowed her eyes. "Her name is Bettina and if you call her anything else, I will be very displeased."

"She don't mind it." He glanced at the gun, then swallowed. "All the same, I'm happy ta call her Bettina."

Necker moaned and put a hand to his jaw.

"What happened to him?" Bettina asked.

Straightening her shoulders, Georgie gave the girl a knowing look. "He refused to do what Luke told him to."

Her eyes widened. "He's tough as a sow's snout, ain't he?"

"Yes, he is." As the shock of seeing Bettina began to wear off, relief set in that the girl wasn't alone on the road somewhere. On the heels of the relief, though, came a feeling of disappointment and deep concern. As soon as she had Bettina alone, the two of them would have a heart-to-heart.

"How vere you going to free us?" Finkel asked. "You haf *die* Keys for these things?"

She shook her head. "No, but Ragston does."

"Vere's Ragston?" he asked.

"Right here." The farmer stepped out from the shrub, pistol aimed at Georgie.

She slowly unfurled her spine.

"Don't make no sudden moves, now." His eyes were so droopy they showed more pink than white. His oversized ears reminded her of the old men outside Schmid's mercantile.

"I'm gonna have to ask ya to put that gun down now," he said.

Her pulse began to race. "I will not."

The men in the hack stilled.

Mr. Ragston gave her an indulgent look. "I know ya don't wanna shoot nobody. So just put the gun down nice and easy."

"No." She tightened her grip on the gun. It was still aimed at Duane, but her focus was on Ragston.

"You're outnumbered, girl," he said. "You cain't really believe the most renowned gang in the state could be rounded up in a single day, by a single man."

"It already has, sir."

He shook his head. "No, ma'am. It hasn't. Frank's disarmed Ranger Landrum. It's over."

Her breaths came in shallow spurts. "I don't believe you."

"I'm afraid you don't have no choice."

"Oh, yes I do. And I choose to wait right here, with my gun, and see who rounds that corner. My money, sir, is on Lucious Landrum."

He cocked his gun. "Put yer weapon down."

Duane twisted around, looking over his shoulder. "Ya cain't hurt her, Clem. I done gave my word."

Ragston's eyes widened in disbelief, their lids lifting momentarily. "Yer an outlaw, Pfeuffer. Yer word don't mean nothin'."

"It does ta me. It does ta her. And it does

ta him. If ya plan ta shoot her, I'll have to dive in front. But my chain's too short fer a proper dive and chances are you'll get my head. Now, that'd be just downright messy. If Comer's really got the upper hand, then we'll wait. If he hasn't, then you can deal with Landrum. But ya leave the hello gal out of it."

"She got into it the minute she agreed to drive that wagon. And yer crazy if ya think I'm waiting around fer Landrum."

She quirked a brow. "I thought you said Luke had been overpowered?"

Hesitating, Ragston darted his gaze about the clearing. "He has."

The men in the hack slumped with disappointment. Necker moaned again. Georgie let out a quiet breath of relief.

Reaching out a hand, Ragston snatched Bettina and put his gun to her head. "Ya give yer word about Hyena, Pfeuffer?"

The girl had no time to scream, much less react.

Gasping, Georgie swung her gun to face Ragston's head, her chest squeezing, her breath trapped. "Let her go."

Bettina held still, her lips screwed up in anger.

"Come on, now, Clem." Finkel frowned. "I haf a *Tochter* about her age. Besides, she's von of us."

"She ain't one of us. She was supposed to come out here and distract the driver so I could knock him out and set you fellers free. Instead she comes out here and 'yes, ma'ams' Miss Gail 'til the cows come home."

Hands shaking, Georgie locked her elbows and looked down the barrel of the pistol. "Let her go."

"She ain't never used a gun a'fore," Duane said, cleaning something from under his fingernail.

Ragston stumbled back a step, hauling Bettina closer. "You put that thing down right this minute or I'll blow this girl to pieces."

Bettina's face lost all color.

"You harm a hair on her head and I'll shoot, I swear I will." Georgie's arms trembled with fatigue and fear.

"You have to the count o' three, missy."

Water rushed to her eyes. "Don't do this, Mr. Ragston. Please."

"Then, put down the gun."

"Will you let her go?"

"Yes," he barked. "Now, put it down."

She reached for the hammer.

"No!" Bettina screamed. "He don't keep his word. He'll kill us both!"

Scrunching up his face, Ragston ground the muzzle into the girl's temple and raised his elbow.

"Don't!" Georgie screeched.

The gun fired, the sound exploding in her ear. She screamed, the gun's kick throwing her backward onto the seat and knocking the weapon from her grasp. She scrambled to get it, but Duane whisked it up and swung it toward Ragston. A livid but unscathed Ragston. He still held Bettina, though the girl had soaked her dress.

Georgie pressed a fist to her mouth.

"Let Hyena go." Duane's voice shook with fury.

Ragston tossed Bettina aside, sending the girl to the ground. "It's about time. I cain't believe you fellers sat here and let a female hold ya prisoner."

"She seemed to hold you prisoner, Clem," Finkel spat.

Ragston holstered his pistol, then yanked a key from his pocket and headed to the wagon bed. Scrambling to her feet, Georgie launched herself through the air and onto the man's back, knocking the key from his hand.

She'd hoped to bring him to the ground, as well, but he did no more than grunt.

"What the blazes?" He stumbled forward.

"Get off me, you confounded woman." He reached around and grabbed her by the hair.

The men hollered, their voices ringing in the morning air.

She wrapped her arms around his neck, her legs about his waist. "No, you can't have —"

A huge explosion sounded by her ear.

Ragston froze. The men dove for cover.

Georgie opened her eyes.

The long barrel of a rifle now rested against Ragston's temple.

At its other end, a very furious Lucious Landrum. "Get off him, Georgie."

Joy burst inside her, despite his strident tone. She decided now wasn't the time to express it, though. Sliding off the man, she waited for her feet to touch the ground, then raced to Bettina and dropped to her knees. She scooped the girl onto her lap, rocking and petting her. Hugging and cooing to her. Her little body trembled with a delayed reaction.

"Put the gun down, Duane." Luke's voice shook.

The boy immediately acquiesced.

Shoving Ragston forward, Luke secured him to the back of the wagon instead of inside it. "You can walk, Clem, and your pace will be set by Miss Gail. It is my deepest hope she wishes to return as quickly as possible, at which point you'll have to step lively or be dragged."

Skirting to the other side, he picked up the gun sitting beside Duane and tucked it in his waistband. Then he grabbed Duane's arm, his chest lifting and falling like bellows, his nostrils flared.

He opened his mouth, but instead of saying whatever he'd planned, he clamped it shut again, his Adam's apple bobbing.

Duane gave him an understanding smile. "Yer welcome, Palmer."

Luke gave a nod, then whirled to face her, his eyes holding a suspicious sheen. He took one step after another, punctuating each with his words. "If you ever, *ever,* do such a fool thing again, I will skin you alive and feed your carcass to the buzzards."

Though he was talking to Georgie, Bettina curled into a ball.

Georgie frowned. "Stop it, Bettina thinks you're serious."

"I am deadly serious." His entire body shook.

She smiled at the telltale sign and placed her mouth next to Bettina's ear. "He's not serious. It's nothing but male bluster. He'd never lay a hand on me with anything but the sweetest, most gentlest of touches." She looked up through her lashes. "Isn't that right, Lucious?"

He didn't answer.

"Tell Bettina it's bluster. She needs to be soothed."

"*She* does, does she?"

"Yes."

"It's not bluster." He handed her the pistol, then strode back toward the bend in the road.

"Where are you going?" she asked.

"To get . . . Comer. He's waiting for me down by the house."

Kissing Bettina on the top of her head, she helped the girl to her feet. "Come on. Let's drive the hack down so Luke won't have to walk back."

By the time they were settled and on their way, Luke and Comer were hiking up the hill. She tilted her head, noting Comer walked as if he'd had a bit too much to drink. When they were within a couple of yards, she pulled to a stop.

Instead of taking Comer round back, Luke stopped next to her. "Georgie, I'd like you to meet —"

"Comer," the man slurred, his face swollen, his eyes heavy. "Name's Comer."

Sorrow etched Luke's features; then he nodded. "Frank, this is Georgie Gail.

She's . . ."

She smiled. "I believe we've met, Mr. Comer. You robbed a train I was on."

He nodded. Though his eyes were glazed with pain, their color was so much like Luke's she drew an unconscious breath.

"I 'member," he said. "The tel'fen operator. The boys here 'bout died when they saw ya step outta the car."

Eyes widening, she turned around. "Y'all were there?"

The men tucked their chins, mumbling indecipherable answers.

"Well, for heaven's sake." But when she turned back around, Luke was leading a weaving Comer to the wagon bed to join the others.

"What happened ta him?" Duane asked, indicating Comer.

"He ran into the butt of my rifle."

Duane grimaced.

Luke secured Comer, jostling Necker in the process.

Necker gripped his knees, leaning against them. "What happened while I was out?"

Blesinger propped him up, while Duane filled him in on all he'd missed.

Georgie kept their pace leisurely so Mr. Ragston could keep up and had Bettina use her lap as a pillow. Stroking the girl's hair, she scanned the trees for birds, listening to every song and puzzling out its owner.

Luke nudged his horse close to her. "I was thinking."

She turned to him. "Yes?"

"Well, I was wondering, I mean."

When he said no more, she gave him a strange look. "Wondering what?"

He pulled at his collar. "I was, um, wondering if you'd like to be my partner?"

She lifted her brows. "Why on earth would you want a partner who can't shoot and who makes you so mad you want to feed her to the buzzards?"

The men in the back quieted.

Luke rubbed his forehead.

Sniggering, Duane leaned forward. "I don't think he meant that kinda pardner, Miss Georgie."

"Oh." Her lips parted. "What kind of partner did you mean?"

Luke scratched underneath his chin. "Same kind as the cardinals?"

A tiny germ of excitement began to bubble inside her stomach. "Cardinals mate for life."

He turned an intense gaze onto her. "Yes."

She pulled the hack to a stop. "Are you proposing to me, Lucious? Right here in the middle of nowhere with a group of men in the bed of the wagon?"

Scowling, he straightened. "I'm not sure when I'll see you next. I have to take them down to headquarters and talk to my captain. Your answer will determine what it is my captain and I discuss."

"What are you saying?"

"I'm saying, if you agree, I'll be turning in my badge. If you don't, well . . . I don't know."

She stared at him. "But you love your job. You told me you did."

Resting his wrists on the pommel, he scanned the horizon. "Not as much as I love you."

She bit her lip. "Can't you have both?"

"No." He shook his head. "My job keeps me on the trail too much. I'm going to want something closer to home."

"What would you do?"

"I don't know. Does it matter?" He looked at her then, his vulnerability apparent.

Smiling, she reached out a hand. "No, it doesn't matter, and yes, I'll marry you."

He grasped her hand and released a pent-up breath. "You mean it?"

"I mean it."

He glanced at the men in the back, then her.

"Go ahead," Duane said, covering his eyes

with his hand, then spreading two fingers so he could peek through.

Smiling, Luke raised her palm to his lips and kissed it, then mouthed, *Later.*

She nodded, faced forward, then gasped. A pair of eagles screeched as they flapped over the prairie, their heads and tails white, their wingspans as wide as Luke was tall.

The men shaded their eyes. Bettina stirred. Luke threaded his hand with Georgie's.

The male and female birds ascended high into the sky, then in a heart-stopping ritual, clasped talons and spun head over tail like a whirligig. Over and over they went, dropping altitude while picking up speed.

The farther they plummeted, the harder Georgie squeezed Luke's hand. At the last moment, the eagles released their hold and spun back up into flight.

Long after they'd flown out of sight, the group sat silent and awed. So beautiful the courtship dance. So close it had come to disaster.

She looked at Luke. "I'm glad I'm a woman and you're a man. And there are some things I do well, and some things you do well. And together, we know when to hold tight and when to let go."

Lifting a corner of his mouth, he gave her

hand a squeeze. "I love you, Georgie Gail."

She smiled. "And I love you, Lucious Landrum. Name and all."

Twisting around, he looked at Ragston. "Hop on up, Clem. I'm anxious to get my gal home."

The men closest to him helped him up onto the flat of the bed.

Once he'd settled and his legs were dangling off the end, Georgie flicked the reins, just as anxious as Luke to return to the home that would one day soon be not only hers, but also his.

Epilogue

"Everybody off the train."

Georgie and Lucious exchanged a glance, then corralled the children and shuffled past the man brandishing a gun. At the door, a man with a neckerchief about his face waved them off.

Jumping to the ground, Lucious turned and assisted her and their five daughters. He gave her waist a squeeze of reassurance, but it did little to comfort her. Would he try to disarm the man?

His job as general manager for SWT&T kept him serving the company in many capacities and occasionally filling in for their lineman and new operator. But it didn't provide much opportunity for disarming outlaws.

Still, he'd kept up his membership in the Gun Club. Had taken the girls hunting every chance he could. And still went everywhere with Odysseus — having retired

Penelope the day they were married, for Georgie was now closest to his heart.

He'd just taken little Julia into his arms when the bandit stationed at the car door stopped him. "Hand over yer gun, mister."

Georgie tensed. Lucious would never willingly give up Odysseus.

He handed Julia to her. "You and the girls go on. I'll be right there."

Swallowing, she took the child. "Here we go, girls. You heard your father."

When they were out of harm's way, he turned back to the man. "You can have my bullets. The gun, however, is mine."

"The only thing what's yers is whatever I say is yers. Now, hand over the gun, real slow-like."

Jaw ticking, Lucious lifted the Colt with two fingers.

The man glanced at it, then took a quick step back and placed both hands on the grip of his pistol. "Where'd ya get that?"

The gun still dangled in Lucious's fingers. "It's mine."

"That there gun belongs to Lucious Landrum. Is part of a pair."

"Yes."

"Well, what're you doin' with it?"

He gave the man a look full of promises. "I own it. Have owned it for nigh on fifteen years. And I don't plan on parting with it anytime soon. The question is, how do you want the bullets? Poured out into your hand, or shot clean through your heart?"

The bandit's pistol began to shake. "Boss!" he shouted.

A man taking goods from the lined-up passengers looked over his shoulder, then jogged to them.

"Take a gander o' that," the one covering Lucious said. "Claims it's his and he'll let us have the bullets but not the pistol."

The boss's gaze went from the bone-handle carvings to Lucious's face. "What's yer name?"

"Lucious Landrum." He smiled. "Would you like me to prove it?"

The question hung in the air, right alongside Luke's pistol.

The boss stilled. "Who's he with?"

"That gal over yonder. The pretty one with the five little girls."

The boss glanced at Georgie, then back at Lucious. "Where's the other pistol that goes with this one?"

"You never know," Lucious answered, his voice dropping. "But he doesn't like to be far from his woman and will go to any lengths — *any* — to protect her."

The boss paled and exchanged a worried

glance with his comrade. Neither made a move toward Luke's pistol.

Georgie could see he was losing his patience. He'd come a long way from the man who charged in first and thought later. But he did have his limits.

"Why're the robbers staring at Pa?" Tina asked.

Georgie looked down at their oldest, not far from the age of the girl who'd been at Georgie's side that long-ago day she'd first laid eyes on the man who would become her husband. "They recognize your father and fear for their lives."

"But there's two of them and only one of Pa."

"Yes."

From the opposite end of the train, a group of men on horseback burst from the forest. *"Get down!"*

The command sailed above their heads and broached no argument.

Spreading her arms, Georgie brought the girls down with her. "Cover your heads," she shouted, then glanced to the side.

The men who'd been with Lucious were without pistols, their hands in the air while he held them at gunpoint.

Good heavens, that was fast. She was sorry she'd missed it. It had been a long time since she'd seen him disarm a man.

Gunshots cracked above them like fire-crackers.

"Mama," Christine cried.

"Shhhh." She reached over and squeezed one of the twins' arms. "I'm right here, girls. Don't worry, help has arrived. Just stay on the ground until they tell us we can get up."

"Where's Pa?" Jessamine sobbed, flinching after each shot.

"He's part of the help. Don't worry. Everything will be fine."

As quickly as it started, the clash between the outlaws and the charging lawmen stopped.

"Can we get up?" Tina whispered.

"Not yet, but soon." The girls scooted closer, their backsides lifting like inch-worms. Georgie stretched her arms as far as she could reach.

"It's okay, folks," a young man shouted, his spurs clinking as he walked the line. "You can get on up now. Danger's over."

The dusty pair of boots stopped beside her. The jinglebobs dangling from the spur's shank still swayed, though the man had quit walking. A thin, youthful hand came into her line of vision. "Ma'am."

Grasping it, she rose, then shook the dust from her skirts. "Thank you."

The girls bounced up beside her like jack-in-the-boxes.

Pushing the brim of his hat back, the young man grinned. "Hey. I recognize you. You're that bird lady."

She scanned the area, then saw Lucious shaking hands with some of the Rangers, clapping others on the shoulders. Once she'd ascertained he was hale and whole, she returned her attention to the lad. "How do you do, I'm Georgie Landrum."

"Yeah. I know." He touched his brim. "I'm Benito von Hiller. But ever'body calls me Hyena."

She stilled, examining the eyes of . . . No, it couldn't be. "Bett —"

"Benito. I'm part of the posse these Rangers put together this morning." Benito's gaze traveled over the girls. "Are all these yours?"

Joy at seeing Bettina filled her. Try as they had, no one in town had been able to tame the young girl or keep her from her tomboyish ways. Her father had died the year Georgie carried her first child. Shortly after von Schiller's death, Bettina had stopped by the cottage to bid Georgie and Lucious good-bye.

"It's time I moved on," she'd said. "There's a whole world out there and I have me a hankerin' ta see it."

"But you're only eleven. Where will you go? What will you do? How will you eat? Wouldn't you rather stay here and live with me and Mr. Lucious?"

"No, ma'am. I like y'all just fine, but I got me some wanderlust what cain't be ignored."

Wanderlust. At the time, Georgie assumed the girl had picked the word up in a saloon of one sort or another. Now she quickly did the math. Ten years of wanderlust. She was twenty-one years old and pretending to be a man?

Good heavens. The Rangers would be horrified, aghast to discover she was a female. Georgie couldn't imagine the rough talk she must have put up with this day.

"I hear tell they just passed a tariff act banning the importation of wild bird feathers." Bettina took out a pouch of Honey Dew chewing tobacco and stuck a wad in her lower lip. "Called it the Georgie Gail Landrum Act."

Ignoring the tobacco, Georgie smiled. "Yes. That's where we were. We're on our way home from Austin right now."

"Congratulations. That'll shore put a crimp in the plume trade."

"Yes. Yes, it will."

"Heard the boys were released a couple o' years back. You ever see any of 'em? Duane?"

Georgie's smile widened. "Duane was released much earlier than the others. He's so respectable you'd hardly recognize him. He married Mattieleene Honnkernamp and preaches at the German Methodist Church over on Quitman."

"He don't, neither."

"He does. And his sermon illustrations are vastly amusing."

Bettina chuckled. "I can just imagine. Mattieleene." She shook her head. "I wonder if he wishes he were back in the calaboose rather than being saddled with that gal."

"They seem to be very happy."

"Well, what do ya know about that? And the rest of 'em?"

"Well, let's see. Lulie Necker ran off with another man while Arnold was in jail. He's back on his farm now but has turned awfully bitter. Mr. Finkel and Blesinger are both home and staying on the straight and narrow. The Ragstons moved to Kansas or some such place. We have no news on that front."

Bettina nodded. "Well, I've always a'wondered."

Fingering a button on her jacket, Georgie hesitated. Luke had told her of Comer's true identity the moment they'd had some privacy that long-ago day of the man's arrest. But while incarcerated, Alec had refused to speak to Luke or interact with him in any way. "You ever hear anything about Frank Comer?"

Bettina shook her head. "Nothin'. After he escaped from jail, it was like he plumb disappeared into thin air."

Georgie's shoulders slumped. "Well, if you ever hear anything, we'd sure appreciate a quick note or telegram."

"You bet." She spit out a wad of tobacco juice, swiping her lower lip with her cuff. "It shore is good ta see ya."

"Same here." Reaching out, she gave Bettina's hand a squeeze. "What are you doing, dressed like this?"

"Seein' the world. Pickin' up jobs here and there."

Georgie shook her head. "Clothes do not make the man, B-Benito."

The girl grinned. "They're sure mighty comfortable, though. Now, ya gonna introduce me ta all these lovely ladies?"

Sighing, Georgie nodded. "Of course." She started with Julia, the youngest, and ended with their oldest. "And this is Tina.

She's ten." Georgie placed her hands on Tina's shoulders. "Her name is short for Bettina."

The young woman whipped her head up, surprise and wonder filling her gaze. "Well, if that don't beat all. I . . . I . . ." She looked again at Tina.

"Hyena," one of the men called. "You gonna jaw all day or give us a hand?"

Lucious whipped his head around at the nickname, his gaze landing on Bettina.

She turned back to Georgie. "I gotta go."

"I understand. If you're ever in Brenham . . ."

The girl shook her head. "Don't know as that would be a real good i-deer." Squatting down to Tina's eye level, she took her by the arms. "I want ya to remember somethin', Miss Tina. Ain't nothing a man can do that a woman cain't do better. Ya hear?"

The girl nodded, her blond curls bouncing. Lucious stepped up next to them. Though he no longer wore overalls on a regular basis, neither did he dress in fancy clothes. Just a string tie, chambray shirt, vest, and denim trousers, with a single holstered gun belt strapped across his hips. He'd never looked better.

Bettina rose, winked at Georgie, then tipped her hat at Luke. "Ma'am. Sir. If

587

you'll excuse me."

They watched her swagger off to assist her fellow posse members.

"Was that . . . ?"

"Yes," Georgie said.

"But she's a —"

Squeezing his hand, she shook her head.

"Mama?"

Georgie looked down. "Yes, Tina?"

"Is that true? What that man said?"

"What'd sh— he say?" Lucious asked.

"That there isn't anything a man can do that a woman can't do better."

Lucious's eyebrows shot up.

"No, dear," Georgie answered. "There's a big difference in reaching for the best we can be and in trying to be something we are not and never will be."

"So women can't do everything men can?" Tina clarified.

"I'm afraid not." A slow grin began to form. "Women can do more."

"Georgie," Lucious admonished.

Laughter bubbled up within her. "Some things are just different, that's all."

He grabbed her around the waist and pulled her close. "I think, Bettina Landrum, your mama is full of sass from getting that piece of legislation named after her."

"She is?" Tina asked.

"She is." He looked over his brood of girls. "But the truth is, your mama can do anything she sets her mind to."

Georgie gave him a playful push. "Don't tease, Lucious. They'll believe you."

"And well they should." Leaning over, he gave her a kiss flush on the lips.

In a cry of protest, their daughters covered their eyes and expressed their disgust at such a display from people so old they didn't even have telephones when they were little.

AUTHOR'S NOTE

This was such a fun book to research. Not only because of the variety, but because I had the good fortune to find some wonderful turn-of-the-century material which I was able to incorporate into the novel. The Frank Comer character was based loosely on an actual Texas train robber who garnered the support of citizens in the ways Comer did and ended up becoming a legend.

Luke's character was loosely based on a combination of real Texas Rangers. I read up on several and took the parts I found most intriguing, then compiled them into one character. We really did have a Ranger who was known for his fancy duds, who had ornate pistols with carvings of a boy and a girl — which he wore closest to his heart — and which he'd inscribed with a motto almost word-for-word to Luke's. (He didn't name his pistols, though. At least, not that I know of.)

The water moccasin incident? Really happened to one of our Rangers when he was a boy.

The speedy disarming of bad guys when the odds were against the Ranger? Really happened — one Ranger being particularly known for this.

The rounding up of the train robbers? Really happened the way I depicted it in the book except instead of posing as a troubleman, the real Ranger posed as a tree salesman and made sales calls to the outlying farms until he could determine which were the gang members and which were not. When he was ready to round them up, no one would join his posse — not unless he planned to bring an army of soldiers along with him (which, of course, he had no intention of doing). After a great deal of effort, he found one man willing to drive the hack; then he rounded up the gang singlehandedly, one by one. The captures of the Comer Gang in *Love on the Line* are re-tellings of the arrests he made back in the day. (All except for Alec's arrest. I made that one up.)

And didn't you just love Brenham? They really did host the 26th Annual Texas State Sportsmen's Tournament. No one cheated, of course, but the 1903 *Brenham Banner* covered the tournament in their newspaper (which was on microfiche), and Kenny Ray Estes of the Trapshooting Hall of Fame had the entire tournament on microfiche as well. It was one of the last tournaments in the country to use live birds.

Brenham still celebrates Maifest every year, so if you're ever in the Houston area around the beginning of May, it's only about an hour and a half northeast of us and an absolute treat. Leaving a Mai tree at your sweetheart's door is a real tradition, but I don't know if it's one Brenham specifically followed. The Brenham festival also has a Maifest King, not just a queen. But we already had a cast of thousands in this book, so I had to leave him out. Sorry about that!

Nellie Bly was, in fact, one of the most famous women in the world and way ahead of her time. There really was a Nellie Bly game and all sorts of things — including a Nellie Bly hat. But I have absolutely no idea if it had any bird parts on it. I made that up.

And how could I set an entire novel in Brenham and not give Blue Bell Ice Cream a shout-out? Their first ice cream was cranked in 1911 in a wooden tub with a maximum output of two gallons per day. But the 1903 *Brenham Banner* advertised an ice cream parlor which opened for the spring and summer months. So I tweaked the name of it to reflect Blue Bell's patriarchs, H.C. Hodde and E.F. Kruse.

The toothache gum and digestive tablets displayed in the book's ice cream parlor were inspired by an old generic tintype I found. I had to get out my magnifying glass, but upon close inspection, that's what they had sitting right up on the counter. LOL. My inclusion of it is, of course, no reflection on the Blue Bell Creamery — as anyone who's had the great privilege of tasting their ice cream knows. As we speak, I have in my freezer a half gallon of their mint chocolate chip, a half gallon of cookies and cream, and a pint of coconut fudge. Yum!

And finally, the bird conservation movement was a hot topic of the time and spearheaded by women. Eventually, a tariff act banning the importation of wild bird parts was in fact passed in 1913 as a result of the pressure the women exerted. (And all before women gained the right to vote!)

I hope you enjoyed reading *Love on the Line* as much as I enjoyed writing it. I would love to hear from you. You can find me on Facebook (facebook.com/DeesCircle) and on my website, IWantHerBook.com. I hope to see you there!

Blessings, Dee